# A House of Cards

# BOOKS BY DOUGLAS J. BORNEMANN

*The Demon of Histlewick Downs* (Book 1 of the Dreamweaver Chronicles). This stand-alone novel explores historic events that set the stage for the Heiromancer Trilogy.

**The Heiromancer Trilogy:**

*Practical Phrendonics*

*A House of Cards*

*The Hanged Man's Gambit*

*Shady Fortunes*

Website: dougbornemann.com
Facebook: https://www.facebook.com/djbornemann/
Twitter @DougBornemann

# A House of Cards

Book Three of
The Dreamweaver
Chronicles

and

Volume Two of
The Heiromancer
Trilogy

## Douglas J. Bornemann

Published by SORCELERITY

First Print Edition
ISBN 978-0-9906281-5-6
Copyright © Douglas J. Bornemann, 2019

*To Marilyn...who knew me before I did*

# Table of Contents

# ÒRAMATIS PERSONAE

**Albert Graves**
> *Curator of Profanities in the Holy City; the Primal's confessor*

**Alexi Reysa**
> *Dona's classmate at Exidgeon University*

**Alistair Nevinander**
> *Aging patriarch of the Nevinander family*

**Alphonse**
> *Alexi's fencing buddy*

**Amanda Merinne**
> *Dona's mother and Rayen's sister and caretaker*

**Amehtan Shoruga**
> *Hathaway Professor at Exidgeon University; Shunese defector*

**Arerio**
> *Marguerite's manservant*

**Arietta Charwick**
> *Dona's gangly and unpleasant classmate*

**Armand Goodkin**
> *Monsignor who arrives to investigate the disturbance at the University*

**Aunt Olivia**
> *Nathalie Nevinander's sister*

**Captain Dunsmore**
> *Captain of Trifienne's Militia*

**Caroline Caldor**
> *Dona's classmate*

**Chancellor Wiggins**
> *Chancellor of Exidgeon University*

**Clarke Reston**
> *Professor of History at Exidgeon*

**Constable Connelly**
> *Constable of Trifienne; Miranda's father*

**Count Lazlo**
> *Blond-haired advisor of Crown Prince Nathan*

**Crown Prince Nathan**
> *Sovereign of Trifienne, father of Princess Julienne*

**Crown Princess Irina**
> *Wife of the Crown Prince*

**Damien Nevinander**
> *Alistair and Nathalie's eldest son*

**Darron Goodkin**
> *Primal and brother of Monsignor Armand Goodkin*

**Dominick Everson**
> *Professor of Grammar at Exidgeon*

**Dona Merinne**
> *Daughter of Henry and Amanda Merinne; student at Exidgeon University*

**Dreamweaver**
> *Legendary niece of Phrendonian, reputed to have invented Daemonology*

**Eloise**
> *Nathalie and Alistair Nevinander's maid*

**Francesca Harcourt**
> *Mother of Jonas and Mathilda; they call her 'Nanna'*

**Father Cartier**
> *Priest of St. Sophia's Church in Trifienne*

**Garvin**
> *Caretaker at St. Sophia's Church*

**Giles Boothby Harcourt**
> *Jonas and Mathilda's dead father*

**Gregory Delauren**
> *Dona's friend and sometimes classmate; an up-and-coming tenor at the opera*

**Helena Dunkirk**
> *Dona's friend and roommate at Exidgeon*

**Jamie**
> *Nephew of Father Cartier, waiter at Tabalaria*

**Jonas Mapleton Harcourt**
> *Traveling merchant dealing primarily in spirits*

**Josephus Vane**
> *Inquisitor with a reputation for ruthlessness and discretion*

**Magister Celeric**
> *A Magister at the Academy*

**Magister Treust**
> *A Magister at the Academy, former mentor to Michlos; creates Amulets*

**Magister Wellsbrough**
> *Provost of the Academy*

**Marguerite Serrola**
> *Matriarch of the Serrola family*

**Mathers**
> *Librarian at Exidgeon University*

**Mathilda (Tilly) Harcourt**
> *Sister to Jonas, owns and runs a brothel in Trifienne*

**Michlos Serrola**
> *Son of Marguerite and Spiros Serrola*

**Miranda Connelly**
> *Dona's friend and roommate at Exidgeon; Constable's daughter*

**Miss Maxtine**
> *House mother of the women's dormitory at Exidgeon*

**Morissant**
> *Gregory Delauren's wealthy patron*

**Mr. Lop Ears**
> *Dona's childhood stuffed toy*

**Mrs. Caldor**
> *Mother of Caroline, Member of the Venerable Assembly of Church Mothers*

**Mrs. Laverne Temrich**
> *Hard-of-hearing member of the Venerable Assembly of
> Church Mothers*

**Mrs. Muscany**
> *Member of the Venerable Assembly of Church Mothers*

**Mrs. Myra Curtsik**
> *Member of the Venerable Assembly of Church Mothers*

**Mrs. Tibbleman**
> *Senile but lovable member of the Venerable Assembly of
> Church Mothers*

**Nathalie Nevinander**
> *Alistair's wife; Member of the Venerable Assembly of
> Church Mothers*

**Newcomb**
> *Princess Celeste's manservant and personal guard*

**Ordinal Bittern**
> *Close ally of Ordinal Laitrech*

**Ordinal Cronsett**
> *Eldest of the current crop of Ordinals*

**Ordinal Isrulian**
> *One of Darron's more recent and regrettable appointments*

**Ordinal Kuypers**
> *One of the current crop of Ordinals*

**Ordinal Laitrech**
> *Advisor of Primal Darron Goodkin; one of his more re-
> cently appointed Ordinals*

**Ordinal Lavicius**
> *Charming and rapacious Ordinal; A patron to the Accipi-
> trines*

**Ordinal Marius**
> *One of the current crop of Ordinals*

**Ordinal Shelby**
> *One of the current crop of Ordinals*

**Ordinal Stohl**
> *One of the current crop of Ordinals*

**Phrendonian**
> *Legendary codifier of Phrendonic Heresy*

**Princess Celeste**
*Sovereign of the Island that is home to the Artist's Colony*

**Princess Julienne**
*Youngest daughter of the Crown Prince and Princess of Trifienne*

**Professor Amberton**
*Scrawny Professor at Exidgeon, confidant to Professor Reston*

**Professor Bartholomew Driessen**
*Professor of Geometry at Exidgeon University*

**Professor Fenton Tamry**
*Professor at Exidgeon, confidant to Professor Reston*

**Professor Rutledge**
*Professor of Music at Exidgeon University*

**Randolph Brent**
*Bursar at Exidgeon*

**Rayen the Magnificent**
*Dona's uncle; subject to occasional seizures, he believes they reveal the future*

**Reginald Nevinander**
*One of the twin sons of Alistair and Nathalie*

**Spiros Serrola**
*Marguerite Serrola's dead husband*

**Terulla Kardell**
*Dona's classmate at Exidgeon*

**Thaddeus Nevinander**
*Alistair and Nathalie's youngest son, younger brother to Verone*

**Thurman Goodkin**
*Armand Goodkin's son and assistant*

**Venji**
*Verone's horse*

**Verone Nevinander**
*Daughter of Alistair and Nathalie Nevinander*

**Zachary Hepplewhite**
*Professor of Rhetoric and Theology at Exidgeon; old friend of the Monsignor*

# TRIFIENNE

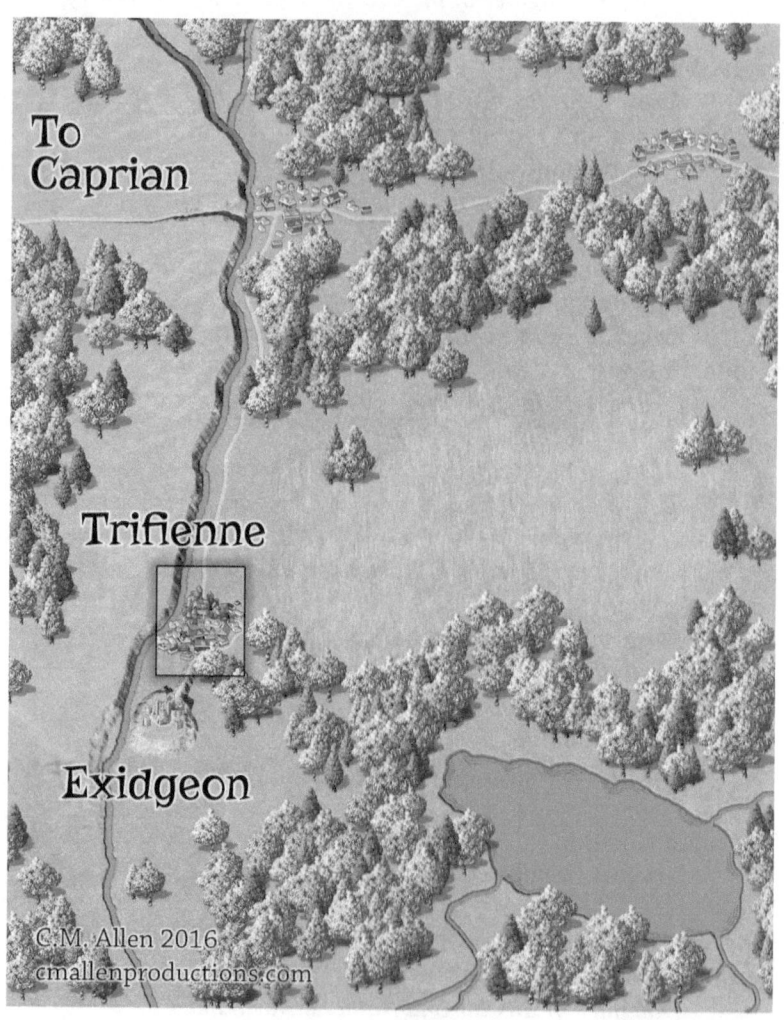

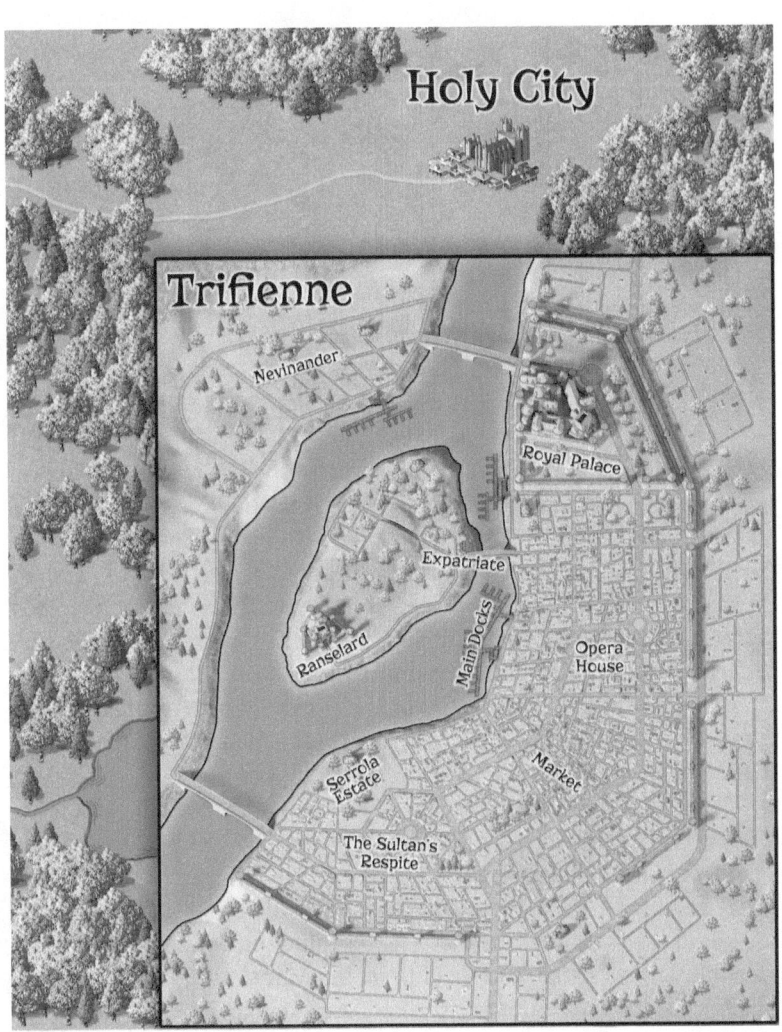

# SYNOPSIS

A *House of Cards* is the second volume of the *Heiromancer* Trilogy, to which *The Demon of Histlewick Downs* serves as a stand-alone prelude that sets the historical stage. The trilogy's first volume, *Practical Phrendonics*, recounts the adventures of Dona Merinne, a college student at Trifienne's Exidgeon University, when she encounters a secret society of scholars led by Professor Reston intent on researching magic, a practice the Church forbids. When, together with classmate Alexi Reysa, Dona finds Reston's copy of the heretical text *Practical Phrendonics* glowing in the library and runs off with it, she becomes the target of threats and a failed kidnapping attempt. The chief suspect is Professor Dominick Everson, who, until recently, had been Reston's uneasy ally. But Professor Everson has himself fallen prey to the machinations of Verone Nevinander, scion of a powerful heretical family, who wants the book for her own purposes.

The situation is complicated by the appearance of the Church's Inquisitor General, Monsignor Goodkin, and his son Thurman to investigate reports of heretical events on campus (instigated by Verone). Dona meets the Monsignor when he sits in on some of her classes, including one in which she gives a presentation about a woman who, unbeknownst to Dona, turns out to be the Monsignor's mother.

Dona soon learns Alexi is Reston's assistant, and Alexi attempts to recruit Dona to Reston's cause during a date at the legendary Sultan's Respite restaurant. Before Alexi clinches the deal, mysterious heretic Michlos Serrola disrupts a meeting at the next table between Thurman and Jonas Harcourt, a local ne'er-do-well. In the ensuing commotion,

Thurman glimpses Dona wearing a glowing necklace Alexi gave her (which marks her as a heretic), the Respite burns to the ground, and Dona is injured. Jonas assists in her rescue and offers to let Alexi and Dona lie low at his sister Tilly's brothel.

On returning to the University, Dona receives a ransom note that seeks Reston's book in exchange for releasing her good friend Gregory Delauren, and she demands that Reston's society help rescue him. When their rescue fails, out of desperation Dona enlists Michlos's aid, despite knowing almost nothing about him. While Michlos temporarily neutralizes Everson as a threat, Dona and Alexi learn that Gregory was never actually kidnapped.

Alexi and Dona regroup at the brothel, whereupon it is raided by the Inquisition. Jonas and Tilly's mother Sacrifices herself to enable their escape, and the four of them go into hiding. Dona's absence causes Reston to contact Dona's mother, who then unexpectedly arrives on campus to search for her. A chance meeting between Verone and Dona's mother (and her seizure-prone Uncle Rayen) alerts Verone that Dona is missing, and Verone offers the aid of her church group to find her.

When the Primal (the Monsignor's brother) calls the Monsignor back to the Holy City, the Monsignor leaves Thurman in charge of the ongoing Exidgeon Inquisition. Thurman aggressively ramps up the Inquisition—an approach the Monsignor had taken great pains to avoid. When the Monsignor discovers this development, he rushes back to Exidgeon, but on arriving, Ordinal Isrulian (who is complicit in Thurman's deal with Jonas) arrests the Monsignor on trumped-up charges. On his assistant Cartier's advice, Thurman flees to the Holy City to report the deed, leaving Cartier in charge of the Inquisition.

Meanwhile, Dona learns that Thurman has engaged Jonas to rob graves in support of a clandestine project, and she convinces Jonas and Tilly to return to Exidgeon. The four of them, together with Michlos and Reston's society, seek a way to use this information to blackmail Thurman and the Monsignor to abandon the Inquisition. Before they can implement their plan, however, a battalion of Inquisitors arrives outside Trifienne, bound for the University.

# A HOUSE OF CARDS

# CHAPTER ONE

## ρυLLING STRINGS

It was mid-morning before Verone finally got a chance to take a break. The ladies of the Venerable Assembly of Church Mothers had been enthusiastic when she suggested they carry signs to help search for Mrs. Merinne's missing daughter, but she had not anticipated how competitive they would be—each group wanted its sign to be a little better than everyone else's. Whenever someone came up with a new idea, all the teams rushed to incorporate it. After several groups had started over more than once, Verone finally insisted everyone make exactly the same sign. By the time they were prepared to strike out across the campus in search of Dona, Rayen had recovered enough from his seizure to accompany them and generously offered to take Verone's place.

Verone's break was short-lived. She barely had enough time to touch up her nails when the chapel door creaked open.

Mrs. Tibbleman called out querulously. "Hello? Is anybody here?"

"I'm here," Verone said, "but it seems the rest of your team has already left."

Mrs. Tibbleman's brows drew together in puzzlement. "Did we win already?"

"It wasn't that kind of team. They went to find Miss Merinne."

"Oh, yes, of course—such lovely signs. I'm sure they'll find her in no time. But what am I to do in the meantime? I so wanted to help."

Verone patted the elderly woman's gloved hand. "Perhaps they'll come back for you once they realize you are missing."

"I'm missing? Where did I wander off to this time?"

Verone tried a different tack. "Perhaps you'd like to join my team to help find Miss Merinne?"

"Oh, that would be splendid, especially since I seem to have misplaced my other team. I do so want to be helpful."

"I don't recall assigning anyone to watch the entrance to the University. Maybe we could be of some use there?"

"Oh yes—it wouldn't do at all to have her leave while we're trying so hard to find her."

"Agreed, but if you're going out in the sun, you'll need a proper hat."

Mrs. Tibbleman's hand went to her tulle-wreathed head. "Oh, I completely forgot about my veil—is it time for services already?"

"Not until after we search for Miss Merinne, which you can't do while wearing that. Fortunately, I brought a spare hat. You wait right here, and I'll get it."

From her things near the sacristy, Verone produced a hatbox. Inside was an enormous straw hat festooned with fake pansies and draped with two lengths of lavender sateen for securing beneath the chin. Humming tunelessly, she slipped a small glass vial from an internal pocket of her pinstriped jacket, uncapped it, and sprinkled its contents over the pansies. Then, she pulled two fist-sized rocks from her leather case, weighed them in her hands, nodded, and shoved them back inside. After tidying her ginger-blonde coiffure and smoothing her coat to ensure it showed her ample figure to best advantage, she snatched up a much smaller box sporting a little purple bow. With the case tucked firmly beneath her arm, hat in one hand and box in the other, she rejoined her companion.

Mrs. Tibbleman clapped excitedly at the sight of the purple bow. "Oh, is it my birthday again already?"

Verone proffered the hat. "Not quite yet, but the gift of a fine hat is an occasion unto itself. Why don't you try it on?"

"Oh, how adorable. I used to have one just like that years ago— they were all the rage when my little Eva was married. I even learned how to make the paper flowers."

Verone helped Mrs. Tibbleman remove her veil. "Let's get this on you, and then we can be on our way."

Mrs. Tibbleman inhaled deeply. "Why, this is delightful. It not only looks all floral, it smells that way too. I wonder how they manage that with paper flowers?"

Verone flashed a little half smile. "They are amazing, aren't they? Shall we head out?"

Clear skies had done little to banish the evening chill, and while Verone welcomed the relief from the heat, Mrs. Tibbleman shivered whenever they passed through a patch of shade.

"You poor dear," Verone said. "I'm not taking another step until we warm you up." She stopped at a bench, put down the box, and rummaged through the leather case. "Aha—this should do it." She draped a floral wrap over Mrs. Tibbleman's shoulders. "Now, please try to remember—the University is not as safe as once it was. While we all want to do our best to help Miss Merinne, we don't want to get ourselves in trouble."

Mrs Tibbleman adjusted the wrap. "Surely not. Isn't that why we have teams?"

"Indeed, it is. Now, we're coming up on the gate, and I think we can best keep an eye on it from just over there by that hedge. You see it?"

"I do—is it honeysuckle?"

"Very possibly. Now, I have a quick errand to run, but I'd like for you to stand right over there by the honeysuckle and keep a close eye out for Miss Merinne. Could you do that for me?"

"Of course. Oh, I do hope she drops by."

"And remember—while I'm gone, if you see anything suspicious, promise me you'll get back to the chapel just as quickly as you can."

Mrs. Tibbleman grew misty-eyed. "Things aren't like they were in the old days, are they? Why, I remember—"

"Mrs Tibbleman—do you remember what you are to do if you see anything out of the ordinary?"

"You mean like this hat?"

"No. I meant more like something threatening or suspicious. Do you remember what you are to do?"

"Why yes, very well. I'm to return to the church at once."

"Chapel," Verone corrected.

"Oh yes, of course."

"Perfect. Now, I'm going to run my errand. I'll be back just as soon as I can."

Mrs. Tibbleman made her way over to the hedge. "Never you worry. No living soul will pass that gate without me knowing."

Verone retraced a few steps and then ducked into an alley. Circling behind buildings, she positioned herself next to Dexter Hall. From there, she could see Mrs. Tibbleman dutifully standing guard. She faced entirely the wrong way, her attention focused on the hedge, apparently attempting to confirm if it really was honeysuckle. Taking a deep breath, Verone stepped out into the open and made a beeline for the front door. It was unlocked, and before Mrs. Tibbleman had any chance to spot her, she slipped inside.

Verone was immediately confronted by a young man arrayed in the embroidered vestments of the Inquisition. "Sorry, ma'am, these premises are not open to the general public."

Verone smiled broadly. "Fortunately, I happen not to be they. I'm here to see Father Cartier. Is he in, by chance?"

The young man looked uncertain.

"I know he's busy. It'll only take a minute. Could you tell him his friend Verone is here to see him?"

"One moment." He took a few steps down the hall and rapped on a door. He leaned in and started a low conversation with someone inside.

"Thank you, sweetie." Verone brushed past him into the room—and stopped short. Ordinal Isrulian looked up in surprise. He sat across from Cartier behind a huge desk. Several other people were scattered around the room as well.

"Verone?" Cartier asked.

"Oh, I'm so sorry. I didn't mean to intrude."

"Not at all," Isrulian said. "We were just finishing up here anyway." He stood. "You find the terms satisfactory, then?"

Cartier nodded. "I do, Your Ordinence."

"Excellent. Don't disappoint me."

"I wouldn't dream of it."

"Come," Isrulian ordered. The others leapt to their feet. Isrulian nodded to Verone as he passed, but the rest of the entourage filed by without acknowledging her.

When they were safely out of the room, Verone pushed the door closed, nearly stubbing the toe of the man who had inadvertently shown her in.

"I am sorry to have interrupted, but as the ladies and I were searching for our young truant, it occurred to me that you might like some of the baked goods they brought with them." She held out the box with the purple ribbon. "It's now a day old to be sure, but still very tasty."

"How thoughtful." He turned to place the box on the desk.

While he had his back to her, she glanced out the window. Mrs. Tibbleman was still standing guard in plain view.

"I'm so glad you're here," Cartier said. "So much has happened since yesterday you won't believe it. Please, have a seat."

"Don't keep me in suspense. What's going on?"

"Thurman, who was running this Inquisition is gone, and his father, the Monsignor, has been arrested for heresy."

Verone spent a long moment blinking. Everson's little heretical misstep delivering that package of hers to Shoruga in the Hathaway compound kept playing out in such fascinating ways. Who could have guessed the repercussions would extend so far beyond provoking the bit of campus-related Inquisitorial activity she'd originally intended? Though dying to hear more, she was careful to maintain a creditable facade of polite but disinterested astonishment. "How did that happen?"

"I'm still not clear on the details, but I think the Ordinal has a grudge against the Monsignor and is trying to discredit him. Likely Thurman was caught in the crossfire."

"But isn't the Monsignor the Primal's brother?"

"He is, but it sounds as though His Primacy may be in extremely poor health. Anyway, Thurman left this morning for parts unknown, and the Monsignor remains in custody, all of which leaves me in charge of the Inquisition. If I can apprehend the heretics responsible for the Phrendonic mischief here at the University, my career possibilities will be limitless. The Shunese suspect's suicide makes that more difficult, but I'll figure something out."

"How fortunate for them that you were here to take over."

"I owe you that, you know."

"Don't be silly. I only did what any friend would have done. I must say, though, with all these machinations, it's starting to seem a little more hazardous than when I first offered my advice."

Cartier shrugged. "Advancement usually entails some risk."

"That may be. However, I hope you will still listen to my advice when I tell you to be careful."

"Sound advice, as always."

"So, is this your office, now?"

"Indeed, it is, at least until Thurman returns, which I don't expect to happen anytime soon."

Verone wandered over to the window. The plaza before Exidgeon's two-story-tall gates buzzed with activity. Students and faculty bound for classes crossed paths with the everyday commercial traffic associated with running an institution of higher learning. A smattering of street performers plied their trades among the traveling vendors who today had chosen the plaza to set up shop. Since the University was situated on a plateau that rose a hundred fathoms above the surrounding plain, the only access to the world beyond lay across the plaza's cobbles. The walls that held the gates surrounded the entire institution—a relic of the fortress that had originally occupied the campus grounds.

"What a splendid view. You can see the gates from here."

"That's why we picked this building."

Verone started in surprise, nearly dropping her leather case. "Oh, my word."

"What's wrong?"

"That woman over there."

"The one in the hat?"

"The very one. If I didn't know better, I'd say she was my Aunt Marguerite."

"What connection does she have with the University?"

"None that I know of. But then, I've only seen her once in years and years. She had a huge falling out with my father. People say they had a disagreement over money, but I don't think that can possibly be—they were far too close for something so inconsequential to come between them."

"So, what do you think it was, then?"

"I'm not sure, but it must have been serious. Her husband died young, and she lived in that old house on the hill, becoming something of a recluse. Those few who did see her now and again whispered she had grown secretive and strange, especially once her children left. And given that outfit, I'd be inclined to agree. We all wondered how she was getting on, but Father forbade us to see her."

"How long have they been estranged?"

"At least twenty years."

"And they never tried to reconcile?"

"Well, she did show up briefly during Father's last birthday party, but there was no reconciliation. In fact, he ordered her off the property. But still, I can't imagine why he'd be so against any of us even talking to her."

Cartier peered out the window, perplexed by the woman's ongoing inspection of the hedge. "What is she doing out there, anyway?"

"I don't know. It does seem unusual, doesn't it? I'd offer to go ask, but I would really feel uncomfortable approaching her, given all the family history."

"No, no, it's quite all right."

"How about we discuss more pleasant topics—like pastries. Are you ever going to open those?"

Cartier strode back to the desk and scooped up the box. "I guess I could try one—but only if you promise to help."

"Well, if you insist."

As Cartier fussed with the box, the corner of Verone's mouth twitched into a half-smile. Events had aligned perfectly—it was time. She reached into her leather case. An instant later, total blackness enveloped the room. Then, there was a crash of shattering glass followed by a thud as something heavy landed on the floor and skidded across to the far wall.

"I can't see," Verone shrieked. "What's happening?"

"We need to get out of here. Take my hand."

"Where are you?"

"Here—I'm right here." Scrambling in the dark, he finally found her. "Quickly, this way."

As he led Verone toward the door, a wave of heat seared their backs. Verone screeched. She scrambled forward, causing Cartier to stumble. Miraculously, he found his way, pulling Verone behind him. Although it took only moments, their rush to the back of the building seemed an eternity.

Once outside, their vision cleared and they looked up at Dexter Hall in awe. A dome of impenetrable blackness engulfed the front of the structure, extending at its highest point all the way to the roof.

"Are you all right?" Cartier asked.

Verone nodded, but tendrils of smoke drifted around her.

"Here, turn around," Cartier ordered. Portions of her dress were smoldering, and he patted out the embers. "How about my back?" he asked, craning his neck.

"You seem fine," Verone said.

Cries erupted in front of the building—plumes of smoke now billowed from the dome.

"My word." Verone said.

The back door burst open, expelling Ordinal Isrulian and his retinue in a most undignified heap. "Cartier, what's the meaning of this?"

"Look for yourself, Your Ordinence. We're under attack."

"Is that smoke?"

"Oh, dear lord," Cartier cried. "The Monsignor." He leapt over Isrulian's minions and dove back through the door.

Isrulian gaped after Cartier as if he'd gone mad. Then he noticed his people staring slack-jawed at the smoking dome. "Don't just stand there, you imbeciles. Fight the fire."

As one, they rushed toward the front of the building.

Isrulian stomped off after them. "Someone's going to pay dearly for this."

Discovering that she was no longer in the company of anyone she recognized, Verone tidied her hair, tucked her empty case beneath her arm, and went blithely on her way as though nothing the slightest bit unexpected had befallen her.

· · · · ·

Moments later, the back door flew open again. The Monsignor emerged, assisted by both Cartier and Chancellor Wiggins. The three of them coughed and wheezed but had escaped the worst of the smoke.

"I see our heretics have made their next move," the Monsignor said.

Chancellor Wiggins winced at the sight of the smoking dome. "You don't suppose they'll burn any more buildings, do you?"

"I wish I could say." He turned to Cartier. "Young man, you have my undying gratitude. Without your selflessness and quick thinking, the Chancellor and I would surely have perished. Is Thurman safe?"

"He is," Cartier said. "He left the University this morning. It seems he was concerned for his uncle's welfare."

"Was he, now?"

"Since I've taken his place," Cartier said, "I'm afraid I will be expected to incarcerate the two of you again once we establish a new base of operations, but in the meantime, I have little choice but to release you on your own recognizance. If, however, you prefer to discuss the matter with His Ordinence, I believe I can hear him cursing at the front of the building. If not, I would certainly understand."

The Monsignor patted Cartier's shoulder. "We wouldn't want to disturb him when he is in such obvious distress. If ever I can return the favor—"

"Now is not the time," Cartier said. "Off with you."

The Monsignor shook Cartier's hand. Without another word, he and the Chancellor headed west—away from the dome, the smoke, and all the indignities of Dexter Hall.

# CHAPTER 2

# OUT OF CONTROL

The bell that tolled the hours in Exidgeon's clock tower had been a gift from the members of the first graduating class. Shortly after it was installed, the clock's mechanism was temporarily disabled for alterations to allow students to enjoy a full night's rest. Since then, however, it had reliably ensured the promptness of generations of students. Thus, when it rang again only a few minutes after striking eleven, Alexi knew something was amiss.

"It can't be noon already, can it?"

"Thirteen o'clock, judging by the number of chimes," Jonas replied. "Oops, make that fourteen."

The fraternity's cellar meeting room, which Professor Reston used for his Secret Society meetings, currently hosted an unlikely assembly of individuals. Dona considered them each in turn. Reston's student Alexi Reysa, who saw himself as Professor Reston's protégé, had been responsible for involving Dona with Reston's group in the first place. Dona had naturally taken refuge with them after an awkward chance encounter with Monsignor Goodkin and his son Thurman. Even though Thurman had every reason to suspect her of Heresy, he hadn't confronted her in front of his father, likely because Dona could implicate him in some shady dealings with another of the room's occupants, Jonas Mapleton Harcourt. Dona had convinced Jonas and his sister Tilly to join forces with Professor Reston to forestall the

Inquisition by using their information to blackmail Thurman, since his father also happened to be the Church's current Inquisitor General.

The clocktower's bizarre behavior had begun while Reston and his colleagues Amberton and Tamry negotiated the plan's final strategic touches. There was much to discuss—Dona's news that an army of Inquisitors had gathered outside of Trifienne made discovery of their Society and its study of forbidden Phrendonic Arts a real and terrifying possibility.

Reston was the first to recognize the bell-ringing for what it was. "It's an alarm." He leapt to his feet and dashed up the stairs.

Other fraternity residents also noticed the unusual chimes, and by the time Reston's group made it outside, quite a crowd had gathered. Although they were nowhere near the front gate, the great black dome that obscured much of Dexter Hall was plainly visible, as were the thick plumes of smoke rising from it.

It took Jonas only seconds to assess the situation. He turned immediately to Dona. "Where did you say your Enforcer was going?"

"He was going to help the constable."

"Apparently, he made a detour."

Dona bristled at the implication. Although Jonas was convinced Michlos was protecting Trifienne's powerful Heretical families at all costs and therefore couldn't be trusted, Michlos had selflessly assisted Dona on several occasions. "You don't know he did this."

"Darkness and flames? Seems to me it has 'Michlos' written all over it."

"Um, in case you've forgotten, you started the Respite fire."

"Well, I certainly couldn't have started this one."

"He'd have no reason to do this."

"Other than to put the entire University on lockdown at precisely the time when he knows we are all gathered here, and coincidentally, just in time for the First Wave. Now the Inquisition has every opportunity to root you folks out as heretics, ruin your lives, and blame you for whatever brought them here in the first place. Wouldn't that be a tidy way to get rid of your Enforcer's thorny little problems?"

Tilly seized her brother by the ear lobe. "One more word, mister, and your ear and I are going to go get a much closer look at that dome."

"Enough—all of you," Reston thundered. "Alexi, see if you can locate Everson, but don't let him know you're looking. The rest of you, get back inside and stay there. I'll be back once I know what's going on."

Alexi nodded and ran off.

Jonas started to say something but stopped when Tilly gave his ear a warning tug. Dona also began to object, but the look in Reston's eye made her think twice. Only once they had all filed back into the fraternity did Reston stalk off in the direction of the dome.

. . . . .

Verone finally caught up with Mrs. Tibbleman in the middle of the park next to the University cafeteria—arrayed in the floral hat and wrap, she was hard to miss. Of course, the fact that she seemed to be engaged in a game of cat and mouse with several park-raised ducks didn't hurt either.

"Mrs. Tibbleman," Verone said. "What are you doing?"

"Oh, Miss Nevinander. Would you be a dear and give me a hand with these? If I'm to get dinner on the table before midnight, I'd best be wringing a neck or two."

"What are you thinking? You can't be wringing necks in your Sunday best. Here, let me help you out of those things."

"Oh, how silly of me. My little Eva would never forgive me if I dirtied them before the ceremony. Listen. They've already started ringing the bells."

Verone lifted the wrap from the older woman's shoulders and slid it back into her case. Then she removed the hat as well.

"There," Verone said. "Now, weren't we on our way back to the chapel?"

"Oh, that's right. Do you suppose they've found that sweet little girl yet?"

"I hope they've had better luck than we have. Imagine, spending all this time looking and finding absolutely nothing."

"Oh, how disappointing. Have we really found nothing whatsoever?"

"I'm afraid not. It's been a very dull morning. But at least we gave it our all."

"Yes, we did, didn't we? I am so glad I got to be on your team."

Verone gave Mrs. Tibbleman a little squeeze as they walked, keeping the hat in her other hand behind her and out of sight. "So am I."

As they passed the cafeteria, Verone flicked the hat into a large, aromatic trash bin.

. . . . .

Professor Hepplewhite set down his teacup and looked up from his text as the belfry sounded the alarm. When the ringing didn't subside, he headed out, but as he stepped into the hallway, he was sidetracked by a familiar voice.

"Hello, Zachary."

The Monsignor stood a short distance away, leaning against the wall.

"Armand? I'd thought you'd left Exidgeon."

"I'm back."

It struck Hepplewhite that something looked different about him. "Where's your cane?"

"I seem to have misplaced it. I find I really do miss it when it's gone."

Hepplewhite's eyes narrowed. "This doesn't have anything to do with this alarm, does it?"

"Would you care for an update?"

"I would, but first, let's get you sitting down." He helped the Monsignor out of the hallway and into his office chair.

"Ooh, that's so much better."

"Now, what's all this fuss about?"

"If you're asking about the bells, heretics have set Dexter Hall ablaze. If, on the other hand, you're wondering about the loss of my cane, until just a short time ago, I was imprisoned there on suspicion of being one. Heresy suspects are not generally permitted to keep anything resembling a weapon, including a cane."

"What?" Hepplewhite cried. "Didn't you leave Thurman in charge of the Inquisition while you were away? You mean your own son imprisoned you?"

"He had little choice, I'm afraid. Ordinal Isrulian ordered him to."

"What's an Ordinal doing at Exidgeon?"

"A very good question, but before we ask it, I must warn you—aiding a suspected heretic can be a very dangerous thing. Are you willing to take the risk?"

"Don't ridiculous. We'll get this straightened out."

"I'm not so sure about that. I doubt Isrulian would be so bold without support."

"Surely His Primacy won't tolerate such insubordination."

"Zachary…my brother is dying."

"Oh, I'm so sorry."

"I would not have mentioned it except to impress upon you that we cannot rely on his aid in this. Are you still sure you want to help?"

In all their years of friendship, Hepplewhite had never known the Monsignor to be this defeatist—the situation was clearly dire. And yet, Hepplewhite's choice was clear. "What kind of friend would I be if I turned my back now?"

"A far safer one."

"Stop with the melodrama. How can I help?"

"I'll need a safe place to work. Our affiliation is well known here, so it shouldn't be anyplace obviously connected with you."

"If Isrulian has accused you of heresy, shouldn't we get you off campus entirely?"

"That may no longer be an option. A battalion of Inquisitors will arrive at Exidgeon any minute now. Once Isrulian reaches them, I'll have no chance of getting past."

"Can you get to them first?"

"Even if I did, Isrulian technically outranks me, and the attack on Dexter Hall has him in a frenzy."

"How does he know heretics were responsible?"

The Monsignor chuckled, but his expression remained grim. "I suppose I should have let you go look. A dome of darkness covers the whole front of the building. They couldn't have been more obvious about it if they'd posted signs."

"I thought you said they'd set it on fire."

"They did that, too. The darkness is no doubt making the flames extraordinarily difficult to fight."

"How did you escape?"

"Thurman's assistant Cartier risked himself to release both Chancellor Wiggins and me. Without him, we would have died."

"They arrested the Chancellor?"

"Isrulian was trying to make the case that the Chancellor and I were colluding to cover up the heresy. Apparently, he got the Chancellor to say things that could be twisted to support such a theory."

"Where was Thurman while all this was happening?"

"He'd already left. If I understood Cartier correctly, Thurman went to inform my brother of Isrulian's treachery. Cartier has assumed nominal control of the Inquisition, but no doubt while Isrulian remains, he'll be pulling the strings."

"What does Isrulian hope to gain?"

The Monsignor paused. "I'm not sure. Isrulian has never been a fan of my brother's policies, or mine for that matter. I could see him wanting to discredit me to embarrass my brother, but with my brother dying, I don't see how he benefits. And if my brother finds out with enough time to spare, Isrulian stands to lose quite a bit."

Hepplewhite raised an eyebrow. "Perhaps he's trying to discredit you to keep you from assuming the Primacy in your brother's place."

"But I have no desire to be Primal. Even if I did, given the current Nine, I'd never muster the votes."

"Does Isrulian know that?"

The Monsignor frowned thoughtfully. "You may have a point."

A knock on the door caused both men to jump. "Professor Hepplewhite? Are you there?"

Dona's mother poked her head in. "I do hope we're not interrupting anything, but this will only take a minute."

. . . . .

The mood was bleak in the fraternity's basement as Reston's compatriots awaited his return. The unrelenting throb of the bell in the clock tower hammered home the inevitability of the Inquisitorial horrors soon to be unleashed upon their little Society in self-righteous defense of incontrovertible truth. Even Tamry was taciturn.

Dona's thoughts kept returning to the shambles of their plan, which had seemed so promising just a few minutes before. But in the face of such a brazen attack, regardless of any influence they might have over Thurman, the Inquisition would have no politically viable option other than to bring the heretics to justice. And just who were these heretics anyway? Did it even matter? After all, what could any genuine heretic possibly stand to gain from an all-out attack on the University? Was Jonas right? Could Michlos have been playing her?

She shook her head. What was she thinking? Michlos had been instrumental in convincing Princess Celeste, ruler of the island that held both the Artists' Colony and Ranselard Keep, to join their cause. Had Michlos simply wanted to stir up trouble, he wouldn't have bothered with Celeste—he would have attacked the Inquisition yesterday and saved himself the effort. It had to be someone else. Everson? That didn't make sense either—he had as much to lose as the rest of them. But who else was there? She couldn't think of anyone who stood to gain from inciting an Inquisition. That is…unless Jonas was right—an enforcer might be able to use such an attack to get the Inquisition to do his dirty work by eliminating Reston's problematic little group in one fell swoop. Once they'd been dealt with, the Inquisition would leave, and the Enforcer's precious *status quo* would be maintained.

"Jonas?" she asked. "How many Enforcers, other than Michlos, would you expect there to be in a city like Trifienne?"

"I have no idea. That's not something they'd advertise."

"But, more than one?"

"It would probably depend on demand."

"But more than one is possible, and maybe even likely, right?"

He eyed her suspiciously. "What are you getting at?"

"Well, if, as you say, an Enforcer would benefit from bringing the Inquisition down on us, and if there exists more than one Enforcer in Trifienne, then any one of them could have committed the attack."

"Except that Michlos had knowledge, motive, and opportunity—there's no need to invent anyone else."

"So, we are to imagine there may be dozens of other Enforcers out there, all of whom, except for Michlos, are just sitting idle. Why couldn't our attacker be any one of those others?"

Jonas squinted as he parsed her theory. "Or maybe they're all working under Michlos's direction."

"I doubt that very much—not when working together means that catching one is the same as catching them all."

"All right, I admit it's possible," Jonas said. "Just not likely, particularly since the whole point of having enforcers is to avoid Inquisitions."

"While we might not agree that Michlos is responsible, I'll grant you that an Enforcer would have quite a bit to gain, provided the Inquisition remains contained at the University."

Jonas packed his pipe with tobacco from a small pouch. "For the sake of argument, let's say we agree. So what?"

"Because once we get past who did it, we can start to focus on what we should do about it."

Jonas tamped the tobacco with his thumb. "I'm open to suggestions."

Amberton shifted uncomfortably, his eyes fixed on Jonas's pipe.

"For one thing," Dona said. "The old plan will have to be scrapped."

Jonas produced a box of thin wooden sticks. "Obviously."

"That leaves two possibilities. We can either try to convince them to abandon the Inquisition, which seems pretty unlikely given the circumstances—"

Jonas lit a stick in a nearby kerosene lamp. "Or?"

Amberton could contain himself no longer. "You aren't actually planning to smoke that thing, are you?"

Jonas applied the flaming stick to the tobacco. "I appreciate your concern. Not to worry though—I don't actually inhale."

Amberton glared, shook out his handkerchief, and held it over his nose.

"Or," Dona said, "we can try to convince them that their attacker has left."

"And how do we do that? We don't even agree on who the attacker was."

"No, but we can agree on at least one of his signature techniques."

Tamry interjected. "Are you suggesting we use Phrendonic Heresy as bait?"

Amberton snorted through his kerchief. "More madness."

"I don't see what we have to lose," Dona said. "The Inquisition knows there's at least one heretic on campus. If we do nothing, they'll meticulously interrogate the entire University. If, on the other hand, we can convince them that their heretic is escaping, they'll have little choice but to pursue. It might at least buy us a chance to disappear into Trifienne instead of simply waiting here for them to arrive with the thumbscrews."

Tamry eyed her skeptically. "As a plan, it seems a wee bit sparse on detail."

"That's deliberate. I don't yet know enough to maximize our advantage."

"Advantage?" Amberton spat. "Wasn't it you who pointed out they have an army practically on our doorstep?"

"The advantage of heresy. Once I'm properly briefed on our potential, I'll be happy to supply the details."

Amberton was so disturbed by the suggestion he dropped his hanky. "Preposterous. We can't use heresy to fight the Church—we'll be crushed."

"That's why we must use it to mislead instead."

The chamber's door rattled, followed by a muffled curse.

"Who is it?" Jonas called out.

"It's me, Reston. Who locked the door?"

"One second." Jonas rolled up his sleeves and fussed at the lock. A moment later it clicked, and the door swung open. "Sorry—I didn't know if it was you or the Inquisition."

"What did you find out?" Dona asked.

Reston looked grim. "The good news is I managed to eliminate the dome, and the fire is under control."

"And the bad news?"

"They've arrived. Now that the fire's out, I shudder to think where all those Inquisitors will be turning their attention next."

# CHAPTER 3

# RELATIVE INTELLIGENCE

Alexi headed for Everson's office, his mind racing. Could Michlos have set them up? He couldn't fathom having been so completely wrong about someone, but try as he might, he couldn't shake the seed of doubt Jonas had planted. No one else had motive. Everson may have had opportunity, but Alexi couldn't imagine he'd want any part of stirring up the Inquisition that way. Hijacking Dona's carriage in an attempt to steal Reston's heretical spellbook was one thing—directly attacking the Inquisition was something else entirely.

He'd hoped to approach Everson's office discreetly, but the warning bell made that almost impossible. Entire classes had emerged from classrooms all over campus to see what the noise was about. At least the spectacle at the gate prevented anyone from focusing attention on him. Everson's office building was no exception. Most of the building's occupants stood on the lawn gaping at the dome and smoke. To his delight, Everson was among them, though Alexi almost hadn't recognized him—Everson's arm was in a sling, and he wore a large bandage across one side of his face. Unlike the puzzled expressions of the others, Everson's was one of shock and dread.

Alexi sidled his way toward the building, doing his best to keep out of sight of his quarry. He was so fixated on Everson that he was startled by a tug on his arm from one of the ladies carrying the crude sign he'd been using to shield himself from Everson's view.

"Excuse me, young man," the lady said. "I'm Mrs. Muscany, this is Mrs. Curtsik, and that's Mrs. Temrich. We were wondering if you happened to know Miss Dona Merinne, and whether you may have seen her recently?"

Surprised, it took him a moment to register who was asking, and several more to ponder why this woman might want to know in the first place. In the meantime, the two other ladies closed ranks on him.

"He's probably hard of hearing," Mrs. Curtsik said. "That seems to be going around lately."

"It's no wonder he didn't hear you, the way you mumbled it," Mrs. Temrich said. "If you're going to ask, then ask. Coy is a tactic better suited to finding a husband than a truant. Here, allow me." She grabbed the sign, waved it in front of Alexi's face, and shouted "Hey, Mister. Have you seen Dona Merinne lately?"

Everson's head whipped around. Alexi dodged behind the sign, keeping his fingers crossed he hadn't been recognized.

"Now you've gone and startled him," Mrs. Curtsik said. "Young man, we're terribly sorry. For goodness' sake, Laverne, will you please stop threatening the poor lad with that sign?"

"No, she's fine. Really," Alexi said, terrified she might take the sign away. "In fact, let's have a closer look at it."

In large block letters, the ladies had spelled out "MISSING." Underneath, Dona's name appeared in bright red, with a fairly accurate description, a plea for help, and a rough map to the campus chapel. A reward was offered, along with what appeared to be an editorial afterthought: *One fresh apple pie every week for three full months, courtesy of Mrs. Laverne Temrich.*

"Apple pie?" Alexi asked.

"I told you not to put that there," Mrs. Muscany said.

"It got his attention, didn't it?" Mrs. Temrich retorted.

Mrs. Curtsik turned to Alexi. "Just ignore them."

"I heard that," Mrs. Temrich said.

Mrs. Curtsik sighed. "Of all things, that, she hears."

"Sorry ladies," Alexi interrupted. "But as tempting as that reward is, I can't say I've seen her."

Craning his neck to peer around the sign, Alexi realized that Everson was no longer standing on the lawn in front of the building. Then, out of the corner of his eye, he noticed a window open in the office building. At first, he was relieved to make out Everson's profile hovering there, but then realized he'd been spotted.

"I'm sorry, but I really need to go." He turned, intending a mad dash for the fraternity. He made it only three steps before his consciousness slipped away.

.  .  .  .  .

Four observers watched from a rise overlooking the surrounding countryside. In the distance, the road from Trifienne wended through the golds, reds, and browns of autumn, up the ramp, and through the great University gates. Beyond those gates, a plume of dark smoke still drifted into the late-afternoon sky. Even from this distance, the ancient ramp, which served as Exidgeon's sole access to the outside world, seethed with activity. Antlike figures disappeared row by row through the gates. When the ramp was empty, the gates, which had stood open for more than a generation, ground slowly closed.

The Crown Prince, in glinting battlegear atop his black steed, wore his displeasure like a shroud.

"My apologies, Sire," Constable Connelly said from astride his bay roan. "We only found out about this force late last night. There just wasn't enough time to raise the militia and intercept them before they made it to the college. We didn't even know that was their goal until a few hours ago."

The Crown Prince rubbed his chin thoughtfully. "Captain Dunsmore, what are our chances of evicting them by force?"

The third observer shifted in his saddle. "Given a little more time to muster, we will greatly outnumber them, but their occupation of the University gives them a tremendous defensive advantage. We know from the successful campaign against the Chervillians that taking the fortress is possible, but only through a protracted siege."

"Do we have any information on the nature of the fire?"

"We don't," Connelly said. "The Inquisition force cut off our ability to investigate."

"Suggestions, gentlemen? How would you deal with these interlopers?"

Dunsmore responded first. "We have the upper hand. While a siege would be long and costly, we would ultimately prevail. Despite the cost, we can't afford to meet such tests of your sovereignty with weakness or equivocation. Use the diplomats, but only to convey our view that they are trespassers who must immediately and unconditionally vacate."

"And if they call our bluff?"

"I did not suggest it as a bluff, Sire. I would make good on the threat. Lay siege, but give them frequent opportunities to surrender their arms and return whence they came. It shouldn't take them long to see the futility of their position."

"Constable? Do you concur?"

The Constable shook his head. "I see the situation as more nuanced. If this were an isolated band of brigands, I might be persuaded, but this force carries the imprimatur of the Church. Not only could the Church send reinforcements in the event of a siege, but also many of our men would be hard-pressed to raise a hand against men of the cloth. In the worst-case scenario, the Church might turn to other kingdoms for aid. Until we know more, I would treat them as unsophisticated foreign diplomats instead of an invasion force. Find out what they want, and see whether we can facilitate it. Perhaps the whole situation can be resolved without resort to force. After all, it's only been a few days since Father Cartier came to me requesting the Crown's assistance in tracking down the brothel heretics."

The Crown Prince eyed the Constable skeptically. "Doesn't that suggest this force may be gathering as the first prong of a full-scale Inquisition to be launched on Trifienne?"

"I can't rule it out, but I'd hate to assume it and be wrong."

The Crown Prince turned to the fourth observer. "Beloved? Your opinion?"

The Crown Princess patted the neck of her restless white mare. "I believe our greatest responsibility lies with the citizens unlawfully imprisoned at the hands of the Inquisition. Whatever our approach, it must ensure their welfare. My heart tells me we must act swiftly: Too much diplomacy would permit the Inquisition to consolidate their position, but too great a show of force may encourage them to use our citizens as hostages. It's a delicate balance, and I would need more information to devise a detailed plan."

The Crown Prince nodded. "I anticipate more intelligence shortly. We camp here." At his signal, grooms stepped forward to attend the horses. The Crown Prince leapt nimbly from his stallion and assisted the Crown Princess.

Below the rise, a flurry of activity erupted as the Crown Prince's regiment set up camp. The Captain and the Constable disappeared to attend to their responsibilities, leaving the Crown Prince and Princess to themselves. They stood, arm in arm in the waning sunlight, gazing at their nemesis in the distance.

Before long, the galloping of a lone horse could be heard above the din of the camping regiment. As the hoofbeats drew closer, the Crown Prince's personal guard drew bows and stepped into formation to bar the intruder. As the rider became visible, however, they lowered their weapons, stood aside, and bowed. Without slowing, the rider sprang past them to the top of the rise. He leapt from his horse and shook the hand of the Crown Prince, concluding with a familiar slap on the shoulder. He then turned to the Crown Princess, who smiled and held out her arms to him.

"My favorite brother," she said as they embraced.

"A role I was clearly born to play," Michlos said, "given I'm your only brother."

. . . . .

Alexi was careful not to move or open his eyes. The ambient sounds were unfamiliar. For that matter, so was the lumpy sour-smelling pallet on which he lay. Numerous women's voices surrounded him at various distances, some vaguely familiar.

"They were emphatic," the first voice said. "Both Professor Hepplewhite and a visiting Monsignor said they saw her only yesterday in two different places on campus, but when we went back to her dormitory, no one there had seen her for a week. Just when it seems we're close, she slips away again."

It dawned on Alexi that the voice must belong to Dona's mother.

"There, there, dear," said another voice. "We'll find her. At least we know she's nearby."

"I'm cursed. First my Henry, and now this."

"You lost a son, too?" a third voice asked.

"No, no—Henry was my husband. He disappeared when Dona was just a girl. I think it was hardest on her. For weeks, she insisted her Da was going to come for her, refusing to believe he was really gone. It was three months before she finally began to doubt. She cried only one night. After that, she wouldn't speak of him again. She tried to act as though nothing had happened, but a mother can tell—she was never the same. It was as though someone snuffed out the joy in her life and left behind only raw determination. She learned to rely on herself, but it was too harsh a lesson learned at too tender an age."

Alexi's heart went out to Dona. No wonder she never mentioned her father.

"What happened to him?" another voice asked.

"We never found out. He disappeared shortly after Rayen came to live with us."

For the first time, Alexi heard a male voice. "I told you, he had no choice."

"Not now, Rayen."

"But Mandy—"

"I said, not now."

The male voice fell silent.

The squeaking of ancient hinges was accompanied by a swirl of chill air.

"Good evening, ladies," said yet another female voice. "Any luck out there?

A chorus of variations played out simultaneously. "Hello, Miss Nevinander."

"No luck yet, I'm afraid," Dona's mother said, "though we know she's nearby."

"Really? Verone said. "And how do we know that?"

"Professor Hepplewhite and his friend the Monsignor confirmed they saw her yesterday."

"You met a Monsignor? How interesting. Where was he?"

"In Professor Hepplewhite's office."

"Well, I'm not the least bit surprised, given all the Inquisitors who have shown up on campus all of a sudden."

"I did warn you," Rayen said. "I hope they weren't any trouble."

Verone paused as Rayen's reminder registered—surely his warning must have been a coincidence. Nevertheless, she filed it away for further consideration once the present situation was managed. "If they step up this Inquisition, we may be forced to abandon our plans.

While we would all surely love to see Mrs. Merinne reunited with her daughter, the University may soon become a dangerous place. Until we know more, I would like everyone to stay put in the chapel. Yes, Mrs. Tibbleman?"

"Does that include trips to the privy?"

"For the time being, the privy is fine. Be sure to take someone with you, though. Any other questions?"

"What have we here?" Miss Nevinander asked, her voice suddenly nearby.

"We're helping him," Mrs. Temrich said proudly. "He had a fit this afternoon just like Rayen had this morning."

"I have water ready," Mrs. Curtsik interjected.

"And I made him some porridge," Mrs. Muscany said.

"He had a seizure here?"

"Oh no," Mrs. Curtsik said. "It happened across campus near some of the offices. "One minute we were asking him about Miss Merinne, and the next, he just fell to the ground. We asked some nice young gentlemen to help us bring him here."

"Did he writhe and froth like Rayen?"

"Not really," Mrs. Temrich said. "Once he fell, he was just out."

"He snored the better part of the afternoon," Mrs. Curtsik offered.

"He doesn't seem to be snoring now, does he?" Verone said.

Mrs. Muscany shuddered. "You don't suppose he's passed on, do you?"

Alexi sat up, stretched, yawned deeply, and opened his eyes. His sudden return to life startled Mrs. Muscany so severely that she dropped the bowl of porridge. It smashed against the stone floor, dousing Mrs. Curtsik in a geyser of gruel.

He blinked at the unfamiliar surroundings. "Where am I?"

"You're at the Exidgeon chapel," Miss Nevinander said. "How are you feeling?"

"A little weak. What happened?"

"It seems you fainted, at least from what the ladies tell me. Do you have a history of seizures?"

"No."

"What were you doing when it happened?"

"I was going off to study."

"By the offices?"

"I had some questions for my professor."

"Which one? It wasn't by any chance Professor Everson, was it?"

Alexi did his best to mask his shock. It had to be a coincidence—there was no way she could have known, and the last thing he wanted to do was draw attention to any connection with Everson. "No, it was a geometry question. I was going to see Professor Driessen."

"I see. Well, I'm glad you are feeling better."

"I should probably get going. I have a test tomorrow, and I'm not even close to ready yet."

"Aren't you the least bit curious how you got here?"

"I am, but I only have a few more hours of study time left. What time is it anyway?"

"Almost six," Mrs. Muscany said.

Alexi leapt to his feet. "That late? I'm so grateful you took such good care of me, but I really have to go."

Mrs. Curtsik's face fell. "Don't you want any water?"

"Well, I could maybe use a sip or two."

Mrs. Curtsik brightened and offered the glass.

Alexi sipped—it seemed so important to her he couldn't bear to turn her down. "Thanks so much. I feel much better now."

Mrs. Muscany paused in patting the gruel out of Mrs. Curtsik's gown. "If you had a little more time, I could put on another pot of porridge. It won't take long."

"Thank you, but I really do have to go."

As he passed Dona's mother, she grabbed his arm. "Pardon me, I know you told the ladies you hadn't seen my daughter, but do you by chance know where I might find a Gregory Delauren?"

"Is he connected somehow?"

"Professor Hepplewhite said this Gregory person was friends with my Dona and that maybe he would know where she was."

"I know of him. He's the new tenor everyone is raving about. I heard he's taking some classes, but I've never met him. Have you tried the music department?"

"No, but I shall. Thank you."

Alexi suddenly realized the man standing next to Dona's mother was staring at him—it made the hairs on the back of his neck stand up. Though that made him even more anxious to be gone, he paused briefly at the door, genuinely touched by the ladies' eagerness to help him. "Thank you all again."

He was greeted by a chipper chorus of "you're welcome."

. . . . .

As the door closed behind him, Dona's mother sighed. "Well, he seemed a nice young man. What was his name again?"

"I don't think we ever asked," Mrs. Muscany said. "Did we?"

Dona's mother shrugged. "I guess we may never know."

"Yes, you will," Rayen muttered, but no one paid him any mind.

# CHAPTER 4

## VINÐICATION

Dona gaped at Reston in disbelief. "That's it? That's all the great and terrible disciples of Phrendonian can muster? No wonder Caprian was such a disaster."

Reston shrugged. "The Phrendonic arts have their strengths, but I never claimed they were all-powerful."

"So, you can't fly?"

"I'm afraid not."

"And you can't become invisible?"

"There has been significant investigative effort into the possibility."

"But without success. And you can't levitate."

"Technically, we could levitate, but given my limitations, it would require some setup."

"But you couldn't levitate some sort of vehicle, say a boat, safely over the precipice?"

"With time, materials, and engineers, we might be able to construct something to do that."

Dona rubbed her hands together. "Now we're getting somewhere. What do we need?"

Reston stroked his chin thoughtfully. "Well, first we'd need to build some sort of track or framework over the edge of the cliff extending all the way to the bottom—"

"Hold it right there. If we could do that, wouldn't it be simpler just to build a ladder?"

"Oh, definitely."

"We can safely scratch that one, then, don't you think?"

"Oh, I wasn't suggesting it as a viable option. I was merely saying it was possible."

Dona sighed. "Since we are under a bit of time pressure, let's try to keep the discussion to viable options, shall we? Can you create illusions?"

"To what end?"

"For example, could you create the illusion of a person creating another one of those domes, and then escaping down the ramp?"

"Not exactly."

"What does that mean?"

"Generating movement in images is difficult and very advanced stuff. I'm sure I couldn't pull it off convincingly. Now if you had some use for a static image, I might be able to manage that. The darkness globe they used on Dexter hall was a simple variant of a static image, with the advantage that you don't need to copy it from anything."

"I thought it was a dome?" Dona said.

"Oh, it looks like a dome, but the spell actually extends in a thirty-foot radius around the object it's cast on. The bottom half was blocked by the ground."

"What about putting Inquisitors to sleep? I know you can do that, I've seen you."

"True, but only one at a time, and I could only do a limited number before I became exhausted. That probably wouldn't be very useful against so many."

"I saw Michlos put five bouncers to sleep at once."

"I've been meaning to ask him about that. In general, vesting theory suggests that a spell vests only on a single target. It's a bedrock Phrendonic principle. I have no idea how Michlos got around it, but I sure would like to know."

"What about mind control? Can you do that?"

"Depends on what you mean. It would be fairly easy to improve someone's mood to make him more friendly."

"I'm not to the point of needing that quite yet, but I'm getting there. Actually, I meant controlling someone's actions. Could we make Thurman order the Inquisitors to leave, for example?"

"That's more akin in difficulty to making a moving image. It's theoretically possible, but it requires all sorts of subsidiary spells to work effectively, many to which I don't have access. Dreamweaver was said to have become adept at that sort of thing, but most with any scruples avoid it. If it gets out that you can do something like that, even your best friends tend to become awfully uncomfortable around you."

Dona leaned in closer. "Dreamweaver?"

Reston waxed didactic. "Dreamweaver gained notoriety for her unabashed practice of the Phrendonic Arts. At the time, the Church had not yet declared it to be heresy, but no doubt her misdeeds were influential in forcing the issue."

"But who was she?"

"We're not exactly sure. The name has been adopted at least three times over the years extending into different generations. Most historians accept the first as *the* Dreamweaver and discount the others as copycats. The first Dreamweaver lived contemporaneously with Phrendonian, and some commentators have speculated that she may have been the niece he refers to in the preface of his Opus. Although we don't know this for a fact, since her real name has been lost to history, it makes a certain amount of sense. At that time, the only way to be an accomplished practitioner was to have close ties with Phrendonian."

Recalling the similarity of the jewelry worn by the Dreamweaver in Celeste's portrait collection to the items in her hope chest, Dona couldn't help wondering if they were somehow connected. "Did she have children?"

"I've never come across mention of it. Why do you ask?"

"Just curious. What did she do that was so infamous?"

"Initially, it was her development and reckless use of emotion and mind control, but she is most universally reviled for single-handedly developing demonology as a Phrendonic discipline. It's tainted the public perception of the Phrendonic arts ever since."

"Demonology? You mean if she were here she could conjure a demon and send it after the Inquisitors?"

Reston laughed. "No doubt she would have fostered that misperception, but no, that's not what demonology is, at least not in the Phrendonic sense."

Tamry adjusted his bulk to fit more comfortably into his chair. "I'll grant that the historical implications of the rise of demonology are fascinating, at least to historians, but may I point out we have a situation that requires our immediate attention. Can we save the lectures for class?"

"I must admit," Dona said, "I'm at a loss here. I really expected you'd be able to use this heresy to do something useful."

Jonas snorted. "Why do you suppose it appeals primarily to academics? The Phrendonics I know of achieve their goals not so much by using what they can do, as by threatening what someone doesn't know they can't do. It's why they keep everything so hush-hush."

"Very well, then," Dona said. "What could we threaten that would get Thurman to call off the Inquisition?"

"It's a little tough to say," Jonas said. "Inquisitions are designed to weather just such threats—it's what they do. In fact, I'm not sure they'd leave even if they were convinced they'd rounded up all the heretics—they maintained a presence in Caprian long after the actual Inquisition was over. My suggestion would be for all the heretics to get out of Exidgeon and plan to stay out. Even non-heretics would probably be better off taking that advice if they can."

"The problem is that they've closed the gate. Even if it were open, the place is crawling with Inquisitors. We couldn't get out if we wanted to."

"They won't keep the gate closed forever. Either find a hiding place and wait it out, or come up with a way to open the gate and escape. That's where I'd put my money."

"Are the gates made of iron?" Reston asked. I've been through it dozens of times, but I never thought to check."

"Why does it matter?" Dona asked.

"Because if it is, I might be able to rust it."

"Wouldn't that just bind the hinges and keep them from opening?"

"That depends on the alloy. If it's pure enough, it might rust clean through."

"What about the Inquisitors? Even if we can get past them, what's to stop them from picking us off one by one as we run down the ramp?"

Reston perked up. "I think I have an idea—"

Another thud rattled the door.

"Who is it?" Jonas asked.

Alexi's muffled voice emanated from the other side. "Ow."

"I'll get it," Reston said. "I have a key, I may as well use it."

Jonas shrugged. "Suit yourself."

As Reston opened the lock, Alexi burst in, still short of breath from the run.

"Well?" Reston asked. "Did you find Everson?"

"I did—by his office while they were still ringing the alarm. Judging by his expression, he wasn't too happy about the attack on Dexter hall."

"Well that's good to know, but it's been hours since then. Where have you been?"

"I got sidetracked by three old ladies. They were looking for Dona as though she was a missing person. They made a sign and everything. While I was distracted, Everson spotted me, and the next thing I knew, I was waking up in a strange place."

"He *Slept* you?" Reston said, incredulous.

"He was probably panicking about the attack. I bet he has no idea who he can trust anymore. In retrospect, I'm not the least bit surprised."

"You should be—I never taught him that. Where did you wake up?"

"It was surreal. I woke up in a chapel filled mostly with elderly women, although Dona's mother was also there. It looked like she'd recruited them to help find Dona, except that someone else seemed to be running things."

"Wait," Dona said. "My mother was there, and someone else was running things?"

"That's what it looked like. A 'Miss Nevinander' was in charge."

"*Nevinander?*" Jonas and Reston said simultaneously.

Alexi nodded.

"The Nevinanders are one of the most powerful families in Trifienne," Jonas said.

"And, if I recall correctly," Reston added, "Everson's new girlfriend went by that name. I guess that explains where he learned the Sleep spell. Come to think of it, he was pretty sophisticated with his little scavenger hunt, too."

"But why is my mother still here?" Dona asked. "Professor, didn't you tell her to see Hepplewhite?"

"I did."

"They went," Alexi said, "but it sounded as though they had just gotten back. Apparently, the Monsignor was with him at the time, and both said they had seen you yesterday."

"Odd," Reston said. "Why would the Monsignor be closeted with Hepplewhite in the middle of this mess?"

Dona buried her face in her hands. "So now my mother is stranded here too? I can't just leave her to the Inquisition."

Jonas harrumphed. "An even more interesting question is how does Dona's mother know this Nevinander woman? I can't say as though I recall Dona ever mentioning her before."

"I don't have any idea," Dona said.

"Seems pretty coincidental, wouldn't you say? Here you are all lovey-dovey with your Enforcer friend, and now it seems Mom has one of her own? I thought you said they would never work together."

A chill went down Dona's spine. All eyes had turned to her, and in many, she saw alarm. Jonas's prattle was clearly having an effect. "I swear—I've never even heard of her before."

"Well, now that we really need him, just where is our Enforcer friend anyway?"

"They locked the gates. He can't get back in."

The room felt suddenly unfriendly. Even Tilly was eyeing her dubiously.

"Dona, where is the book?" Reston asked quietly.

"It's locked away in my hope chest."

"You're sure it didn't somehow make its way into Everson's hands?"

"I'm sure." Dona's mind raced, but she could think of nothing else to say to reassure them.

"If you're telling the truth, then having my copy of *Practical Phrendonics* at your dormitory is a huge threat to you, and we should get it out of there before the Inquisition finds it. If, on the other hand, you're using it in some sort of nefarious Nevinander plot, we'll know soon enough. Alexi, are you up for taking another walk?" Reston picked up his coat. "We'll be back shortly. I don't suppose I need to tell you to lock the door behind me, do I?"

Jonas just smiled and puffed on his pipe.

. . . . .

"Ladies," Verone called out. "Ladies, if I might have a moment of your time?"

The Venerable Assembly of Church Mothers gathered round.

"After considerable thought, I've decided to declare our efforts a success."

Polite applause broke out.

"Have we found the girl, then?" Mrs. Caldor asked.

"Not precisely, but we now have it from reliable sources—one of them a Monsignor no less—that Miss Merinne was safe and present here on campus as recently as yesterday. While we'd all dearly love to see the girl and her mother reunited with our own eyes, we certainly don't want to get in the way of an ongoing Inquisition. Therefore, I'd like everyone to be ready to leave by dawn tomorrow morning. I'll arrange with the nice Inquisitors to open the gates. Any questions?"

"Oh, I have one," Mrs. Muscany said. "Will the girl be leaving with us?"

Verone blinked twice before answering. "I'll see what I can do."

Mrs. Caldor stepped forward. "Would it be all right if I took my daughter with us? I'm not sure I want her attending classes here in the middle of an Inquisition."

"If she's here and ready on time, I doubt the Inquisitors will object. Anyone else?"

"If I may?" Rayen asked. "I want to thank you from the bottom of my heart for all the tremendous work you and the ladies have done on our behalf. You are as compassionate as you are beautiful."

Once again, polite applause broke out. Verone seemed momentarily at a loss. A hint of color tinted her cheeks, but she recovered quickly. She drew herself up and executed a dramatic bow. The ladies responded by increasing their applause, which continued until Verone gave in and bowed again.

"That's enough of that. Go to bed. Dawn comes early. Now go."

The applause faded, and the ladies went about their business.

Verone's mother Nathalie was waiting for her by the Chapel door. "He is a handsome one, isn't he?" she said, eyeing Rayen.

"Mum, don't start with me."

"What?" she asked innocently.

"You know very well what."

"Well, you can hardly blame a mother for trying."

Stepping outside, Verone once again scanned the ground for rocks. She slipped several that suited her into her leather case, checked to be sure it also contained the floral wrap, and stalked off into the twilight.

. . . . .

Alexi, Dona, and Reston approached the dormitory through the darkness. They detoured several times to avoid being seen, since the campus was unusually active. Apparently, the Inquisitors were not finding it trivial to locate reasonable accommodations. While many had chosen to occupy classrooms, some diehards had pitched tents and started small campfires as though stranded in the wilderness. The flickering flames begat sinister shadows that danced among the buildings.

The dormitory, by contrast, was uncharacteristically quiet, and the reason became clear when Dona tried the door—it was locked. She knocked for several minutes before Miss Maxtine's throaty voice called out, demanding she identify herself.

"It's Dona. Let me in."

The cacophony of turning bolts and dropping chains suggested Miss Maxtine had wasted no time in taking the necessary steps to ensure the safety of her charges. Finally, the door swung inward.

"It's so good to see you, child—we were worried half to death."

"Since when are we locking the door?"

"I've instituted a curfew. Under the circumstances, you can't be too careful. Of course, since you haven't been here, you couldn't have known, but until this unpleasantness blows over, I'm insisting everyone be in by eight o'clock sharp. Oh, and that means no visitors after curfew either." She eyed Reston and Alexi.

"Oh, I've forgotten my manners. Allow me to introduce Professor Reston and his assistant Alexi."

"Pleased to meet you," Miss Maxtine said.

"Professor Reston has agreed to help me with an extra-credit project, and I need to pick up some of my textbooks."

"Oh, that reminds me," Miss Maxtine said. "You had a visit from the campus librarian some days ago."

"I did?"

"Yes, his name was 'Mathers' or some such. He was an odd-looking man, nasty scratch on his face, but very polite—"

"Excuse me, ma'am," Alexi said. "Do you happen to remember which side of his face?"

"Let's see. It was on my left as I was facing him, so that would be on his right, I think. Anyway, I wouldn't normally have let him in, but he had a warrant from the Chancellor, so I didn't have any choice."

"You let him into my room?"

Alexi caught Reston's eye, and traced a line along his right jawline with his finger, mouthing the word "Everson."

Reston nodded, and his eyes narrowed.

"Well, I wasn't happy about it, I can tell you," Miss Maxtine said. "But whether I like it or not, I don't have the authority to override a warrant from the Chancellor."

"What did he want?" Dona asked.

"He was looking for a library book. Said it was a rare one and never should have been lent. I suggested he just wait for you to return it, but he would have none of it. I should warn you that he was obliged to break into your hope chest."

"You just stood by while he broke in and took it?"

"Well that's the odd thing. He never did find any book, and he looked mighty hard for it. I know because I insisted on watching him the whole time."

"So, he took nothing from Miss Merinne's hope chest?" Reston asked.

"Nothing."

"Did anyone else have access to her room?"

"Well, her mother tried to get in for a look-see, but I couldn't let her. It caused quite a row when I mentioned that I had to let the librarian in because of the warrant. I see her point, but my responsibilities on the matter are clear."

"And it was locked when the librarian tried to open it?"

"Yes, it was. He had to force the lock with a pry bar."

"That can't be," Dona cried. "I put it in there and locked it myself."

"I'm only saying what I saw."

"And what day was that?" Reston asked.

"Last Tuesday morning, I think"

"I can't believe you let some stranger paw through my things," Dona said. "And then you let it sit there unlocked for a whole week? That does it. Out of my way."

Dona forced her way past Miss Maxtine, but the startled house-mother recovered in time to block Reston and Alexi.

"I'm sorry, Professor—rules are rules."

Dona rushed up the stairs to her room and threw open the door. Miranda and Helena looked up in surprise—Miranda from her reading and Helena from her stitchery.

Dona inspected the chest's broken lock and ran her fingers over the pry marks. The contents had clearly been rummaged. A copy of the Chancellor's warrant lay on top.

"Miss Maxtine said Mathers searched it for a book," Helena said. "Neither of us was here when it happened. Where have you been?"

Dona ran to the windowsill and retrieved the key. It was exactly as she had left it. "All right, where is it?"

"What's gotten into you?" Helena asked.

"One of you has it, and I need it now."

"What are you talking about?"

"My book. Which one of you took it?"

"I don't know what you're talking about. If there's a book missing, Mathers almost certainly made off with it. Why don't you try yelling at him?"

"Miss Maxtine was watching. He didn't take it."

"Well, it was clearly locked when he got to it, or he wouldn't have needed the pry bar."

"Exactly, which means one of you must have gotten to it first."

"That's a terrible thing to say. We're your friends. We would never violate your privacy like that, would we, Miranda?"

Dona folded her arms.

"Miranda?" Helena asked.

Miranda hunched down behind her book. "Don't hate me."

Dona's eyes narrowed. "So, you do have it."

Miranda lowered her book, nodding slowly, her lip quivering.

Dona sighed in relief. "I don't hate you. In fact—I love you. If they had taken it when they broke open the chest, I'd be up to my neck in hot water. Now quickly, get it for me."

"I don't have it here anymore."

"What?"

"When I heard about all those Inquisitors arriving today, I thought it would be too dangerous to keep it here, so I hid it."

"Where?"

"In the library—in the theology wing near where you spent all that time on your talk. I just slipped it into the stacks."

Dona whirled to go.

"Are you coming back?" Helena called after her, "…ever?"

.  .  .  .  .

Downstairs, Reston and Alexi waited patiently for Dona to reappear. Miss Maxtine had politely but firmly closed the door in their faces and had just finished the arduous task of relocking it when they heard Dona's voice on the other side. After several more minutes of bolt-flicking and chain-sliding, the door stood open once more.

"I've found it," Dona said. "It's in the library."

"Inside or out." Miss Maxtine said.

Dona stepped outside. "Sorry."

Miss Maxtine had barely started the relocking process once more, when they heard her sigh. In a few more moments, the door stood open again, and Caroline Caldor emerged, accompanied by a lady who resembled her so strikingly that she simply had to be her mother.

Alexi and Reston stepped aside to let the women pass, but once Caroline's mother saw Alexi in the light from the doorway, she paused.

"Look, Caroline, it's the young man I was telling you about,"

"Oh, that's just Alexi," Caroline said. "I have some classes with him." She held her hand up in a shy little wave. "Hi, Alexi. Feeling better?"

"Hi, Caroline," Alexi said. "Yeah, I'm fine."

"Oh, and that's her, right there." Caroline said. "That's Dona Merinne."

Mrs. Caldor squinted through her spectacles. "Is it really? Oh, now that you mention it, I really do see the resemblance." She took Dona's hand. "I'm Mrs. Caldor, Caroline's mother. I'm so happy to see you safe and sound. I know it's late, but you really must come to the chapel and let your poor mother know you're all right. She was dreading leaving tomorrow without seeing you. It would mean so much to all of us."

"Leave?" Dona asked. "How? The Inquisition closed the gates."

"Well, I don't know all the details, but Miss Nevinander assured us we'd all be leaving at dawn. I confess this Inquisition has me on pins and needles, so Caroline is coming with us, at least until things settle down. Maybe you should come with us too."

"Perhaps I shall. Listen, I have a few things I need to get ready first, but I'll try to visit the chapel a little later, if that's all right?"

"The ladies will be so excited. We'll go let them know. Come along, Caroline."

Once the Caldors were safely out of earshot, Reston eyed Dona and stroked his beard. "It seems you've acquired a bit of a fan club."

"Yeah, it's a little weird," Dona said. "Now, about the book—it turns out it's not here."

"So you said. You expect us to believe Mathers took it, even though your housemother was very clear that he didn't?"

"No, that's not it—Miranda swiped it out of my hope chest first, so it wasn't there when Mathers, or whoever he really was, searched for it. I know it seems far-fetched, but it's the truth."

"Miranda Connelly?" Reston asked.

"Yes, she's my roommate."

The sound of Miranda's name jogged something in Reston's memory, and he recalled the troubled look on her angelic face as she asked him about Dona's *Practical Phrendonics* extra-credit project.

"Anyway," Dona said. "I know you think I've double-crossed you, and now I can't even get you the book like I promised. Still, you deserved to know what really happened, even though it's too wild a story for you to possibly believe. So, I guess I'll just leave tomorrow morning with Ma, then."

The pain in Alexi's eyes broke Dona's heart. Without Reston's trust, she couldn't stay, and as long as Alexi felt his reckless behavior with Reston's book made him responsible for endangering the Society, she knew he'd never leave them. Blinking back tears, she turned to go.

"I believe you," Reston said quietly.

"Wait—you do? Why?"

"Corroborating evidence," he said mysteriously. "Shall we continue our discussions in a less public place? We don't want to risk happening across any more of your fans, do we?"

Relief flooded through her, followed by something else. Now that she had to face the decision head on, the thought of turning down the opportunity to leave with her mother filled her with dread. Stay with Alexi and brave the maelstrom or abandon him to save herself? She'd have expected the answer to be obvious, but the thought of choosing—now that both options were before her—left her paralyzed. She'd only just learned she had fans, but already she felt unworthy.

"No, I suppose not," she said.

·  ·  ·  ·  ·

Sitting at their window overlooking the front door, Miranda and Helena exchanged puzzled glances.

"What was that all about?" Helena asked. "And why would Professor Reston think Dona double-crossed him?"

"I'm not sure," Miranda said. "But did you hear Mrs. Caldor say they'd be leaving at dawn?"

"So?"

"So, have you seen any militia here from Trifienne?"

"No," Helena said, "why?"

"Because there's no way the Crown would have allowed the Inquisition to gather such a big force here without militia oversight."

"Aren't they supposed to work together?"

Miranda pulled out a canvas bag and began tossing things into it "In theory, but in practice, it almost never works that way. If the Inquisition brought this many people here without permission, you can bet there's serious trouble brewing. Daddy will need to know."

"What are you doing?"

"Unless I miss my guess, those gates are not going to open very often in the next few days. If they really are going to let people through at dawn, I intend to be among them."

# CHAPTER 5

# RECKLESS ABANDONMENT

Jonas slapped his hand over his face and shook his head. "Are all academics this naïve? So, she tells you her roommate hid it somewhere, and you believe her? I suppose you also give her full credit when the dog eats her homework."

"Her story was corroborated not only by the house mother," Reston said, "but unintentionally by Miss Connelly herself, and before any of us knew anything about a Nevinander being involved."

"Either that or the roommate is in on it, and the book is still hidden in her room."

Tilly could contain her annoyance no longer. "I've had just about enough of your attempts to sabotage everything, mister. You sit here and talk big like you have some sort of superior insight, but you contribute no reasonable alternatives of your own. Well, just for the record, your 'superior insight' destroyed my livelihood, got us branded as heretics, and got our mother killed. I think I speak for everyone in this room when I say that if you can't come up with a constructive suggestion, keep your trap shut."

Jonas opened his mouth to say something but ended up puffing on his pipe instead.

"I apologize for my brother's lack of manners," Tilly said.

"As I was saying," Reston said, "there is a chance that the Nevinander woman will prevail upon the Inquisition to open the University gates at dawn to permit Alexi's elderly rescuers to go back to Trifienne.

I've been trying to think of a way to take advantage of the opportunity, but I'm concerned we might endanger the ladies."

Jonas choked a little, but Tilly's admonition held.

"Since Dona's mother is a member of the group," Reston continued, "Dona might be able to accompany them. Under the circumstances, I think she should try."

Dona whirled on him. "What? I can't leave you all behind."

"Besides," Alexi said, "what if this Nevinander woman is working with Everson? Wouldn't that put her in more danger?"

"Even if she is working with him, she'll probably just want the book, which Dona doesn't currently have anyway. I don't know when there'll be another opportunity to get someone out of here. Maybe she could get word to the Constable. Besides, don't you think she's put her poor mother through enough?"

She'd countered Reston's suggestion reflexively. He had no business making her decisions. Alexi siding with him only strengthened her resolve—it wasn't his place either. Besides, Alexi was in far more danger than she was. To escape the Inquisition unscathed, he was going to need help, but Reston's track record in that department was less than stellar. She doubled down. "I said I would go visit her tonight, and I will, but I never said I would go back with her. My life is here. And besides, it was you who involved my mother in the first place."

"Life as a victim of the Inquisition is not worth it," Tilly said. "You'd be better off starting over someplace new."

"I'm not a victim yet, and if I can do anything to save this place, I have to at least try. Exidgeon is by no means perfect, but by admitting students like me, they're bucking eons of tradition. Losing that now would be a giant step backward."

"I can't force you," Reston said, "but if I were you, I'd think long and hard before giving up an opportunity to get out of here. Things are likely to get far worse before they get better."

Reston's pleas to consider her safety were beginning to grate. If Alexi had the chance, would Reston be advising him to leave, too? Somehow, she thought not, but since clearly neither she nor Reston were going to reconsider, Dona resorted to an approach she often used to end futile arguments with her mother.

"All right," she said. "I'll think about it. In the meantime, I'd better get this visit to the chapel over with."

"I'll go with you," Alexi said. "Under the circumstances, you shouldn't be traveling alone at night."

Dona took his hand. "That's very sweet of you."

Alexi winked at her. "And here I thought I was being selfish."

She glanced back at Reston. "We'll be back shortly—Ma willing."

. . . . .

It didn't take Verone long to determine that the Inquisition had transferred operations to Canasty Hall, which was right next door to Dexter Hall. She had to get a bit short with the Inquisitors standing guard, but she eventually wrangled a meeting with Cartier. His new office was makeshift, with a table serving as his desk. He was seated in an old wooden chair, and they were interrupted every few minutes by Inquisitors either reporting on the status of something or requesting guidance on some detail for adapting the new building to their needs.

"I'm sorry—I don't have long," he said. "As you can see, things are still a bit up in the air. Did you ever find your missing person?"

"We came across reliable witnesses who had seen her on campus yesterday," Verone said. "Since we determined she was safe, we've decided to call off the search."

"Congratulations."

"I thought it might be easier on everyone if the ladies and I got out of your way. Do you think I could prevail upon you to have the gates opened for us?"

"I think we could arrange something. We'd have to make it quick, though—I'm told the Crown has amassed a welcoming party, and I haven't figured out how to spin this situation yet. I'm sure they'll view closing the gates as an act of aggression."

"Have you found the heretics?"

"Not yet. Thurman really didn't bother to do much investigating once he got the confession, and now that the prisoner is dead, there isn't much to go on."

"So, can you pick up the investigation where Thurman left off?"

"We can, but I'm not much of an expert on Phrendonic Heresy. I'll need to check among the newcomers for someone with experience in that area."

"Perhaps you can send someone to tell the Crown that you only closed the gates to make sure potential suspects couldn't escape. If they feel they're a part of the process, they wouldn't be so quick to believe the worst."

"I'm not sure they would buy that. I think they'd feel uncomfortable with any large occupying force stationed in Exidgeon. After all, it's really more a fortress than a university.

"So, let them send in observers. Once they see what you're doing here, how could they not be thankful you're trying to keep their citizens safe?"

"You'd be surprised. So, when did you want the gates opened?"

"How about just before dawn? That way no one will be any the wiser."

"All right, just before dawn it is."

"Thank you, Father. I'll have the Ladies assembled and waiting."

Cartier kissed her hand in farewell. "It's the least I can do."

. . . . .

Overcast skies would have made the evening trip to the chapel treacherous if it hadn't been for the multitude of campfires dotting the landscape. Dona and Alexi picked their way among them, careful to stay out of sight, flitting like ghosts, shadow to shadow. It wasn't until they found themselves in a secluded alley that Alexi broke the silence.

"So, are you going to leave with your mother tomorrow?"

Dona paused, then turned to face him. "Do you want me to?"

He met her gaze for only an instant. "I think it's your safest option."

"That's not what I asked."

"You'd be foolish to stay and risk capture by the Inquisition."

She straightened his collar. "I want you to say what you feel—not what you think is safest or least foolish."

"I can't ask you to stay. If you were hurt because of me, I couldn't live with myself."

"I didn't ask you to work out all the possible repercussions. I merely asked you to tell me what you want. But, like most men confronted with their feelings, you're overcomplicating and overrationalizing to the point you're answering a completely different question."

"All right then, if I could guarantee—"

Dona touched her finger to his lips. "Shh, no ifs."

"Fine. I want you to stay."

There, that wasn't so hard, was it? You really can be very endearing—"

A disturbance at the far end of their alley caused them to leap for cover, but it was merely a cat stalking dinner. They made it the rest of the way to the Chapel without difficulty, but he stopped her as they reached the door.

"So?" he whispered. "Are you staying or leaving?"

"I'm still considering." She felt a twinge of guilt for not telling him her decision, but she couldn't help it—the extra attention was as addictive as it was charming.

Cheers erupted as Dona and Alexi stepped into the chapel. Dona's mother rushed from the crowd to embrace her daughter. "I was so worried."

"I don't know what Professor Reston was thinking," Dona said. "He really shouldn't have put you through this—I can take care of myself. But it is so good to see you."

Standing a bit back with the others, Rayen beamed and waved.

She ran to hug him. "And you too."

"I told her you were fine," Rayen said. "But you know your mother…"

"I do indeed. Thanks for watching out for her anyway."

Rayen smiled. "I couldn't very well let her worry her way around Trifienne all by herself, could I?"

Dona gaped at the welcoming crowd, humbled that so many had gathered on her behalf. "Well, this is very flattering." Then she did a double take. "Miranda? What are you doing here?"

Miranda raised a glass. "I came for the party."

"She wants to go with us when we leave tomorrow," Mrs. Caldor said.

"Are they really going to open the gate for you?" Dona asked.

One of the ladies extended her hand to Dona. "I don't see why they wouldn't. My daughter has gone to arrange it. I'm Mrs. Nathalie Nevinander. On behalf of the Venerable Assembly of Church Mothers, I want to welcome you. You led us on a merry chase, but we are all overjoyed that it has ended so well."

Dona started at the Nevinander name, but the woman's smile conveyed a caring warmth that struck her as entirely genuine. "I'm truly touched."

"Please, come in and make yourself at home. We'll see about getting you set up for the night. My daughter would like us to be ready to leave at dawn."

Dona spied Alexi leaning against the wall, arms folded, staring at her as though he was waiting for her to say something in return.

"I'd like to thank Alexi here, for letting me know you were all looking for me."

The ladies applauded him politely.

Mrs. Temrich pumped Alexi's hand. "Welcome back, young man. I do hope this visit won't interrupt your studies." She spoke so loudly, her voice drowned out the applause, and all eyes turned to her.

"Poor dear," Mrs. Tibbleman said. "She's a little hard-of-hearing. I suppose sooner or later we all must face the prospect of age catching up with us—knock wood."

"The interruption won't matter," Caroline Caldor said. "They've cancelled all classes until this Inquisition thing is sorted out."

Nathalie turned to Alexi. "Will you be coming with us, young man?"

"I—I hadn't really thought about it."

Dona donned a smug grin—now it was his turn to decide. "Take your time. Sometimes the right answer isn't immediately obvious."

"Are you leaving?"

"Of course she is," Dona's mother said. "If they are canceling classes, this Inquisition isn't anything to trifle with."

Dona's smile faded. Though she'd known this argument was inevitable, she hadn't expected it to start so soon. If she wasn't careful, her mother was going to ruin everything. "Ma, I'm perfectly capable of making my own decisions."

"Then I'm not saying anything you haven't already considered. Rayen, help her find a suitable pallet. Dawn will be here before we know it."

"That may be, but that still doesn't mean I've made up my mind."

"Allow me to help. Your arguments in favor of staying are what?"

"None of your business."

Rayen grimaced, and a little vein pulsed on Dona's mother's neck. "I see. Well whoever the lucky boy is, I'm sure he'll still be here when this all blows over."

"I never said it was a boy. I told you, it's none of your business."

Rayen winced again, and the venerable ladies murmured among themselves.

At last Alexi spoke. "Your mother's right. You really should go."

Dona's eyes flashed. Managing her mother was trying on the best of days and, even had he agreed with her, none of Alexi's business. But to publicly sabotage her efforts—that was completely over the line. "Fine. Since my opinion doesn't seem to matter, I guess I have no choice. Best of luck to you Mr. Reysa."

She sniffed and stalked through the assembled ladies.

Dona's mother shrugged. "She always did get a little cranky past bedtime."

. . . . .

While Alexi fully expected Dona to argue with him, the shock of her decision to actually leave him stung. He silently cursed himself for overly romanticizing their bond—deep down, he had fully expected it to effortlessly survive such trivial challenges as safety, common sense, and even his own repeated urgings for her to leave. Disappointed and deeply shamed by his misperception of her feelings, he suddenly felt the walls closing in.

"I'm sorry," he croaked. "I need to go."

"Thank you for your help," Dona's mother called after him.

He slammed the door behind him so hard it dislodged bits of plaster from the frame.

# CHAPTER 6

# ⲘIRAⲚⲆA WARNINGS

It had been some time since Dona had witnessed a predawn hour later than three, and she was finding it difficult to adjust. While Miranda and Caroline kept trading yawns, the industrious Church Mothers were chipper and efficient, packing their things and cleaning the chapel in record time.

"How do you do it?" she asked Mrs. Curtsik, who had just finished rolling up and storing the last pallet.

"Do what, dear?"

Dona stretched and blinked. "How are you so awake?"

She patted Dona's arm. "At my age, I'm so thankful for every remaining hour that I am eager not to miss a moment."

Verone had been readying the carriages, and only now did she happen across the group's new additions. She squinted at Caroline Caldor. "I'm sorry, have we met?"

Mrs. Caldor placed her hands on Caroline's shoulders. "This is my Caroline. "Remember? You said she could accompany us."

"So I did, but I don't recall you mentioning you'd be bringing three daughters."

"Oh, didn't anyone tell you? That's Miss Merinne. She showed up last night after you went out to make arrangements."

"So, this is the elusive Miss Merinne. Now, that's unexpected."

Dona curtseyed. "I understand you are to thank for organizing the efforts on my behalf. My mother thought it would be best for me to accompany you back to town, if you don't mind."

Miranda gave Dona a little nudge.

"Oh, and this is my roommate Miranda. She'd like to go with us too."

"She's the Constable's daughter." Mrs. Caldor pointed out.

Verone gave Miranda a closer look.

Miranda nodded. "Pleased to meet you."

"Here's the challenge," Verone said. "Mum's carriage can hold four and a driver. Mrs. Curtsik's carriage can hold two and a driver—three if we squeeze them—for a total of nine. I will be riding my Vengi. It seems we have two more riders than we have seats."

"I'd be willing to walk if it would help," Rayen said.

"And I can keep him company," Dona added.

"I don't know," Dona's mother said. "It's a pretty long walk."

"Maybe someone would be willing to drop off passengers and come back for us?" Dona suggested. "We should be easy to find along the road."

"I'd be happy to," Mrs. Curtsik volunteered.

"If we are all agreed, let's get to the gate," Verone said. "I told Father Cartier we'd be there before dawn."

Dona had forgotten how bone-chilling the early morning hours could get. By the time she and Rayen reached the gate, she was already regretting her offer to walk. She also wondered whether she'd been too hard on Alexi. While his meddling was inexcusable, he only had her best interest at heart. But it was too late to turn back now—another row with her mother would only jeopardize everyone else's chance to leave.

The carriages were dimly visible in the pre-dawn twilight, and several of the ladies milled about, rubbing their arms for warmth. Verone was off to one side holding the reins of her horse and chatting with a priest. Once Dona and Rayen arrived, Verone nodded to the priest and approached the group.

"All right ladies—"

"And gentleman," Rayen interrupted.

"Yes, of course, how could I forget? Before we leave, Father Cartier has asked that we line up for inspection. It's merely a formality—

since we're in the midst of an Inquisition, they're obliged to make sure nothing heretical leaves the University."

The ladies, and Rayen, hastened to comply. Two Inquisitors stepped up to search them—one started with the carriages while the other searched the ladies themselves. Dona's heart almost stopped—Father Cartier was the same man they'd almost trampled during their escape from the brothel. She gulped and did her best to look the part of the innocent schoolgirl. For a few moments, Cartier's brow gathered, and his gaze kept darting back to her as though he was trying to place her, but if he came to any conclusions, he kept them to himself.

Shortly after the search began, an older man still wearing his night-clothes appeared. Only his hat betrayed him as someone important with the Church.

"Cartier," he yelled. "What's going on here?"

"I'm sorry you were disturbed, Your Ordinence. I'm just letting the elderly ladies of my Church head back to their homes, since they were successful in locating the young lady who went missing. They were staying at the old campus chapel in circumstances that were less than suitable for ladies of their advanced years."

"Are you out of your mind? That gate is the only thing standing between us and Trifienne's militia."

"Your Ordinence, I've checked, and they have not yet approached the ramp. In this darkness, the gates should be difficult for them to see. We can have them open and closed again before Trifienne has any chance to respond. And I believe we only strengthen our position by convincing the Crown we are running a civilized operation here. You know, one that can reasonably be negotiated with?"

Cartier's explanation calmed Isrulian's panic, but not his irritation. "Who are these people anyway? How do you know you aren't releasing a masquerading heretic?"

"These are ladies of my Church, many of whom I've known all my life and most of whom have never set foot on this campus before."

Isrulian stalked over to inspect Rayen. "This one doesn't seem so ladylike to me."

Verone stepped forward. "If I may, Your Ordinence, this is the uncle of the missing girl. He's here because he has a medical condition that requires constant monitoring. His sister is the missing girl's mother, and she couldn't leave him behind."

He inspected Rayen even more closely. "Is that so?" Then he moved to Dona. What about this one? I doubt you've known this one all your life."

"She's the missing student," Verone replied. "And this is the girl's mother. If you would like, Your Ordinence, I can take a moment to introduce them all."

"That won't be necessary," Isrulian said. "The others I can well believe are Church Mothers, except for this one." He pointed to Miranda. "To whom does this one belong?"

There was a long pause.

"Surely someone must claim her. What's your name, young lady?"

"She's my roommate," Dona said.

"Did I ask you?"

Dona dipped in a contrite curtsey. "No, Your Ordinence."

"I trust, then, that you have learned from this little outburst and, in the future, will keep a tighter rein on your exuberance?"

"Yes, Your Ordinence."

He raised an eyebrow at Miranda. "Now, young lady, I caution you not to make me ask you again."

"My name is Miranda—Miranda Connelly, Your Ordinence."

"There. That wasn't so hard, was it?"

Isrulian wandered back over to Cartier just as the Inquisitor who was patting down the ladies reached Dona. Although she wasn't carrying anything suspicious, she was still thankful he wasn't doing a thorough job, until she glimpsed a long red scar on his right jawline. Her eyes widened in recognition. A slight turn of his head told her he'd noticed.

"Well then, Father Cartier," Isrulian said. "Here's a blunder to match allowing Monsignor Goodkin and Chancellor Wiggins to escape."

"I don't follow," Cartier said.

The scarred Inquisitor patted his way around Dona until his breath was hot on her neck.

"Then allow me to spell it out for you," Isrulian said. "Miss Connelly, do you happen to know a Constable Connelly?"

"Yes," she said quietly.

"And precisely how do you know the Constable?"

"He—he's my father."

"Let that be a lesson to you, Cartier. Never conduct an Inquisition without familiarizing yourself with the families of your potential adversaries."

It was all Dona could do to keep from pulling away from the scarred Inquisitor's invasion of her space, but she held perfectly still.

"One word…" he breathed into her ear. "One word and we all burn."

"Take the Connelly girl to Canasty as our guest," Isrulian said. "If the rest pass inspection, they may go." He wrapped his nightshirt more tightly and stalked back the way he'd come.

The carriage inspector approached Father Cartier. "The carriages pass."

"Take the girl then," Cartier said.

Miranda whimpered as the Inquisitor approached, but she allowed him to escort her away. Dona was powerless to stop him.

The scarred Inquisitor moved on to inspect Rayen and pronounced them all clear. He then started a second inspection on the carriages, this time on the outside surfaces, and underneath.

Dona leaned over to Rayen. "You take the vacant spot."

"I knew we wouldn't be walking," he whispered. "That's why I offered to do it."

Cartier signaled to an Inquisitor stationed near the stone building that housed the gate mechanism. The gates ground slowly open.

Somberly, the ladies climbed into the carriages. Isrulian's interrogation had delayed their progress, and dawn was now almost fully upon them.

"Quickly now," Cartier shouted. "We don't have all day."

"Does anyone else smell smoke?" Mrs. Temrich asked.

Mrs. Caldor slapped her hand over Mrs. Temrich's mouth, and Nathalie, who was driving her carriage, looked wildly toward Cartier, but the moan of the gate's ancient hinges had apparently drowned out the stray comment. The instant the gate was open, Nathalie rushed her team forward, and Mrs. Curtsik's team followed close behind. With a farewell wave to Cartier, Verone followed on Vengi as the first rays of light appeared over the horizon. Then the great gates ground closed once more.

The moment they clanged shut, the now-familiar clock-tower bell rang out a new warning.

"Dona?" Dona's mother cried out over the reverberating bell as the carriages flew down the ramp. "Dona? Are you with us? Dona!"

. . . . .

From their vantage point atop the rise, The Crown Prince, his wife, and her brother could just barely make out the closing of the gates and the wild flight of the carriages. By contrast, the plume of thick black smoke rising over the University was plainly visible.

The Crown Prince pointed it out. "Where is that coming from?"

Michlos squinted. "I think that's where the Hathaway Scholars are housed."

"I pray they can contain it without our help" the Crown Princess said.

. . . . .

Dona strove to be inconspicuous as she stole her way back to the fraternity. Sticking to the morning's longest shadows, she almost tripped over the body of a man lying just off the path. He had been stripped nearly naked, and at first, she was terrified he might be dead—until over the raucous calls of early morning birds she heard his snore. Then, startled by the clock-tower alarm, she abandoned all thoughts of stealth and simply fled.

. . . . .

By the time Dona made it to the fraternity, most of the residents had gathered on the front steps, where they stood watching smoke billow from the Hathaway compound. She had been smelling the smoke since Mrs. Temrich first mentioned it, but only now, when she climbed the steps and gawked with everyone else, did she see the dome. One of the Hathaway Scholars' buildings was almost completely obscured by it. And, as with Dexter Hall, the dome apparently concealed a fire. However, this fire was already too large to be easily contained.

"Welcome back, Miss Merinne," Reston said. "Some of the others are downstairs, if you care to join them. I'll be back as soon as I see if there's anything I can do in the Hathaway compound."

"There's no time for that, Professor."

"The building is already lost, but maybe I can help to keep the fire from spreading."

"You don't understand—we have a more pressing problem."

Reston glanced anxiously back at the smoke. "All right, downstairs. Quickly."

After letting them into the chamber, Jonas resumed dragging on his pipe, while Tilly tended her pot of tea. Both had enough sleep in their eyes to suggest the alarm bell had been their wakeup call.

"Where's Alexi?" Dona asked.

Tilly poured a cup. "Last we saw him, dear, he was leaving with you."

Reston closed and locked the door. "All right, what's the problem?"

"The Inquisition has taken Miranda."

Reston's jaw dropped. "Miranda Connelly? The Constable's daughter?"

"Yes. It happened just now."

Reston dragged his hand down his face and groaned.

"And that's our problem, how?" Jonas asked.

"She knows about the book," Reston said. "She thinks I lent it to Miss Merinne for an extra credit project. If they question her about heresy, she'll lead them right back here."

"Oh, I can see where that might be our problem."

"We may have a little time," Dona said. "There's an Ordinal at Canasty Hall, and he only seemed interested in her because she was the Constable's daughter. If we're lucky, they might not think to ask her about heresy right away, particularly if most of the Inquisitors are off fighting the fire."

"A little time for what?" Jonas asked. "We can't run—the gate is closed."

"To rescue her, of course. If we don't, we risk being accused of heresy by an Ordinal. We'd be fugitives the rest of our lives."

"An Ordinal?" Reston asked. "Where was the Monsignor?"

"Oh, I forgot to mention that the Ordinal seemed upset that the Monsignor had escaped custody. It sounded as if he had been arrested."

"The Primal's brother arrested by an Ordinal? That seems unlikely."

"I'm only saying what I heard."

"Where did you hear all this?" Jonas asked.

"At the gate this morning. My mother and the church group were trying to leave the College. Miss Nevinander had it all arranged, but things fell apart when the Ordinal showed up. The Church group ended up leaving, but not before the Ordinal took Miranda hostage. Oh, and Professor Everson is masquerading as an Inquisitor now. He searched everyone before they were permitted to leave."

"No doubt failing to notice anything incriminating that Miss Nevinander may have been carrying," Reston said.

"He never even searched her."

"He may have finally found his calling," Reston said. "It took him almost no time to go from Priest to Inquisitor. No doubt next time we see him, he'll be Primal."

"We'd best act fast. The longer Miranda remains the Ordinal's guest, the greater the chance they'll learn about the book. If we move soon, most of the Inquisitors will be fighting the fire."

"Just what are you suggesting?" Jonas asked. "Mount an assault on Inquisition headquarters?"

"I don't care what we do, so long as Miranda is free when it's over."

"Free to do what? Sit here at the fraternity with the rest of us until the Inquisition finally tracks her down? It's not like we've come up with any sort of plan to get anyone out of here."

"Maybe it's time we did. The longer we stay here, the worse our chances get. Have you considered what happens when Everson gets discovered?"

"Then we're fugitives anyway," Reston said.

Jonas puffed out a smoke ring. "Maybe we should take a cue from this Everson character."

"How so?"

His eyes twinkled. "Listen up, folks. I've got an idea."

# CHAPTER 7

# CLOAK AND DAGGER

Alexi trailed his toe in the duck pond. The ice-cold water stung a little, but he barely noticed. Complex aromas wafting from the cafeteria announced lunch was imminent, but even had they been appetizing, he wouldn't have been interested. All around him, students were returning from canceled classes wearing expressions that ranged from relief to righteous indignation, but he didn't care.

Alphonse sat beside him. "You might improve your chances with a worm and a hook."

Alexi grunted.

"Let me guess. She decided you weren't the one?"

Alexi stared into the water. "How could I have been so naïve?"

Alphonse chuckled. "Naiveté is part of the game, my friend. Without it, you aren't really playing, and if you don't play, you can't win."

"But at least you can't lose."

"You never really lose, you know, at least not if things end early and cleanly. It may be painful, but the pain is brief"—he tossed a pebble into the pond—"and the pool of eligible fish is vast."

Alexi shook his head.

Alphonse clapped Alexi's shoulder. "Look, the good news is that if you just keep playing, winning is inevitable. How many games can claim that? The only way to really lose is to prolong a bad fit."

Alexi looked up from the pond. "But I didn't think it was a bad fit. How could I not have known that?"

"Oh, now I understand. You're upset because you were the one who was dumped."

"Yeah, that's it. Thanks for understanding."

"Hey, anytime things don't work out, someone has to realize it first. Why would you assume it should always be you?"

"It always has been before."

Alphonse flashed a wry smile. "And so naturally, it should work that way every time? You'll never pass logic with reasoning like that. I'd say this means you are getting better at selecting candidates. You've managed to find one you didn't want to ditch. Now all you have to do is find one who doesn't want to ditch you."

"And go through this all over again? No thanks."

"Well then, there's always the monastery."

"Oh, now there's a good fit."

"Job security, three meals a day, all the beer you can brew, and absolutely no chance of having to suffer through the pain of getting dumped."

"Oh, I wouldn't be so sure about that."

"You really are in a bad way if even the monks wouldn't have you."

"Thanks, I feel so much better now."

"Face it, my friend—it's going to be a while before the sun comes out from behind these clouds. In the meantime, what could be more distracting than a sabre winging its way toward your jugular? Let's get in a bout or two before lunch, shall we?"

"I can't do it."

"I'll let you win."

Alexi snorted. "You say that every time, and then you pummel the daylights out of me."

Alphonse shrugged. "What can I say? Helplessness brings out my killer instinct."

"I am not helpless."

"And now you have the perfect opportunity to prove it."

Movement behind Alphonse caught Alexi's eye. "Hey, what's going on over there?"

"Nice try, but you aren't getting out of this that easily."

"Seriously, there's a mob gathering, and it's coming this way."

Alphonse finally allowed himself to look. "Are those nuns?"

"Sure looks like it, though I don't think I've ever seen them driving a cart before."

"Forget the nuns," Alphonse said. "What's that they've got in the cart?"

Alexi shaded his eyes. "I'm not sure, but unless I miss my guess, I'm going to be taking a rain check on the pummeling."

"All right, then," Alphonse said. "I suppose if it occasionally takes a strange nun to take your mind off being ditched, who am I to judge? Just don't get in the habit."

Alexi groaned.

. . . . .

Cartier paced his makeshift office, trying to work out some way to repair the damage the meddling Ordinal had done to his plans. While the Inquisition remained bottled up in the University, he couldn't make any progress in his investigation, and once the Crown found out they were holding the Constable's daughter, it would be impossible to establish the amicable working relationship he'd envisioned. Without it, he'd never be able to discover the evidence he so badly needed— evidence that would make even the unpopular Inquisition seem the preferable alternative.

The knock on his door was long overdue. He'd expected this new fire to be under control more than a half hour ago. The prospect of the Ordinal accusing him of failing again was one he didn't want to contemplate. "Come in," he yelled. "Is it out yet?"

The young Inquisitor who entered was covered with ash and grime. "No, Father, the darkness is complicating our efforts, and now the fire has spread to another building. We need more manpower."

"Take more men, then. The place is crawling with them. Get that fire under control."

"Yes, Father."

"Well, what are you waiting for?"

"There is one other thing…." The Inquisitor opened the front of his grimy vestment and removed a long floral length of fabric. The pungent smell of smoke mingled with the faint scent of roses. "We found this caught in one of the hedges near the burning building, I kept it as clean as I could."

Cartier took it from the young man and inspected it.

"I think it's some sort of ladies' cloak. At least, I assume it belongs to a lady. I don't know any men who would wear such a flowery thing—or want to smell like that."

Cartier thought it looked somehow familiar. It had a tag sewn into a seam at the neck. Taking it to the window, he made out tiny embroidered letters. Once he'd read them, and then reread them, he threw back his head and laughed.

"I knew I'd seen this before."

"What does it say?"

Cartier grinned ear-to-ear. "It's a name. It says Marguerite Serrola."

Distracted by a small crowd gathering near the gate, Cartier opened the window and leaned out. He immediately recognized several of Isrulian's sycophants. "Now what?"

The question was rhetorical, but the young man answered anyway. "I think the Ordinal is up on the barbican speaking with someone outside the walls."

Cartier threw him a sidelong glance. "I don't suppose he's threatening to jump?"

"I don't think so, Father."

Cartier sighed. "As if I don't have enough fires to put out. Speaking of which, you'd best get back to the Hathaway compound."

"Yes, Father." The young man bowed and left.

Cartier took a deep breath and ducked outside. It wasn't long before he heard Isrulian's booming voice echoing above the gate. "I assure you, we have the situation well in hand."

A man's voice, amplified by a speaking trumpet, responded. "We have men with training, experience, and equipment ready to assist, Your Ordinence. Such fires can be treacherous. Are you certain you don't wish to reconsider?"

"The University is currently under the jurisdiction of the Inquisition. Until our investigation is farther along, these gates must remain closed for security reasons. I'm sure you understand."

Cartier took the barbican steps two at a time. Isrulian leaned out through one of the arches, speaking to a small delegation of men bearing the standard of the Crown of Trifienne. At the group's forefront, a powerfully built man with hair and a goatee so blond they were nearly white, lifted an eyebrow at the Ordinal.

He raised the trumpet once more. "I'm sure you can appreciate my position as well, Your Ordinence. We have no desire to impede your investigation, but without our help, the Crown is concerned the fires may rage out of control. If you refuse our assistance and that should happen, I'm afraid he will have to hold the Church financially account-able. May I tell him you find that arrangement agreeable?"

Isrulian snorted. "Don't be ridiculous. Not only does the Crown stand to benefit from our apprehension of these dangerous heretics, but we've already expended considerable Church resources fighting their fires. The Crown would be better served by appreciating what it's been given instead of threatening to charge its benefactors for their freely given aid."

"The Crown appreciates your efforts on its behalf. However, now that we are aware of the problem, we can track down the arsonists without further assistance. Of course, we could do that more effec-tively if we had access—"

"Which we will not be able to grant until we have apprehended the heretics. These sacrilegious attacks on the Church cannot go un-punished."

"Perhaps we could compromise and open the gates very briefly," Cartier interjected. "Just long enough to admit a small number of the Crown's agents to observe our efforts. If we did it quickly, we'd minimize any chance that the heretics could escape. At the same time, the Crown could rest assured that we are doing everything possible to resolve this crisis expeditiously. Would that be acceptable?"

"I believe the Crown Prince would be agreeable to that arrange-ment. I will relay the proposition and return shortly with his answer. In the meantime, should you reconsider our offer to assist with the fires, we will stand ready below." The blond man bowed to Isrulian and then to Cartier, and the delegation retreated down the ramp.

Isrulian's eyes narrowed. "I don't recall asking for your opinion."

Cartier smiled brightly. "Why thank you for noticing, Your Ordi-nence. I pride myself on anticipating people's needs." He dashed back down the stairs before Isrulian could formulate a suitable response.

Upon reaching the plaza, Cartier noticed another crowd gathering in front of Canasty hall. As he drew closer, he could make out a crude horse cart parked in its midst, with two women seated at the front. They wore the distinctive red-trimmed amber habits of the Sisters of Solace.

As Cartier pushed his way through the crowd, one of the Sisters rose from her seat. Her voice was heavy with a Caprian accent. "Can anyone tell me who is in charge? I have grave tidings to bestow."

"Can I be of service, Sister?" Cartier asked.

"Are you in charge then, Father?"

Cartier was hesitant to offend Isrulian further, but since Isrulian seemed not to have followed him, he felt safe risking a quick nod.

"Oh, praise be." The Sister touched her lips and then her forehead in thanks. "I am Sister Matriana, and this is Sister Cappeletrea from the infirmary. We come to warn you—we are doomed."

Cartier sighed. "Doomed in what way?"

"Do you know not of the curse then?"

"Curse? What curse?"

"The Curse pronounced by Omenahm Mavrenuto, High Priest of the death god Chervil, cut down before these very gates by the combined might of Trifienne and the holy Church." At Cartier's blank look, she went on. "It is written that with his last gasp, he laid a curse on these gates, that if ever they be closed, a great plague shall decimate the usurpers, sparing only those who remain true to the death god."

Cartier rubbed his temples. "Meaning no disrespect, Sister, but surely you don't believe this nonsense?"

"Once, I too thought as you, back when I was a wee lass in Aylesford, the village of my youth."

"I'm sure it was all very tragic. and I assure you we'll do our best to be careful, but if you'll excuse me, I have an Inquisition to run."

"I was afraid you'd not take me seriously. Only those of us who lived through it can know its terrible power."

As she spoke, students and Inquisitors continued to gather.

"When the Aylesford town fathers discovered the Ossarium, they did not heed the warnings either. In their pride and their greed, they defiled Chervil's sanctum and incurred the death god's wrath."

Cartier turned slowly back. "They found an Ossarium?"

"Aye, and their deaths."

"Just how did they die?"

"The death god's vengeance was swift as it was terrible—he unleashed the Red Death."

"What are you talking about?"

"Aye, I'm not surprised you do not know. Few who encounter it survive, and those who do are loath to speak of it. I was one of the lucky ones, and in thanks, I have dedicated my life to the calling. But I know when I am overmatched."

She inclined her head toward the sheet covering the bed of the cart. "Sister, if you would."

Her fellow Sister stepped into the back of the cart and whisked away the sheet to reveal an emaciated husk of a man. He shivered and moaned at the exposure, covering his face in shame with stick-like arms. The assembled crowd gasped. Cartier had seen sick people before and had even tended them, but this was something completely outside his experience—every inch of the man not concealed by his infirmary robe was a deep crimson. Even the whites of his eyes were red.

"Five so far have sought our aid. Four have succumbed. This is the other."

"Is there anything that can be done for him?"

"You can pray. The Red Death has no cure, it kills nine in ten who contract it, and it spreads like a wildfire."

"What are the early symptoms? We may need to institute a quarantine."

"The first sign of infection is feeling faint, for many, to the point of passing out. After that, the telltale red color spreads quickly. The afflicted may then recover for a short time, even thinking they'll survive despite their ruddy complexions, but alas, not for long. For then the wasting begins, and the organs fail. Vomiting is not uncommon, and in later stages, vomiting of blood. It's particularly hard on the men, though."

"The men? Why is that?"

"Because they are ever so sensitive about their manliness. I've never seen such terrible shriveling in all my life. And once the putrescence sets in—and it always does—amputation is the only thing for it. Even those few who recover never recover from that."

The man in the cart moaned and buried his face in the straw on which he lay. A murmur rippled through the growing crowd.

"Why did you bring him here?"

"To convince you that you must not open the gates again until the plague has run its course. Quarantine is our only hope. We all stand exposed."

The murmur in the crowd became significantly louder.

Isrulian pushed his way through. "Cartier, what's the meaning of this?"

"Stay clear." Cartier warned. "It's the plague."

"The plague?"

Cartier pointed at the man in the cart. "The Red Death."

Isrulian snorted. "Red Death? Really, Cartier—I can understand this kind of superstition coming from the Sisters, but I thought you were a man of letters."

"I don't know, it looks like it could be pretty serious."

"Nonsense. Allow me to prove it to you." Isrulian languidly raised his hand. "Knife."

A member of his retinue rushed forward with a dagger.

He addressed the wretch in the cart. "Now then, come over here."

The patient's terrified eyes fixed on Isrulian's blade. Instead of moving closer, he cowered in place.

Isrulian pointed the knife at one of the assembled Inquisitors. "You there, bring him to me. Drag him if you have to."

The Inquisitor gaped as though Isrulian had just sentenced him to death. Trembling, he slowly shook his head.

Isrulian sighed. He pulled his bulk up onto the cart. The poor wretch scuttled farther back until he cowered at the feet of the younger Sister. As he gazed up at her with pleading eyes, Isrulian seized him by the hair and sheared off a handful. The lock in Isrulian's hand flickered from crimson to dull blond. He held it aloft in triumph.

"There, you see? Proof."

"You're terrifying him," the younger Sister cried. "Leave him be."

Startled by the outburst, Isrulian eyed the younger Sister He squint-ed, first in suspicion, and finally, in recognition.

"Well, well, well, when last we met, you promised to keep that an-noying exuberance of yours in check. How fitting, then, that breaking your word is what betrayed you. I do hope you'll bring the same level of enthusiasm to your interro—"

The Ordinal dropped the dagger. He frowned and shook his head, as though trying to clear it. He blinked several times, then his eyes lost focus and rolled back into his head. Finally, he collapsed, narrowly missing the wretch he had just shorn.

The elder Sister gasped and rushed to his aid. After only a brief inspection, however, she drew back in horror. Eyes wide, arm trembling, she pointed at the stricken Ordinal. "Chervil's wrath has claimed its next victim. Fear the Red Death. Pray for deliverance."

Several members of the Ordinal's retinue leapt to assist their master. As they lifted him down from the cart, they were greeted by the crowd's collective intake of breath—the Ordinal had turned a brilliant shade of crimson.

"Quickly," Cartier said. "Take him to the infirmary. He must be quarantined as soon as possible. Any of you who touched him are to report there as well."

Cartier's barrage of orders was interrupted by an ear-splitting groan from the gates. At first the left door leaned inward, then the right side broke free from its hinges entirely. The ponderous slab of wood and iron teetered on edge for a long moment before it fell, striking the earth with such force that windows rattled and a cloud of dust obscured the entire archway. The left-hand door wavered, then followed, smiting the ground next to its mate.

Stunned silence was broken by the sound of a single set of galloping hooves. The crowd only got a brief glimpse of the horse's two riders—one with golden ringlets, the other trailing tobacco smoke—before they disappeared into the billowing dust. Then, a second horse followed, the rider's academic robe flapping in the wind.

"Stop them," the elder Sister yelled. "The quarantine must hold." She hopped into the driver's seat and urged her team to action. They surged forward, nearly throwing their patient from the cart. Inquisitors scattered before them—many only narrowly avoided being trampled.

A voice screamed after them from the crowd. "Dona—wait up."

The younger Sister looked up from her charge to see a man sprinting all out toward them.

"Alexi," she cried. "Hurry."

She made it to the back of the cart just as he attempted to jump in, but his grip was unstable. The Sister braced herself with one hand and grabbed his shirt with the other, but he was heavy. Desperate, she heaved with both hands. By the time they disappeared into the dust, he was nearly in the cart. Then a wheel struck the fallen gate. The cart lurched. She lost her grip. He cried out as he fell. She winced at the impact as he struck the ground.

"*Alexi!*" Without hesitation, she leapt after him.

. . . . .

Jonas eyed his surroundings and whistled appreciatively. "Not bad for a tent."

It spanned twenty feet on a side and was more lavishly draped than the Sultan's Respite. Tilly and Amberton were seated on silk cushions of red, blue, and yellow around a low central table covered in fabric with the luster of spun gold. Amberton huddled in a blanket, a knit cap pulled down over his forehead. Jonas lounged off to one side against a stack of spare pillows, while Reston paced the plush carpets, his agitation plain.

"Are you saying she jumped off?"

"I don't know," Tilly said. "I heard her scream 'Alexi' and the next chance I got to look, she wasn't there. We hit something pretty hard in the gateway. Maybe she was thrown."

Reston rounded on Amberton. "What about you? You must have seen something."

"I was far too busy choking from the dust to notice anything else. All I can say is, the next time you need an emaciated plague victim to do your dirty work, don't look at me. Do you have any idea how long I'm going to be stuck wearing this ridiculous hat? And I'd just been to the barber, too."

"I swear," Jonas said, "the man would complain if he found a bag of gold under his pillow. Can you find no bright spot to lighten the burden of your miserable existence?"

"Easy for you to say. All you had to do was pick a few measly locks while Mathilda, Dona, and I kept everyone distracted. And you even had Reston to back you up. If there was a bright spot, though, it was Mathilda's gripping performance. Absolutely riveting. That bit about shriveling and amputation was positively inspired. And your accent was flawless."

Tilly blushed. "In my business, you need to know a thing or two about managing men. As for the accent, well, I hail originally from Caprian."

"Well, brava, even so," Amberton said. "And Reston's timing was impeccable. If he hadn't shown up in the nick of time, there's no telling what else that crazed clergyman might have tried to cut off."

"What clergyman?" Reston asked.

"I think he's talking about the Ordinal," Tilly said. "You know, the one who gave him the tonsure? Once you Slept him, all I had to do was touch him with Jonas's wand like I did for Amberton, and presto—insta-plague."

"I never Slept the Ordinal. Once we released Miss Connelly, I went directly to work on the gates."

Amerton scowled. "Well, if you didn't Sleep him, who did?"

Tilly's eyes widened. "He didn't die for real, did he?"

Amberton rubbed his hat. "Would serve the butcher right. Why'd he want to go and cut my hair off like that anyway?"

Michlos slipped in through the tent flaps. "Presumably to prove you were afflicted by heresy rather than the plague."

Tilly's brow furrowed. "How would a haircut show that?"

"It's an application of the 80-percent rule," Reston said. "If you sever something on which a spell is vested, the spell only survives on pieces that retain at least 80 percent of the original."

"Quite so," Michlos said. "Though it works a bit differently for spells vested on people, the result in this case is the same: The spell on the severed hair breaks, but the remainder of the spell on Amberton continues. It's a subtle technical point, but I suppose an Inquisitor who specializes in Phrendonic Heresy might be aware of it. And, it's a pretty definitive test."

"So the Ordinal saw through it?"

Michlos scratched his ear. "I'd be shocked if he didn't, but judging by the number of Inquisitors we've caught sneaking out past the fallen gates, it doesn't look like his demonstration convinced many they weren't actually doomed. You've done the Crown quite a service. By holding Miss Connelly hostage, the Inquisition acquired considerable leverage. Even if the Church declined to exercise it, the Constable's decisions would be suspect. Not only that, you've greatly reduced the stronghold's defensive advantage. The Inquisition will be far more amenable to compromise now that those gates are down.

"What about Miss Merinne?" Reston asked. "I don't suppose you've caught her sneaking out of the gate, have you?"

"Not so far as I know."

"Which means she's still trapped in there, with an Ordinal hunting for her who knows she's working with heretics who attacked him."

"So it would seem. If it comes to that, at least we now have a better position to negotiate her release."

"Not before they torture out of her what she knows. We were in a better position before. They had no real reason to question Miss Connelly about heresy. For Miss Merinne, they have every reason. We have no choice—we must rescue her."

"That could prove difficult. They've stationed archers on the barbican. No doubt they have taken other precautions as well. A surprise attack is unlikely to succeed now that they know they need to guard the gates, and under the circumstances, any more overt uses of Phrendonics is ill-advised. The last thing we need is for the Church to send reinforcements."

"What if it's not an attack? You said the Crown was going to try to negotiate. We can be part of the negotiating team."

"And risk having the Church uncover a conspiracy of Crown-sanctioned heresy? I'm afraid the Crown is unlikely to find that possibility appealing."

"What do you suggest, then? We can't just sit here and do nothing."

"Until something changes or we come up with a better idea, that's exactly what I suggest. By overreacting, we could cause far more damage than we stand to correct. We don't even know whether she's been taken captive. If she hasn't, where does that leave you and your rescue party"

"She'll still need to get out of the University."

"As will every other person currently trapped there. If that's all she really needs, we must be patient and rely on the negotiators to do their jobs. Count Laslo is very good at what he does. If there's a way, he will find it."

"Speaking of finding things," Amberton interrupted. "You haven't come across any clothing that might fit me, have you? This infirmary garb is a little breezy for my taste."

"Oh, I'm sorry Professor," Michlos said. "It slipped my mind. I'll see to it immediately." He ducked back outside.

Reston resumed his pacing.

"I don't get why you're so worried about her specifically," Amberton said. "She's not the only one with toxic knowledge who's trapped in there."

Tilly laid a sympathetic hand on Reston's arm. "You feel responsible, don't you?"

"I can't help it," Reston said. "The others knew they were taking a risk when they got involved, but Miss Merinne had no choice, and ultimately, that was my fault."

"She's a resourceful young woman. Maybe with the Inquisition suffering from the ill effects of our 'plague,' she'll be able to give them the slip."

"If Jonas were stuck in there, could you just sit by and hope for the best?"

Tilly eyed Jonas disapprovingly where he lay snoring against the stack of pillows. "It depends on the day. But for the time being at least, it seems we have no other choice."

# CHAPTER 8

# POETIC JUSTICE

Verone peered over the artist's shoulder. "I'm shocked the oils aren't rock solid at this temperature."

The hills of the Artists' Colony provided many splendid vistas of the river below, and Verone's brother Thad had staked out a spot that afforded a stunning view of a particularly gorgeous fall-scape.

"Verone—I didn't see you there."

"That, I assumed after the first ten minutes."

"You've been standing here for ten minutes?"

"Of course not—just checking to see if you were still as gullible as you used to be."

"It's what makes me so insufferably cute. Even you can't resist plying me with offerings. Now, what did you bring me?"

She held up a woven basket. "Lunch. Do you have time to eat, or will your light change too much?"

"Do I look like I can afford to worry about the light?"

She smoothed his tattered, paint-stained smock. "I'd like to be able to say you look like you can afford something, but that's about the only thing I can think of."

"I'd love to exchange 'cheap' shots with you all day, but I smell baked apples. As much as I love taking verbal abuse, I love baked apples even more—nothing personal."

"Apple pie, to be precise. I stopped by the Church on my way here.

I also brought some sandwiches and a bottle of wine, just in case the pie isn't quite filling enough."

Down the hill they found a bench, and Verone threw a towel over it. Next, she arranged place settings and brought out the sandwiches. Finally, she set out the pie and poured two glasses of wine, offering him one.

"You spoil me."

"I know."

"But only when you want something. So, tell me—if I accept the bribe, what have I agreed to?"

"'Bribe' is such a nasty word. I prefer 'incentive.' Now, should I pretend you aren't going to eat half the pie at once and cut it into wedges, or just draw the knife across the middle and call it good?"

"Just draw the knife across it. We should keep it as sharp as possible. I'll probably need it for putting myself out of my misery, when, in a moment of confectionary weakness, I end up taking whatever deal you're offering."

"Stop being so suspicious—this one's right up your alley. You'll probably even enjoy it."

"If that were true, I wouldn't need the bribe."

"Oh, good point." She reached for the pie.

"All right. Whatever it is, I accept."

"You always were a hard sell, but this time you got a good deal—I just want your interpretation of a little bit of prophecy."

"Prophecy? I didn't think you went in for that stuff."

"I don't, but a self-styled seer gave this to me specifically. I found the document wholly inscrutable, but if there's any chance he touched on something important, I'd hate to miss out. Here—let's see if you actually learned anything useful in all those poetry classes." She handed him a piece of folded parchment.

He opened it and read aloud:

> *The echoes of her empty heart grow still,*
> *The phoenix embers die a final time.*
> *The cold resolve that's left cannot fulfill*
> *The soul that longs to bask in love sublime*
> *Strategically she plucks the skeins of fate*
> *Defiant rage begets a cunning mind*

*So focused on the just it's just innate*
*Reflecting back what she was dealt in kind*
*The seeds of discontent take root and grow*
*Though twisted things of thorns and bile unfold*
*Their magic lies in that which none yet know*
*Their flower is a wonder to behold*
*When healing blooms and embers re-ignite*
*Remember fondly he who claimed the sight.*


"Hmm, interesting."

Verone leaned forward. "Yes? Is there something I missed?"

"Just who is this seer, anyway?"

"Someone I met doing charity work. Why?"

"Charity work? Since when do you do charity work?"

"Don't sound so shocked. I was helping Mum's church group."

"So, what made you think there might be predictions in this?"

"Not much, really, just little things he said."

"Like what?"

"Like warning me to be careful of all the Inquisitors right before a whole bunch of them showed up."

"You mean at the University? What were you doing up there?"

"I told you—charity work. We were searching for the seer's missing niece."

"If he's really a seer, what did he need you for?"

"Well, he wasn't really the one looking. We were there helping the girl's mother."

"While he stood by and watched with that 'knowing' look in his eye?"

"That's the interesting part. He maintained all along that she wasn't really lost, which turned out to be true."

"But he didn't deign to tell you where she was?"

"Look, are you going to tell me if there's anything in there, or not?"

"Oh, there's clearly something here, but it's probably not what you expect."

"If you ever want to see this pie again, now would be a good time."

"All right, all right. It has a rhyme scheme of abab cdcd efef gg, and the meter is iambic pentameter."

"What does that tell you?"

"That this prophecy is not so much a prophecy as a sonnet, and it looks like he's pegged you pretty well. If I didn't know better, I'd say our seer has fallen for you."

"What?" She ripped the parchment from her brother's hands. She scanned the document again, mouthing the words as she went. Finally, she crumpled the parchment into a ball and tossed it over her shoulder. "You've got to be kidding me. What a waste of pie."

"You got one thing right, though. I really did enjoy that."

"Oh, knock it off."

"If I write you a sestina, will you bring me a trifle? Or maybe a limerick for a cookie?"

"Don't you have a painting to finish?"

"I might. If only I had the proper—what's that word again? Oh, yes—*incentive*."

Verone glared.

He waved his finger at her sandwich. "Speaking of which, are you going to eat that?"

"Take it—and go."

He gathered up the rest of the pie and both sandwiches, but it got to be quite a lot to carry. "Are you going to need that basket?"

Her eyes narrowed.

"Never mind, I can manage."

He trudged back up the hill toward his easel. At the top, he turned to look back. "Thanks again for lunch. Oh, and give my fond regards to your boyfriend, assuming, of course, he doesn't already know."

She lingered on the bench, alternately sipping her wine and shaking her head, until her glass was empty. Then she shot a glance up the hill. Satisfied her brother was truly gone, she approached the crumpled parchment where it lay on the grass. She stared at it for a long time before finally picking it up. Returning to the bench, she smoothed the parchment on the towel, pressing out the wrinkles as best she could. When she had read through it one more time, she folded it and slipped it back into her leather case. Then, she gathered her things and headed toward the bridge back to Trifienne.

. . . . .

Even with all the desks pushed against the wall, the classroom was cramped and ancient. The rough-hewn stone of the walls radiated a chill that would have made Dona shiver under the best of circumstances. Next to her, Alexi rubbed his swollen ankle. Dona was sure his trek from the gate had been agonizing, but he had protested little. Of course, the crossbows had provided ample discouragement. Unfortunately, some Inquisitors' faith seemed to have survived the test of Tilly's plague. Two of them had held fast in their determination to bring her to justice, even as many of their brethren slipped quietly out through the fallen gates.

The man seated next to Dona couldn't seem to stop staring, though he looked away every time she caught him at it. Finally, she could stand it no longer. "Can I help you?"

"I'm sorry Sister, I couldn't help wondering what threat the Inquisition might think one such as you would pose. Did they arrest all your patients as well, or just this one?"

"Believe me," Dona said. "They're trying all my patience."

The man looked horrified until he caught the joke—then he chuckled nervously. "You're like no Sister of Solace I've ever met."

"You've got that right."

"I'm Professor Garamon. It's a pleasure to meet you." He extended his hand, but the movement dislodged his cane, which had been resting against his chair. He dove from his seat to catch it.

"Are you all right?"

"Fine, fine," he said, brushing himself off. "How clumsy of me."

"That's one elaborate walking stick."

Garamon eyed the door as he returned the cane to its spot against his chair. "Yes, I suppose it is. Gaudy old thing, really. I probably should get a new one."

Dona took a closer look. "Actually, it's fascinating." The bottom of the cane had a metal tip, perhaps gold or polished brass. The wood was dark and very smooth, suggestive of lacquered ebony. Along half its length were a series of rings crafted from the same metal as the tip, graven with symbols. The top of the cane was covered with a makeshift leather pouch, presumably for a more comfortable grip.

"What do the symbols mean?"

"I don't know. Decoration, perhaps. What did you say you were in for?"

"I didn't, and I'm not really sure."

"As I understand it, they are rounding up everyone at the University for questioning. Those who are considered high risk end up here."

"Why are you here, then?"

"The same reason as many of the others—I'm a Hathaway scholar, and this mess apparently started over in the Hathaway compound."

The door flew open, and two Inquisitors shoved another man into the room. He stumbled and fell heavily to the floor. The Inquisitors slammed the door behind him. Dona rose from her seat to help him, but Garamon caught her arm.

"Careful, Sister. Sharing his burdens may earn you complicity for his sins."

Dona shook off his grip. "If helping people is a sin, I'm already guilty." She bent to help the man up and was shocked to find herself staring into the kindly eyes of the Monsignor. He was dressed as a professor, and his head was shaved, but there was no mistaking him. He smiled in recognition, but gave a warning look and a subtle shake of his head when she started to speak.

"Thank you, Sister," he said.

"You're welcome, sir. Are you hurt?"

"I'm all right."

"Have a seat over by us. There's plenty of room."

"Don't mind if I do."

The wait was awkward. The Monsignor didn't volunteer anything further, and she didn't know what she could safely ask. When Alexi finally recognized him, his eyebrows raised quizzically, but she could only shrug in return. Assuming the Monsignor must be a Hathaway Professor, but puzzled that he didn't recognize him, Garamon tried to engage him in conversation. After the Monsignor politely evaded his efforts several times, he gave up, and the room fell silent.

The door opened again, admitting three Inquisitors. Two younger ones remained by the door, but the older one took a step into the room. He pointed at one of the other prisoners.

"You," he said. "Come with us."

The man strode over to the Inquisitors. "It's about time. I thought you'd never get around to clearing this up."

One of the younger Inquisitors cuffed the man on the side of the head. "Show respect." The prisoner's eyes widened in righteous indignation, but the young Inquisitor's hand strayed to his sword, and the man blanched.

"My apologies, Inquisitor," he said, as they escorted him out.

The Monsignor cringed but remained silent.

When the door finally slammed shut, another of the prisoners stood and faced the rest. "You saw how they treated him. Are we all going to just sit here and let them take us one by one?"

"Sit down," another said. "They'll hear you."

"I know they aren't likely to punish the whole University, but we have to face facts—they've designated us high-risk for a reason. Do you really think they'll just confirm we are innocent and send us on our way?"

"Shut up," another prisoner hissed. "You'll get us all killed."

"Don't you see? You're as good as dead anyway. We need to band together. Fight our way out. It's our only chance."

The door burst open, and the two young Inquisitors stepped inside. One of them pointed to the vocal prisoner, who swallowed hard and pointed to himself. The Inquisitor smiled crookedly and nodded.

The prisoner turned to the rest of the prisoners, his eyes pleading, but no one moved a muscle.

At last, the Monsignor struggled to his feet. "Perhaps I could go next, if it wouldn't be too much trouble?"

The Inquisitor drew his blade. "Sit down, old man."

The Monsignor gulped and sank into his chair.

The prisoner shot his fellows a final forlorn look as the Inquisitors led him away. "Fools," he breathed. Then he was gone.

The room's silence became deafening. At one point a prisoner began tapping his foot but stopped immediately when he realized everyone was staring at him.

The door opened again. This time, the three Inquisitors entered. The eldest pointed to Professor Garamon.

Garamon got to his feet. "It was nice meeting you, Sister."

Despite the perspiration on his forehead and the trembling in his hands, he put on a brave face. With head held high, he approached the Inquisitors. "Thank you for taking time to speak with me."

The elder Inquisitor inclined his head to indicate that Garamon should go first, and the three Inquisitors followed.

He'd been gone perhaps three minutes when Dona noticed Garamon's cane was still leaning against his empty chair. She considered running after him to return it, but then had a better idea—she passed it to the Monsignor, who eyed it in surprise.

"Might this be of use?"

"That's very kind of you, but I think your friend may need it more."

"What he needs is a crutch, and this is not that. Ideally, we should get him home and give him a chance to heal, but in the meantime, he can lean on me."

Silence fell, then grew oppressive. Dona felt herself sweat despite the chill as she dwelt on the fates of those whom the Inquisitors had chosen before her. The twisted landscape of her fears echoed with their agonies. The haunted visage of the prisoner who had urged them to fight tormented her. Her heart pounded. The line between reality and imagination seemed to blur until she was half convinced she could actually hear their cries.

Alexi stirred. "Do you hear that?"

"I do," the Monsignor said. He hobbled to one of the shuttered windows and listened intently. "And I don't like the sound of it."

"What is it? What's happening?"

The Monsignor's jaw tightened. "The fools running this Inquisition have gone and caused a riot. The mess they've already created will take years to clean up. If they overreact now, the damage could be irreparable."

The shouting grew louder, punctuated by the occasional crash of breaking glass. The other prisoners held steadfastly to their seats, though they stole nervous glances toward the shutters.

"It's getting closer," Dona said.

A crash rattled the shutters near the Monsignor, splintering one of the slats. "It would seem they're here," he said.

"What do we do?" Alexi asked.

"What can we do? Our hosts—"

The door burst open. Both Dona and Alexi jumped. Even the Monsignor looked startled.

"Alexi? Are you in here?"

"Alphonse? I'm here."

Alphonse poked his head in. "Oh, there you are. Well, what are you waiting for?"

"What happened to the Inquisitors?"

Alphonse shrugged. "They're otherwise occupied. Are you coming, or would you prefer I rescue someone else?"

"I'll be right there."

Dona supported Alexi as he limped toward Alphonse. While a few other prisoners took advantage of the opportunity to slip out, most stayed put, torn between the promise of freedom and the potential for a harsher fate if caught.

"Am I ever glad to see you," Dona said.

Alphonse bowed. "Always a pleasure, my lady."

The four of them fled down the hallway as fast as Alexi's injury and the Monsignor's infirmity would permit. Even so, they were only halfway to the exit when behind them they heard the hiss of drawn steel.

"Hold it right there." The two younger Inquisitors had returned.

"We can't outrun them," Dona said.

Drawing his own blade, Alphonse turned to face the Inquisitors. "Oh, yes you can. Go. Now."

"You can't take two at once," Alexi cried.

"Alas, no. The hallway is too narrow. I shall have to best them one at a time." He saluted the closest Inquisitor with his blade. "I trust your prayers are up to date?"

"You wouldn't dare," the Inquisitor said. "It's sacrilege to strike the clergy."

Alphonse advanced a step. "I hope you didn't skip any fencing classes relying on that nonsense."

The Inquisitor seemed suddenly less certain. "Drop the weapon."

Alphonse advanced again. "But I'm not done with it yet."

The Inquisitor took a step back. "I'm warning you. Drop it."

"If you insist." He lowered the tip of his blade until it touched the floor, leaving himself wide open for an attack.

Dona paled. "Alphonse, no!"

The Inquisitor lunged.

With blinding speed, Alphonse's blade swept upward. It deflected the Inquisitor's weapon to within a hair's breadth of Alphonse's shoulder. In one fluid motion, Alphonse rotated his blade and stepped forward, driving his guard into the overextended Inquisitor's chin. The Inquisitor's head snapped back, and he collapsed at Alphonse's feet.

Alphonse shook his head. "Seems he skipped the class on feint retreat—what are the chances?"

The second Inquisitor eyed his fallen comrade in stunned disbelief.

Alphonse saluted him with an intricate flourish. "*En garde*, sir."

The man blanched and dropped in a senseless heap.

"That's unexpected," Alphonse said. "Apparently, I'm even more impressive than I thought."

Dona shot Alexi a suspicious glance, but he just winked.

Alphonse kicked the blades away from the fallen Inquisitors. He handed one to Alexi and one to the Monsignor.

"Hey," Dona said. "Why does Alexi get one? He can't even walk."

"True, but he has at least some meager training, which I'm sure you'll agree is important. Besides, you'll have your hands full helping him."

"Typical," she muttered.

Outside, the riot continued. Hordes of angry students surged through the streets. Small pockets of armed Inquisitors pushed through the fracas, dodging thrown debris and clubbing any students they caught into submission. Dona's group skirted the edges of the violence and kept to the shadows of buildings. Despite their efforts, a stray rock struck the Monsignor in the back. It took several moments for him to catch his breath, and Dona feared he'd broken a rib, but he'd soon recovered enough to signal they should keep moving. They made better progress after that, finally reaching a spot the protesters had deserted. Desperate to find a safer place to wait things out, they rushed around the next corner, only to find themselves facing an advancing wall of armed Inquisitors. They ducked back immediately, but they had clearly been spotted, and the Inquisitors were moving fast.

Alphonse brandished his sword. "You go. I'll delay them."

"Don't be ridiculous," Alexi said. "They have crossbows."

Dona yanked on the first door she came to. "There's no time for that. We have to get inside." The door was locked, but she persisted, pounding with both hands. "Let us in." A tiny grate opened in the door, and an eye peered out.

"Open up." Dona cried.

The grate closed again.

"So much for the direct approach," Alexi said.

"Over here," a voice called out. "Quickly."

Across the street, a wizened man waved to them from beside an open door. The pounding beat of marching Inquisitors grew louder.

They rushed for the door, which the old man slammed and bolted the instant they'd crossed the threshold.

Several small desks were scattered about the tightly shuttered room. A large drafting table sat off to one side, and a door at the back led to another room.

When his eyes adjusted, Alexi recognized the pinched little man who'd beckoned to them as Old Mr. Brent, the University Bursar.

"Thank you," Dona said. "That was too close."

Brent peered disapprovingly over the tops of his spectacles. "Sister, forgive me if this is none of my business, but what on earth were you thinking going out in the middle of that?"

She nodded toward Alexi's swollen ankle. "I was called to the aid of the injured. When called, I go."

The Monsignor stepped forward. "Thank you for opening the door. It pains me to say, but nowadays most would not have bothered."

Brent snorted. "Few enough are called to serve with the Sisters. I can at least do my part to preserve the ones we have. The name is Randolph Brent. Now—young master Reysa I know already from his errands on behalf of Professor Reston—who, may I ask, are the rest of you?"

Dona struggled unsuccessfully to recall her alias. "I am called Sister Cappelletti. Allow me to introduce my friends, Armand and Alphonse.

Brent nodded. "Pleased to meet you. It may be some time before the streets are safe again. I apologize the office is not designed for lounging, but at least while the school is closed there are plenty of available chairs. If you'll excuse me, there is work to be done and no one but me to do it."

Brent took a seat on his stool and began wading through neatly organized mounds of paperwork.

The four of them selected desks at the opposite end of the room from Brent, ostensibly to avoid disturbing him in his work. Despite Brent's presence, Dona could wait no longer for answers, and she hoped the background noise of the ongoing riot would cover her whispers.

"What's going on here? Why are you dressed that way, and why are you running from your own Inquisition?"

The Monsignor sighed. "The short version is that I've run afoul of a political opponent who outranks me."

"Outranks you? I thought your brother was the Primal?"

The Monsignor laid his cane across the desk. "He is, but he's ailing, and I think Isrulian is betting he won't survive long enough for the backlash from framing me for heresy to catch up with him."

Alphonse nearly dropped his blade. "Your brother is the Primal?"

"As far as I know, he still is. I was hoping to lie low and pray that my brother lasts long enough for the Ordinal's transgressions to catch up with him."

"Is that why they put you with the high-risk prisoners?" Alexi asked. "Because they framed you for heresy?"

"Oh, I doubt they would have chosen to put me there if they'd known who I was. While I'd intended to simply stay out of sight until Isrulian was brought to justice, the recent fires in the Hathaway compound changed my mind. You see, I'm still trying to identify the heretics responsible for the disturbances at the University. Since it seems Isrulian has no intention of doing so, I was hoping to find evidence at the site of the most recent fire, trusting that my disguise would be sufficient to avoid suspicion. Unfortunately, my loitering in the area was deemed suspicion enough. I was elevated to high-risk status when they discovered I was wearing my stole under my cloak. Stupid, I know, but after all these years, I feel naked without it. Apparently, they've had issues with heretics masquerading as clergy."

He raised an expectant eyebrow at Dona. "You wouldn't happen to know anything about that, would you?"

She blushed. "It's a long story."

"It would seem we have time."

"It started when the Ordinal took my friend Miranda hostage."

"Hostage?"

"Well, hostage might be too strong a term, but she certainly didn't choose to be his 'guest' as he put it."

"Do you have any idea why the Ordinal would be interested in your friend?"

"Her father is the Constable."

"Oh, I see. Is the Crown already responding then?"

"I don't know, and my friends and I didn't think we had the luxury to wait, so a friend and I dressed up like this as a diversion while some other friends attempted a rescue."

"Why would you think dressing as a Sister would be a diversion? Given that the campus infirmary is run by the Sisters, I'd expect they'd be a frequent sight."

Dona scratched her ear. "Well, it wasn't so much the habit. It was probably more the plague."

"Plague?"

Dona's mouth went dry. "It wasn't only my idea, you know."

"What wasn't your idea?"

"The plague. We needed a diversion that would be effective."

"Oh, what have you done?" The Monsignor bowed his head and covered his eyes.

"We had no choice."

"Am I to understand that you exploited the Sisters' good name to spread false rumors of a plague?"

Dona shrugged. "It did make for an effective diversion."

"But at what cost? I suppose we need look no further to explain the riots."

"You don't think they are rioting over that, do you?"

"I wouldn't be at all surprised. It touches on a very base fear, and it's not like they're permitting anyone to leave." He abruptly turned his attention to the cane. "Hello, did you see that?"

"See what?" Dona asked.

"One of the metal rings—I think it just turned."

The Monsignor took a closer look. "Sure enough, these rings rotate."

Dona leaned against Alexi for a better view. "What do the symbols mean?"

"I haven't really had a chance to look."

Alphonse tilted his head. "You never examined your own cane? Wouldn't that be a little like failing to test your own blade for an edge?"

"It's not his cane," Dona said. "One of the Hathaway Professors accidentally left it behind."

The Monsignor squinted to make out the symbols. "Oh, I wouldn't be too sure it was an accident."

"Why do you say that?"

The Monsignor placed the cane's metal tip on the floor and worried the thongs holding the leather sheath. "Because of this," he said, slipping it off.

He revealed a glimmering golden skull, beautifully crafted, its eyes set with rubies. As he moved it, the skull seem to grin mischievously.

"Whoa," Alphonse said. "Why would he want to leave that behind?"

Alexi whistled low. "Because, regardless of its value, a Chervillian symbol is a bad thing to be caught holding during an Inquisition."

Brent's gasp startled all of them. He'd approached unnoticed during the discussion and was now staring at the golden skull, his eyes wide, his expression skeptical, as though he simply could not believe what he was seeing.

"The Morgatuan."

"I think that's what they called it," the Monsignor said.

"This thing has a name?" Dona asked.

The Monsignor nodded. "It was among the pieces of regalia recovered when the Chervillian fortress that pre-dated the University fell to Trifienne and the Church. It's not so much a cane as a scepter."

Dona shook her head. "What was a Hathaway Professor doing with such a thing? It makes no sense."

"Based on its history, I can venture a guess. The Morgatuan was taken by the Trifienne Crown as spoils of war. As I understand it, Hathaway research is also funded by the Crown."

"Even if you think Professor Garamon was researching it for the Crown," Alexi asked, "why would he take it with him to be interrogated?"

"Oh, I'm sure he didn't choose to take it with him. My guess is that his office was in a building affected by the recent fire. He probably rescued it, only to be arrested before he could find a safe place to stash it."

"But why would the Crown spend money researching a cane?" Dona asked.

The Monsignor peered closely at the scepter. "A very good question."

The door was struck by something so hard it shuddered. The blow was followed by a hoarse cry. "Open up, in the name of the Inquisition."

The Monsignor's eyes darted from the Morgatuan to the door, and then to Brent. "You don't by any chance have a back door, do you?"

Brent shook his head. "Very few of the older buildings had them."

Another resounding blow—this time, the whole building shuddered.

"Just a moment," Brent cried.

Dona leapt up. "They're going to break the door."

"Not to worry," Brent said. "This is the Bursar's office. That door is built to take abuse—even a battering ram—at least for a while. We have some time, but none to waste. Quickly, this way."

He led them to a back room stacked floor-to-ceiling with decades of well-organized records. One entire wall consisted of a great metallic door boasting numerous dials and keyholes.

Another thud rattled the building. Unperturbed, Brent leafed through a file drawer. From a folder, he retrieved a brass key. He repeated the process several times, retrieving keys of various shapes and sizes.

Another thud, louder still.

"Was that the door cracking?" Dona asked.

"Patience," Brent hissed. He spun dials and turned keys according to rules he didn't see fit to share. At last, he cranked a metal wheel in the door's very center, and it creaked open.

"Welcome to the University Vault," he said, stepping inside. The others followed, single file.

Alexi peered through the gloom. "It's huge."

The room contained an even larger collection of files and supplies, as well as coffers of coin labeled with the flags of various nations.

"All very impressive," Dona said. "But with no back door, how does it help us?"

In the distance, they finally heard the main door give way. "This is the Inquisition. You're all under arrest," a voice called faintly.

"We shall see," Brent said. He caught hold of the vault door and tugged it closed.

As it locked into place, Dona felt a twinge of panic. Darkness enveloped them. The closed Vault blocked all sound—all evidence of the world outside.

"When do you suppose it will be safe to leave?"

"What do you mean?" Brent asked.

Dona struggled to reign in her growing unease. "I mean, how long will we have to wait before the Inquisition leaves and we can open the door again?"

"I don't think you understand, "Brent said. "The door opens only from the other side."

# CHAPTER 9

---

# FIAT LUX

Cartier stepped forward to greet the Crown's delegation as they passed beneath the arch that had once held Exidgeon's gates. Although the cries of rioters still echoed throughout the University, Cartier smiled as though he didn't hear a thing.

"Count Laslo. A great pleasure to meet you."

"The pleasure is mine, Father. Will His Ordinence be joining us?"

"I'm afraid His Ordinence is currently indisposed."

Laslo frowned. "Nothing serious, I hope?"

"Nothing a little time spent in the care of the good Sisters can't fix. Has the Crown had a chance to review my proposal?"

"It is being considered as we speak. While I expect the Crown will be pleased with it, I admit to scratching my head at the abrupt change in plan."

"It's simple. Upon further reflection, we thought it prudent for the Crown to play a more pivotal role in managing University affairs during this difficult time. After all, Exidgeon clearly falls within the Crown's jurisdiction."

"Jurisdictional issues are often among the most difficult to resolve, particularly when they involve the collective spiritual well-being. In the past, the Church has frequently claimed the right to intervene without secular interference. Am I to understand that, with respect to this matter, you don't share that view?"

"Come now, Your Excellency. Like you, I'm Trifienne born and bred. The Crown and the Church have a long history of mutual respect and beneficial collaboration. Who better to entrust with the welfare of our people?"

Laslo raised an eyebrow. "So, the riots were more than you bargained for, eh?"

Cartier shrugged. "Perhaps."

"I figured. Is the Church planning a total withdrawal, then?"

"Oh, not at all, Your Excellency. I'm serious about undertaking a coordinated effort. I'm sure neither of us would care to see the University become a hotbed for heresy. To that end, the Church will happily provide the manpower and expertise to conduct a thorough investigation, while the Crown uses its authority to keep order among its citizens and protect University property."

"That's very generous of you. I anticipate the Crown will be amenable. Shall we set it to parchment?"

"The sooner the better. Step into my office and we'll finalize the terms."

Laslo tilted his head to gauge the distance of the rioters' cries. "Indeed, the sooner the better."

. . . . .

Brent shuffled through the vault's contents, his frustration growing. "*Consecrated damnation.*"

"What are you looking for?" Dona asked.

"My lucifers. I've kept a box of them in here for years, just in case something like this happened. It had to be that Hanstead boy. More than once I've caught him with the smell of tobacco smoke about him. Now I know how he was lighting up without a lamp. I suppose it's too much to hope for that any of you happened to bring some with you?"

There was a long moment of silence.

"Figures," Brent muttered.

"Perhaps it's just as well," the Monsignor said. "A fire in this confined space could foul the air, and there's no telling how long we may need to breathe it."

"How are we going to see anything, then?" Brent snapped.

"What do we really need to see?" Alexi asked. "We're locked in a vault, and the only way out is for someone to open the door from the other side."

"So, you plan to just sit here and wait for someone to rescue you?"

"What other choice have you given us?"

"I suppose you would have preferred explaining away your possession of the Morgatuan to those friendly Inquisitor folks who battered down my front door."

"How did you know about this Morgatuan thing anyway?" Dona asked. "Did Professor Garamon tell you about it?"

"Well, it's not like it isn't distinctive."

"Are you saying it's a matter of common knowledge?" Alexi asked.

"Is that really so odd? After all, your friend here seemed to know a thing or two about it as well."

"Armand has a prodigious memory for stray facts," Dona said.

"Speaking of whom, I don't believe we've met—and I know every Professor on the payroll."

"I'm just visiting," the Monsignor said.

"Are you, now? And I suppose you stumbled across the Morgatuan and ended up visiting this old Bursar by mere happenstance?"

"Is there some scenario you think would be more plausible?"

"Do you really think we'd be here if there weren't? I saw you reading the Morgatuan's symbols. It was barely a week ago that Professor Reston was here, no doubt making certain he had found the right spot. That would certainly explain his strange behavior."

"The right spot for what?"

"Don't patronize me. I've served a lifetime never daring to hope this moment would come. Spare me the fabrications and just get on with it. Use it."

"You mean the Morgatuan?"

"Of course. What else could I mean?"

"There's only one small problem," the Monsignor said. "I can't see it."

"In that case, I'm afraid we are doomed."

"Won't someone come to open the vault once they realize you're missing?" Alphonse asked.

"The Chancellor's office may still have the directions I sent them some 40 years ago, but even if they do, it won't help us."

"Why not?"

"Because they are wrong."

"You sent the wrong directions?"

"Chancellors come and go. Allowing unconditional access posed too great a risk."

"There may be another way," Dona said. "What if Armand could see the Morgatuan?"

"Without lucifers to light a lamp?"

"Alexi? Will you do it?"

Alexi gasped. "Dona, don't."

"We have no choice. It's either that or starve to death."

"I can't. I don't have the right."

"If you're worried about the others, you might stop to consider that the entire University is being held hostage by the Inquisition. Their discovery is just a matter of time."

"I won't do it."

Dona took his hand and pressed her locket into it. "Once, in a sumptuous restaurant, a handsome man I barely knew asked me to take a leap of faith with him. I didn't know where he would lead me, but I had a feeling it wasn't going to be to safety. And yet, when he asked, I jumped with both feet. I jumped because, even though I didn't know the danger, I'd peered into his eyes, and thought I knew him. Wherever he was going, I couldn't bear the thought of being left behind. I know what I'm asking isn't easy, and it seems risky, but that's what life is. We don't have the luxury of knowing every little consequence each time we make a decision, but that doesn't mean we should ever stop choosing."

"I can't betray them."

"Alexi, if you don't help us, we are all going to die, including the Monsignor. Do you really think your friends will fare better with Isrulian?"

"Monsignor?" Brent asked incredulously. "What do you mean by Monsignor?"

"Oops," Dona said.

"But—but—the *Morgatuan*."

"We never intended to mislead you," the Monsignor said.

"But the Inquisition…they pursued you."

"A minor misunderstanding…"

"A whole lifetime—wasted."

"I'm sure this seems worse than it is."

"Whole generations—*lost*."

"Look, it can't be that bad."

"You'll never use it. Not while I draw breath, heathen."

A crash echoed in the darkness as Brent threw himself at the Monsignor's voice.

"Where are you, heathen? You can't hide from me forever."

There was another crash and a curse as Brent stumbled over something.

The sibilant sound of steel on steel echoed through the vault as Alphonse drew his blade. "Stop right there, old man."

"Alphonse, no—" Dona's cry was cut short as Brent collided with her.

"Ooomph," the Monsignor grunted.

"There you are, heathen."

"Monsignor," Dona cried. "Did he hurt you?"

"Let go, heathen. How dare you defile this sacred relic?"

"Unhand him," Alphonse said—his blade useless in the dark.

Brilliant golden light illuminated Alexi's pale features with an almost beatific radiance. He held the glowing locket aloft.

Instantly, Alphonse's blade found its mark just beneath Brent's chin. Ever-so-slowly, Brent relinquished his hold on the artifact.

Brent squinted against the light. "What sorcery is this?" His eye strayed from the glowing locket to Dona, who now stood at Alexi's side, and his jaw dropped in sudden realization. "What a fool I've been. Who else could bend a Monsignor to her will? Why else would a Monsignor flee the Inquisition? The Mistress lives. She has returned."

Alexi finally finished mouthing his mnemonic, and with a wave of his hand, the overwrought Bursar collapsed.

The Monsignor stooped to examine Brent and was relieved to find the man still breathed. He then eyed Alphonse, Alexi, and Dona in turn. At last, he took a seat on a file cabinet, resting the Morgatuan across his knee.

"Well," he said, "this is a little awkward, isn't it?"

. . . . .

Laitrech hummed to himself as he turned his key in the lock of the ancient door that stood as the first line of defense for the Chapel Ordinalis. His spirits were high of late. He hadn't realized how much the dread of Armand's impending Ascendency weighed on him until it was canceled. And he hadn't even had to lift a finger.

He'd already closed the door before he realized something was amiss. He'd caught a dim impression in the hallway in the flicker of the lamplight, but it was so unexpected that it took a few seconds to register. He locked the door anyway.

"You're taking quite a risk," he said.

"Hardly."

As Laitrech's eyes adjusted, he could make out the speaker sitting squarely in the middle of the hallway, leaning against the unseen barrier with both knees pulled up. The figure slowly rose, throwing back a heavy cloak to reveal priestly vestments, a pate of close-cropped white hair, and an ancient face.

"How is he?"

Laitrech slipped his key into his pocket. "Stable, but weaker than he was. He took his brother's desertion pretty hard."

"How much weaker?"

"It's hard to say. Some is mood, and some is illness. At this stage, they can be difficult to distinguish. Why are you here?"

"This charade has gone on long enough. I need access."

Laitrech was beginning to regret his dealings with this old has-been. Though the deal's payoff was improbable at best, even a slim chance of success had been too tempting to pass up—he still shuddered when he imagined the consequences of the promised information falling into Lavicius's hands instead. But Thurman's repeated delays only bolstered Laitrech's initial suspicions—they would never be able to deliver. And after making him wait this long, they had temerity to make additional demands? He wouldn't have entertained the request even if current circumstances hadn't made granting access unthinkable.

"I'll see what I can manage." Laitrech said. "I'm sure he'll be delighted to see you again."

The priest's aged eyes narrowed. "I meant while he's asleep."

Laitrech frowned. "What on earth for?"

"I need to diagnose him myself. Your vague descriptions are of no use to me."

"That's easily arranged, assuming you fulfill your end of the bargain first."

"You'll have it just as soon as I get the raw materials."

"Forgive me, but I don't see that happening anytime soon. Last I heard, your lackey succeeded in buying himself a fake soul. Correct me if I'm wrong, but that is a key component, right?"

"A fake? How do you know?"

"Because I sent Isrulian to test it."

"And you relied on his judgment?"

"It's a pretty simple test. Even he could probably manage it."

"Then I definitely can't afford to wait any longer. If you force me to find another way, the deal will be off."

Laitrech snorted. "If you can't deliver the goods, it hardly matters, does it?"

"What if I were to give you the scroll now and deliver the rest when I could?"

"You miss the point. How can I verify the scroll's authenticity without a suitable test?"

"You might want to hedge your bet. I'm not getting any younger. If something happens to me, the knowledge dies with me."

"Not to worry—the Chapel's repository of knowledge is vast. It's only a matter of time before I discover what I seek there. Now, if you'll excuse me, you've inspired me to take another look."

Laitrech held aloft his Relic and spoke the prayer to abate the Bastion. Behind him, his elderly companion's lips moved as well—but the words they formed did not match Laitrech's.

The Ordinal held out his hand to confirm his success. When it met no resistance, he bowed superciliously. "I trust you'll be able to find your own way out."

With that, he strode off down the hallway toward the Chapel.

. . . . .

Alexi's eyes glistened in the locket's golden glow. "I'm sorry, Dona, but I couldn't stand by and let him attack the Monsignor. I know how much you wanted to be a professor someday. I've ruined everything."

Dona took his face in her hands. "Alexi Reysa, that was the bravest, most selfless thing I've ever seen anyone do."

His mouth trembled. "I've betrayed us all. If we don't die here, the Inquisition will make us wish we had. Either way, our lives are over."

Dona met his gaze with a look of sympathy and admiration. "Not yet..." Her own eyes began to well as she gently brushed Alexi's tears away. "There's one more thing I have to do before my life can be over." She pulled him close, willing their lips to meet. For a long bittersweet moment, they stood lost in each other's arms.

Finally, Alexi pulled away and faced the Monsignor. "What happens now?"

The Monsignor sighed. "I'm sorry, Alexi. This is a very serious matter. There's only so much I can do."

Dona took a step forward. "But you're the Inquisitor General. He was trying to help you."

"And I feel terrible about that, but this goes far beyond just heresy. At least one man is dead, several buildings are destroyed—and I shudder to think what's going on outside right now."

"You can't possibly believe Alexi had anything to do with those things."

"I'm not sure I know what to believe anymore."

"Who died?" Alexi's voice was hoarse.

"A professor. His name was Amehtan Shoruga."

"How?"

"He was being held for questioning about an incident involving Phrendonic Heresy that took place at the Hathaway compound—he took his own life."

"Forgive me, Monsignor, but doesn't that say more about the Inquisition than it does about Alexi?"

"Had there been no heresy in Exidgeon, there would have been no Inquisition. Shoruga would still live."

"And had this Inquisition been anything remotely like the one you described in class, he'd have had no need to kill himself." Dona jabbed a finger toward the vault door. "You saw what they're doing out there. You can certainly imagine what they did to this poor professor of yours. For the love of all that's holy, look what they've done to you. How can you support what they do to people and still live with yourself?"

Alexi put his hand on her arm. "Don't."

Dona pulled away. "Don't defend the finest man I know from the one who should be?"

The Monsignor shifted uncomfortably. "The Church suffers from all the same flaws and foibles of those who make it up. Although not perfect, the vast majority of us are honorable men who strive not only to make this world a better place, but also to protect and prepare the souls of our charges for the next."

"Like you protected and prepared Shoruga's?"

"No one regrets that more than I, but Phrendonic Heresy is insidious. It seduces its victims with the promise of power and at the same time provides the ability to conceal it. And if we do manage to track it down, it gives the heretics weapons against which we have little defense. Casualties are inevitable."

"How is that any different from what Isrulian does?" Dona asked.

The Monsignor's jaw dropped. "You know about that?"

"He flaunts his power like a badge of honor, and no one has any defense against it, apparently not even the Primal's brother. You're no different from the people you torture, unless, of course, you count the torture."

Alexi took Dona's arm. "Stop. You're only making it worse."

"But I'm right."

Alexi gave her a wild look. "He doesn't agree."

The words seemed to hang in the air. Dona heard Hepplewhite's voice admonishing her once more: *A manifest injustice can be a powerful motivating force, but if, and only if, the vast majority of your audience is on board about the injustice.*

Suddenly she was ashamed. She swallowed, took a step back and straightened her dress. "Very well then, as you wish."

Alexi faced the Monsignor. "Please—don't hold her defense of me against her. She didn't mean those things."

Dona touched Alexi's arm. "Don't—this is my responsibility." She took a deep breath. "Monsignor, even when I gave you no reason to, you have only ever treated me with kindness. I repaid you by holding you accountable for the misdeeds of the entire Church. I know I don't deserve it, but I am sincerely sorry, and some day, I hope you can forgive me."

The Monsignor eyed Dona pensively. "Miss Merinne, you are a difficult person to know. The very first time we met, I was forced to face my lifelong failure to address the injustices that had been visited by the Church, not just on women in general, but on my own mother."

"I know, Monsignor, and—"

The Monsignor held up his hand. "I'm not done yet. Today, you ask me to justify how what we seek to prevent is any different from what we actually do, and once again, I find myself at a loss. I am somehow left with the feeling I wasted my entire life seeking to reform what I should instead have sought to abolish. When I raised this very issue with the Primal and he disagreed, instead of persevering, I apologized for being too argumentative. What I didn't have the guts to say to my own brother, you were brave enough to say to the Inquisitor General. Miss Merinne, facing you is like staring into a mirror that reveals the cancers of one's soul."

"I promise I'll work on that if I am given the chance."

"Please do. The world could stand a little more self-reflection. In the future, though, might I suggest a gentler touch?"

"Yes, Monsignor."

"For my part, I shall take your words to heart. In the future, I promise to choose the right way, even if it also happens to be the hard way. And as for you, Alexi, although I have no idea what my status will be if we ever make it out of here, you have my word that I shall do everything in my power to ensure that you are treated fairly."

Alexi bowed his head. "Thank you, Monsignor."

"Now, how long will the Bursar remain asleep?"

"At least an hour."

"And the light?"

"Also an hour, but I can recharge it if necessary."

The Monsignor eyed Alexi sidelong. "We'll cross that bridge when we come to it. Alphonse, could you see if you can find some cord to bind the Bursar—there's no telling what he'll do when he wakes up. Alexi, could you bring the light closer. The Bursar seemed convinced there was a way to use this thing. Maybe I'll be able to tell something from these symbols."

"Do you recognize them?" Dona asked.

"I do. When I was a student back at the seminary, they made everyone memorize the Canticle of Obsequy. It was just my luck to have the one instructor who required it to be memorized in the original Tep'Chuan."

"Tep-*what?*" Alexi asked.

"Tep'Chuan," Dona said. "It's an ancient pictographic language adopted by the Chervillians for sacred writings."

"Very impressive," the Monsignor said. "I doubt even most seminary graduates would remember that detail. Did Professor Reston teach you that?"

Dona shook her head. "I learned it as part of my project for Professor Hepplewhite—your mother reportedly mastered Tep'Chuan in only two semesters. It was one of the things that first got her noticed by the Abbot at the seminary."

"Really? I never knew that."

"So, you can read these markings?" Alexi asked.

The Monsignor shook his head. "Not exactly. I was only required to memorize the symbols that appeared in the Canticle, and that was long before either of you were born. Chervillian Heresy hasn't really been my focus."

"What's a canticle?"

"It's a little hymn. The Chervillians often inscribed them on monuments."

"I've found some rope," Alphonse said.

"Excellent. Would you mind seeing if you can get him bound well enough so that we'll at least have some warning when he wakes up?"

"I'll see what I can do."

The Monsignor focused on the scepter. "These rings almost look like a locking mechanism, but the markings are a little small for old eyes in dim light."

"Just what we need," Alphonse said. "Another lock."

"I hope I'm wrong. With all these symbols, it could take forever to test every combination." He rotated the bottom-most ring. It made a tiny click as its symbols aligned with those the next row. He paused and listened intently, but nothing further happened. "Well, that's one down."

"Can you make the symbols say something?" Dona asked. "Even if we don't know what the combination is, whatever rules they use for syntax might cut down the number of possibilities."

"Let me see," the Monsignor said. He started turning the rings back and forth, arranging the symbols into a pattern that was meaningless to the others. "Hmm, now that's interesting. We might just be in luck. I think the combination might actually be the Canticle of Obsequy. I found the first symbol on the first ring. Then I found the symbol closest to what I thought should be second. That's when I noticed the next row of symbols seemed to be forming into the next line of the Canticle."

Alexi frowned. "What are the chances you would have memorized the one Canticle you happened to need?"

The Monsignor turned several more rings. "There aren't really that many to choose from, but I would think the odds would still be astronomical against. After all, the Canticle of Obsequy is usually inscribed only above the entrance to an Ossarium, which is why we had to memorize it. I've never heard of it appearing on a piece of Regalia before, but—there it is." He carefully nudged the last ring into place.

The instant the final symbols aligned, the cabochon rubies that filled the eye sockets of the Morgatuan's skull flickered with a blood-red glow, as though something malevolent had awakened. Simultaneously, radiant Tep'Chuan symbols etched themselves across the floor at Dona's feet. At that moment, a fierce blast of stale air and dust buffeted her, scattering the contents of the vault in fetid swirling eddies. Covering her ears against the pressure change, she stepped back, only to discover that a large section of floor behind her had simply vanished. Her foot missed the edge—she lost her balance, and with a shriek, she toppled into the abyss.

"Dona!" Alexi screamed. Oblivious to the pain in his ankle, he dashed to the brink and held aloft the Lighted locket.

The circular pit's walls were roughly carved from bedrock. A narrow stairway spiraled along them into the depths, beyond the ability of the locket to illuminate. The stairs were interrupted at several points by landings, each with its own archway framing a tunnel leading into deeper darkness.

"Dona!" Alexi yelled.

A moan echoed from below.

"Don't move. I'll be right there."

"You can't run those stairs with that ankle," Alphonse said. "Hand me the locket. I'll go."

Alexi paused, glancing from Alphonse back to the pit.

The Monsignor peered downward. "He's right. He can make it faster. Let him go."

Alexi thrust the locket into Alphonse's outstretched hand. "Be careful." He turned back to the pit. "Dona, hold tight. Alphonse is coming."

Alexi and the Monsignor hobbled after Alphonse, but it wasn't long before he was too far ahead for them to see their footing. Pausing, Alexi cast a furtive glance over his shoulder at the Monsignor, who was trying desperately to place each step using the Morgatuan's feeble glow. Alexi held up the Inquisitor's sword. "Forgive me, Monsignor." In full voice, he recited a series of mnemonics he'd gleaned from Reston's book. Brilliant golden light streamed from the blade. Alexi resumed his slow descent.

For several moments, the Monsignor stood blinking in shock. Then, as Alexi's light left him behind, he called out. "I forgive you. Hold up."

Far below, Alphonse finally reached the layer of moldering straw that blanketed the pit's lower reaches. Although he couldn't see Dona anywhere, a haze of dust and mold still lingered.

"Dona, are you there?"

Another moan—from beneath the straw. He placed a tentative foot on its surface, but it failed to support his weight.

As he drew back his foot, Dona screamed.

Setting his jaw, Alphonse leapt. He sank up to his waist. Dust billowed around him. He struggled for breath.

"Hold on," Alexi cried. "We're coming."

Dona's head surfaced. "There are bugs in here." She flailed and swatted, raising noxious clouds of dust and decay.

Alphonse held out his hand. "Are you hurt?"

"Just the wind knocked out of me. I'm bruised, but I can walk—if the bugs don't get me first." She swatted a few more times and reached for Alphonse's hand.

Alphonse helped drag her back through the straw to the stairway. "You're lucky to be alive."

Once their feet hit stone, Dona dusted the dirt and straw from her habit and evicted as many bugs as she could find.

When Alexi and the Monsignor finally made it down the stairway, Alexi rushed to embrace Dona, but backed off when he caught a whiff.

He settled for picking stray pieces of straw from her hair. "Don't ever do that again."

"Don't worry. What is this place, anyway?"

The Monsignor had a seat on the steps. "Unless I miss my guess, we've discovered the long-lost Exidgeon Ossarium."

"Ossarium?" Alphonse asked. "What's that?"

"Chervillians don't believe the soul moves on to a new realm after death. Instead, they're convinced it is destroyed unless extraordinary steps are taken to preserve it."

"So…this is a cemetery?" Dona asked.

"Not exactly. An Ossarium is more like a temporary storage area for the dead."

Alexi shuddered. "What do you mean temporary?"

"There'd be no point in storing them unless you were planning to revive them, would there? They believe a great savior will one day arrive to rescue them from their slumber."

"I don't suppose there's another exit?" Alexi asked.

"I have no idea."

Dona brushed off her hands. "It's not like we have any other options. We'll have to look."

"We'll need to be extraordinarily careful. Ossaria have historically been prime targets for looters, and the Church long ago deemed them anathema. As a result, the Chervillians became quite adept at concealing and protecting them. Under normal circumstances, when the Church discovers an Ossarium, only trained experts are authorized to enter and neutralize it. Even then, there are occasional…accidents."

The light on the locket suddenly winked out.

Dona rubbed Alexi's arm. "Can you light it up again?"

Alexi looked to the Monsignor, who, after a long pause, shrugged. "Go ahead. We can worry about our penance later. I very much doubt we'd survive in the dark."

Alexi took the locket from Alphonse, and a moment later, the glow resumed. As he placed it around Dona's neck, something smote the straw next to Alphonse, raising a telltale puff of dust.

Alphonse peered upward. "Ack, the Bursar."

"I thought you tied him up?" Alexi said.

"I thought I did too, but I've never had to tie anyone up before. It's not as easy as it sounds. Not to worry—I'll get him." He drew his sword and sprinted up the stairway. He took six steps and stopped. "Um, I'll need a light."

"We should all go together," the Monsignor said. "If you take off after him, there's no telling what you might run into."

"He's already attacked you once," Dona said. "We can't just let him get away."

The Monsignor was adamant. "We are better off staying together."

"I'll go first," Alphonse volunteered.

"He'll need my light," Alexi said. "I'll go second.

With Dona following the Monsignor, who leaned on the Morgatuan as a cane, they limped their way upward. Despite a brave show, Alexi had irritated his sprain to the point where he could barely put weight on it. Dona was terrified he would lose his footing. The distraction proved disastrous—the arm around her throat came as a total shock.

Instinctively, she tried to twist out of her attacker's grasp. "Hey—"

Her struggles were cut short by a sharp pain in the small of her back—to avoid skewering, she allowed herself to be dragged into an archway and out of sight.

The cry alerted her companions, but their positions on the stairway made coordinated response difficult. The Monsignor whirled toward the archway, but Brent's voice froze him in place.

"That's far enough, gentlemen."

"I can't get to him," Alphonse said. "Back up."

"Don't move," Dona cried. "He has a blade."

Alphonse gaped at the Monsignor. "Where's your sword?"

The Monsignor reddened. "I left it above."

"Don't you worry," Brent said. "It's in good hands."

"What do you want?" the Monsignor demanded.

"The same as you do—to get out of this place alive."

"We aren't stopping you." Alexi said. "Let her go."

The Monsignor held up his hand and Alexi fell silent. "How does taking the girl help with that?"

"Would you have negotiated if I hadn't?"

Alexi handed off his glowing blade to Alphonse and slipped silently past him up the steps.

"What did you want to negotiate?" the Monsigor asked.

"A truce. I can't make it out of here without your light, and you'll never make it out without my help."

Alexi crept farther up the stairway.

"What about your help would make it worth the risk?" the Monsignor asked, "keeping in mind you've threatened to kill me."

"That was before I knew we had a source of light. I thought we were all dead. Even with the light, you'll never make it out of here unless you work with me."

By now, Alexi had made it up the stairs to the opposite side of the pit and was on his hands and knees trying to get a good view down through the archway, but so far, all he could see was Dona's feet off to one side. The Monsignor glanced up to him with a hopeful look, but Alexi shook his head.

"Really?" the Monsignor asked. "What's so dangerous?"

"Nice try, but you aren't going to get the milk for free."

"Well then, at least name the cow. Why should we believe a University Bursar would know anything useful about an Ossarium he couldn't even open?"

Alexi moved a bit farther up the stairs, but to no avail—the Bursar had moved far enough back into the corridor that Alexi couldn't get a bead on him. Once again, he shook his head at the Monsignor.

"I recognized the Morgatuan," Brent pointed out.

"As you mentioned before, it is distinctive. You'll have to do better."

"I knew it could be used to open the Ossarium. That's why I locked us in the vault."

"Then again, you might simply have decided that starving to death would be better than what the Inquisition had in store for you. If you aren't lying, we'll have to find out how you know what you claim to know sooner or later."

The Monsignor shot Alexi a frustrated look. All Alexi could do was shrug—Brent was not visible from his vantage point.

Brent sighed. "Very well. One of my ancestors survived the defeat of the Chervillian enclave here by escaping through the Ossarium. I have his journal."

"An intriguing story, but awfully convenient."

"He does have an old-looking book with him," Dona said.

"Then, hold it out where we can see it."

"I'm not falling for that one," Brent said. "Here." He thrust the journal into Dona's hands. "You hold it out."

Trembling, and with the point of the sword still making its presence known, Dona moved forward just enough so that her companions could see the crumbling journal. In doing so, she moved just enough for Alexi to glimpse the top of Brent's foot through his sandal.

"I've kept my part of the bargain," Brent said. "Do we have a deal?"

"We'll need to discuss it."

"Take your time. I'm not going anywhere."

"I vote 'yes,'" Dona said.

And then Brent's sword clattered to the floor. Dona snatched it up and whirled to face her assailant, but he offered no resistance. For the second time in as many hours, Brent lay unconscious.

"About time," Dona said.

Alexi started back down toward them. "You were in the way—"

"The journal," the Monsignor said. "Do we have the journal?"

Dona held it up. "Right here."

"So, he was telling the truth," Alphonse said. "There is a way out."

"And if what he says is true," the Monsignor said, "with the journal, we won't have to rely on Brent's cooperation. Call me uncharitable, but I'm not particularly comfortable placing my trust in people who've attacked me."

"Um, I wouldn't be so sure," Dona said, paging through the journal.

"You mean, he lied to us?"

Dona held up the open journal for them to see. "I can't tell. The whole thing's written in Tep'Chuan."

# CHAPTER 10

---

# SACRED AND PROFANE

It was proving to be a late night for the Curator of Profanities. When he was younger, completing his lesson plans on time had been something he took for granted, but in those days, he hadn't been prone to nodding off while writing them. He surveyed his handiwork and shook his head. In three separate places, his crabbed handwriting trailed off into an incoherent line, and he had several pages still to go. He shuddered to imagine what the bright-eyed seminary students must think of the doddering old priest who did his best to spoon feed them everything they needed to know on the dangers of heretical artifacts. He couldn't afford to be incoherent—many of these students were destined to become Inquisitors—their very lives could depend on knowing what he had to teach. He tried to shake the sleep from his eyes, but it wasn't working. He picked up his guttering lamp. Perhaps a walk to the kitchens would help lift the fog, and if that wasn't enough, he could always grab a cup of tea.

The instant he stepped into the gallery, he knew something was amiss. The front door, which he had locked behind himself on the way in, was standing open, allowing light from a hallway lantern to stream into the room. Holding his lamp aloft, he scanned the myriad display cabinets and pedestals, looking for anything that might have been disturbed. Then, somewhere in the darkness he heard something—the subtle sound of cloth on cloth, as of someone shifting position.

His heart raced. He swung his lamp toward the noise and squinted into the semi-darkness. "Who's there? You're not allowed here."

His voice held more authority than he felt. He waited, listening intently, but heard nothing else. The silence was so complete he began to doubt his memory of locking the door. If his mind could shut down on him during lesson plans, why not at other times? He laughed nervously and forced himself to breathe.

It's not as though the door had been forced. Or, had it? He needed to be certain. But as he got close, it creaked closed, revealing a figure swathed in priestly vestments whose dark eyes glittered in the lamplight.

"Albert?" the figure asked. "How have you been?"

The Curator's eyes widened in recognition. "What are you doing here? I was told you'd been shipped off to spend your final years in quiet contemplation."

"So I was. The contemplation was fine, but the quiet grew interminable."

"And so you snuck away? Is that why you're dressed like that?"

"They say clothes make the man."

"Very funny. May I call you 'Father,' then? I wouldn't want to give anything away."

The old priest nodded. "That might be safest. So, what's new in the world of Profanities?"

"Very little, actually." Most of the things you see on display here still date back to Caprian. Fortunately, Armand hasn't had to deal with any issues of that magnitude."

"Now that you mention it, many of these things do look familiar. Is that the same old set of Harcourt wands?"

The Curator chuckled. "The very ones. I still can't believe you actually triggered one. I thought Roman was going to have me defrocked. He had only just appointed me Curator."

The old priest snorted. "I was only green for an hour or so. He would never have needed to know."

"But even if he'd never found out, that kind of secret would have eaten away at me."

"Where's the prize of your collection?"

"You mean the Vis-à-vis wand?"

"As I recall, it used to take center stage here."

"That hasn't been out for some time. Since I've been teaching seminary students in the gallery, I've tried to display only those artifacts I know are mostly harmless, and we never really did figure out exactly what that wand was made to do."

"I've been thinking about that," the old priest said, "and I've come up with a new hypothesis. Could we take a look?"

The Curator sorted through the keys on his chain. "Well I suppose so, as long as we don't spend all night at it. I have to teach come the morning, and I'm not done planning the lecture yet. So, what is this new insight?"

"I was trying to remember how it was put together. Didn't it have an unusual handle?"

The Curator slipped on a pair of cotton gloves and unlocked a musty cabinet. "I always thought the whole thing was unusual. Ah, here it is."

As the Curator reached into the cabinet, he felt something cold press against the side of his neck. He stiffened and sank to the floor.

The priest slid a ring onto a gnarled finger. "I'm sorry Albert, but I can't risk your overactive conscience. And for future reference, Samulian's Signet, in the wrong hands, is far from harmless."

Reaching over the fallen Curator, the old priest carefully retrieved the precious wand from its resting place. The main shaft was light-colored and solid, possibly hickory, with the words Vis-à-vis emblazoned along its length. Even in the dim light there was no mistaking it—whereas most wands had an obvious handle and an equally obvious tip, Vis-à-vis sported handles at both ends. This odd configuration was itself enough to drive the Curator to touch it only using special precautions, such as the cotton gloves—he had no desire to trigger it, and there was no telling which end was safe.

Harboring no such qualms, his priestly friend grasped it by one handle and pressed the other firmly against the flesh on the back of the Curator's wrist, just above the glove.

. . . . .

The discussion concerning what to do with the Bursar had been brief, and in Dona's mind, disturbing. The thought of cooperating with her attacker galled her. Rubbing her back at the memory of his blade, she considered their predicament one more time in the hopes of finding a plausible strategy that didn't include him, or failing that, a more convincing argument that he couldn't be trusted. Alphonse had sided with her, but then, Alphonse was known for brandishing a sword to distract men with crossbows. The Monsignor's position was simple: without a guide, their chances of navigating the hazards of the Ossarium were negligible. Besides, the Bursar had incentive to act in good faith, since the journal's information was probably useless in the dark. Dona expected such arguments from the Monsignor, but she hadn't foreseen Alexi would side with him as well. As much as she tried to tell herself Alexi's defection wasn't personal, that certainly wasn't how it felt.

When Alexi nodded off in the middle of the argument, they woke him long enough to have him refresh the light and agreed to let him rest until the Bursar regained consciousness. The pain from Alexi's swollen ankle and the intense mental effort required for working his heresies were taking their toll, and he was central to every option they could think of.

In the quiet they provided for Alexi, it wasn't long before the Monsignor began to nod as well, but Alphonse showed no sign of fatigue. His eye never left their prisoner, and his hand never strayed far from his blade. The set of his jaw made it clear he had no intention of letting them down again, and when the Bursar finally stirred, it was the sound of Alphonse drawing his blade that gave warning.

"Alphonse, please," the Monsignor said. "There's no need for that."

He lowered the blade but did not sheath it.

Brent sat up. "You're still here?"

"We'd like to discuss your truce," the Monsignor said.

"Where's the journal?"

The Monsignor nodded to Dona. "Give it to him. It's no use to you."

She balked. "But you know some Tep'Chuan. You might be able to piece it together."

The Monsignor shook his head. "For a truce to have any chance of working, it will require good faith on both sides."

"That's assuming it has any chance of working, period. This man held a sword to my back—"

"Which is precisely what makes returning the journal such an exemplary show of good faith."

Dona turned to Alexi for support, but he simply stared at her expectantly, as though waiting for her to comply.

Fuming, she tossed the journal to the Bursar. "I hope you know what you're doing."

"There, now," the Monsignor said. "I propose we accept Mr. Brent's offer of cooperation. I think it's obvious that we'll all be better off if we can set aside our differences and work together toward the common goal of getting out of here alive."

"Just a moment, Monsignor," the Bursar said, peering over his glasses. "There are conditions."

The Monsignor's eyebrows raised. "There are?"

"First, you must all swear that you won't breathe a word about the existence of this Ossarium to anyone."

The Monsignor shifted uncomfortably. "Mr. Brent, I'm sure you can appreciate that as a representative of the Church, I—"

"Ever," Brent said.

Dona eyed the Monsignor sidelong. "It would be an exemplary show of good faith to agree, don't you think?"

The Monsignor sighed. "I asked for that, didn't I? Very well, I agree."

"Make it reciprocal," Alexi said. "You can't tell a soul about anything we did here either."

The Bursar shrugged. "Your heresies, you mean? They don't concern me, and so long as you stop using them on me, I'll happily agree—but you may want to exact the same promise from your Monsignor friend while you still have the chance."

"That's between the Monsignor and me."

The Bursar shrugged. "Suit yourself. Second, I get custody of the Morgatuan."

The Monsignor hesitated.

"The Monsignor needs it to get around," Dona said, "but if your help turns out to be essential for getting us out of this place, I think that would be a small price to pay. If not, we keep it."

The Bursar stepped aside and gestured toward the side passage. "Fair enough. This way, then."

"You first," Alphonse said.

"Whatever you say." The Bursar stepped into the darkness of the passage, with Alphonse on his heels.

Dona offered Alexi an arm for support. "He doesn't waste any time, does he?"

The Monsignor steeled himself and followed Alphonse. "Let's pray his enthusiasm stems from his shared desire to escape. I'd just as soon not contemplate the alternative."

.  .  .  .  .

The two guards stationed at the rectory entrance bowed politely. "Good evening, Curator," one of them said.

The Curator scowled. "Well this is new. When did His Primacy decide he needed round-the-clock surveillance?"

"Ordinal Laitrech's orders. Rumor has it His Primacy is not well."

"So I've heard. Be that as it may, I need to see him right away."

"I'm sorry, Curator. No one can see his Primacy without Ordinal Laitrech's say so."

The Curator pushed forward. "I'm sure his Ordinence did not intend to bar access to His Primacy's trusted advisors."

The two guards stepped together to block the old man's passage. "Our orders are clear—no one is allowed in without the express approval of His Ordinence."

"And what if an Ordinal needed to see His Primacy?"

The guard shook his head. "We can't let anyone in without approval, Ordinal or no. We'd have to turn away his own mother if she didn't carry the right papers."

"I see," the Curator said.

"Nothing personal."

"On the contrary. Loyalty is a virtue. I just hope it isn't misplaced in this instance. No matter. It seems a little visit with His Ordinence is in order. I'll be back."

"I'm sorry." The guard's apology echoed down the hallway as the Curator stalked away, but no response echoed back.

.  .  .  .  .

As they progressed deeper into the Ossarium, the brick walls of the passage gave way to a natural cavern. The overwhelming scent of straw mold had lessened, but the air became clammy, and Dona rubbed her shoulders in a futile attempt to stay warm. The Bursar halted abruptly. An ancient brick archway loomed before them, built to conform to the natural walls of the cavern.

"There it is," Brent said. He strode forward for a better look.

"Slow down," the Monsignor warned. "The light is pointless if we don't use it. There's no telling what we'll run into down here."

"What's the matter, Monsignor? Don't you trust me?"

"I'd prefer to retain the option of continuing to trust you, if you don't mind."

The Bursar was too busy inspecting an inscription over the archway to answer. He scratched his head and consulted his journal several times as he puzzled over the Tep'Chuan symbols.

"What's wrong?" Alexi asked.

"Probably nothing."

"Probably?" Dona asked.

The Bursar drew himself up in indignation. "If you would prefer to do this, be my guest."

"I'm sure she meant no disrespect," the Monsignor said, "and I'm sure we would all like to know what has you so puzzled."

"The inscription doesn't match. It translates roughly: '…and where the faithless find perdition, the faithful shall find life anew.'"

"What's it supposed to say?" Alexi asked.

The Bursar frowned. "According to the journal, it should say something to the effect of '…and the faithful shall abide in joyous repose.'"

"Are we in the right passage?" Dona asked.

The Bursar bristled. "The archway is here as described, and these are both common scriptural references. The journalist probably just misremembered the specific verse. It's not like they would have had time to jot it down while they were fleeing."

"I was merely asking."

Alexi held up his blade to illuminate the space beyond the archway. "Where do we go from here, then? This looks like a dead end."

The Bursar smiled. "For that, I'll need the Morgatuan."

"Not yet," Dona said. "We had an agreement."

The Bursar shrugged. "If our good Monsignor would prefer to handle this next part, I have no objections."

The Monsignor placed his hand on Dona's shoulder. "We must learn to trust." He handed the Morgatuan to the Bursar.

Dona's eyes narrowed, but she held her tongue.

The Bursar carefully read and reread several pages of the journal before he continued. Then he turned one of the rings on the Morgatuan, and the flickering light in the eye sockets winked out.

"All right. Everyone stay close." Starting at the arch, the Bursar paced his way into the darkness beyond, counting quietly. The others followed in a tight cluster, and though Dona didn't trust a word the Bursar said, she was careful to follow directions.

The Bursar held up his hand. "Far enough." Ahead, the passage ended in a natural cave wall.

"But this is a dead end," Dona said.

"Observe," the Bursar said. He held the Morgatuan aloft and clicked the errant ring back into position.

The eyes flickered back to life. A swirling burst of dust and debris buffeted them. Dona instinctively covered her face, but still ended up with a mouthful of grit. It took several seconds for the pressure to equalize.

Dona spat several times into her kerchief. "Was that really necessary?"

"See for yourself," the Bursar said.

The floor before them had disappeared, revealing a stairway leading down into darkness.

"All that drama for a stairway?" Dona asked. Next time can we just approach it the normal way?"

"If you like," the Bursar said. His enigmatic smile only annoyed her more.

Alexi tapped her on the shoulder. "Um, Dona...don't step back."

Mere inches from where her heels were planted, the floor had ceased to be. But instead of a stairway, there was only a pit, and even when Alexi held his blade over it, they still could see no bottom.

Dona gulped. Coloring only a little, she smiled sweetly and addressed the Bursar.

"Well, then, Mr. Brent. What did you say our next move was?"

. . . . .

Laitrech looked up from the stack of scrolls he'd pulled. He could have sworn he'd heard footsteps. Only rarely did any of the other Ordinals venture here, and certainly not at this late hour. There must be some emergency.

"Who's there?"

The door to the Chapel Ordinalis creaked open.

"I'm sorry to bother Your Ordinence…"

"Albert? Is that you?"

The Curator stepped into the Chapel. "In the flesh."

"What are you doing here? Who let you past the Bastion?"

"I just let myself in. I hope you don't mind."

"Don't be absurd. Only an Ordinal can bypass the Bastion."

"I don't know what to tell you. As you can see, I am alone."

"Impossible," Laitrech said. Then he raised an eyebrow. "Unless… you didn't, by chance, bring any Profanities with you?"

"As a matter of fact, I did."

Laitrech smirked as he considered the potential implications. "Excellent. Bring it to me."

"If you insist."

"Which one is it? Do you have any records detailing its manufacture?"

"It's a simple ring," the Curator said, removing it from his finger. "I'm afraid we don't know much about it."

"Let me see."

"As you wish." The Curator pressed the ring into Laitrech's outstretched palm.

Confusion spread across the Ordinal's face. Then he stiffened and collapsed across the desk.

"As simple as that," the Curator said. From his vestments, he produced an oddly shaped two-handled wand and touched it to the back of the Ordinal's hand.

. . . . .

Without hesitation, the Bursar strode down the stairs and threw open the door. The warm glow of a lighted chamber spilled into the stairwell. The others followed, but tentatively, with Dona assisting Alexi, and the Monsignor leaning heavily against the wall for support.

The chamber's peculiar walls soared to a vaulted ceiling and were honeycombed, top to bottom, with hundreds of alcoves, most of which were lit by a faint radiance. The combined effect rendered the light from Alexi's blade unnecessary. In the chamber's center, a stone structure—perhaps an altar—rested on a raised dais. Grinning skulls decorated its edges, and various unidentifiable implements and containers lay scattered across its surface. Two stone effigies flanked the altar, their impassive expressions giving no clue as to their identity or significance. Several stone sarcophagi occupied places of prominence, one of which lay open, its lid resting against its side.

Dona gaped in wonder. "What are all the lights?"

The Monsignor's eyes flicked nervously about the chamber. "I believe they are called 'vigil lights.' Only the most wealthy or powerful Chervillians were accorded such honors. Am I correct, Mr. Brent?"

The Bursar, who was frantically flipping pages in his journal and shaking his head, ignored the question.

Dona was beginning to suspect he had overstated the journal's value. "What is it this time?"

The Bursar continued to flip pages. "This isn't right. There's no mention of this place anywhere."

"So we took the wrong passage after all?"

"No matter," Alexi said. "Can't we just backtrack and start again in a different passage?"

"We could—if a bottomless pit didn't block our way."

"Well, doesn't the journal say anything about getting past the pit?"

"No. In the journal, they only went one way."

Alexi frowned in thought. "Can we use something to span the pit?"

Dona put her fists on her hips. "Just how do you expect to hobble across a rickety makeshift bridge with that ankle? And what about the Monsignor? How do you expect him to get across?"

Alexi stared blankly for a moment, then shrugged. "I'm too tired to think straight."

"And how much time do we have left on the light?"

"I don't know. A few more minutes, maybe."

"We can't do this tonight. Alexi, you need to rest."

The Monsignor shook his head. "I'm not so sure this is a good place for a rest. In theory, the most prominent will also be the best protected."

"It's also got light. Alexi is in pain and can barely keep his eyes open. Once that sword goes out, he's not going to have the wherewithal to light it again, and I, for one, would rather face the rest of the night here where I can see, instead of someplace else in pitch darkness."

The Monsignor eyed his surroundings uneasily. "Very well, let's make ourselves as comfortable as we can here, then. Mr. Brent, if I might trouble you for my cane, please?"

Sullenly, the Bursar returned the scepter. "In this place, of all places, you would do well to keep your blasphemies to yourself, Monsignor."

"I'll keep an eye on him," Alphonse said.

The Monsignor regarded Alphonse for a moment and nodded.

Dona and Alexi huddled together for warmth, and the Monsignor settled down nearby. The Bursar found a spot some distance away, while Alphonse, his sword still unsheathed, hunkered between him and the others. A few moments later, the light from Alexi's sword finally winked out, leaving only the vigil lights and the flickering eyes of the Morgatuan to illumine their uneasy dreams.

· · · · ·

The guard snapped to attention. "Good evening, Your Ordinence." The second guard, who had been resting against the wall with his eyes closed, heard his partner's greeting and jumped into position.

"Gentlemen," Laitrech said with a nod. He hesitated, and when the guards did not react, he reached for the door. "Carry on," he said. Then he stepped into the rectory and closed the door behind him.

The room was dark, except for the moonlight streaming through the high windows of the hall. Finally satisfied that nothing was amiss, he cracked open the door to the gardens. There was no sign of life, other than the rasping of crickets in denial that summer had left them. On the desk, he found a candlestick in a brass holder and set it alight. Careful not to douse the fragile flame, he climbed the steps to the room where his Primal lay in fitful slumber.

The Ordinal gazed at the Primal for a long moment, a tender smile playing at the corners of his mouth. Then, he shook his head, as if clearing away the remnants of an unwelcome memory, and strode to the nightstand. He picked up a goblet and sniffed intently at its dregs.

Puzzled, he rubbed the rim with his little finger and touched it to his tongue. He wrinkled his nose at the taste and placed the goblet back on the nightstand.

At last, he rolled up his vestments' oversized sleeves, clutched the silver snake pendant on the cord around his neck, and began mouthing prayers. At one point, the Primal stirred and changed position, causing the Ordinal to freeze mid-stanza, but when the Primal showed no further sign of movement, the silent recitation continued. The prayers ended, and the Ordinal closed his eyes in silent meditation. Suddenly, he gasped. Outrage flared across his face. His eyes narrowed and his jaw set, his expression now one of grim determination.

"What is it my friend?" the Primal wheezed.

Laitrech started at the words but retained his composure. "How do you feel?"

The Primal's smile was pained. "I've been better. I am always so tired now, and with so much still to be done. Has Armand returned?"

"Not yet."

The Primal's eyes welled. "I could have handled that better, couldn't I?"

"I suppose so. Do you think you can walk?"

"The vertigo makes that difficult. Walk where? What time is it anyway?"

"It's late, but I may have found a new treatment. There is no time to lose."

"What kind of treatment?"

"There isn't time to explain."

"Why can't you just bring it here?"

"If that were possible, don't you think I would have?"

The Primal's eyes widened. "Mind whom you address, Ordinal." In a milder tone, he added. "Are you all right?"

"I'm sorry. I just don't want us to be too late."

"Very well. Help me up." Once they had him sitting on the edge of the bed, he continued." I'll need my vestments."

After a brief search, Laitrech located some hanging in an armoire.

The Primal raised an eyebrow. "You really think I'll need the formal set for this?"

"I don't think it matters, so long as we get you into them quickly."

"You sure you're all right?"

"Put your arm through here."

After a few more minutes of struggling with the vestments, the Primal reached for the cane by the edge of his bed and tried to stand. After two attempts, and with a little help from the Ordinal, he got to his feet.

"Will I need anything else?"

The Ordinal shook his head. "Once we get you downstairs, I'll ask the guards to send for your carriage."

"Guards?"

The Ordinal paused. "Since you've gotten so frail, I've asked someone to be on duty at the door at all times, just in case you need something and I'm not close by."

"I see. I guess that makes sense."

They made it down the stairs, but the effort took its toll on the Primal, who gasped and wheezed from the exertion. "They just don't make Primals like they used to."

"True. The previous ones couldn't hold a candle to the current model."

The guards snapped to attention as Laitrech opened the door. "Quickly, fetch the Primal's carriage."

The guards saluted. "Right away, Your Ordinence." One scurried off down the hallway.

"You—assist His Primacy." The other guard rushed to support the Primal, but their progress was still slow.

After a few minutes, Laitrech shook his head. "This isn't working. Carry him."

The guard hesitated, but once the Primal shrugged his permission, he lifted the Primal off his feet, and they made better time.

"Have you left instructions with the Secretary?" the Primal asked. "I'll need to be notified as soon as possible if Armand arrives."

The Ordinal mumbled something unintelligible.

"Laitrech?"

The guard stopped and glanced over his shoulder. He caught only a brief glimpse of an ancient withered face beneath a shock of white close-cropped hair before something solid took him in the cheek and swung his head around. He staggered, nearly dropping the Primal, until he steadied himself against the wall.

The man in the Ordinal's vestments stepped around to confront the guard and his precious cargo. The guard nearly dropped the Primal a second time, for the Ordinal now wore a face that precisely matched his own.

"Listen carefully," the guard in Ordinal vestments hissed. "You're not sick, you're being poisoned."

The Primal's eyes went wide with horror. "What have you done with Laitrech, *demon?*"

"Superstitious fool. Listen to me. I've done all I can—the rest is up to you. Trust no one, particularly not Laitrech." With that, he sprinted down the corridor, his vestments fluttering behind him.

# CHAPTER 11

---

# REINFORCEMENTS

**R**andolph Brent opened one eye ever so slightly, and what he saw through his lashes made him smile. Alphonse sat propped against a sarcophagus, sword in hand, his chin resting on his chest, his breathing slow and rhythmic. Peering past his self-appointed jailor, he could see the girl and her beau. The boy snored deeply, while the girl's slumber was more fitful. More than once, she spoke in her sleep, but Brent had been unable to make out the words. Beyond them, the Monsignor slept, looking perversely peaceful, considering his surroundings. At the sight of him, Brent's smile evaporated. The Morgatuan was cradled in one arm. To Brent, it seemed its glowing eyes fixed him with an unrelenting accusatory glare. He shook his head to dismiss the unsettled feeling, knowing it was foolishness—but the guilt did not abate.

Silently, he rose and tiptoed to the altar. Other than a metal prybar, he recognized none of the implements strewn across it, but the grinning golden skull embedded in its surface was a symbol he knew all too well. It was reminiscent of the Morgatuan, but on a larger scale. As he got closer, he noticed the altar was not smooth as he had first thought. Instead, much of it was covered with finely graven symbols much like those that filled his journal. He leaned in as far as he could without stepping onto the dais and adjusted his glasses.

"Can you read it?"

The surprise of Alphonse's whisper nearly made him lose his balance. "Don't sneak up on old people like that."

"Sorry—I'm trying not to wake the others. Can you read it?"

"Not from this distance."

"If you got closer?"

"Why the sudden interest in ancient Chervillian script?"

"I was wondering if it told us a way out. This place makes my skin crawl."

"Surely there's nothing lurking here that blade of yours can't handle."

"You mean like the floor dropping out from under you?"

"Except for that."

"There has to be a way out, doesn't there? Tell me my girl won't have to live out her days wondering why her man abandoned her."

Alphonse's earnestness softened the old man's heart. "We'll figure it out. These alcoves weren't all filled at the same time. There must be a way back."

"That's good—I'm too young for perdition."

"You and me both. Should we wake the others?"

"I don't think we need to. They will only want to know what this writing says, and they can't help you with that. May as well let them rest."

"As you've seen, Ossaria are known for dangerous little surprises. I've been hesitant to step on the dais for fear of triggering something, but I don't see an alternative if I want to read the writings."

"Do you think it might disappear like the floor in the passage?"

"I can't rule it out, though the two pits we've seen so far seem only to react to the Morgatuan. Of course, that pattern may itself be part of the trap. Notice how the dais is made of several wedges, any one of which could conceal another pit."

Alphonse rubbed his chin. "True, but it might also conceal the way out."

"You have a point. I suppose I do tend to view my cup as half empty."

Alphonse grinned. "Probably you've been drinking from it longer."

"Let's wait to wake them until after I've had a look at the writing. Here, give me a hand with this coffin."

Together they approached the open sarcophagus and inspected its lid. There were chips out of one edge, but it was otherwise intact.

"What do you want to do with it?"

"I'd like to lay the lid across several of the wedges. If one disappears, maybe I won't disappear with it. The lid ought to be heavy enough to trip anything set to trigger from someone's weight."

Alphonse lifted his end without difficulty, but Brent managed only with much grunting and puffing. The noise of their exertions finally woke Dona and the Monsignor, who approached to see what they were up to. With effort, Alphonse slid the coffin lid close enough to the altar for Brent to read the altar etchings. The dais seemed unaffected. Brent tested with his toe, and when it held, he tested his full weight. He shrugged, had a seat, and began reading to himself.

"What do they say?" Dona asked.

Brent peered at Dona over his glasses. "I don't know—it's not like I've had much chance to digest it yet."

She blushed but met his gaze. "Well, there could have been a title or something."

Brent huffed and went back reading.

Steeling herself, Dona peered into the open sarcophagus. "This is empty. Do you suppose it was robbed, or was it never filled?"

"I hope it was robbed," Alphonse said. "It would be great to know that someone else who made it in here also made it out."

The Monsignor cleared his throat. "Assuming he did make it out."

"It was filled." Brent said.

Dona inspected the sarcophagus more closely. "How can you tell?"

"The lid was inscribed, and there are signs it was sealed."

"Whose coffin was it then?"

"Some long-dead Chervillian's, I would imagine. I can only translate one thing at a time."

"Well, pardon me." Dona shook her head and turned her attention to a statue the Monsignor was studying.

"Gracia Terrati, if I'm not mistaken," he said.

"Who is that?"

"The Chervillian equivalent of a Saint. A fairly typical representation—note the open book in the right hand and the skull in the left. Legend tells us she was a pivotal figure in the Schism."

"Schism? From whom did they split?"

"Oh, the Church, of course. Officially, it never happened, but numerous historic sources suggest the Chervillians were once a sister organization. To this day, a similar relationship exists between the Church and the Sisters of Solace, whose habit you currently wear."

"The Sisters aren't a part of the Church?"

"Technically no. They collaborate closely with the Church, but they do not answer to the Primal."

"If you are quite done with your lecture," Brent interrupted, "I have a rough idea what these etchings are about."

"By all means, Mr. Brent."

"They outline some sort of procedure—I can make out several distinct steps, but their purpose is never explicitly stated."

Alphonse brightened. "Maybe it's telling us how to get out."

The Monsignor rubbed his chin. "I don't know. This place was likely home to quite a few procedures, most of which are probably best avoided."

"Think about it, though," Alphonse said. "The faithless get perdition and the faithful get new life. Who, other than the faithful, could even read this writing? It's got to be the way out."

The Monsignor still looked dubious. "What do the etchings instruct you to do, exactly?"

"They speak of several rods and the order in which they are to be used."

The Monsignor was nonplussed. "What do you mean by rods?"

"I'm the translator, not the author. How should I know?"

Dona pointed at the altar top. "Are they talking about those?"

The Monsignor stiffened in shock. "Those aren't rods—they're *wands.*"

Brent snorted. "Rods, wands, sticks, whatever."

"You don't understand. A wand is a uniquely Phrendonic tool. I've never heard of them being found in a Chervillian stronghold before, much less being described in Tep'Chuan inscriptions. A Chervillian-Phrendonic alliance would be a disturbing development, indeed."

"I'd see it more as the natural consequence of the Church's actions." Brent said. "After all, when haven't the persecuted sought out the enemies of their enemy and called them friends?"

"Are we following the instructions, or aren't we?" Alphonse asked.

The Monsignor took a step back. "I'd first need a far better understanding of these wands and their purpose."

"Agreed," Dona said. "How do we find that out?"

The Monsignor exhaled slowly. "I'm not sure. You can test them, of course, but that's tantamount to using them, and depending on what they do, may not be informative. Perhaps there are other writings?"

"Should we fan out and search?" Alphonse asked.

The Monsignor frowned. "I'm not sure that's such a good idea either—there may be other traps."

"Well, what then?"

Alexi hobbled over to join them. "I say we try them. What's the worst that could happen?"

The Monsignor raised an eyebrow. "I take it you aren't familiar with the Phrendonic practice of Infernal Sacrifice?"

Alexi swallowed. "Not really."

"I thought not. At the end of the Caprian Inquisition, when it was clear the Church would prevail, some heretics resolved they would sooner die than recant. They devised a way to incinerate themselves upon capture. They perished in flames of their own making, taking everyone nearby with them."

Alexi and Dona's gaze met in horrified epiphany.

The shared moment wasn't lost on the Monsignor. "Oh, so you are familiar with the practice?"

Alexi shrugged. "I guess I didn't know that's what it was called."

The Monsignor bowed his head. "It was a dangerous time to be an Inquisitor. Anyway, you asked what's the worst that could happen. Not all those who Sacrificed were capable of the heresies required to set it up. Worse still, not all the participants were willing."

Dona's jaw dropped in revulsion. "They turned people into bombs?"

"As I said, it was a dangerous time."

Alphonse's brow furrowed. "But why would the Chervillians bother writing directions for something like that? If they wanted to kill us, couldn't they have done that when we walked in?"

"I'm not saying that's what these wands actually do, I'm just saying they should not be treated lightly."

Alphonse scratched his head. "Maybe we can get a better idea of what they do from how they're used?"

Brent felt all eyes turn to him. "If my opinion matters," he said, "I think the Monsignor has a point. Ossaria are nothing to trifle with. We already have a blueprint for getting out of here, if only we can retrace our steps. At very least we should make sure that's not an option first."

"We haven't tried going back to the pit and turning off the Morgatuan," Alexi offered.

"I don't believe we have," the Monsignor said. "I guess we were all pretty tired last night. It's worth a shot."

"We should first make a plan for getting across the pit," Brent said. "What if the Morgatuan closes the entrance to the chamber but leaves the pit open?"

Alexi shifted uncomfortably. "I suppose we're going to need another light?"

Dona peered into an alcove. "Can't we just use one of these vigil lights? Here, let me get one." With both hands, she retrieved a sturdy cage—in its center floated a glowing human skull.

The Monsignor scrambled toward her. "No, don't."

"Whoa," Dona said. Regardless how she tilted the cage, the skull remained suspended in the its center. "How does it do that?"

The Monsignor mopped his brow. "In the future, I'd really appreciate more warning before you touch anything."

Her eyes narrowed. "You knew the lights were skulls all along, didn't you?"

"I saw no reason to make anyone more uncomfortable. I was concerned you might find the presence of so many human remains disturbing."

"If we are quite finished desecrating graves," Brent said, "perhaps we can get down to business?"

Dona put the cage back "Fine by me. This thing is way too clumsy to use as a light anyway. Alexi, can you make another?"

Alexi set his sword alight once more, and together they filed up the stairwell.

Alexi eyed the pit. "With a good ankle, I might have been able to jump it."

"I don't know," the Monsignor said. "The ceiling is pretty low."

Brent kicked a pebble into the abyss. "Do we have rope? Perhaps we could swing across?"

The Monsignor shook his head. "I don't think we have the materials for that. I'm fresh out of ideas."

"All right," Dona said. "Let's try turning off the Morgatuan, then. Are we agreed?"

Everyone nodded.

"Here goes," The Monsignor said. He held aloft the Morgatuan, flicked a ring out of alignment, and waited expectantly.

Nothing happened.

His face fell. "I was afraid of that."

"I guess that leaves only the wands." Alphonse said.

The group trudged back into the chamber.

"Let's hope they still work after all this time," the Monsignor said. "What must we do?"

"The procedure requires only one operator," the Bursar said. "It would be safest if the rest of you stayed well away, maybe even back up the stairs—just in case."

Alexi shivered. "If the wands don't us get out, surviving them probably does no one any favors."

"I'll do it," Alphonse said. "Tell me what I must do."

The Bursar shook his head. "I appreciate your bravery, lad, but we may only get one shot at this. I'll need to see what's happening to make sure the directions are followed precisely."

Alphonse shook his head. "But they'll need you to lead them out if this doesn't work."

"If this doesn't work, there may not be a way out. Go on, now. Up the stairs with you."

The Monsignor remained behind. "You don't have to do this."

"We both know I do. No one else can translate Tep'Chuan."

"You could write it out."

"And risk a translation error? It's not worth it. Now, get up those stairs before I lose my nerve."

With a heavy sigh, the Monsignor withdrew. At the base of the stairs, he paused. "My sincere apologies for having misjudged you, sir."

Brent nodded and faced the altar.

· · · · ·

Cartier appraised the Inquisitor from behind his makeshift desk. The man was tall, heavily muscled and, so far as Cartier could tell, humorless. "You come highly recommended."

"I have no doubt."

"As you would have discovered shortly, I have agreed to dismiss the Exidgeon Inquisition."

The Inquisitor raised an eyebrow. "How does his Ordinence feel about this development?"

"His Ordinence is not currently in charge of operations here. Is that a problem?"

"Not in the least."

"Good. Despite this small concession to the Crown, the search for heretics will be far from over."

"So, there is to be a clandestine operation?"

Cartier leaned forward. "If there were, I would need a capable person to spearhead it."

"Understood. And what would be the goal of such an operation?"

"To bring a certain suspect into Church custody."

"Sounds simple enough. What's the catch?"

"The suspect would have to be apprehended without being harmed and taken directly to the Holy City under conditions of utmost secrecy."

"Such a suspect would be politically sensitive, I take it?"

"So sensitive, in fact, that if something were to go wrong, there must be no evidence to suggest any Church involvement."

"Which means that if something were to go wrong, the Church would disclaim all knowledge."

"Precisely."

"And the rewards would be commensurate with the risks?"

Cartier leaned back and put his feet up. "Of course."

"In that case, I think I know a suitable someone. Is there any reason to believe this suspect might actually be a heretic?"

"Oh yes. That's the beauty of it."

"And, does this heretic have a name?"

"She does—she goes by Marguerite Serrola."

.  .  .  .  .

"They've agreed to what?" Reston asked. Confinement to the lavishly appointed tent was beginning to chafe, and his frustration showed.

"I have no reason to doubt the veracity of my sources," Michlos said. "The Inquisitors will be leaving, starting this afternoon."

"But that makes no sense. Why send those Inquisitors all this way only to send them right back again?"

Michlos shrugged. "Perhaps breaching the University gates made their position untenable, or maybe they didn't expect such an immediate response from the Crown."

"Or they got what they came for," Reston said. "Has there been any news of Alexi or Miss Merinne?"

"Nothing."

"You realize if they're captured, the repercussions will be unthinkable."

"I am well aware—what would you have me do?"

"Set up a checkpoint at the gates. Search everyone who leaves."

"And what would the Crown's justification be for that?"

"He's the Crown. They trespassed. Does he need a better reason?"

"If the Inquisitors haven't already discovered something, the longer they stay, the greater their chances. I'm afraid the Crown will hesitate to jeopardize this concession without very good reason."

"The University is in disarray. You could always spin it as looter deterrence."

"Publicly accusing the Church of looting would not be viewed as a viable option."

"What I meant was, you'd use it to discourage looting. You wouldn't have to actually accuse anyone."

"And if we find Alexi or Miss Merinne is in their custody? What then? Technically, they do have the right to arrest suspected heretics."

"Then, you let me deal with that." Reston said.

"Just to be clear, you would not have the backing of the Crown."

Jonas took a heavy drag on his pipe. "I'd help."

"I would too," Tilly said.

Jonas turned to Amberton. "What about you, stick man?"

Amberton's glare could have peeled paint. "Well, I can't imagine why you'd need me, but of course I'd do what I could."

"Splendid," Michlos said. "I'll see what I can arrange."

. . . . .

Brent took a deep breath and stepped onto the coffin lid. For a second time, he read through the instructions emblazoned across the altar, correlating the text with the implements. Next, he turned his attention to two of the altar's three containers. One was quite large, the second comparatively tiny, and the third, broad and flat. All three had hinged lids. First, he opened the small one, which appeared to be a jewelry box. Inside, nestled in black velvet, was a striking gold ring set with a large crimson stone. He put the small box aside. Next, he flipped back the lid of the larger box. From its depths, a gentle glow lit his face. Reaching inside, he reverently lifted out a cage, complete with a glowing, floating skull, and set it on the altar. He glanced over his shoulder—he was still alone.

After several minutes of fussing, he discovered the trick of the cage. He tugged the lynchpin rod, and the cage flew apart. Component rods clattered in all directions. The skull dropped to the altar.

The Monsignor's voice echoed down the stairwell. "Are you all right down there?"

"Fine," Brent called back. "I'm just a little clumsy is all."

"Should we come down?"

"No—I'm not done yet."

Brent next arranged the wands on the altar in a specific order. Bracing himself, he picked up the first wand and applied the tip to the skull. When nothing happened, he breathed a sigh of relief. He then took up the second wand and touched that to the skull. The skull shuddered and flattened, taking on a metallic sheen. Brent compared the result to the golden skull mask embedded in the altar—it had become an exact match, though, unlike the altar's skull mask, the new mask still glowed. All was proceeding as expected.

Again, the Monsignor interrupted. "Are you sure you're all right down there?"

"I've begun the procedure, but there are several steps to go. When I'm done, I'll let you know."

Setting the new mask aside, Brent removed the ring from its velvet repository and laid it on the altar. When its position satisfied him, he took up the third wand and applied its tip to the ring. A brisk whirlwind swirled his hair and stirred the dust blanketing the room. On the altar, a man now rested, his chest rising and falling rhythmically. The ring was the only thing he wore.

This time, the Monsignor's voice brimmed with concern. "What was that?"

"I'm fine," Brent yelled. "Almost done."

Brent grabbed the fourth wand and touched it to the body, without apparent effect.

The Monsignor's concern became alarm. "I'm coming down there."

"Not just yet. Only one more to go."

Brent set the wand aside and snatched up the mask. Gently he laid it over the face of the man on the altar. Just as the Monsignor appeared in the doorway, he touched the final wand to the masked man.

The Monsignor roared in horror. "*Brent, NO!*"

The glow from the mask seeped into the man's body, filling it with light. He reached up, lifted the mask from his face and set it aside. As he withdrew his hand, the mask's light winked out.

Brent was exultant. "True," he cried. "The scriptures, Chervil's Promise, all true. My sacrifice was not in vain."

Behind the Monsignor, the others crowded into the chamber.

"Get back," the Monsignor cried.

The man on the altar sat up and faced the Monsignor. "You have something that belongs to me." Although his accent was strange, his words were clearly understandable. He lowered himself onto the dais.

Brent opened the third box and retrieved a black cloak, which he threw over the man's shoulders.

"What do you think of your specious little faith now, Monsignor?" Brent sneered.

The Monsignor didn't take his eyes from the cloaked figure. "I don't know what you think you've accomplished here, Brent, but your complicity in creating this demon is unlikely to shake my faith."

The daemon took a step toward the Monsignor. "The Morgatuan. It is mine."

Brent bowed obsequiously. "He doesn't understand, Vismort."

The daemon turned on Brent. "What is there to understand? He holds my property in my domain."

The Monsignor paled. "You demonized a Vismort?"

"Yes," Brent hissed. "As we agreed. He's our only hope of getting out. Now, give him the bloody scepter."

The Monsignor backed against the wall as the daemon approached him, but Brent's logic proved inescapable. Reluctantly, he placed the Morgatuan into the outstretched palm of its rightful owner.

Next the daemon turned to Dona, who was watching wide-eyed from the doorway. "Mistress, I would have words with you in private. The rest of you, begone."

"Regarding that," Brent interjected. "The hallway pit is open and blocks our exit."

The Vismort shrugged. "A small matter." With a swirl of his cloak, he strode past the Monsignor and the others into the stairwell and up the steps, followed closely by the Bursar. The others waited nervously for the Monsignor's guidance. He hesitated only a moment, and then, with Alphonse's assistance, he hobbled after Brent.

When they reached the top of the stairs, the daemon turned again to Dona, who was assisting Alexi. "Mistress, if you would be so kind as to await me in the chamber, I shall meet you there presently."

Dona froze.

The Monsignor attempted a diversion. "Perhaps the Mistress would prefer to witness first-hand the wonders of this installation's defenses."

The daemon rounded on the Monsignor. "I expect the Mistress is well enough familiar with the defenses she designed and implemented."

"My apologies, Vismort. Still, it can be quite satisfying for a skilled craftsperson to witness her handiwork in action."

The daemon's eyes flashed. He shouted something incomprehensible—the Bursar cringed at the sound of it. The Monsignor's features tinged blue, and he sank to the floor, twitching violently.

"My apologies, Mistress," the daemon said. "Please, wait below. I shall not be long."

Terrified, Dona retreated down the stairway.

Once she was out of sight, the daemon reached above the keystone over the stairway entrance. Again, the gritty blast of air assailed them, and when it died down, the pit and the stairway were gone—the corridor appeared exactly as it had before they had activated the Morgatuan.

The Monsignor continued to convulse but instead of rushing to help, Alexi stood immobile, his glare fixed on the Vismort, his jaw working silently.

The daemon waved dismissively. "See to it this one troubles me no more."

Alphonse dropped to his knees at the Monsignor's side. "I think he's dying."

Brent feebly attempted to drag the Monsignor by his shirt. "Don't just sit there, help me."

"We can't move him like this. Please Vismort, sir, can't you help him?"

The daemon sighed. "Oh, very well. Anything to expedite his miserable departure."

He barked something in his strange tongue, and the Monsignor's torments ceased.

At that instant, the daemon wavered, his jaw slackened, and he collapsed.

Alexi beamed in triumph. "Take that, you monster. You're not the only one with the wherewithal to work a spell."

# CHAPTER 12

## VISITATIONS

Thurman sat bolt upright on his pallet as the door to the one-room cottage burst open. His initial terror gave way to recognition as a lone figure entered and latched the door.

"Where have you been?" Thurman said. "I've been waiting here for hours, and what I have to say can't wait."

The figure threw back an oversized hood revealing an ancient face and close-cropped white hair. Thurman's hackles rose as the figure ignored him to peer out through each of the shutters, careful not to be visible to anyone who might be outside.

"What are you doing?"

"Making sure I wasn't followed."

"Who would follow you?" Fixed by a look that combined condescension, pity, and indignation in equal measure, Thurman felt color creep into his cheeks. "That didn't come out right."

"Clearly."

"I'm sorry."

The old priest threw off the cloak, revealing the Ordinal vestments beneath.

Thurman's eyes nearly popped out of his head. "Promotion?" His voice held a note of sarcasm.

"Long story. Now, tell me, what are you doing here? Where is your father?"

"He's still in Trifienne. Isrulian accused him of heresy and took him into custody. I came as soon as I could."

"Isrulian? Are you sure?"

"I was there. We have to tell Darron right away."

"That may be difficult under the circumstances."

"You don't mean…"

"No, he still lives, but only barely. Laitrech has taken over in all but name."

Thurman shuddered. "If it's gotten this serious, can you convince Laitrech to give you access in advance of payment?"

"Is there some reason we can't pay him now?"

Thurman colored again. "I was in the middle of completing the deal when we were interrupted by heretics, or I would have it by now, I swear."

"Heretics? What nonsense is this?"

"Powerful. One of them killed five men with a wave of his hand. Another set the whole building ablaze with her locket and blinded everyone with darkness. I barely escaped."

"*Phrendonic* Heretics? Is that what you mean? Be clear."

Thurman nodded.

"Hmmm. It would appear our friendly neighborhood spirits merchant is not the innocent nouncer he pretends to be. Isrulian doesn't know, does he?"

"Not about the heretics at the restaurant, or at least I don't think he does. Of course, he does know we were investigating allegations of Phrendonic Heresy at the University. There was no concealing that."

"What was Isrulian doing there in the first place?"

"I presume Laitrech sent him. I had written that I would be closing the deal shortly, and all of a sudden Isrulian arrived, wanting to confirm the goods, which, of course, I still didn't have."

"So, you showed him a fake?"

Thurman gulped. "I had to. I couldn't very well tell him the deal had been interrupted by the merchant's heretic friends. I even tried to track down the merchant. We had him cornered at a brothel, but when our men went in to apprehend him, there was another fire. Several Inquisitors were killed."

"A Sacrificer?"

Thurman shook his head. "I wasn't there, I can't say for sure. Say, shouldn't we be coming up with a way to get you access to the rectory before it's too late?"

"Things have changed—I no longer need access to the rectory. Your Uncle isn't sick."

"I thought you said he was barely alive?"

"Poison will do that to a person."

"Poison? I knew it. Was it Laitrech?"

"You have a better candidate?"

"But can you be sure?"

The old priest patted Laitrech's Relic. "Let's just say I had to resort to extreme measures, but yes, I'm sure."

"Does Darron know?"

"He was warned, but given Laitrech's hold on him, I doubt he'll believe it."

"Where is Laitrech now?"

"When I last saw him, he was napping in the Chapel."

"You took his clothes and just left him there?"

"I didn't know about the poison at that point."

"So, when he wakes up and finds out someone is on to him, what's to stop him from finishing the job?"

"The Bastion of Bethany, for one. He needs his Relic to get out, but that still may not give us much time. When Laitrech is missed, you can bet someone will look there. Once that happens, I doubt your uncle is long for this world."

"Couldn't you just go to him and warn him?"

"Given our history?"

"I could go."

"And tell him what? That Laitrech is poisoning him? And when he asks how you know, what will you tell him?"

"The truth," Thurman said.

"No offense, but Laitrech would almost certainly be able to convince him that you had simply been duped. It's not so much a matter of truth—the problem is Laitrech's considerable influence. In retrospect. he's done a marvelous job both of isolating your uncle and making himself indispensable. I can't believe I didn't see this coming."

"We can't just stand by and let this happen."

"No, we can't. But the only person I can think of with sufficient sway to counter Laitrech's influence is your father."

Thurman gasped as the rationale for Isrulian's bizarre behavior in Trifienne finally sank in. Isrulian was in on Laitrech's plot, which meant he would try to keep Armand and Darron separated at all costs—at least until the poison did its work. "What do we do, then?"

The priest collapsed wearily into a nearby chair. "That's a very good question."

· · · · ·

The thunderheads began building early in the morning, and it didn't take a seer to predict there would be weather. In the face of nature's gathering wrath, Princess Celeste's subjects were scrambling to put the scant remaining moments of sunshine to good use. They scuttled about, securing ships, shuttering shops, and bustling to shelter that which could not survive wind or water. Not one to miss an opportunity, the Princess secured an easel to the parapet atop the north tower and, with energetic strokes, was committing it all to canvas. From her vantage, she couldn't miss the lone horsewoman winding her way up the long road to Ranselard Keep. An almost-imperceptible lifting of an eyebrow accompanied recognition of the incipient visitor. She made no move to set aside her brush.

When at last the plumes of Newcomb's hat made an appearance at the trapdoor, she surveyed her artistic progress and sighed in resignation. "Such a pity—it might have been magnificent."

"Yes, Highness," Newcomb said dutifully.

"Please, show Miss Nevinander in—" Then her eyes glinted mischief. "Or rather, up."

"You mean…up to the battlement?"

"If you would, please."

"As your Highness wishes."

The Princess resumed her art with a vengeance. Although she did her best to put the additional time to good use, it was clear it would not be enough. Indeed, only minutes passed before she heard footsteps in the chamber below.

"I don't understand," Verone said. "Is this some sort of joke? Where is the Princess?"

"The Princess has requested that you join her on the battlements," Newcomb replied.

Verone's voice rose nearly an octave. "Where?"

"I'm up here," the Princess said.

"You mean, up this ladder?"

"You won't regret it—the view is amazing."

After a momentary pause, Verone started up the ladder. Almost immediately, her dress boot slid forward until the rung caught her heel. She would have fallen had Newcomb not steadied her. She set her jaw and continued without further mishap until her head popped through the opening. After several moments' consideration, she placed her leather case to one side and twisted sideways to seat herself on the roof. She then rolled away from the hole and struggled to her feet with as much remaining dignity as she could muster.

The Princess permitted herself a secret guilty smile. Only once Verone had made it fully to her feet did she pull herself away from the canvas. "Verone, how delightful of you to visit."

Verone curtseyed. "Thank you for agreeing to see me, Your Highness."

The Princess turned back to her canvas. "Don't be silly. You're always welcome here. I trust your parents are well?"

"Both fine. They were a little disappointed you didn't make it to the party, though."

"I would have loved to come, but there were two parties that day, and as you know, I refuse to play favorites."

"Pity. Mum outdid herself." Verone stepped forward and peered over the Princess's shoulder. "Interesting subject matter. Political allegory, per chance?"

The Princess furiously dashed on brushstrokes as the approaching clouds threatened the last vestiges of sunshine. "How do you mean?"

"Clearly, the escalating tensions between Church and Crown have not escaped your notice."

"Oh, I see. You think perhaps this represents the gathering storm?"

"It certainly is suggestive, under the circumstances."

"I was under the impression those tensions were little more than a misunderstanding well on its way to being resolved. Is there something I don't know?"

"Do you by any chance remember Father Cartier?"

The Princess shook her head. "Should I?"

"Well, for several years, now, he's run my mother's Church. During that time, I've gotten to know him fairly well."

"Oh, wasn't he the celebrant at Reginald's wedding?"

"Indeed, he was. I mention him because he's been tapped to run the Inquisition up at Exidgeon. Last I spoke with him, he seemed pretty concerned about Trifienne's Church-Crown relations. He couldn't give me any details, but his expression spoke volumes. I got the distinct impression he thinks this situation could get pretty bad."

The Princess's brush came to an abrupt halt. "You don't think they know, do you?"

Verone shrugged. "Maybe it's nothing. All I can say is that Father Cartier sure seemed worried."

A low rumble rolled in, accompanied by a chill breeze off the river.

The Princess dropped her brush in a waiting crock. "Is the Crown aware?"

"I'm not sure. We aren't exactly on speaking terms. And even if we were, it's not like I could just go warn him about my inferences from Father Cartier's grim expression."

"But you think perhaps I could?"

"Oh, no, of course not—at least, not until there is something more definite."

"Then why tell me?"

"I thought perhaps I could offer my assistance. I got to thinking about how you've been embroiled in this petty little feud with the Church for some time. It struck me that now might be a good time to repair it. That way, if it turns out they need someone to mediate this dispute, you'd be an obvious choice."

"Me? Why on earth would they would they come to me?"

For one thing, you're royalty. That counts as credentials with anyone. For another, the Crown respects you, and everybody knows it. Not only that, but you aren't particularly threatening to either side, and you have a vested interest in seeing both sides get along."

"Don't be ridiculous. The Church would never go for that."

"Well, not as things currently stand, but suppose you and the Church had just gone through a very public reconciliation?"

"They would have to agree to some very stringent conditions for that to have any chance of happening. I won't sacrifice the Island's artistic freedoms, and neither will I cede one iota of my sovereignty."

Verone patted her arm. "That's precisely where I can help. If there really are serious problems between the Church and the Crown, I'm sure the Church would love to make a big show of reconciling with you. In fact, you'll probably never get a better chance to name your terms. I can use my influence with Father Cartier to help shape the Church response. He's not particularly dogmatic, and he was born and raised here in town—he understands how important the Artists' Colony is to Trifienne."

"And if the problems turn out to be…irreconcilable?"

"Let me put it this way. If by some horrible twist of fate, the Church has discovered the Crown's dirty little Phrendonic secret, would you really want to be both this close to the Crown and on the wrong side of the Church?"

The Princess blanched. "I see your point."

"So, I take it I can tell Father Cartier you'll meet with him?" Despite the careful phrasing, she clearly intended those words as a statement rather than a question. It was Verone's turn to sport a secret smile—negotiating this reconciliation would provide Cartier ample gravitas to maintain his new position in the face of all but the most formidable of challenges. And, although the crack the reconciliation would create in the Crown-Island alliance was tiny, it was only the beginning.

Forked lightning flashed amid the bruise-colored clouds that loomed over Ranselard Keep—and the thunder it unleashed followed immediately. The storm was nearly upon them.

. . . . .

After what she'd seen that thing upstairs do to the Monsignor, Dona was less inclined than ever to meet with it—particularly not alone. Feeling helpless and exposed, she cast about for something with which to defend herself. Her eyes fell on the altar. Without regard for any traps that might be lurking on the dais, she rushed over and grabbed the prybar, but it proved to be too unwieldy to be an effective weapon. She dropped it in the open coffin and returned to the altar to scoop the neatly ordered wands into her habit's ample apron pocket. Maybe she could somehow use them to undo what they had done.

She took several deep breaths, but before she could come up with a plausible plan, the stone blocking the stairwell vaporized once more.

Weapon drawn, Alphonse took the stairs in a single bound.

Alexi's voice echoed after him. "Dona? Are you all right?"

"I'm fine. Where's the Vismort?"

Alexi finally appeared, leaning on the Morgatuan. "He's having a little nap."

"You mean—that actually worked on him?"

"So far."

Dona rushed into his arms. "Oh, well done! And the Monsignor?"

"He's still a little pale, but I think he'll be all right."

"And the pit?"

"We know its secret now, but we all need to be upstairs to try it."

"What are we waiting for? We'll want to be as far away as possible when Mr. Congeniality wakes up."

"I think the Monsignor needs a few minutes."

The Monsignor sat propped against the wall looking pale and uncomfortable and holding his shoulder—it had borne the brunt of his weight in his fall.

Dona knelt beside him and touched his arm. "Is it broken?"

The Monsignor grimaced. "I don't think so."

Alexi rounded on the Bursar. "You have some explaining to do."

Brent sniffed. "I don't know what you're talking about. I did exactly as we all agreed."

"You deliberately withheld information."

"You didn't ask. And, in case you haven't noticed, the plan worked. If it weren't for me, we'd all still be trapped in that chamber waiting to add our corpses to the collection. Do you really think you'd be better off if I'd told you more?"

Alexi huffed. "Alphonse, keep a close eye on him."

The mood was tense, but there was little else to do but wait for the Monsignor's status to improve. Fortunately, by the time the blade's light failed, he'd fallen asleep and his color had returned. Alexi muttered, and the blade resumed its glow.

When the Monsignor awakened, Dona was the first to notice. "How are you feeling?"

He sat up, still favoring his shoulder. "Better."

"We should move on, then. We need water, and I'm getting pretty hungry, too."

"I have supplies upstairs," Brent said. "We can stop there first."

The Monsignor shook his head. "Not yet—we need to destroy that chamber first."

Brent's mouth fell open. "What are you talking about?"

"We can't let this abomination stand."

Brent crossed his arms. "I won't permit it."

"You saw what that demon was capable of. It would be irresponsible to allow something like that to get free."

Brent didn't budge. "I also saw what young master Reysa is capable of. Does the same argument apply?"

"Alexi is compelled to do what he does to keep us alive. Are you suggesting he shouldn't defend us?"

"From what I saw, Alexi did what he did the instant the Vismort reversed what he'd done. And, I might add, the Vismort was engaged in saving our lives at the time. That doesn't sound like defense to me."

"Miss Merinne was trapped."

"On the contrary, he asked her politely to remain behind, and she consented."

"Yes, but only after the demon demonstrated what it does to those who displease it. Could she really have refused its request?"

"Enough already," Dona cried.

At that instant, there was another blast of air and grit. When they opened their eyes, the daemon had vanished.

"How did you do that?" Alphonse asked.

"It wasn't me."

"Can it come back?"

"The Monsignor shuddered. "I'm not sure."

Alexi handed Monsignor the Morgatuan. "With all due respect, sir, I don't think we should wait to find out."

The Monsignor rotated one of the rings. "Perhaps you're right. Let's find that mechanism."

"While Alexi held the blade aloft, the Monsignor and Alphonse searched for the concealed switch. As Dona gathered up the daemon's cloak, she felt a hard lump in the fabric. Suddenly aware that she had become the subject of the Bursar's scrutiny, she nonchalantly maneuvered the lump into her apron pocket and donned the cloak.

"So, I was right about you after all," Brent whispered.

"I don't know what you're talking about."

"Don't worry, your secret is safe with me—Mistress."

"Got it," Alphonse called out.

Once again, they were engulfed in a whirlwind of dust and grit.

. . . . .

Marguerite almost never had time for needlepoint anymore, but the storm's incessant howling had been so distracting she'd finally been forced to give up work on her more demanding projects. Needle and sampler in hand, she settled into her favorite chair beside the great hall's roaring fireplace. There, she stitched and watched through tall leaded windows as the tempest's incandescent fury lashed the heavens. The simple sampler afforded a rare opportunity to let her mind wander. She smiled, recalling the wonder that fierce storms had always evoked in Spiros when they were young, and how cross she would get when he pulled her away from her work to watch. If only she'd known how little time they would have.

A pealing bell jolted her back to the present. Even over the moaning of the wind, she recognized the doleful clang of St. Sophia's pride and joy.

*What disaster does it portend this time? Has the lightning touched off another fire?*

She was tempted to climb the stairs and look for smoke, but even if there were a fire, by the time she got there it would either already be out, or well beyond her ability to extinguish.

Instead, she let herself fall into the rhythm of the stitching, giving herself over to the delicious freedom of not having to think.

Arerio startled her—his silhouette only erratically realized by the relentless flickering of the storm.

"You have a visitor, Mistress."

"A visitor? In this weather?"

"A young militiaman by appearance. I showed him in to the parlor. He seems a bit…distraught."

Marguerite's heart skipped a beat—in the distance the bell still rang.

"Did he say what he wanted?"

"Only that his message was urgent."

"See that he's comfortable. I'll be out presently."

"Very good, Mistress."

Marguerite retreated briefly to her chambers to freshen up, trying not to contemplate what dire message might await her. Casting a critical eye over the woman she faced in the mirror, she nodded, drew herself up to her full height, and strode downstairs to face her fears.

She found the young man warming himself before the fireplace. His ill-fitting uniform had created a pool on the hearth that threatened an heirloom rug.

"My apologies," she said. "Didn't Arerio offer you dry clothing?"

The young man turned. "He did, ma'am, but I'm on duty. Are you Marguerite Serrola?"

"I am. How can I help you?"

The young man fidgeted with a button on his coat. "I don't know how to say this in a good way, but the Crown Prince, well—it ain't good. The Crown Princess wants you to come right away."

Marguerite struggled to keep her composure. "Can you tell me what has happened?"

"Assassin's bolt, or so folks are saying. I didn't see it myself or anything."

She clutched her mouth in shock. "Nathan? Is he…?"

"I'm sorry, ma'am."

Marguerite did not reply.

"I gotta go, ma'am. I'm still on duty. I'm real sorry."

He made for the door, his every step wringing a puddle from his sodden boots.

Marguerite stared blankly after him.

And then, shock gave way to rage.

"Arerio."

The manservant stepped from the shadows. "Yes, Mistress?"

"Have the driver prepare the carriage. Someone is going to pay."

# CHAPTER 13

## REVERSALS

**B**rent cupped his hands around his mouth and shouted upward. "Just bring a few bottles—it doesn't matter which."

Once they had made it back to the stairway beneath the vault, Brent reminded them again of his store of supplies. The problem was that neither Alexi nor the Monsignor was eager to limp all the way back up, and no one was comfortable sending Brent alone. Finally, they decided Dona should go. Alexi relit her locket to light her way. Rummaging with the aid of the Bursar's shouted directions, she'd located his stash of wine and a few wheels of cheese, which she dutifully lugged back to her grateful companions.

"Well, here we are," Alexi said between mouthfuls. "Right back where we started."

"Only now we no longer have a journal to rely on," Alphonse said.

Brent scratched his head. "I don't understand—I followed the instructions precisely."

Dona handed him a bottle. "That only helps if they were written with the same precision. Perhaps the account was reconstructed after the events?"

"Then why give all the detail? If you were simply conveying the basic story, wouldn't you just say 'we took a passage,' instead of 'we took the second passage from the bottom?'"

"Are you sure you read it correctly?" Alexi asked.

Brent fixed him with a withering glare.

The Monsignor cocked his head. "Did you say the second passage from the bottom?"

Brent held out the journal. "That's what it looks like to me, but if you can read it better, be my guest."

The Monsignor held up his hand. "Relax, Mr. Brent—I'm not impugning your literacy. Miss Merinne, how deep would you estimate the layer of straw at the bottom of the stairwell to be?"

"Pretty deep. I fell a long way."

Brent peered over the landing's edge. "Are you suggesting the straw conceals another passage?"

Alphonse drew his blade. "Well what are we waiting for?"

Dona's brow furrowed. "Hold on, if there's one, couldn't there also be two passages under the straw?"

Alphonse considered that. "Yes, but the right one will have an archway with the proper inscription."

"Unless there's more than one with the same inscription," Alexi said.

Alphonse scowled. "Is there anything you can't overthink? Let's just go look."

Brent stood. "I'm game."

The Monsignor still moved slowly, even with the Morgatuan to lean on. Before they made it to the straw-level passage, Alexi had to renew the light again—from his expression, his efforts were taking a toll.

When the sword's glow revealed an archway, the Bursar rushed forward, leaving the others to catch up as best they could. "The inscription matches—this must be it. Hand me the Morgatuan."

They passed it forward. Brent checked it briefly and began counting paces.

"Stand here," he said, waiting until everyone had gathered around his mark.

Finally satisfied, he clicked the scepter's bottom ring.

As the swirling dust settled, they saw that once again a deep pit had opened behind them and the wall ahead had disappeared. Beyond, instead of a lighted chamber, they beheld a narrow passage leading into darkness.

The Bursar nodded. "That's more like it."

Floor-to-ceiling alcoves lined the musty passage, although these were unlit. The passage intersected several others, but Brent chose their route with confidence. In one spot, he had everyone step over a loose stone. In another, he bid them squeeze one at a time into an alcove that concealed a tight passage near the floor. It was easy to spot, since it billowed dust and grit as they approached. Still, Brent meticulously counted the alcoves from the last fork to confirm. Alexi didn't know which was worse—the thought of what else might occupy the alcove, or the thought of squirming through the narrow cleft beyond. It took several deep breaths before he calmed enough to make the attempt, but he made it through without difficulty. The Monsignor was not so lucky—for a few heart-stopping moments he got wedged, but with concerted tugging, Alphonse pulled him free.

Past the alcove, the passages lost their rough-hewn character and became more cave-like. In places, Alexi caught the distant echo of rushing water, and occasional unwelcome droplets smote him from above. Soon, the passage gave way to an expansive cavern. Dona drew her confiscated cloak tight against the deepening chill. As they picked their way downward, the musty smell gave way to one far more cloying and intense. A high-pitched chittering erupted overhead, and when Alexi held his sword aloft, the cavern's roof twinkled like the sky on a moonless night.

He strained his arm for a better look. Lost in the distraction of the roof, he failed to notice the steeply sloped floor had become slick. Despite Dona's support, he slipped. Dona screeched as he dragged her down with him. Together, they slid past Alphonse, who leapt out of their way, and into Brent. The air about their heads churned—the chittering became deafening.

The Monsignor shielded his eyes with the crook of his arm. "Bats."

Alexi, Dona, and Brent's willy-nilly slide ended as they plowed into a pungent mass the consistency of curdled milk.

"Ugh, guano." Alexi said. "I think we've found the source of the smell. Is everyone all right?"

Brent clambered to his feet "No, you oaf, everyone is not all right. Look what you've done." He held out his muck-slathered journal. "How do you expect me to read this?"

"It's not like I did it on purpose. And you could have warned us that the floor was getting slippery."

Brent sputtered "Oh, so now it's my fault?"

"I didn't say that."

The Monsignor intervened. "Done is done, gentlemen. Let's see if we can clean it up."

Brent grudgingly relinquished the soiled journal.

The Monsignor produced a strip of white fabric.

Dona recognized it immediately. "Oh, Monsignor, not your stole."

"There are more where this came from." He dabbed away the worst of the malodorous grime and wrapped the journal in the cloth. "I'll need to wet it for the rest. For that matter, the three of you could also stand a good rinse. From the sound of it, water can't be far off. Shall we make for it?"

Brent gaped at him. "Are you mad? We dare not deviate from the path."

"Without the journal, do we even know where that is?"

"Don't say I didn't warn you."

"So noted, Mr. Brent."

They picked their way carefully around the edge of the cavern until they came to a narrow side-passage. The sound of rushing water was louder here, and the air from the passage comparatively fresh. It took very little encouragement for even the sullen Bursar to nod his assent.

"But I'm not going first," he said. "Not without the journal."

Alphonse stepped forward. "I'll go first."

Since it took a bit of climbing, the side passage proved difficult for Alexi and the Monsignor, but with grim determination and a few bumps and bruises, they made slow progress. Alexi had to renew the light several times, but eventually the difficult stretch was crossed by a trickle of fresh water. It emerged from a broad cleft and disappeared into another in the passage's opposite wall. They followed the trickle's channel down a shallow slope, hoping to discover a pool large enough to meet their needs. The omnipresent rumble of rushing water told them it couldn't be far, but the sound proved deceptive. After a short stretch, the trickle disappeared down a hole they couldn't follow. They were forced to retrace their steps.

"I told you so," Brent said. "You can't expect to navigate this maze without a guide."

The Monsignor paused. "Using the journal while soiled might end up obscuring more information. Are you suggesting we try?"

"Can't we just find some water first?" Dona asked. "There must be some nearby. I'm not sure how much longer I can take this stench."

Alexi peered into the opposite cleft. "Maybe there's a pool upstream? The water must be coming from somewhere."

The Monsignor eyed the slope dubiously. "All right, then. Upward it is."

Brent shook his head, but followed.

After a short climb, the passage widened. The farther they went, the more the ceiling dripped. Subtle colors played across the occasional gleaming stalactite. The passage was anything but even, and the path was made more treacherous by odd shadows and reflections. They slowed to a crawl. Eventually, the walls of the passage fell away, revealing an immense cavern. The ceiling, now far above, dripped stalactites to either side like the ribs of some great sea creature. A multitude of pools lay before them, stretching beyond the power of Alexi's blade to illuminate.

"Finally," Dona said. "Alexi, can you make me a new light?"

Alexi sighed wearily. "Do we really need another?"

She patted his cheek. "Even though I love you all, a bath is not something I'm willing to share."

He was too tired to fight. In short order, the glow from her locket added to that of the blade.

Dona strode off among the pools. "I'll be back in a bit."

Alphonse crossed his arms. "Do you really think it's safe for her to go alone like that?"

The Monsignor shrugged. "There's been no sign of Chervillian construction for some time. We're likely beyond the range of any deliberate traps. If she watches her step, she should be all right. Why don't you gentlemen clean up, and I'll see what I can do about restoring this journal."

. . . . .

Dona looked forward to getting clean again, even if it meant a quick dip in a bitterly cold cavern pool. After only a few minutes, she found one appropriately out of sight. The sound of rushing water thundered through a broad fissure on the pool's opposite side.

After a glance over her shoulder, she reached into her habit pocket for her collection of odds and ends. Despite her collision with Alexi and the Bursar, the wands from the altar were unscathed. Setting them aside, she examined the Vismort's ring—and nearly dropped it—the resemblance to the jewelry in her hope chest was uncanny. It could almost have been a matching piece. There was something odd about it. She turned it back and forth—and then she had it. She tucked her locket into her habit, dousing the light. Despite the sudden darkness, she could still see the ring plainly. It had a faint glow—much fainter than her locket—but unmistakable.

*That's odd.*

The allure of getting clean was too strong for her to dwell on the ring. She stripped off her soiled clothes and rinsed the habit in the pool repeatedly. Satisfied the fabric was as clean as she could get it, she stepped into the pool. She could only tolerate the frigid water for a minute or so, but despite the bone-chilling cold, she felt much better for it. She slipped into her clothes again, but since they were still wet, they offered precious little warmth—she would need to stay active. She vigorously swished the cloak, which had been far more thoroughly soiled than the habit, but the water numbed her hands. When the cloak snagged a branch, she snatched it up and swirled with that instead.

Idly, she wondered what kind of tree it could have come from. With sudden realization, she drew back the branch for a closer look—it wasn't so much a branch as a bone, and she had a sickening feeling it was probably human. Tossing it aside, she held the locket over the pool. Its bottom was littered with bones. Wide-eyed, she backed away.

"Alexi." Her voice echoed across the chamber.

"Are you done?" he asked.

"Oh, I'm done, all right. Could you come over here? And bring Alphonse with you. I'm not sure we're alone in here."

"What do you mean?"

Alphonse's blade sang free of its scabbard. "Are you all right?"

"I think so." Keeping a close eye on her surroundings, she snatched up her collection and stuffed it in her pocket.

"Are you coming?" Her voice held an uncharacteristic tremor.

When Alphonse finally appeared, he carried Alexi's lighted sword. Dona was still peering about with the locket held high.

"Are you looking for something?" he asked

"I'm not sure. Take a look in that pool, and you tell me."

Alphonse approached the water.

Dona shivered. "Don't get too close."

He held out the sword. "Are those bones?"

"They sure look like it to me."

Brent arrived next. "Bones?"

A plume of water shot out from a fissure across the pool. Alphonse leapt back, but too late to avoid a soaking. The passage gurgled, spilling into the pool several more times before settling down to its customary roar.

"In the pool," Dona said. "At the bottom."

Brent approached the water. "The light, if you please."

The fissure sputtered again, and more water spilled out. Alphonse edged forward to light the Bursar's view.

"They're human," Brent said.

Dona nodded. "I thought so too."

Alexi limped closer for a look, while the Monsignor sidled toward the fissure to see what lay beyond. He stepped back just in time as more water gushed into the cavern.

"Why does it keep doing that?" Dona asked.

"You mean the water?" Alexi said. "It probably always does that."

"It didn't do that the entire time I was bathing."

The fissure surged again. The pool was noticeably deeper than it had been.

"We must be very close," the Bursar said.

"Close to what?" Alexi asked.

"The funerarium—where the souls of the dead are prepared. We might be able to find our way from there, assuming the journal is readable again."

A rushing torrent interrupted Alexi's next question—the fissure's flow was now constant and increasing.

The Monsignor had to shout. "We'd better find it soon—or be ready to swim."

Dona's shoes were already partially submerged. "We won't last long in water this cold. Let's get out of here."

"We can't," the Monsignor said. "Once this water hits the sloped passage, it could fill completely. Even if we didn't drown, we'd be dashed to death."

"There," Brent cried, pointing upward.

Alphonse held up the sword. Far above, where wall met ceiling, they spied another opening, partially blocked by a railing.

"The funerarium," Brent said. "It has to be."

Dona's heart sank. The frigid water was already lapping at her ankles, and the railing was 30 feet up. With two of them unable to climb, it might as well have been a mile.

Alphonse switched swords with Alexi again. He then turned to Dona. "May I?"

She passed him the locket.

"I'm going to see if there's something up there that can help us."

The climb's first few feet were easy, but as he got higher up, the cave wall curved outward over the cavern floor. He got stuck once, and at another point he nearly lost his grip, but by the time the water reached Dona's calf, he was waving at them from the railing.

"I'll be back," he said. And then he was gone.

Dona approached the wall. "Bring the sword over here."

Alexi eyed her quizzically as he approached.

"Perfect," she said. She began to climb.

"What are you doing?" Alexi asked.

"I'm going to see if he needs help."

"You'll never make it. You'll break your neck."

She inspected the wall intently for fingerholds. "Alphonse didn't."

"Alphonse is—"

"A man?" Dona asked.

"—an athlete."

"I guess we'll see if that makes a difference, then. Move the light."

Grudgingly, Alexi shifted the sword. "This is crazy."

"So is standing around waiting to drown. I'd rather die trying."

The Monsignor cleared his throat. "Alphonse may find something to help. Shouldn't you give him a chance?"

"If he does, I'll be one fewer person to pull up. Light, please."

Alexi adjusted his position.

The Monsignor tried again. "But if you're injured, you may not be able to help."

Dona didn't reply. She had reached the difficult stretch and was discovering that Alphonse had made the climb appear much easier than it was. Her fingers had gone numb—she had lost any sense of precision.

She pushed forward on determination alone, struggling to follow Alphonse's trail. Inch by painful inch, she dragged herself upward. She looked down only once and was horrified by the drop. But the sight of Alexi standing in frigid water above his knees steeled her resolve. Stretched to her absolute limit, she grabbed the railing.

Applause and a collective sigh of relief rose up from below. Then she lost her grip. With a shriek, she fell away from the wall and dangled by one hand from the railing. Her fingers dug into rusty, flaking metal. She tightened her handhold. Forcing herself to focus, she stretched her free hand toward the railing, but no longer had the strength to reach that far. The wall was also out of reach. With nowhere left to turn, she looked down. She was out of options.

"I'll catch you," Alexi cried.

"Alexi," the Monsignor said, "back away. If she hits you, you could both die. Let her try to hit the water."

"It's not deep enough."

"It's her only chance."

Alexi hesitated.

The Monsignor spoke with quiet intensity. "Alexi, you must give her space."

His eyes fixed on Dona, Alexi swallowed hard and took several steps back.

The Monsignor called out. "Fall backward, but don't overdo. If you hit flat, the water may break your fall."

Dona stared at the water and whimpered. With what little feeling remained in her fingers, she sensed the railing slipping away.

Viselike fingers encircled her wrist. "Give me your other hand," Alphonse ordered. Within moments, he lifted her to safety.

Alexi whooped with joy. Even Brent applauded. The Monsignor sighed and bowed his head in silence.

Weeping openly, Dona threw herself into Alphonse's arms.

"You're safe," he said, "but we need to hurry if we hope to help the others."

She sniffled a few times before she caught her breath, mortified she'd allowed her pride to circumvent reason—but she didn't have the luxury to dwell on it. "Did you find anything?"

Alphonse held up the locket. The room was small. Tiny alcoves carved into the walls held old candles in various stages of consumption. Near them stood a metal brazier. A circle of corrosion by the railing suggested that Alphonse had moved it from the balcony. Perhaps it had been placed there to vent its smoke into the larger cave beyond. Dona longed for a means to light it, if only to recover the feeling in her fingers.

A stone platform occupied the room's center. In some respects, such as a frieze of skulls around its edge, it resembled the altar from the Vismort's chamber. But unlike that altar, this platform's top was tilted and its surface inscribed with deep channels that converged to a lip on its lower end. Implements of cruelty hung from the walls. Knives, tongs and hooks were all represented. Many had corroded, but a few still seemed pristine. Dona took down a corrosion-free knife.

"Brass, I think. And coated with something. Some sort of resin maybe."

Alphonse struggled to open an iron-bound door that now stood slightly ajar. The hinges had rusted tight. "The water is loud over here. Good thing you yelled. If you hadn't, I would never have heard you."

"What's this?" Dona asked, inspecting a large furry lump resting amongst the cobwebs on the platform."

Alphonse shuddered. "If you want to know, you are braver than I am."

She prodded it with the knife "No, seriously."

Alphonse yanked the door again, but it didn't budge. "I was serious. Hey, I could use a hand over here."

Dona didn't reply. She was staring in shock at the ball of fur. For one who had lived her entire life under his reproachful eye, there was no mistaking the distinctive face of Mr. Lop Ears.

"What is it?"

"Oh, nothing," Dona said.

"Hey—isn't that just like the one you have?" Alphonse said. "You know—the stuffed toy on your hope chest. Helena said it was yours."

"I guess there's a slight resemblance. They must have been popular back in the day... Wait, what were you doing in my room?"

"Just visiting."

"You could be expelled for that."

"If we don't get out of here, the point will be moot. Could I get a little assistance, please?" Alphonse grabbed a hammer. "You pull, while I pound the rust off these hinges."

The rust fell away more easily than expected, as did one entire hinge. With it gone, they pried the door open enough to squeeze through. The sound of rushing water was deafening.

Alphonse went first. Before them, a great chasm reached upward into darkness. The channel below churned with raging water. They stood atop a rock outcrop that jutted out over the flow. A narrow bridge suspended from thick ropes spanned the chasm, reaching across to a ledge that followed the river.

Alphonse tugged on a rope. "How is this still standing? It must be at least as old as the door."

Dona inspected the fibers. "Resin again, I think. The ropes are caked with it. And look, so are the slats."

"Do you think it would still bear a person's weight?"

"I have no idea. It seems to be in good shape, but how do you tell if they missed a spot?"

"We'll need a piece of that rope."

"I see what you mean—we can't untie it from this side."

Alphonse cocked an ear. "Did you hear that?"

"All I hear is water."

"I'm going back to check on them."

Together they made their way back to the balcony. The water had risen to Alexi's waist. Alexi and the Monsignor supported Brent, who shivered violently.

"Alphonse," Alexi cried. "Where are you?"

"I'm here. What's happening down there?"

"He's freezing to death," the Monsignor said. "And I daresay Alexi and I are soon to follow. If you are going to find anything to help, it had best be soon."

"Hold on a little longer," Alphonse said. "We've found rope."

"We need it now."

Alphonse and Dona rushed back to the bridge. "I'm going across," Alphonse said.

"Plunging to your death doesn't help anyone," Dona said. "See if you can find something back in the room to test it first."

Alphonse couldn't argue with her logic. "Wait here."

When he returned a with a hook, Dona was already halfway across.

"What are you doing?" You could be killed."

"I weigh less—it only makes sense that I should cross. And they need your strength. We can't afford to lose you."

"We can't afford to lose anybody." He cast frantically about for something to help, but there was nothing. He couldn't even pursue her—adding his weight might push the bridge over its limit. All he could do was watch.

Moments later, Dona had made it across.

"Don't ever do anything like that again."

"Don't worry," she called back. She began sawing at the thick fibers of one of the handholds to the bridge using the funerarium's brass blade. After a few more minutes the rope's tension dropped.

"All right," Alphonse said. "Now let go and I'll pull it over here."

"Just a second," Dona said.

"Hurry."

After several minutes, Dona started sawing again.

Alphonse held up the locket. "Wait, what are you doing?"

Half of the bridge dropped toward the rushing water. "I'm cutting down the bridge." She started sawing the other half.

"Why?"

"Because we need to save them as soon as possible."

"But how will you get back?"

"We'll have to cross that bridge when we come to it."

The second half was severed, and the entire bridge, save a single length of rope that had served as a handhold, dropped into the churning rapids.

"But we could have saved them with just the first rope."

"Not in time. We've seen how well you tie knots."

"You could have tied them."

"I was joking—even with perfect knots, you couldn't lift the Monsignor to the balcony, and he's in no condition to climb a rope. Now, listen carefully. I've tied the guide rope I cut first to the last slat on the bridge. If you pull that rope, you can now pull all the bridge slats up onto the landing. Then, free the bridge by cutting the ropes on your side, and the slats will be strung between the ropes like rungs on a ladder. Drag the improvised ladder to the balcony and tie one end to the railing. Then, throw the rest of the rungs over the railing down to Alexi and the Monsignor—they should be able to climb right up. I'm not sure what you'll do about Mr. Brent, but I'm sure the three of you can work something out."

"I can't just leave you there."

"I'll think about what to do while you rescue the others. Now go."

Seeing no reasonable alternative, Alphonse did as he was told.

·  ·  ·  ·  ·

Lightning split the sky as the carriage surged through the gates. Ahead, Trifienne's silhouette flickered against a backdrop of electric gloom. Gale-force winds raked the carriage with watery talons. The driver hunched in his greatcloak to present a smaller target. He only barely controlled his team—his four black steeds snorted and foamed, their eyes white-rimmed with fear.

Marguerite Serrola, fury etched in every line of her face, steadied herself as the carriage was bounced from below and buffeted from above. The instant they left the gate, the howling winds extinguished the carriage lanterns, leaving them at the mercy of intermittent semi-darkness. Perversely, the carriage increased speed, since the lantern light, reflected by the lashing rain, had only served to decrease visibility.

A fortuitous lightning strike revealed a donkey-drawn cart blocking the road. The driver avoided a collision only by throwing his full weight against the reins. Inside the carriage, Marguerite skidded across the floor. She threw open a small window in the front of the carriage near the driver.

"Now what?"

"Cart in the road, ma'am. Couldn't hardly see it for the rain."

Marguerite's jaw clenched. "And just what is a cart doing in the road in this weather?" The moment she asked, she knew.

The driver cried out. The carriage lurched to one side. Something scratched at the doors. She touched one of her rings and lunged for her seat. A panel in the wall fell open, but it was too dark to make out its buttons. A familiar creak signaled the door latch was turning. She slapped the panel, pushing several buttons at once.

With a satisfying click, all the carriage doors locked. At the same time, the carriage lanterns lit, not with flame, but with an unearthly glow far brighter than fire. The carriage rocked. Through the window she spied a dark figure struggling with the latch. Marguerite's pulse quickened—his features were completely obscured by a hood.

"They know," she breathed.

She jabbed another button.

A moment later, the man cried out and dropped. The door latches sizzled and sputtered. At the touch of another button, the windows darkened, becoming one-way mirrors. Satisfied she could no longer be seen, Marguerite risked a peek outside. Several hooded figures skulked around the carriage, the closest shaking his hand—now conspicuously gloveless. She muttered something, and the man dropped.

"One down."

A struggle near the front of the carriage caught her eye. Her driver Maxwell was grappling with another of the attackers.

Her eyes narrowed. "Poor dear—I bet they told you that hood would protect you."

Moments more, and the grappler lay motionless.

"Two."

Maxwell scrambled toward the carriage. Marguerite reached for the panel to let him in, but just as he made it to the door, he toppled forward.

She cried out, thinking he'd been shot, but the light revealed no evidence of a wound. Either he'd been knocked cold, felled by a wound she couldn't see, or....

For the first time, she was genuinely afraid.

Behind her, a window shattered. Marguerite dropped and rolled away. A gloved hand darted through the opening, thrashing, feeling about until it struck the panel.

The carriage was plunged into darkness. As the hand continued its frantic flailing, Marguerite groped for the opposite lock—until she remembered she needed the panel to release it.

To her surprise, the darkness suddenly vanished. The gloved hand seized the nearest latch and wrenched it.

Confident the lock would hold, Marguerite danced her mind through the requisite mnemonics. The arm went limp and slid back out the window.

"And that's three."

As she struggled to regain her feet, the locks released—all of them.

Ignoring the scattered window shards, she pounded the button again. The locks did not respond.

Over the storm's relentless wail, she heard a man laugh. He stood in the open, hood thrown back, arms raised. As she watched, he clapped.

"That was quite a show."

Marguerite's jaw tightened. "Wait until you see my encore." From behind the relative safety of the reflective glass, she compelled her mind to weave the requisite patterns.

"And, four."

But, she'd spoken too soon—the man still stood, a sardonic smile on his lips.

"Marguerite Serrola, we need to talk. May I come in?"

"Who are you?" She was stalling—buying time to determine why her spell had failed her.

The man bowed deeply. "My name is Josephus Vane."

The surname struck a chord. "Vane? Of the Pemberton Vanes?"

He strode briskly toward the carriage. "As fond as I am of my Pemberton brethren, I can't say I generally number myself among them."

"Stay back."

"I think not." His pace didn't slow.

As he reached for door, Marguerite slapped the lock into place manually.

Vane stifled a momentary scowl. "Please don't make this more distasteful than it already is."

"What do you want?"

"We need to talk—and I'm not about to do it standing in the rain. I can, however, resolve the matter without your input, if you prefer."

"What matter?"

"You have been Noticed."

Marguerite blanched. "That's impossible—I have been absolutely meticulous."

"Really? And I suppose this carriage is a testament to your powers of circumspection. I'll say it one time and one time only. Open this door."

"Not without proof."

Vane sighed. "As you wish." He stripped off his left glove, held out his hand, and closed his eyes.

In the next flash, she saw it. Perched on his flesh was a great fanged monstrosity. Simultaneously awful and magnificent, its eight pallid appendages spanned his entire palm.

Marguerite gasped. "The White Spider." Overcome with revulsion, she turned away. When she looked again, it was gone.

With trembling hands, she released the lock.

The latch hissed as he threw open the door. Unperturbed, he whisked off his remaining glove and took a seat. The wind slammed the door shut behind him.

"Please," he said. "Make yourself comfortable." Once she sank onto her seat, he continued.

"As you know," when a Santine learns someone has been Noticed, he is oath bound to eliminate all evidence of the breach, or barring that, to minimize its consequences."

"Mr. Vane, spare me the patronizing lecture. Who claims Notice, and have you confirmed it?"

Josephus stood and threw off his cloak to reveal the vestments concealed beneath. "It's *Inquisitor* Vane, if you please. As for the Notice—I was informed by Father Cartier directly. There's no telling how high this goes. Given your familial entanglements, I'm sure you realize how devastating this breach could become."

Marguerite failed to contain her sarcasm. "I suppose you'll be recommending the Sacrifice, then."

"Out of the question. That would be tantamount to an admission. You would only succeed in dragging the Crown down with you. Might I suggest instead a less flamboyant option?" He flicked open a small box to reveal a white tablet nestled inside.

Marguerite paled. "So, it's to be poison?"

"Yes—shortly after I deliver you to the Inquisition. In return, I shall see that your estate is properly sanitized. Assuming Cartier's evidence is sufficiently flimsy, that would provide the Crown an opportunity to turn the tables and accuse the Church of abduction and murder for political gain. Perhaps the Crown could even survive it."

"My apologies, Inquisitor Vane, but am I to understand that you are—and here I quote—'assuming their evidence is flimsy?' Does that by any chance mean you don't actually know?"

Josephus shifted uncomfortably. "I haven't managed to extract all the details yet, but there is no doubt that they believe you to be a

Phrendonic Heretic. Since you clearly are, is it really such a leap to assume they have evidence to support the notion?"

"And whom exactly do you mean by *they?* I thought you said this Father Cartier knew, and beyond that, there was—what was it again? Oh yes, 'no telling' who knew."

"I seriously doubt Father Cartier has time to investigate such matters on his own. The order must have come from higher up."

"So, as I understand it, based on the mere possibility that there exists at least one priest who might possess some potentially incriminating evidence, whose nature as yet happens to be unknown, you think this plan of yours is justified?"

Josephus frowned. "I don't think you understand. I'm not bargaining for your participation—I merely extend the option as a courtesy. Do you want the pill, or don't you?"

"So you can claim credit with all your little Inquisitor friends for capturing me?"

Josephus shrugged and snapped the pillbox closed.

"Wait. You'll make certain they can't trace anything to my children?"

"I guarantee nothing other than that I shall make the attempt."

"I have your word?"

"Of course."

"Very well, then—I'll take it."

Vane cracked a wan smile. "I thought you might."

As she took the pillbox, she flexed her wrist, and one of her rings brushed against his finger. Belatedly, he realized his error, but before he could react, his eyes lost their focus, and he slumped in his seat.

Marguerite pocketed the pillbox and shook her head in disdain.

"Four," she said.

# CHAPTER 14

# MACHINATIONS

The Curator of Profanities lifted his head from his desk, stretched, and opened his eyes.

"Good afternoon, sleepyhead," the old priest said.

The Curator started, but relaxed when he realized who sat across from him. "Did I nod off again?"

"I'm afraid so, and for quite some time, too. I was beginning to worry."

"What time is it?"

"Late—four or five, I'd expect."

"My class?"

"It's all right. I sent them away."

"Why didn't you wake me?"

"You looked exhausted. I thought you could use the rest."

"I suppose I was a little overextended. I don't remember ever sleeping this late. I had such odd dreams."

"I'm not surprised. You need to take better care of yourself. What if someone needed you in the field?"

"Those days are long gone."

"I wouldn't be so sure about that."

"Look around you. In the minds of the youngsters who will soon be running things, I'm a pitiable old man spending his declining years dusting a room filled with irrelevant curiosities. Caprian isn't even a memory for them—it's ancient history."

"History has a way of repeating itself."

The Curator sighed. "I know. I do my best to impress upon my students the importance of learning the lessons the Profanities teach us, but it's an uphill battle."

"I didn't mean that rhetorically."

The Curator roused himself from his nostalgic fog. "What are you saying?"

"Thurman is back from Trifienne. Armand has need of your expertise there."

The Curator blinked in surprise. "He does? Whatever for?"

"I'm sure he'll brief you fully once you get there, but rumors of Phrendonic Heresy are rampant."

"How soon does he need me?"

"Immediately. Thurman has a carriage waiting."

"And you let me sleep all this time? I have so much to prepare."

"You needed the rest—it's several days' ride. Everything else you'll need is already in the carriage. I'll be sure to cancel your classes."

"Where is the carriage?"

"There's some drill taking place in the palace complex. To keep from getting caught up in that, Thurman has the carriage waiting by Yanshee's pub. Simply show the driver this letter, climb aboard, and you're off."

The Curator's hands trembled with excitement. "I hope this turns out to be a false alarm, but would it be a sin to say it's wonderful to feel needed again?"

The old priest ushered the Curator to the door. "If it is, I'm happy to absolve you."

"Very funny. Any messages for Armand?"

"Thurman's already left one for him in the carriage. Travel safely."

"You'll lock up?"

"I'll take care of it."

"Thank you for all your help."

The old priest waved as the Curator ambled off to find his carriage.

.  .  .  .  .

"Welcome, my boy," the Primal said.

As Thurman approached the Primal Throne, he took careful note of his Uncle's circumstances. Pale and weak, His Primacy sat upright, a posture he maintained using a bevy of strategically positioned cushions. Flanked by armed guards, he presided over a bustling chamber—messengers came and went, dropping sealed missives into a bin at the Primal's left hand. A thin-lipped secretary primly opened each and skimmed its contents, occasionally leaning to whisper into the Primal ear. Small groups of grim Inquisitors milled about, awaiting an audience. A flurry of servants flitted throughout, seeing to the needs of the assembled and slaving tirelessly to ensure the chamber remained seemly.

"Why all the commotion?"

The Primal struggled to his feet. He leaned heavily on Thurman as they embraced and then sank back into his pillows, wheezing from the exertion.

"We've been invaded."

"By whom?"

"A demon in Laitrech's skin tried to make off with me—stole me right out of my bed."

"A demon? How do you know?"

"It changed form as I watched."

"Where is it now?"

"Escaped, and no one has seen Laitrech since. I've initiated a search of the palace, but it's a big place."

"What makes you think he's in the palace?"

"You've got to start somewhere. Where's your father? Did he come back with you? I could use him."

"Actually, I wanted to talk to you about that—is there somewhere we could speak privately?"

Murmurs erupted from nearby Inquisitors whose place in line Thurman had usurped.

"It would be a little difficult for me to get away just now. Is there a problem?"

Thurman leaned in close, but before he could say anything, a booming voice echoed through the chamber.

"Gentlemen. The call has gone out, has been heard, and has now been answered. As once I served the father, now, humbly, I shall serve the son."

"Oh, you didn't. Not him?" Thurman whispered.

Into the chamber strode a caped figure. His black boots were polished to a mirror-like sheen, and the starched collar of his crisp white shirt stood tall and proud. Dangling from his neck was an outlandish golden trinket, and his left eye played host to a sparkling crystal monocle. Atop his head an enormous broad-brimmed hat trailed vermillion plumage. He paused briefly for dramatic effect, stroking his waxed mustache. He might even have been dashing in an over-the-top sort of way, if only his head had reached higher than Thurman's nose and if he'd been somewhat less stout.

Jostling Thurman aside and sweeping off his hat, he dropped to one knee.

"It is I, Your Primacy, Thoren Theratigan, Demon Hunter Extraordinaire. Now and ever, at your service."

"Oh, give me a break," Thurman muttered.

Theratigan's head snapped toward Thurman, his visible eye skewering him with a look of intense suspicion. He rose to his feet and replaced his hat.

"If I may be so bold, Your Primacy, just who might this be?"

The Primal eye twinkled. "May I present my nephew, Father Thurman Goodkin."

"Nephew, eh? We'll see about that." Theratigan produced a jar, removed the lid, and held it out, but when Thurman reached for it, he drew it back. "Don't touch." He presented the jar a second time "Spit, please."

Thurman stepped back. "What?"

With barely concealed amusement, his uncle mouthed the words "humor him."

As Theratigan's polished toe tapped impatiently, Thurman felt every eye in the room fix squarely on him. Shaking with indignation, he felt his mouth go suddenly dry. "I'd rather not."

Theratigan turned sharply back to the Primal. "In that case, Your Primacy, I cannot rule him out as a suspect. Guards, take him."

Everyone started whispering at once. The guards flanking the Primal exchanged glances, as though uncertain whether to comply.

The Primal held up his hand. "Quiet."

Silence fell.

"Thurman," he said, no longer smiling, "might I prevail upon you to reconsider?"

Thurman's cheeks colored. This ridiculous little man was going to succeed at subjecting him to this gross public indignity, and there was nothing he could do to stop it. He spoke between clenched teeth. "If that is your wish, Your Primacy."

Theratigan thrust the jar at him once again. "Spit, please."

After several intensely embarrassing moments, Thurman managed to hack out a small driblet of spittle, which caught on his chin on the way out. It hung there for an eternity before, finally, falling free.

The disgusting little man caught it deftly in his jar. After a moment's examination, Theratigan clicked his heels and faced the Primal. "He passed. He's not a demon."

The whispering resumed at once, and Thurman couldn't shake the feeling that everyone in the room was laughing at him. The thought of it made him physically ill. Even though his business with his uncle was far from over, he bowed stiffly and fled the chamber.

. . . . .

The old priest padded softly down the long marble corridor until, just ahead, in the sputtering lamplight, an ancient metal-bound door loomed. Intent listening revealed only silence. The key felt leaden, but it still turned the lock, and the door creaked inward. A few swift, silent steps and the door clicked back into place against the frame. Each step grew more reluctant—and rightfully so. Murder was grim business—one never got used to it. The dust-laden corridor stretched ahead into darkness, the unseen Bastion an oppressive reminder of the sanctity of this ancient place and of the enormity of the impending deed. Other than its effect on the conscience, the Bastion offered up no resistance this night. Step by agonizing step, the old priest moved forward, half wishing the ward had failed and the way had been barred.

Every imaginable scenario lacking this single critical act had played out with disastrous outcomes. Yet, doubt circled, vulturelike. Could Laitrech himself have been duped? Was it possible he was unaware of the taint in his concoctions? Doubtful, of course—Laitrech was no rube. And yet, how easily he had fallen prey to the Curator trick. But then, what of his diagnosis? Could he possibly have gotten it so drastically wrong by accident? What if his only sin was misrepresenting his skills?

And there stood the final door, an arm's-length away. The old priest breathed deeply, banishing all distraction and uncertainty. No use in dithering—there was, quite simply, no other way. The door flew wide, and the old priest, wearing an expression both bleak and terrible, stepped inside—only to gape in surprise.

The desk, where by all calculations Laitrech should still lie sleeping, was empty.

. . . . .

"Young Goodkin, if I could beg a moment of your time?"

Fresh from his mortifying encounter with Theratigan, Thurman was in no mood to chat. But scion of a house of Primals and Ordinals though he was, even he thought twice before refusing an Ordinal's overture.

"Of course, Your Ordinence," Thurman said. "How can I be of assistance?"

Ordinal Lavicius smiled expansively, putting Thurman instantly on his guard. Tall and trim, with glittering eyes and a touch of grey at the temples, Lavicius had a charm about him that most found difficult to resist. It was a trait he exploited ruthlessly.

"Walk with me," he said. "What's the news from Trifienne?"

Thurman struggled to keep up with the Ordinal's brisk stride. "The heresy investigation continues."

"I understand you were instrumental in extracting a confession."

"It was a team effort."

"That's not what I heard."

"I'm just a cog in the great machine of justice," Thurman said.

"Come now—no need ply me with false modesty. You hail from extraordinary stock and are destined to do great things. The sooner people realize that, the sooner they can get out of your way. Take credit where it's due."

Thurman blushed. "You are too kind."

"Nonsense, I call things as I see them. I've been privileged to know quite a number of great men in my time. Do you know what sets apart those who attain their dreams from those who merely show potential?"

"I really haven't given it much thought."

"It's the company of other great men."

"I suppose that makes sense."

"Of course it does. Great ideas are synergistic, and so are the efforts of those who think them. That's why my heart goes out to the gifted man who struggles to make a name in isolation. I've made it a mission of sorts to help such men if ever I should happen across them. Thurman—may I call you Thurman?"

Thurman nodded.

"I think you are just such a man."

"I...I don't know what to say."

Lavicius displayed one of his glittering smiles. "Humble to the bitter end. Have you by chance heard of the Accipitrine Order?"

"Wasn't that one of the heretical groups ordered to disband during the Caprian Inquisition?"

Lavicius frowned. "Yes, well, those were dark days, and people are always suspicious of what they don't understand. Fortunately, the Order survived in spite of that little misunderstanding. Anyway, I'd like to invite you to attend one of our meetings. I think you will find membership has much to commend it."

Thurman saw no way to politely decline. "I would be honored."

The Ordinal picked up on his hesitation. "I know you're wondering what a humble young priest such as yourself would have to offer such an august group."

"Well, actually—"

Lavicius held up his hand. "Say no more. While a little humility can be an endearing trait, until you are better established, you are going to have to fight that urge. After all, not only do you have a remarkable pedigree, you also have a swift and definitive Phrendonic Heretic's confession to your credit. Combined with the fruits of your recent efforts to recreate an Ordinal's Relic, I'm sure you would be a shoe-in for membership."

Thurman's jaw dropped. "Who told you about that?"

Lavicius took a step back. "My apologies if I've somehow violated a confidence. I presumed it was common knowledge."

"It isn't," Thurman said. "Or at least, it shouldn't be. Who else knows?"

Lavicius shrugged. "Who can say? These things have a way of getting around. Now that it has, the real question is what do you plan to do with the information? If you haven't already sold it to Laitrech,

I'm sure I could arrange a more attractive offer, including, should you require it, the protection of the Accipitrines. I assure you, their good will is vastly preferable to their animus. Besides, given Laitrech's unfortunate disappearance, what guarantee do you have that he will be able to fulfill any promises he may have made?"

"I appreciate your kind offer, Your Ordinence, but there's one small problem. I haven't succeeded, so as of right now, there isn't anything to sell."

"I'm sorry to hear that. I do hope, however, that you will keep me in mind if you succeed. The Accipitrines would no doubt be very disappointed if they discover they were overlooked as potential purchasers for this information, should it become available."

"Thanks for letting me know."

Lavicius flashed another smile. "I'm already looking forward to our next meeting. I do hope you'll make it sooner rather than later."

"I'll do my best."

Lavicius patted Thurman's arm affirmingly. "I know you will."

As the Ordinal wandered off to engage another potential victim, Thurman was left with the distinct impression he would have been better off had he stayed put in Trifienne.

. . . . .

It seemed like forever since Alphonse had pulled up the bridge and dragged it through the doorway. Dona was beginning to second-guess her impulsive sacrifice. The non-stop chattering of her teeth made it impossible to concentrate and devise a way back across the gorge. After her harrowing experience at the balcony, she wasn't about to try climbing hand-over-hand, and forging her way alone in total darkness through treacherous caverns was unthinkable.

The glowing locket suddenly appeared across the water.

Dona had to shout to be heard over the rushing cataract. "How's it going over there?"

"We've made progress," Alphonse called back. "Alexi found some flint, and we're trying to start a fire. We split some of the slats for kindling, and we tore up the stuffed toy to catch the sparks. I think it's going to work."

Dona groaned. "You're starting a fire without me?"

"The Monsignor thinks it might be the only way to save Brent. Have you thought of a way to get back?"

"Not yet."

"Well, when the Monsignor brought the Morgatuan up onto the balcony, it opened another passage. He thinks it leads back into the Ossarium. The sooner you get back here, the sooner we can get out of here."

"Don't tell me we have to start over?"

Alexi joined Alphonse on the outcrop. "We got a fire started. The Monsignor is trying to revive Brent. You and Alphonse saved our lives."

Dona hugged herself for warmth. "Now if only I could save my own. It's freezing over here."

Alexi nudged Alphonse, who raised the locket in Dona's direction. "I can't do anything about that, but...hold still."

By now she should have expected it, but she was still startled when her cloak began to glow.

"There," Alexi said. "At least you don't have to plan in the dark."

"It's not a warm bath," Dona said, "but it's still a big improvement. Thank you."

Alexi bowed. "It's the least I could do for the woman who saved my life."

"Yes, and you're not off the hook until you return the favor, so start thinking. In the meantime, as long as I have light, I'm going to see where this ledge leads. Someone built that bridge for a reason."

"No, stay where you are," Alexi said. "The light will only last for an hour, and you could get lost. All these tunnels look the same."

"I'm just going along the ledge a little ways. I'll be back in twenty minutes, tops."

"Dona, come back here."

She glanced over her shoulder. "Twenty minutes."

Alphonse shrugged at Alexi, as if to say I told you so.

Alexi pointedly ignored him.

. . . . .

The ledge was wide and flat, and with the light from her cloak, Dona moved quickly. She wanted to make her twenty-minutes count—

and a brisk pace might warm her up a little. She only made it five minutes before she stopped—above her loomed an enormous machine. The wheels, chains, and gears reminded her of a clock mechanism, but there was no face. She knew it couldn't be the guts of the Exidgeon clock tower, since she had seen them once, and they were sensibly deployed within the tower proper, not unaccountably buried in a cave. Perhaps the chains that reached up out of sight were attached to some other less-well-known clock inhabiting one of Exidgeon's ancient pre-campus buildings. If that was true, it had stopped keeping time, since the mechanism showed no signs of movement.

In a thicket of chains on the far side, she spied a waist-high mound piled high with a small library of moldering books. She was instantly among them, eager to determine whether they held the key to the mystery of the mechanism or a way out of the caves. To her great disappointment, the first book she seized was covered with the inscrutable symbols she had come to recognize as Tep'Chuan. The same was true of the second, and the third.

Aware her time was slipping away, she rummaged through the stacks. With the books that didn't fall to pieces at her touch, it was the same each time—those maddening unreadable symbols. Since the books in the center of the pile seemed to be in better shape, she tried examining their spines for any sign of a readable language, but they were too closely stacked. She moved some of the crumbling books off the mound but still couldn't see the spines at the bottom. After wasting precious time removing some of the outer books, she braced her foot and put her hip into trying to slide them apart. When they hit an obstruction, she lost her balance. Books toppled in all directions, raising a great cloud of dust and mildew. Sprawled amongst them, she felt a most unsettling tremor, accompanied by the screech of strained metal and a rattling of chains. The gears of the great contraption hiccupped.

She froze, not breathing until the chains were perfectly still. Then, she struggled to regain her feet, but the chains jerked once more. As eager as she had been to know the machine's purpose, she had no desire to see it in operation until she was at a much safer distance.

Once the mechanism settled, she rose slowly, careful to avoid any sudden movements. This time the mechanism behaved, but as she tried to step away, her cloak toppled a precariously balanced stack. The machine screeched, the gears whirled, and the chains pulled taut.

The floor lurched, and Dona fell again. Only now did she realize she was on a platform, and it was rapidly lifting her into the air.

As she clambered to one side to look down, several volumes tumbled off the edge. She peered over in time to see them swallowed by the raging river below. Terrified, she shrank back from the edge, holding fast as the platform shot upward. Vaguely, she was aware of a large shape passing her in the void and wondered whether it could be some form of counterweight.

With a shudder, the mechanism ground to a halt. The platform swayed gently. Inching back to the edge, Dona could see a bin of rocks suspended just below her. If it was a counterweight, it had stopped in an odd spot—as had she. She could see nothing to suggest she'd reached a destination. With a sinking feeling, she realized the contraption must have gotten stuck.

She rocked the platform—slightly at first, but with effort that increased with her frustration. Whatever was blocking the mechanism held fast. After a few minutes, she stopped, since she was making no headway and was uncomfortable with the thought of the extra strain on the ancient chains. Her eye strayed to the bin of rocks. If she could get rid of some of the rocks, her platform might be heavy enough to reverse direction, but she could think of no way to do that. Her only option was to add to the counterweight—to go forward rather than back. One by one she tossed books toward the bin. With luck, she might change the balance enough to overcome the obstruction.

Unfortunately, the platform wasn't a very stable place for book-tossing, and she was still chattering from the cold. Even though most of her tosses missed, they still lightened her platform—but the obstruction held. She tried rocking the platform again. At last, terrified the chains would snap, she risked hopping. The mechanism heaved and squealed. Once again, the platform rose.

Dona hugged her knees, relieved she was moving again. She dreaded her destination. Would it be any better than being stuck? Finally, the platform came to rest against the cavern wall. The ceiling at this point was unnaturally flat, perhaps hand hewn, and close enough so she couldn't stand without hitting her head. Centered above the platform was a pair of oval holes large enough to squirm through. The air was fresher, and she heard the deep rumble of thunder. Upon worming her way through a hole. she found herself in a tiny, oddly familiar room. As she pondered it, the door was wrenched open from the outside.

Dona had nowhere to go. She stood, eyes wide and heart pounding, helpless against this new threat. Then her jaw dropped—there, in the doorway, stood her gangly dormitory nemesis, Arietta Charwick.

In a flash, the pieces fell into place—she'd climbed into the garderobe. Even Arietta's sour face couldn't spoil her delight.

Dona's still-glowing countenance had a vastly different effect on Arietta, however. With an earsplitting shriek, she bolted down the hallway.

Dona poked her head out and watched her flee. *And to think they told me Phrendonic Heresy wasn't useful.*

. . . . .

Arerio inclined his head briefly. "The room is prepared."

Marguerite looked up from her writing. "And our guests?"

"Awaiting your arrival."

"Well, we mustn't keep them waiting. And our special guest?"

Aerio kept a respectful pace two steps behind her. "Resting comfortably, as you directed. If you prefer, I could see to it that he rests through the night."

Marguerite stopped short. "Arerio, did you just make a suggestion?"

Arerio blushed furiously. "Forgive me, I have overstepped."

"It's fine—I am just not accustomed. By all means, speak plainly. Why would I want him to rest through the night?"

Arerio swallowed hard but forced himself to continue. "Might it not be preferable for Master Michlos to be present for the proceedings?"

"To talk me out of this, you mean?"

Arerio said nothing, but his raised eyebrow suggested that it might not be such a bad idea.

"I know you don't approve, but our options are limited. What would you have me do? Toss them off the cliffs?"

"Sometimes simple solutions are the most effective."

"You don't mean that. Though I admit the temptation is great, we can never afford to become that which we despise, even in the name of opposing it."

"There may be other simple solutions, though. Perhaps if Master Michlos—"

"Michlos has his hands full with too many other things to concern himself with a minor matter such as this."

"As you wish."

Marguerite sighed. "I don't like it either. I've thought this through a hundred times—the situation is too complex to involve the Constable, we don't have the wherewithal to hold them indefinitely, and that wouldn't solve the problem anyway. You'll just have to bear with me. They arrived at a door, and she threw it open. Ah, here we are."

Multiple lanterns cast flickering shadows throughout the parlor. Marguerite strode between two men armed with wicked-looking blades. Neither of them actually had a clue how to use one, but Marguerite wasn't relying on them for protection anyway. The guards had served their purpose—the three prisoners squirmed in their seats, casting the occasional resentful glance their way. Behind the prisoners, a great velvet curtain cloaked the wall, giving the room a theatrical flair. From the prisoners' expressions, it was clear they were anticipating a tragedy.

Marguerite cleared her throat. "Good evening, gentlemen. I trust you have found the amenities to your liking?"

The sullen men did not respond.

"Well then, as long as there's nothing else you require, I was wondering if we could chat about our little misunderstanding on the road?"

"You'll get nothing from us, witch," said the first of the three. His right hand was swathed in bandages.

"Oh, so that's what this is about? Someone made accusations of heresy, and you believed them? Someone affiliated with the Church, perhaps?"

"After what you did to us, you have the gall to deny it?"

"If you're referring to clothing and feeding you after you assaulted my carriage on the road, then indeed, I am guilty."

The prisoner held forth his bandaged hand. "You forgot to mention this."

Marguerite nodded. "I did have it bandaged. It looked like it needed it. Is that such a terrible thing?"

"Don't mock me, witch. You did this."

"I don't even know you. Even if I were a witch, why would I have bothered?"

"To escape justice."

The man next to him leaned over. "Shut up, Aaron."

Marguerite addressed him next. "You, sir, I do know. Even without the militia uniform beneath the cloak and hood, I would never forget the face of the man who told me my son-in-law had been murdered. What could possibly compel a man to commit such a heinous deed?"

The man looked away.

She turned to the third man. "And you. How could any righteous man accost an old lady in the dark of night? Are you claiming some sort of higher purpose like your friend here? Or are you the common thief you appear to be?"

Anger flared in the man's eyes, but he mastered it.

"By all rights, I should have the Constable slap you in chains. He takes a dim view of highway robbery. And if I thought for one minute you were responsible for your actions, I'd have done it already."

"I saw your witchlight," Aaron said. "And the ensorcelled slumber. I know you for what you are."

Marguerite nodded. "That's your one saving grace. I saw it, too. That's how I know you were deceived."

"She's trying to confuse us. Don't listen to her."

"You haven't asked what happened to the last member of your little band," Marguerite said. "You were hoping he escaped, weren't you? That perhaps he's rallying to your rescue as we speak. You must think very highly of him to have risked your lives like this. Did it not occur to you that he might have ulterior motives—ones he maybe didn't deign to share?"

Aaron growled. "If you captured him, it only confirms the power of your witchery."

"Actually, I think our friend Josephus was a bit surprised when my armed retine showed up. They were only a few minutes behind my carriage. I don't normally employ one, but then, I don't normally find myself in the position of rushing to the scene of an assassination. I have you gentlemen to thank for ensuring I arranged for backup. Poor Josephus seemed reticent to argue with their crossbows and accompanied us placidly enough."

The second man stirred. "Do you honestly expect us to believe these lies? Josephus is the most righteous man I have ever served under. You're asking us to believe he engineered everything for some hidden sinister purpose?"

"Why, yes," Marguerite said. "To frame me."

Aaron snorted. "That's ridiculous."

"It does seem farfetched, doesn't it? But I'm not asking you to take me at my word."

"Then, why are we here?"

"Why, for the show of course." She tugged a nearby cord. A cacophony of bells sounded. One by one, Arerio extinguished the lanterns.

"I direct your attention to the window behind the curtain that Arerio will open shortly. Things may take a moment to get going, but once they do, I expect you'll find the performance fascinating. Please don't think of leaving your seats until the show is over. I assure you the swordsmen are very skilled and their blades are very sharp—it would only take me opening this door for them to have plenty of light to do their business."

A slight rustle marked the curtain's movement, but since the room was pitch black, there was nothing to see.

"This is pointless," one of the men said.

"Patience," Marguerite replied.

Through the window, a golden light flared, revealing a small bedchamber. Next to the bed stood a tall, heavily muscled man in a glowing nightshirt, his wrists bound in great iron shackles. The glowing man closed his eyes, held up his hands, and the shackles crumbled.

The three men gasped.

Next, the man inspected the room, stopping for several seconds to examine the window.

At that moment, Marguerite opened the door, and light flooded the parlor. "Gentlemen, I give you your heretic. Not even iron shackles can bind him."

With the light from the hallway, the three men stood revealed to Josephus as well, and the horror and betrayal in their eyes was plain. For a fleeting instant Marguerite met Vane's gaze, which burned with an intensity of loathing she had rarely seen in anyone, save, perhaps, her brother. Then Vane's light went out.

"Anyway," Marguerite said, "based on the evidence I've seen here tonight, I can certainly see how easily this man could have misled you, and I therefore forgive you all. You're free to go. Since I didn't expect him to escape the shackles so easily, you might want to be on your way as quickly as possible. There's no telling the lengths to which he'll go to preserve his terrible little secret."

"You did this," Aaron cried. "You set this all up."

"If you wait a few more minutes, perhaps Vane would be willing to address that accusation personally, but I really wouldn't advise it."

The second man tugged the first's arm. "Aaron, c'mon. Let's get out of here."

Once the three had fled into the remnants of the storm, Marguerite sensed Arerio standing nearby.

"How far did he get?" she asked.

"Just into the hallway."

"Once they have a substantial lead, leave him down by the bridge. He can sleep it off there."

"We'll need to replace the lock and the hinges."

"When you do, make them brass."

"As you wish."

As he padded away, Arerio shook his head, but said nothing further.

# CHAPTER 15

# ḥAUNTED

The common room of Exidgeon's girls' dormitory was unusually crowded. On another night, the young women might have been scattered across campus, but this was not just any night—the storm had interrupted Inquisition's evacuation, and though the worst was now past, ominous rumblings still rattled the rafters at regular intervals. On such inclement evenings, Miss Maxtine recruited her charges to decorate the common room, light a cheery fire, make treats, and mull cider. Ostensibly she touted the festivities as a bonding opportunity. Secretly, though, thunder scared her silly, and she couldn't abide the thought of enduring it all night alone.

Typical activities on storm nights ran the gamut from needlepoint, to games, to all-out song and dance. But dancing was out of the question tonight, given the somber mood from recent events. In a valiant effort to engage her gloomy companions, Terulla Kardell volunteered to tell a story. It began as a simple romance, but grew increasingly spooky, eventually crossing the line into a full-blown ghost story. Arietta left the room abruptly just as Terulla voiced the moans of the hungering wraiths of the bog sisters—young maidens mercilessly drowned by the same villainous beast that held prisoner the hero's beloved.

Though on edge from the storm, Miss Maxtine was nonetheless captivated. But as the tale continued, Terulla's embellishments became ever more gruesome. Her hero braved the swamp's perils, arriving at last at the lair of the ravening beast, only to find the beast was prowling elsewhere. Finding his beloved asleep in the cave, he embraced her—but it was a trap. No sooner did their lips meet than illusion failed. Instead of his beloved, he held the hideous bloated corpse of a bog sister.

Curiously, though, his horrified scream emanated not from the storyteller, but from outside the common room entirely.

Everyone in the room jumped, including Terulla. Once they had a moment to recover, several of the girls giggled.

Miss Maxtine laughed with the rest. "Oh, well done. How ever did you work out the timing?"

Terulla brought a trembling hand to her mouth. "I didn't."

Miss Maxtine looked at first puzzled, then alarmed. "Then what was that?"

"I don't have any idea. Arietta maybe?"

Miss Maxtine leapt to her feet. "Where did she go?"

"I don't know. She just left."

"Everyone is to stay right here." Miss Maxtine's tone brooked no disagreement. "Understood?"

The young women nodded. Miss Maxtine strode to the fireplace and retrieved a poker. As she approached the door, it burst open. Arietta collapsed in a mound at her feet.

The girl struggled to catch her breath between sobs. "Dona Merinne. Her...she's a...wraith..."

Miss Maxtine eyed her skeptically. "A wraith? What are you talking about, child? Are you hurt?"

Arietta shook her head.

Miss Maxtine took the gangly girl by the wrists. "Now what's this all about? You've scared us half to death."

"The...gar...garderobe," Arietta said faintly. "Dona Merinne's ghost."

Miss Maxtine's eyes narrowed. She leaned close to sniff Arietta's breath, and her lips pursed.

"Well, it seems pernicious spirits are at work here after all, but I seriously doubt they have anything to do with Miss Merinne."

"But the garder...the ghost."

Miss Maxtine held out her hand expectantly. "All right, hand it over."

Grudgingly Arietta produced a flask from her reticule. Miss Maxtine removed the cap and peered inside. "Good gracious, it's empty. Is it any wonder you needed a visit to the garderobe?"

Arietta's indignation supplanted her terror. "What about the ghost?"

"You expect me to believe your rantings while you're in this condition?"

"I know what I saw."

Miss Maxtine sighed and grabbed the poker. "Oh, very well. Show me this ghost—and then it's to bed with you. Terulla, lass, lend her a hand."

"Yes, Miss Maxtine."

By now several students were curious to see the ghost. Miss Maxtine, poker at the ready, led a tight cadre of cautious young women through the doorway. Others stayed behind, their curiosity firmly subordinated to their anxiety. When the door finally closed, only Helena had chosen to neither stay nor follow. Instead, she quietly ducked out another door and headed to her room, which by now she fully expected to be haunted. And, as she saw it, this ghost had quite a lot of explaining to do.

She caught the spook red-handed.

Dona slammed shut her ravaged hope chest. "Oh, it's only you."

Helena crossed her arms. "What do you think you're doing?"

Dona rummaged through the room, dumping random things into her satchel. "What do you mean?"

"Scaring Arietta like that. She has Miss Maxtine chasing after your ghost with a poker. Aren't you in enough trouble? And, what are you doing here? I thought you left the University with Caroline and her mother."

"Who told you that?"

"I heard them ask you myself."

"It's a long story, and I'd love to tell you the whole thing, but there isn't time. Do you have any rope?"

"Whatever for?"

"How about in your sewing kit?"

"I have cord, and maybe some twine."

"That might work. Bring it."

"The whole kit?" The fabric too?"

Dona thought a moment and then nodded. "Good idea. Bring the whole kit, fabric and all."

"Bring it where? We're not just talking a needle and some thread here. That's a lot of material."

"We'll have to hope it's enough. We'll need lanterns too."

"What do you mean we? In case you haven't noticed we're in the middle of a storm and an Inquisition. I'm not going anywhere."

Dona opened the satchel and peered inside. "As you wish. I'll be sure to give your regards to Alphonse, assuming, of course, I make it back in time to save him."

"Alphonse? He's in trouble?"

"Alexi too."

"Why didn't you say so? Here, let me grab another satchel."

"Hand me that," Dona said. "You head over to the garderobe and watch for them to leave. When they're gone, come back and get me."

"Can't the garderobe wait? I thought this was an emergency."

Dona sighed. "I don't have time to explain. Are you going to help me or not?"

"Fine, but you better be quick about it, then."

"Oh, and stop by the common room and grab up as many logs as you can carry."

"Logs?"

"Just do it—and hurry."

Helena ducked out the door. "Fine, I'm going, but you'd better be here when I get back."

Dona finally finished gathering as many of Helena's sewing supplies as she could stuff into the satchels, as well as lanterns and a few apples. She plopped on the bed and blew stray strands of hair from her face as she waited for Helena to return. Her eyes fell on Mr. Lop Ears, staring disdainfully up at her. For the first time in her life, she found his presence disconcerting—as though she'd just learned her most trusted friend lived a secret life about which she knew absolutely nothing. He'd been a part of her earliest memories. Once, she had lost Mr. Lop Ears and overheard her mother wondering whether he been burned with the trash. Even after all this time, the memory of that cold empty feeling still made her shudder. And then, her father was there, pressing the stuffed bunny into her arms, hugging them both and promising that Mr. Lop Ears would never ever leave her. Even now, the irony stung that he'd never made the same promise for himself.

Helena reappeared, her arms loaded with split wood. "Are you all right?"

"The coast is clear?"

"Currently, yes. Miss Maxtine is still dealing with Arietta, who's not being terribly cooperative. She may be occupied for some time."

"Good. Let's go."

"If you're planning to go outside, I hope you have a nice quiet way to get through all the locks. It's after curfew, you know."

"I know."

"One more thing," Helena said. "Have I mentioned how happy I am to see you home safe?"

Dona stopped short. Tears welled, but she was too loaded down to brush them away.

"You sure you're all right?"

Dona stifled a sniffle. "I am now. I'm so lucky to have you."

Helena winked. "You certainly are—and likewise. Now, shall we rescue those silly men?"

"If we don't, who will?"

. . . . .

The corridor was lit only at rare intervals. Night visitors to the garderobe generally carried a lantern, but Dona and Helena didn't have any hands free. Fortunately, Helena's assessment was still accurate—the garderobe was clear.

"I'm going to set these logs down here," Helena said. "I'll pick them back up when you're done."

"No, don't."

"But they're heavy."

"Take them in with you."

"But I don't have to go."

"Yes, you do. Take them in and set them to one side."

"Why?"

"You'll see."

Helena shrugged. "Very well. If you insist."

Dona followed her in and set down the satchels. "Now, go light one of these lanterns off a hallway lantern and bring it back."

While Helena was gone, Dona dropped a coin into the garderobe and was relieved to hear it clink on the platform. She lowered herself through the seat, feeling for the platform with her toes. She was half-way through when Helena returned with the lantern.

"Have you lost your mind?"

"Quiet. Get in here and lock the door."

Helena engaged the latch. "I think it's about time for an explanation. Do you have any idea how far down that goes?"

"Things have changed. There's now a platform right beneath my feet, and I'm going to drop onto it. You'll need to hand me all the stuff we brought. I'm hoping it will be enough."

"Enough for what? And why would you want to stick a platform down there?"

Dona's feet finally touched. "Hand me the lantern first."

Too astonished to argue, Helena held out the lantern.

"Right. Now the stuff from the satchels."

Helena passed Dona the larger bolts first, and once the satchels were down to a manageable size, she passed her those as well.

"Now the logs."

One by one, Helena gave them to Dona.

"Is that everything?" Dona asked.

"Yup, that's it."

"Oh no," Dona said. "It's not enough."

"Enough for what?"

Before Dona could answer, the door rattled, and a voice filtered in. "How long will you be?"

"At least fifteen minutes maybe longer," Dona said. "I'm not feeling well. You might want to use the privy instead."

The voice turned petulant. "But it's raining."

"Sorry."

"Dona, is that you?"

Dona signaled Helena with a finger to her lips.

The door rattled again. "Dona? Dona Merinne? Are you there? Are you all right?"

The first voice was joined by a second. "Hey, I'm trying to sleep."

"I swear I heard Dona Merinne in here, but now she won't answer. She said she wasn't feeling well."

"Dona hasn't been here in days. You're starting to sound like Arietta."

The door rattled again. "Look, it's locked from the inside. Someone's in there."

The second voice grew louder. "Who's in there? Hello? This isn't funny anymore."

"That does it," the first voice said. "I'm getting Miss Maxtine."

Five minutes later, when Miss Maxtine pried open the door, the garderobe was empty.

. . . . .

Lavicius strode into his colleague's office with open arms and a broad smile. "Ordinal Bittern, so good see you again. How is your guest doing?"

Bittern rose from his desk. Middle-aged and portly, Bittern was prone to comfort his nervous disposition with a ready supply of sweets concealed nearly everywhere he happened to frequent.

"Still out cold. I couldn't find any injuries, so I expect he was drugged. Must have been a potent one, too. I'm shocked it didn't wear off before you got here. What took you so long?"

"I came the instant I received your message. Wherever did you find him?"

"Face down on a desk in the Chapel, dressed in nothing but his skivvies. He told me he was heading down there last night. When I heard he was missing, it was the first place I checked."

"And his Relic?"

"Nowhere to be found."

"Pity. It might have come in handy. Did you find any evidence to identify his attacker?"

"I presume it was the same demon that attacked the Primal. Where else would it have gotten his vestments?"

Lavicious pulled up a chair. "Ordinal vestments are easily duplicated. But the fact that Laitrech's were missing supports the notion the same culprit attacked both Laitrech and the Primal. I'm afraid, however, that I just don't buy the idea it was a demon. There are too many more-probable explanations."

"Well the Primal certainly seems convinced."

"Yes, but as you know, the Primal, bless his soul, is not a well man. Who knows what hallucinations might be brewing in that drug-addled brain of his? You're certain Laitrech's attacker left no evidence behind?"

"Frankly, when I found him unconscious, that wasn't the first thing I thought of."

"Apparently alerting the Primal wasn't the first thing you thought of either."

"Actually, it was, but then another possibility occurred to me, so I brought him here instead."

"Really? And what possibility was that?"

"The possibility that you might prefer to find out first."

"I'm flattered, of course," Lavicius said. "But I'm also a bit puzzled. Why would you think I'd want that?"

"I thought you might like to make a deal."

"What sort of deal did you have in mind?"

"It occurred to me you might be interested in taking credit for his rescue."

"How curious. Why would you think I'd want to do that?"

"Perhaps the two of you would end up being on better terms, then."

"I don't know what you mean. I happen to pride myself on being on good terms with all my esteemed colleagues."

"Do I really need to spell it out? I'm sick to death of all this duplicity and I want out. Take him, take the credit for saving him, and in the future, you can find out whatever it is he's up to directly. In return, any debts you think I may still owe will be considered paid in full."

Lavicius regarded Bittern for a long moment. "Duplicity? That's the word you choose to describe the essence of our long and profitable friendship?"

"Don't bother playing the martyr with me. It doesn't work anymore."

"All right, let's assume I agree. Even if I took credit for rescuing him, what makes you think he'd confide in me? I'd merely get credit for dragging him out of the Chapel. Is that really a rescue?"

"Weren't you listening? His Relic is missing. Without it, he couldn't get out on his own. If one of us hadn't happened across him, he'd have starved to death. I'd be pretty grateful to be rescued from that. Wouldn't you?"

Lavicius nodded. "True, but once he turned up missing, it would only be a matter of time before someone thought to check the Chapel. He does spend considerable time down there after all."

"You seriously expect me to believe you can't turn this situation to your advantage? I've seen you transform slung mud into spun gold without even breaking a sweat."

"Ah, but fool's gold doesn't confound an able jeweler, and I'm afraid our friend Laitrech has a practiced eye."

"I expect it would be worth the risk. After all, the Primal isn't expected to last much longer, and you want his job so bad you can taste it. Do you really want to let Laitrech grab all those sympathy votes unopposed?"

"Laitrech isn't even in the running. The Primal is expected to support his brother to replace him. Whether he has the votes to win remains to be seen, but Laitrech doesn't stand a chance."

Bittern popped a caramel. "I'm afraid your information is out of date." He held up a parchment. It bore Isrulian's seal, now broken.

Lavicius snorted. "You expect me to give Isrulian's assessment more credence than my own?"

Bittern handed him the document. "Here, decide for yourself."

After reading a few moments, Lavicius looked up in disbelief. "Is this some sort of joke?"

"Have you ever known Isrulian to display a sense of humor?"

"The idiot actually charged the Primal's brother—who also happens to be the Inquisitor General—with heresy? This is madness. Isrulian's days as an Ordinal are numbered. The Primal will have his head—probably literally."

"Doesn't that depend a little on the timing? As you just pointed out, our Primal is not a well man. What if he should happen to pass sooner rather than later?"

"You mean before Armand is cleared of these charges?"

"Precisely. Any idea how that might affect the election?"

Lavicius rubbed his chin. "It could eliminate Armand as a candidate."

"And then who would step in as the Primal's anointed?"

"Oh, I see—Laitrech, of course."

"Given that possibility," Bittern said, "let me renew my offer. Why not be the one to rescue Laitrech?"

Lavicius shook his head. "I'm sorry. I know you'd like me to accept, but I really can't, especially if all you say is true."

Bittern scowled. "Why ever not?"

"Because if Laitrech becomes a viable candidate, I will need to know what he is up to more than ever. I'm afraid our current arrangement will have to continue a bit longer."

"You don't understand. I'm done. If you don't want to consider it a deal, view it as a parting gift."

Lavicius gave his arm an empathetic pat. "I understand the desire for a fresh start now that your dear friend may be a viable contender for the Primacy, really I do."

"So, you'll take the deal?"

Lavicius sighed. "I'm afraid not."

"Let me rephrase. Take it or leave it."

"Before you make any hasty decisions, you might want to consider the consequences if this morning's letter were to fall into the wrong hands. Its details are a bit vague, but given the publicity surrounding today's events, it wouldn't take a genius to put two and two together. I expect Laitrech would be very curious to know why your announcement of his rescue was delayed until after you first consulted with me."

"You wouldn't dare."

"Of course, if that were to happen, I would probably find it more difficult to stay up to date on Laitrech's daily activities. But, then again, if you really do decide to call it quits, I suppose it wouldn't really change anything at all, at least from my perspective."

"Damn it, Lavicius, I've paid my dues."

"Oh, I wouldn't lose sleep. I'm sure Laitrech views you as a trusted friend. He'd never believe you'd allow him to fall into the hands of a bitter rival who could quietly dispose of him—particularly during circumstances where everyone would simply assume the demon got him."

"You would never."

"Of course not. Tempting though your offer was, I clearly managed to resist."

"That wasn't my intention, and you know it."

"And I believe you. I'm sure Laitrech will too, once you explain it all to him."

Bittern pointed to the door. "Get out."

Lavicius didn't budge. "Such a lot of bother, though. Who could blame you for choosing a simpler path—one where such explanations wouldn't be necessary, especially if, as you say, Laitrech may have a shot at the Primacy?"

"I said, get out."

Lavicius smiled sympathetically. "You've had a rough day and still have quite a lot to think about. Don't worry, though. If you should need any more help deciding what to do, I'll be in touch…as usual."

Once Lavicius was gone, Bittern, his features ashen, sank heavily into his chair.

# CHAPTER 16

# SOME DISSEMBLING REQUIRED

The cottage door slipped silently open, revealing a shadowy presence barely visible against the Holy City's evening twilight. It closed just as silently, followed by a dull thud and a muffled curse.

Bedsheets rustled as the old priest sat up. "It's all right, I'm still awake."

"You moved the chair," Thurman said. A lucifer flared, and he stopped rubbing his shin long enough to light a lantern.

"I didn't expect you would be here to notice. Your father generally stays in the guest room when he visits the palace. I take it you didn't receive the same courtesy?"

"I didn't get to see Darron that long. He's mobilized half the city trying to find Laitrech and capture this demon. He even called in that moron Theratigan."

"They haven't found Laitrech yet?"

Thurman frowned in puzzlement. "Why does that surprise you? I thought he was safely tucked away in the Chapel."

"Not anymore...someone must have gotten to him."

"But I thought you took his Relic."

"I did, which whittles down our list of suspects considerably."

"Well, if he's been found, I don't think Darron knows it yet—or he's putting on a good show."

"Did you tell him about Isrulian's little ploy?"

Thurman shook his head. "I never got a chance. He was holding court in the throne room. Just as I got his attention, that fool Theratigan showed up and demanded I contribute to his drool collection."

You mean Thoren Theratigan, the Demon Hunter?"

"The same twit Grandfather had tagging along during that scare they had with that demon in Histlewick Downs."

The old priest regarded him intently. "Does he still wear a monocle?"

"That's him, and he's grown a ridiculous mustache to go with it."

The old priest paused, lost in thought. "So, he never returned it then. That may complicate matters."

"Returned what?"

"The monocle—and probably several other Profanities as well."

"The monocle's a Profanity? How can he be carrying around a known Profanity?"

"By dispensation. The matter of Histlewick Downs was a bit of a desperate case. By the time Theratigan got involved, they were willing to resort to almost anything."

"Including passing out Profanities to charlatans? It couldn't possibly have been that desperate."

The old priest raised an eyebrow. "Theratigan may be peculiar, but he's no charlatan. Born of a family of Phrendonic Heretics, he was not yet of age when they were brought to justice by your grandfather. It was about the time Armand was first beginning his work with the Inquisition. He took pity on the young man and interceded with your grandfather for mercy on Theratigan's behalf, arguing that repentance should surely suffice in one so young. By all accounts it was Theratigan's expertise that turned the tide at Histlewick Downs."

"But that was ages ago. Surely the dispensation no longer applies."

"Well, other than Theratigan himself, the only person I can think of who might recall the specific terms is well on his way to Trifienne, and I doubt your uncle would take him to task for it in any event. Still, it's a good thing you told me. With Theratigan snooping about, I'd best keep my forays into the palace to a minimum. I can't afford to risk him seeing through one of my little disguises. Fortunately, you still have the run of the place."

Thurman snorted. "For what it's worth. It's not like I can keep an eye on him from here."

"We'll just have to hope Laitrech doesn't turn up until tomorrow at the earliest, or better yet, that he never does. In the meantime, there's something else you can do that might help your uncle." The old priest handed him a key ring from the nightstand. "I need you to get something from the Hall of Profanities. Do you remember the Harcourt wands?"

"Vaguely. It's been a long time since I've been in that place."

"You can't miss them. Albert has them on a pedestal in a little rack. I think he even has them labeled."

"What do you want with those?"

"We can only afford to take one. Taking all of them would be too obvious."

Thurman yawned. "I'll get one first thing in the morning."

"That may be too late. Even if Laitrech hasn't reappeared yet, it won't be long before they notice Albert is missing. Once they do, your chances of getting anything out of the Hall plummet."

"I'll go tonight, then. But what are we going to use it for?"

The old priest smiled. "I think it's time we gave our friend Theratigan a little test. If his powers of observation are any match for his self-proclaimed powers of deduction, this could get interesting."

"I take it you're not going to tell me."

"I'm still working on the details. Now hurry up, before Laitrech shows up and makes things that much harder. And Thurman?"

"Yes?"

"Whatever you do, don't touch the tip."

. . . . .

With Helena's added weight, the platform sank at a steady pace. As the garderobe ovals receded, they found themselves suspended in a featureless abyss, their progress impossible to gauge by anything other than the sound of rushing water. Helena sat hugging her knees. The thought of looking over the edge made her dizzy. Dona inched as close as she dared and peeked. Far below, a point of light wandered slowly about the cavern.

"It's Alphonse. He must have crossed the rope to look for me."

Helena brightened. "He's here?" Forgetting her fear, she leaned toward the edge.

"I can't tell for sure, but we should be there in no time."

The platform ground to a halt.

Helena's brow furrowed. "Are we there?"

Dona caught a glimpse of the counterweight nearby in the lantern light. "Not yet."

"I don't understand. Why have we stopped?"

"I think we're stuck."

"Stuck?"

"Shh," Dona said. "They'll hear you all the way up to the garderobe."

"Isn't that exactly what we want?"

Alphonse's point of light was now moving away. In seconds, he would be out of sight entirely. Dona grabbed a spool of thread and threw it.

Helena gaped in horror. "Hey, what are you doing?"

The light stopped moving.

Dona lobbed another spool. "I'm getting Alphonse's attention."

After several more spools, the light finally moved closer.

"I think he's seen us," Dona said.

Alphonse held the locket aloft and peered up through the gloom.

"What are you doing up there?"

"Catching up on our needlepoint. What does it look like?"

Helena crawled to the edge. "We're stuck up here. Can you get us down?"

"Binky?" Alphonse said. "Is that you?"

Dona gaped openmouthed at Helena. "Binky?"

"He calls me that sometimes. Isn't it sweet?"

"How did you get down here?" Alphonse asked.

"It's a long story," Dona said. "Right now, we need you to see if you can get this contraption unstuck."

"What do you want me to do?"

"There's a big flywheel on one side. See if you can get it to turn."

"Found it."

The platform lurched. Helena screeched, and Dona flattened herself against the cold metal.

Released from whatever had been binding it, the flywheel once again spun freely. Moments later, the platform settled amid the scattered books. Helena threw herself into Alphonse's waiting arms. The instant she stepped off, the platform shot upward. It was several feet in the air before Dona had the presence of mind to leap. She landed in an ignominious heap.

Alphonse dashed to her aid. "Are you hurt?"

She brushed herself off. "I'll live."

"My sewing kit," Helena cried.

"Don't worry," Dona said. "We'll retrieve it once the counterweight arrives.

"You're sure?"

"Here it comes now. Alphonse, would you be so kind as to remove some of the ballast?"

"Let's have a look." He strode off toward the counterweight's expected destination.

Once he was out of earshot, Helena touched Dona's arm. "What's that thing around his neck?" she whispered. "And where's Alexi?"

"I presume Alexi is waiting for us across the fallen bridge. Isn't that right Alphonse?"

Alphonse nodded. "It was all I could do to keep him from trying his luck with the rope. He got a bit agitated when you missed your deadline."

Dona perked up. "He did?"

The counterweight planted itself on the cavern floor in front of him. "I didn't mean to imply it was in a good way. I don't think I've ever seen him quite that upset. You might want to tread lightly for a bit."

"I'll keep that in mind. Now, if I can persuade you to unload some of those rocks, we can retrieve Helena's sewing kit and be on our way."

"Happy to oblige," Alphonse said. "Maybe while I'm doing that, you could tell me where you've been?"

"The women's dormitory is somewhere up there," Helena said. "The platform comes to rest beneath the garderobe. Dona figured it out and asked me to come help. So, what exactly am I helping you do?"

Alphonse removed another rock, and the counterweight heaved "Could one of you hold that down, please?"

Helena sat on its edge.

Alphonse removed a few more rocks. "All right, try hopping off."

The counterweight began to rise.

"We can control it, then," Dona said. "That's a relief."

As before, the mechanism seized when the platform was about halfway down. A few nudges to the flywheel got it moving again until it landed safely amidst the chains and books.

Helena climbed aboard and began gathering.

"What are you doing?" Dona asked.

"Getting my things," Helena said. "Why?"

"It's not quite that simple. If you don't take it all at once, the platform might rise again when you step off."

"Perhaps if we all three gathered and stepped off at the same time?" Alphonse suggested.

She examined the mechanism with a critical eye. "Maybe—but there's got to be an easier way."

"We don't have much time. The bursar isn't doing well, and if I don't show up soon, Alexi may try something rash."

Dona pulled back a stout lever with both hands. "I bet this is it. Now try unloading."

Helena stepped off the platform, and it didn't budge.

"Excellent," Dona said. "Let's gather and go."

Moments later, the heavily laden trio arrived at the bridge. Across the gorge, Alexi, bathed in the glow of his sword, rose stiffly to his feet.

"He looks mad," Helena said.

Dona huffed. "He'll be fine. After all, I found us a way out, didn't I?"

"What is that thing he's holding? It looks like no lantern I've ever seen."

"We'll have plenty of time for explanations later. Right now, we have sick and injured people over there, and we must find a way to get them over here. Can you use your kit to craft a harness?"

Helena frowned. "I'll have to think about it. I've never tried anything like that before. Under normal circumstances, I'd use hemp instead of twine and fabric. How many people are we talking?"

"Just Alexi, the Monsignor, and the Bursar."

Helena's jaw dropped. "Monsignor Goodkin?"

"I'm afraid so," Dona said, "so you'll want to make it sturdy. Alphonse, do you think you could find a way to get some of that firewood over to them? It's got to be better than bridge slats for keeping them warm."

"I'll tie it in bundles with the twine," he replied. "Maybe I can hang it from the rope across the chasm and Alexi can pull them over to him. I'll also reinforce the rope with twine."

"Good plan. If it works for the wood, maybe we can pull the others over here in a harness in the same way. See if you can get a bolt of fabric over to them too. They can use it as a blanket."

Alexi's voice echoed across the chasm. "So nice of you to drop by."

Dona sighed. "I'm sorry I'm late, but I found a way out. We need to get the three of you over here as quickly as possible."

"So, you didn't have time to let us know about that, but you had plenty of time to check in with your girlfriends?"

"We can fight about this later. Right now, we have people relying on us. See if you can help Alphonse get things over to you. Helena's trying to make a harness to ferry people across."

Alexi's eyes flashed. "Whatever you say, Mistress, but first, allow me to alert the rest of the rabble you have arrived and will deign to see them shortly. It's the sort of thing polite people do."

"He'll come around," Alphonse said. "You had him pretty worried."

"Clearly."

Although Dona assisted Helena's harness efforts, the set of her jaw informed them that she was in no mood for idle chitchat. Alexi, who emerged a short time later to work with Alphonse on rope reinforcement, was equally dour.

When they were finished, Alphonse hung one of the bundles of wood on the rope using a twine loop. He tied another length of twine to the bundle, then tossed the end over to Alexi, who tugged the hanging wood over to his side. Although the process was slow, all the wood made it across long before Helena finished her harness. A bit later the Monsignor ventured out, still pale, but in high spirits.

"Miss Merinne, thank you so much for your timely efforts. Mr. Brent's condition has improved, and I'm feeling much better myself. Alexi tells me you've found a way out of these caves?"

"I have. It's not far, but we have to get you over to this side. It takes us back into Exidgeon, though. I hope that's not a problem."

"Is there any chance of avoiding the Inquisition? I'd hate for all of this spelunking to have been for naught."

"The passage leads to the women's dormitory. So far, the Inquisition has left them alone."

Helena chimed in. "The Inquisition is leaving Exidgeon anyway. Last we heard, they struck a deal with the Crown to evacuate the college."

The Monsignor raised an eyebrow. "Leaving? I wonder how they got Isrulian to agree to that?"

"Finally." Helena held up a complicated network of twine, leather, and bright floral fabric. "Who wants to try it first?"

The Monsignor squinted across the gorge. "What is it?"

Dona caught Alexi's dubious expression and snatched the harness out of Helena's hands. "I will."

Helena frowned. "But, weren't we trying to get them over here?"

"We'll need a test first, and I'm the lightest. Besides, they'll need help from someone who isn't hurt."

"If they need help, I'll go," Alphonse said. "There's no need for you to risk it."

Dona wriggled into the harness. "Not true. They are going to need your help on this end to pull them up. I'm not big enough to do that. Helena, could you help me get this on the rope?"

"Sure," Helena said. "This wide leather strap here hangs over the rope. Now we tie it securely through the grommets with several thicknesses of twine and it should give a smooth surface for sliding over the rope. Here, let me sew through it a few times with some cord to make it more stable."

Alexi could contain himself no longer. "Don't you dare risk yourself in that thing."

A satisfied smirk crept across Dona's face. "The time to volunteer has passed." She handed Alphonse the pull cord and stepped out over the gorge.

She bounced several times as the rope took her weight, sliding partway across until she found herself suspended over rushing water.

As he had done with the twine for the firewood, Alphonse threw the weighted end of the pull cord across the gorge over to Alexi. He hadn't anticipated how difficult even Dona's weight would be to drag across the rope, and ultimately, it took the Monsignor's help to pull her the rest of the way.

Once she was safely across, Alexi rounded on her "What do you think you're doing? You could have been killed, and for what?"

"For this, silly." She threw her arms around him and kissed him deeply. "There," she said. "I think it was worth it, don't you? Now, put on your harness. In the meantime, I'll see to our friend the Bursar."

She was already gone before Alexi could respond. He turned to gape at the Monsignor, as if seeking an explanation.

The Monsignor politely pretended not to have noticed. "Need any help with that harness?"

· · · · ·

The funerarium had been transformed since Dona had last seen it. The brazier held a cozy fire that cast dancing shadows on the rough-hewn walls. Broad swatches of colorful fabrics had been spread across the floor—the spot seemed almost inviting, at least to someone whose teeth were still chattering. The biggest change was the presence of a new archway in what had previously been solid wall. In the darkness beyond, she thought she caught a dim flicker.

And then it hit her—the Bursar was missing.

"Mr. Brent?"

An echo was her only answer.

"Mr. Brent, are you all right?" Had he awakened disoriented and wandered off by mistake? She stepped through the arch. "Mr. Brent? Are you in here?"

Ahead she heard the clink of metal against stone and a muttered oath. She sprang toward the sound. "Don't move, Mr. Brent—I'll be right there."

For an instant, a dim red glow reflected off the wall. She squinted against a brief gale of musty air, and as it died, darkness enveloped her.

Dona scrambled backward, but the archway was gone. From behind, measured footfalls approached. A lantern flared. She blocked its glare with her hand.

"Mr. Brent?"

"Your timing is impeccable, young Mistress, and most unfortunate."

"Maybe we can pound on the wall to let them know we're stuck. Even if they can't hear us, where else could we have gone? All we have to do is wait for the Monsignor to use the Morgatuan again, and we'll be fine—I've found a way out."

"So I heard, but I'm afraid the Monsignor will not be coming to your rescue. You see, he no longer has the Morgatuan."

The pieces came together. "The red glow. You stole it."

"Not so fast, young Mistress. You'll recall that, according to our agreement, I was to receive the Morgatuan in return for my assistance. Now that we've come to the exit, it is mine by right. I never promised to accompany them beyond that point."

"Well, I'm not out of here."

"No, but you were. Once that happened, my end of the bargain was fulfilled."

"Then if you would be kind enough to open the passage, I'll just be on my way."

"You know I can't take that chance."

"What chance? All you have to do is open the passage, I'll leave, and then you can go off and do whatever you want—even take the Morgatuan with you."

"I think you even mean that, but so long as the Monsignor commands the swordsman and the sorceler, I can't trust him. Do you really think if I opened the arch that he could afford to honor his side of the bargain?"

"I don't think he would have made a promise he didn't intend to keep. Besides, Alphonse is already on the other side of the gorge, and the Monsignor is probably helping Alexi across as we speak."

"I doubt it. Not once they noticed the disturbance from sealing the arch."

Dona's mind raced. "Isn't keeping me here a bigger risk? After all, maybe the Monsignor intends to honor his promise to keep this place secret. But if I'm lost, Alexi won't let him rest until they mount a rescue. Would you really prefer having the entire Inquisition down here?"

"That would have been a better threat if you hadn't been fleeing the Inquisition when we met."

"That was just a misunderstanding."

"Well, we certainly don't want any of those. In fact, why don't we just take this opportunity to clear the air? Let's start with the real reason for your visit here."

"You just pointed it out yourself—we were fleeing the Inquisition."

"Or making it look like you were fleeing. Was that part of your plan to encourage my cooperation?"

"We really were fleeing. The Monsignor was traveling incognito. We couldn't have known you would offer to help."

"So, you expect me to believe that of all the doorways in all the world, you just happened to wander through mine, conveniently pursued by the Inquisition and carrying the Morgatuan? What kind of fool do you take me for?"

Dona shook her head. "Mr. Brent, at this point all I want to do is get out of this cave. I couldn't care less about whether you go your own way or whether you take the Morgatuan with you."

The Bursar regarded her thoughtfully. "If that's true, you must have already gotten what you came for. But what could that be? You are quite the enigma, young Mistress."

"Why does everyone keep calling me that?"

The Bursar laughed. "At first I thought you might actually be the Mistress, returned to us to fulfill Chervil's Promise. Who else could have retrieved the Morgatuan and conscripted both a Monsignor and a heretic to her cause? And maybe that is who you really are, but if so, you are either a very convincing liar, or you're completely unaware of it—I eventually dismissed the whole idea. Now, given the Vismort's reaction, I'm not so sure."

"Chervil's Promise? What are you talking about?"

The Bursar regarded her for a long moment. "All right. I'll play along. Chervil's Promise is the reason for this Ossarium as well as the countless others that were built and hidden away over the years. You see, unlike the Church, which holds that the soul is eternal and eventually passes to a better place after death, Chervillians believe the soul is fragile and easily lost if not preserved."

"Isn't that the same thing?" Dona asked.

"On the contrary—it's the difference between eternal life and total annihilation. Chervillians believe that the Church, through a tragic misunderstanding of the nature of the soul and a perverse elevation of faith over common sense, systematically exterminates its own followers."

"You mean Chervillians don't believe in an afterlife?"

"Actually, that's the essence of Chervil's Promise—which is that if the souls of the dead are preserved long enough, the faithful will eventually acquire the means to restore them to life."

"But isn't that every bit as far-fetched as the Church's position?"

"Is it? I may not be expert in the intricacies of Chervillian dogma, but I found the Vismort's little demonstration quite convincing."

"The Vismort?" Dona said. "Are you saying he used to be dead?"

The Bursar nodded. "So it would appear, and judging by the date on the coffin lid, I'd say he'd been dead for a good long time."

"But I thought he was supposed to be some sort of demon?" Dona protested. "Isn't that what the Monsignor called him?"

The Bursar snorted dismissively. "And just what exactly do you suppose a daemon is?"

"I guess now that I think about it, I'm not really sure," Dona said. "But I thought they were all supposed to be wretched and evil. Yet, if what you say is true, almost anyone could end up a demon."

"That's precisely the point. The Mistress offered the Chervillians of Exidgeon hope that the Pledge could actually be fulfilled in their lifetime. But of course, given that the Church would view such individuals as having been denied an oh-so-glorious afterlife through the application of dangerous heretical practices, is it any wonder they paint them as wretched and evil? For that matter, isn't that exactly how they characterize Chervillians?"

Dona's eyes widened in sudden realization. "And Dreamweaver too."

Brent paused, adjusted his spectacles, and leaned forward with the lantern for a closer look. After an eternity of scrutiny, he smiled. "It seems we are not so naïve after all."

Dona silently cursed her inability to keep her mouth shut. "Why do you say that?"

"Let me see. On the one hand, you profess your ignorance of the Pledge and are mystified as to why someone might confuse you with the Mistress, and yet, by some miracle you are familiar with her alias, which I am quite certain I have never once mentioned."

"Well, isn't she the obvious suspect any time someone brings up a mysterious woman who traffics in daemons?"

The Bursar raised an eyebrow. "The obvious suspect, even to a young lady who professes to be nothing more than an eager young college student? I think it's time you told me who you are and why you're really here."

Dona bristled. "Are you sure you can afford to take that tone with whoever it is you think I might be?"

The Bursar sighed. "Let me put it this way. If you really were the Mistress, you wouldn't be relying on me to let you out of here."

Although he said it with conviction, Dona heard something wistful in his voice, perhaps a twinge of doubt, a tremor of disappointment that made her feel that he would have liked nothing better than to be wrong. An idea took shape, and out of desperation, she seized on it.

"So, you are willing to take the risk she didn't send me? I suppose it never occurred to you that she might want an assessment of whether now would be a good time to continue her work on the Pledge. Think about it. That would explain my uncanny resemblance, not to mention my possession of the Morgatuan."

The Bursar hesitated. "If that's true," he said slowly, "then why the Monsignor?"

"I don't presume to know her mind, but I would guess that whom-ever she sent would need the assistance of an expert in Chervillian Ossaria. Let's face it, actual Chervillians are currently a little hard to come by."

"Are you suggesting that's why he was traveling incognito?"

"I suggest nothing. I just think a person should consider the poten-tial consequences of his decisions before he makes them. Speaking of which, are you going to open this arch or aren't you?"

Again, the Bursar hesitated. At last, he shook his head. "I can't risk it. I've spent too many years protecting this place to allow the Morgatuan to fall into Church custody."

Dona shook her head. "Only to throw it all away for lack of a few lucifers. Don't you see? I'm your only hope. If I am just a naïve col-lege student, you lost everything the moment you threw in your lot with the Monsignor to save yourself. If the Church learns this place is here, do you really think they'll need the Morgatuan to destroy it? On the other hand, if the Mistress did send me, would you really want the Monsignor to leave here without my constant supervision?"

The lantern wavered in Brent's trembling hand. "You'll see he keeps his end of the bargain?"

"I make no promises."

He nodded as though he'd expected as much. Setting down the lan-tern, he peered through his spectacles at the Morgatuan's rings, align-ing their mysterious markings to recreate the Canticle of Obsequy.

. . . . .

St. Sophia's caretaker rolled over and groaned. Although he frequently rose with the dawn, he had been counting on today being an exception. It was bad enough an Inquisitor had dragged him out of bed to toll the bell for over an hour during the storm, but then the storm kept him awake into the wee hours. At first, he ignored the pounding at the door by dragging a pillow over his head, but the unwelcome visitor was simply unwilling to go away. After indulging himself with a good stretch and an expansive yawn, he pulled a robe over his nightshirt, thrust his feet into a pair of well-worn slippers, and shuffled to throw open the vicarage door. "What in blue blazes is so important that it can't wait for a reasonable hour?"

Two soaked and bedraggled men stood before him on the stoop, one of them sporting a militia uniform.

"Is Father Cartier here? We have to see him right away."

The other man nodded. "It's urgent."

The caretaker scratched his head. "Last I heard, the good Father was still up at the College, though I hear tell he could be coming back any day now. Best to try again tomorrow, say, around noonish."

The uniformed man blocked the door with his boot. "Can we leave a message? It's really important."

The caretaker sighed. "If you must. What is it?"

"It's for Father Cartier's eyes only. Do you have pen and parchment?"

"I reckon I can dig some up."

He bid them wait at a small table in the dining room while he found the supplies. The militiaman took them without comment. He dipped the pen and paused to look up at the caretaker, who stood watching over his shoulder.

"Could I also trouble you for sealing wax?"

The caretaker frowned. "If you really think it's needed."

The uniformed man waited expectantly.

The caretaker grumbled and ambled toward Cartier's office. "All right, I'll see what I can find." By the time he came back with wax and candle in hand, the parchment was folded and ready for sealing.

Once he'd imprinted the seal with his signet, the militiaman held out the letter. "See that he gets this as soon as possible."

The caretaker graced them with an ill-concealed yawn. "The very moment he arrives."

On the stoop, the uniformed man turned to face him one last time. "Remember—as soon as possible."

The caretaker's response was interrupted by a brilliant flash, followed by shrieks from all three men. The visitors' soggy clothing hissed and steamed, and the caretaker's robe and nightshirt erupted into flames. The sealed letter fell blazing from his grasp. Several more flashes cut the men's screams short and set the entire dining room alight.

.  .  .  .  .

The rising sun crested the horizon, revealing an ominous finger of dark smoke reaching high over the city. Supervising the Inquisition's departure from Exidgeon's barbican, Father Cartier immediately took it as an ill omen, but it would be some time before he learned just how close to home it had touched.

# CHAPTER 17

---

# EXEUNT

Alexi reached out to Dona as the dust cleared. "What happened?"

Dona shot the Bursar a significant look. "Mr. Brent must have awakened disoriented and wandered through the arch. When I went after him, that wall appeared out of nowhere."

Brent scooped up the lantern. "I didn't have any idea where I was. I guess I panicked."

The Monsignor crossed his arms. "How fortunate you still had the presence of mind to take the Morgatuan with you."

"Yes, it was."

Dona nudged Brent's arm.

"Oh, here you go," Brent said, handing over the scepter.

"The Monsignor eyed him dubiously. "That's most gracious of you."

"Well, then," Dona said, "let's get out of here, shall we? I'm freezing."

Alexi pulled her in close. "Now that's something I can help with. I'm sorry for getting mad before."

Dona ogled him in surprise. "Alexi Reysa, are you apologizing?"

Alexi shrugged. "I thought I'd lost you and that it was my fault. I crossed the line—the surest way to lose a free spirit is to cage it, even if it is for its own good."

Dona smiled up at him. "That's pretty sophisticated thinking for a man. Maybe that's why I'm so inordinately fond of you."

"You mean, it's not my raw animal attraction?"

She caught hold of a bright floral stretch of harness. "Ah yes, a trait rivaled only by your unerring sense of style."

"This old thing? I can't take credit—it was a gift from someone I care about."

"You must love her very much."

Brent tapped his toe. "How about we get out of this funerarium before we age enough to need it?"

"All right," Alexi said. "We had to cut the the harness to get it off the rope."

"I saw how Helena sewed it," Dona said. "I should be able to fix that."

Despite its makeshift appearance, Helena's harness made the process of crossing the gorge relatively straightforward. Alexi crossed first, while Dona stayed behind to help the Monsignor and the Bursar. With both Alphonse and Alexi to pull them across, they all stood on the far side in short order.

"What's next?" the Monsignor asked.

Dona pointed "There's a contraption around the bend ahead that lifts a platform to a place where we can get into my dormitory It's pretty rickety, but it got me up there and Helena and me back, along with everything we were carrying."

Brent raised an eyebrow. "The Scales of Ossary, I'll wager."

"You already knew about it?"

Brent felt his pockets. "There's a reference—"

The Monsignor held out the journal. "Looking for this?"

"Yes, thank you." Brent flipped through its pages. "Ah, here it is."

Translating on the fly, Brent read a passage:

> *The Vismort held forth the Morgatuan, and the funerarium was suddenly revealed. At last, Mazaharian saw fit to share his designs: Once assured of the safety of his charges, he would return to this place and, by means of the Scales of Ossary, re-enter the fortress. On this, he was adamant over even the ardent pleas of the Mistress, whom he had ever been*

*loath to deny. And when she declared her intention to accompany him, he denied her yet a second time—for while his duty bound him to the fortress, hers now lay in securing the welfare of their child.*

Dona blinked. "You mean that Vismort and the Mistress had a child?"

The Bursar shook his head. "It's not the same Vismort. The name on the sarcophagus is different, and the journal recounts the fortress's final days—there wouldn't have been time to process anyone who died after this point."

"Does it say anything more about these so-called scales?" the Monsignor asked.

The Bursar scanned the next several pages. "I don't think so. It looks like the Vismort escorted them out and then returned alone—so that part wouldn't have gotten recorded."

"The mechanism's really not that complicated," Dona said. "We should be able to get by without directions. After all, I've already used it twice now."

As they rounded the bend, their lanterns lit up the monstrosity of chains and gears.

Alexi snorted. "Not that complicated, eh?"

"It looks complicated, but it really is just a scale. You have the platform there, which is opposed by the counterweight hanging somewhere up near the cave's ceiling. If the counterweight is heavier than the platform, the platform rises, but if the counterweight is lighter, the platform drops back down. The gears probably slow the process. And this lever here freezes everything in place."

Helena peered upward. "But what were they weighing?"

Alphonse gulped. "Corpses, probably. They had to get the dead down here somehow."

Helena shuddered. "Sorry I asked."

Dona inspected the lever. "I'd suggest only one of us go at a time to minimize the stress on the machine. Since Helena and I came down together, it ought to be able to hold any one of us without breaking."

The Monsignor paused to eye Brent. "What are you doing?"

"Just cleaning up around the platform."

"Are those books?"

When Brent didn't answer, the Monsignor inspected them himself. "This is written in Tep'Chuan—as is this one."

"I think you'll find most of them are," Brent said.

"These appear to be scriptural."

"Some are, but they address other subjects as well."

The Monsignor flipped from one title to the next. "This is incredible. It's a treasure trove of early Chervillian texts. We must get them back to the Holy City for study."

Brent looked up from his gathering. "You will do no such thing."

"Well, we can't just leave them here. Many have already suffered irreparable damage."

Brent crossed his arms. "The books stay here."

The Monsignor's eyes flashed. "I don't see how that is your decision to make."

"I didn't make it, you did—when you agreed to keep this place secret in return for my aid. Or hadn't you considered that your scholars might want to know where these books came from? Which reminds me—it's time you made good on the rest of your bargain. The Morgatuan, if you please."

"We could say we found them in a different cave."

"And start a rush to find additional caves stuffed with ancient treasures? I think not. Please don't make me ask for it again."

Dona put her hand on the Monsignor's arm. "We can't take them right now anyway. The Inquisition is still up there."

The Monsignor sighed and handed Brent the scepter. "Very well—a deal is a deal. I appreciate your upholding your end."

Brent's hands trembled as he took it. "Thank you." Ostensibly Brent said it to the Monsignor, but his eyes were on Dona.

Helena rubbed her shoulders. "Can we go? It's really cold down here."

"All right," Dona said. "I'll go first. Helena, you come next, followed by the Monsignor."

"How does the next person get the platform back?" Brent asked. "If it works like a balance, won't you have to load the platform with something up there?"

"Oh, I think you're right," Dona said. "Last time I just brought Helena with me, but it can't have been convenient for the Chervillians to load it every time they wanted to use it. Let's have a look."

They studied the scales for several minutes before Alphonse pointed out a gear with a handle. "What about this?"

"I don't know. Try it."

"It won't budge."

"Oh—just a second." She released the safety lever. Immediately Alphonse's gear spun, and the platform rose.

Seizing the handle, he stopped the platform's ascent, and with concerted cranking, reversed its direction until the platform sank onto its customary spot on the cave floor. The instant it touched, Dona engaged the safety again.

"There's your answer. We'll load the counterweight with just enough rocks to lift one person, and then as each person gets off the platform, Alphonse will ratchet it back down, engage the safety, and start the process over again. "

"Who releases the lever for Alphonse?"

"Hmm, good question. Helena, do you have any more of that twine?"

"Just a second," She rummaged through her bags. "Here's some."

Dona looped the twine and slipped it over the lever. "Let's see if this works." Stepping on the platform, she gave the twine a stiff tug, releasing the lever.

Nothing happened.

"Now what?" As she stepped off it to investigate, the platform shot upward.

"Oh, that's right. We need to refill the counterweight."

Once they dealt with the counterweight and waited for Alphonse to ratchet the platform down again, Dona was ready to test it for real. A quick tug on the twine, and up she went. At last, the platform came gently to rest beneath the garderobe. She remained there only long enough to make sure the platform was descending once more, and then she was off down the hallway, wracking her brain for a solution to her next problem. She obviously had to involve Miss Maxtine, but she hadn't the foggiest notion what she could possibly say that would convince her to harbor four fugitive men in her all-female dormitory.

. . . . .

Long lines of Inquisitors and their associated horses stretched down the Exidgeon ramp. First, they waited near the entrance to be searched by their appointed brethren for anything that could be deemed heretical, and then they waited again near the bottom of the ramp to be searched by representatives of the Crown for evidence of looting. Cartier and Verone threaded their way slowly among them, conversing amidst the chaos.

"Thank you again for seeing me," Verone said. "From the look of it, evacuations are exhausting."

"You have no idea," Cartier said. "For every decision I make, at least five more demand my immediate attention. Be that as it may, I'd be foolish to turn away my best advisor."

"You are too kind. I trust the Ordinal is pleased with your progress?"

"I suspect very little pleases His Ordinence at the moment. Last I heard, the Sisters had him quarantined in the infirmary as an exotic-disease risk."

"They can keep an Ordinal against his will?"

"Their rules on quarantine are quite explicit, although I confess I might have provided a little encouragement. Of course, I had only the best interests of the University at heart."

"Oh, of course. Can they keep him indefinitely?"

"Alas, all good things must come to an end. With any luck, though, we'll be long evacuated by then."

"Where will you house all these Inquisitors, if not at the University?"

"Oh, most of them will head back to the Holy City. I'll keep only a small contingent, most of whom I'll house at the vicarage. All these Inquisitors only served to antagonize the Crown and distract me from the investigation."

"So, I take it you haven't yet captured the heretics responsible for the attacks?"

"Not yet, but I'm pursuing some significant leads."

"Well if anyone can get to the bottom of these crimes, it's you. I certainly hope the Church appreciates your value."

"Just doing my part."

"Listen. I know you're dreadfully overbooked, but I wonder if you'd be interested in taking on just one more little task?"

"I'd be happy to help, provided I can fit it in."

"Well, I was chatting with Princess Celeste over at the Artist's Colony yesterday. She expressed an interest in reconciling with the Church, but she wasn't sure how best to go about it. Of course, I immediately suggested you as the perfect candidate to mediate the discussions, since you are familiar with both the situation and the relevant Church doctrines."

"If she's serious, I'd be a fool not to. Bringing the Princess and the Colony back into the fold would be a noteworthy achievement."

"I thought the opportunity might appeal to you."

Cartier paused. "Wait a minute. You encouraged her to reconcile, didn't you?"

"I suppose it's possible I pointed out it might be a good idea."

"Once again, I am in your debt. If ever there's something I can do in return—"

From the crowd, a bedraggled man in a filthy hooded cloak lurched directly toward Cartier. His boots held enough moisture that the leather spit bubbles where they flexed. His white-rimmed eyes bulged with either desperation or madness.

"I have to warn you."

Cartier had barely enough warning to sidestep. The man stumbled and sprawled in the dirt. Several Inquisitors threw themselves on top of him.

"Did he touch you?" Cartier asked.

"Don't worry about me," Verone said.

The Inquisitors dragged the man to his feet. Once again, he tried to speak. "Father, you must listen—"

"Silence," Cartier bellowed.

When the man ignored Cartier's command, an Inquisitor struck him across the face. "What do you want done with him, Father?"

"Poor soul," Cartier said. "He's probably just looking for his next drink. Give him a few coins and help him get a good start back to Trifienne. Let's hope our charity inspires him to greater wisdom in the future. In the meantime, please see to it that he meditates on his good luck—silently."

"As you wish, Father." Two Inquisitors dragged the whimpering man down the ramp.

Cartier shuddered and mopped his forehead. "My apologies."

"None necessary," Verone said. "Are you all right?"

"Just extremely busy is all. Please convey my regards to the Princess, and assure her I would be delighted to assist in her reconciliation."

"It will by my pleasure."

"Now, if you would be so kind as to excuse me, I have an Inquisition to run."

Verone nodded and waved her goodbyes, uncertain whether she fully understood what she had just witnessed. The more she thought about it though, the more certain she was that she wanted to.

. . . . .

Several attendants helped Thurman's uncle ascend the Primal Throne, and Thurman was relieved to see Theratigan was not among them. Although it was still early, the throne room hummed. No formal announcement had been made, but the palace was rife with the rumor that the missing Ordinal had been found at last. Despite the throngs vying for the Primal's attention, the secretary announced Thurman's name first. He approached the throne, grateful that familial bonds still seemed to carry at least some weight in his uncle's increasingly 'enlightened' administration. As he bowed, to his dismay, an assistant thrust a jar beneath his chin.

"Spit please," the functionary intoned.

"Sorry, my boy," the Primal said. "Theratigan's orders. Everyone is to be tested."

Thurman grimaced, but complied. He was determined to prevent Theratigan's mischief from distracting him again. "Your Primacy, I hereby request an audience *in camera*. My situation involves a private family matter."

"Well, in that case, I hereby grant your request. We can retire to the rectory at ten. By then, I will have either exhausted today's petitions, or they will have exhausted me."

Thurman bowed in acquiescence, but he was less than pleased. His request for privacy, though unquestionably necessary, had just landed him at the end of the line. For a while, he loitered nearby, fearful that if he left, he might miss an announcement on Laitrech's whereabouts. When no such announcement was forthcoming, he ducked out of the throne room and into the square. Once outside, he took a deep breath and exhaled slowly, hoping to release some of his pent-up anxiety. The air was fresh from the evening storms, and the sun was warm on his face. He closed his eyes and imagined, for a moment, lounging at the family villa, and that the past week had all been a bad dream. When he opened his eyes again, the square stretched out before him, bustling with vendors hawking their wares to well-dressed passersby too preoccupied with their own importance to acknowledge their existence. He wandered among the vendors until, tired of deflecting their insistent offers, he took a seat on a shoeshine bench. The bench's aged but spry proprietor immediately set about buffing his boots.

Thurman sat up in in surprise. "What are you doing?"

"Keeping up appearances," the cobbler said. "You would do well to do the same."

Thurman sighed and leaned back again. "I guess I should be thankful—at least you're not still decked out in that Ordinal outfit. All right then, how's business?"

"Just peachy, as a matter of fact. I've already had twelve customers this morning, and at least seven of them entered the palace complex. At this rate, we might even earn enough to buy another Relic—in ten years or so."

"Very funny."

"Any word on our friend Laitrech?"

"Nothing official yet, but all the gossip says he was found sometime last night. Apparently Theratigan ordered him sequestered until he had a chance to be tested and questioned."

"And your uncle allowed that?"

"He's not a fool. Even if Darron still trusts Laitrech implicitly, he can't argue with the wisdom of making sure whomever they found isn't just another Laitrech impersonator."

"And did you get your audience?"

"Not yet. He agreed to meet with me in the rectory at ten."

"Excellent. I suspected he'd postpone an *in camera* petition. And now we have our time certain."

"I would rather have gotten this over with as soon as possible. Let's just pray he gets to my petition before Theratigan shows up again,"

"Worry not. Thanks to your late-night handiwork, I suspect Theratigan will be the least of our worries."

"It's working then?"

The cobbler held up a slender amber-tipped wand. "Like a charm. The miraculous properties of a Golden-Shine shoeshine are unlikely to be lost on our friendly neighborhood demon hunter."

Thurman snatched his feet away. "You didn't, did you?"

"That would have defeated the purpose, now, wouldn't it? I'm afraid your shoes will have to make do with something a bit more conventional. Now if you don't mind, I have paying customers to attract."

. . . . .

It took several minutes, but Miss Maxtine eventually recovered from the shock of seeing grown men emerge from her dormitory's garderobe. It took several more to recover from the shock of recognizing one of them as the well-respected Bursar of her University. The shock of learning that one of them was brother to the Primal was, however, almost more than she could bear. Afraid she might faint, Dona guided her to a chair, while Helena fanned her with a swatch of starched cotton from her sewing kit.

Taking the seat next to her, the Monsignor tried gently to engage her in conversation, first by thanking her for her assistance, and then by asking if she might have a spare room to house them for a few hours' rest. She managed a nod, but paled further as she wondered which of her rooms could possibly be suitable for the Primal's brother. To minimize contact with other residents, Dona suggested a room in the unoccupied south wing, which was being held in reserve for anticipated increases in female enrollment.

Miss Maxtine's objections were immediate. "But they don't even have bedding."

Helena raised her hand. "I'll take care of that."

"At this point, even a straw pallet would seem a luxury," the Monsignor said, "and privacy would be most welcome."

"Of course, Your Grace," Miss Maxtine stammered, "whatever Your Grace prefers."

The Monsignor stood. "It's settled then. Once Alphonse arrives, we'll move to the south wing. Miss Dunkirk, if we could prevail upon you to make good on your kind offer to locate some bedding, we would be eternally grateful."

Helena nodded. "My pleasure, Monsignor. I'll see what I can find."

As Helena strode off, Brent took her place. "What are you planning to use to sink the platform?"

The Monsignor's brow furrowed. "I'm sorry, what are you talking about?"

"Well surely you don't plan to leave it docked under the garderobe waiting for a misguided student to use it to strand herself in the caves below."

The Monsignor sighed wearily. "No, I suppose not. Perhaps Miss Maxtine could locate some firewood to donate to the cause?"

Miss Maxtine dipped in an awkward curtsey. "If it pleases Your Grace, I'll see to it immediately."

The Monsignor rewarded her with a warm smile. "You are very kind. Once again, my apologies for the inconvenience."

"It's an honor to serve Your Grace. I'll be back shortly."

As she disappeared down the hallway, Alexi emerged from the garderobe. "I can't believe we're finally out of there. Is the campus safe yet, or is there still rioting?"

"I think it best we rest here for a few hours," the Monsignor said. "I'm having trouble keeping my eyes open, and that will give us time to assess the campus situation."

Alexi raised an eyebrow. "Strange men sleeping in Dona's dormitory? Isn't that against the rules?"

"Miss Maxtine already gave her consent," Dona said. "Apparently 'His Grace' transcends the usual rules."

The Monsignor winked. "Poor thing seemed so bebothered, I didn't have the heart to correct her."

"I think I would sleep a whole lot better in my own bed," Alexi said. "If it's all the same to you, once Alphonse gets back up here, we'll have a look outside, and if it's clear, we'll head for home."

The Monsignor frowned. "I'm afraid it's not all the same to me."

"What do you mean?"

"We still have the matter of your heresy to resolve. I'm going to have to ask you to accompany me to the Holy City."

Dona's jaw dropped. "Are you serious?"

"I'm afraid I am. Phrendonic Heresy is a very grave offense."

"Need I remind you he used that heresy to save your life down there? In fact, if I remember correctly, you even gave him permission."

"I am well aware. Those heresies committed with dispensation will not count against him, but I obviously wasn't there to grant dispensation when he first learned them."

Dona's eyes narrowed. "I thought you told us in Professor Reston's class that nowadays all a heretic had to do was renounce the heresy and maybe do some sort of penance. Are you saying that wasn't true?"

"In simple cases, that would be true, but this case is far from simple. Phrendonic Heretics are clearly responsible for setting fire to two University buildings, and one of those was likely intended as a direct attack on the Church itself."

"And you think Alexi is your arsonist?"

"I don't, but he had to learn the heresy from someone, and that person could be. Or it could be the person who taught that person. We need to catch the arsonist as quickly as possible before more buildings are set ablaze, and this is the best lead we've had so far."

"Then wouldn't it make more sense to just interrogate him here, where you can put the information to immediate use?"

"It would—but I can't afford to stay here as long as Ordinal Isrulian is in charge."

"Which brings up another point," Dona said. "With precious gems like your Ordinal Isrulian running things, what makes you think Alexi will be treated fairly?"

"I have already given my word that I would do everything in my power to see that he is."

"And if I understand the situation correctly, that fact alone would be enough for Isrulian to make a special example of him."

"What would you have me do?"

Alphonse finally stepped from the garderobe. "I have a suggestion. It seems to me the Monsignor is right to worry about catching the arsonist, but at the same time, Dona's fears that Alexi may not get a fair shake are also valid. Since everyone agrees a penance is necessary, why not just tailor it to address both concerns?"

"Tailor the penance?" the Monsignor said. "I'm not sure how that gets us any closer to finding the arsonist."

"If you really think Alexi's contacts could lead you to the arsonist, wouldn't it be more efficient if he used them? He is, after all, a little less obvious."

Dona nodded. "And unlike you, he doesn't have pressing reasons to leave the University."

"Out of the question," the Monsignor said. "Investigating Phrendonic Heresies is a dangerous proposition."

The Bursar snorted. "Unlike his prospects if the Ordinal catches wind of him, you mean?"

"It's not like he's defenseless," Alphonse said. "You saw how he dealt with that Vismort fellow."

The Monsignor shook his head. "That's precisely the sort of thing that got him into trouble in the first place. He can't go about doing such things indiscriminately."

Dona raised an eyebrow. "So he was wrong to try to save you?"

"It's never wrong to try to save a life, but the use of Phrendonic Heresy to do so can be condoned only under the most extreme circumstances."

"Such as when trying to catch a dangerous arsonist?" Alexi asked.

"You too?" the Monsignor said. "You aren't actually serious about this, are you?"

"Given the choice, I would absolutely stay and defend my University."

"Do you have any idea what you'd be up against? You've seen perhaps only a fraction of what this person is capable of. Even assuming you could bring your unique defenses to bear, the odds of you succeeding alone would be slim at best."

Dona took his hand. "He wouldn't be alone."

Alphonse stepped forward. "He can rely on my blade as well."

The Monsignor eyed Alexi appraisingly. "You would really prefer this?"

"I would."

The Monsignor sighed. "Something tells me I'm going to regret this. Very well, your penance shall be to seek sufficient evidence to identify the Phrendonic Heretic responsible for causing the fires that burned the two University buildings."

Alexi bowed his head. "Thank you, Monsignor."

Dona beamed. "I knew we could trust you."

The Monsignor's tone grew stern. "Let me be clear. Under no circumstances are you to confront any suspects directly. You are to search for evidence only. Do you understand?"

The three nodded solemnly.

"And if we find evidence, what do we do with it?" Alexi asked.

The Monsignor thought a moment. "Take it to Professor Hepple-white. Ask him to see that I get it as soon as possible. And Alexi?"

"Yes?"

"I truly appreciate the courage it took to save my life. Thank you."

. . . . .

"I'm sorry, ma'am," the guard said gently, "but we have strict or-ders not to let anyone in to see the Primal without Ordinal Laitrech's permission."

The lady placed her gnarled hands firmly on her hips. "Well, then, I suppose His Ordinence expects the Primal linens to be changing themselves—or will he be doing it himself today?"

The guard laughed nervously. "Just following orders, ma'am."

"You think this is a laughing matter, do you? Do you have any idea how the bed linens of an invalid get after a few days of neglect?"

The guard looked across to his buddy and shrugged. "No ma'am."

"Well, unless you want to find out, I suggest you find His Ordi-nence and get his permission straight away. I am not dragging this cart all the way up here again."

"Haven't you heard? His Ordinence is missing."

"Missing? Ach, isn't that just like an Ordinal? I suppose he just up and left, giving nary a thought to the state of His Primacy's linens. Perhaps under the circumstances you might consider asking His Pri-macy himself whether he would care to skip today's linen change, on the off chance he hasn't managed to soil himself again."

The guard's eyes widened. "The Primal soils himself?"

"Have you never seen an invalid before? It's not every day, of course, but lately it's been two days out of every three. I should think there's a good chance he might welcome a change before His Ordi-nence deigns to put in another appearance."

"We can't ask him," the second guard said. "He's out taking peti-tions."

"He's feeling a mite better then? Well that's good news at least. But if the Primal is out, whom exactly are you protecting?"

"We're just following orders, ma'am."

"So I gathered. After all, someone has to protect the Primal's linens from the threat of a much-needed changing. Do you two always get picked for the really important missions?"

The guard reddened. "I'll have you know we have both earned multiple commendations during our tours of duty."

"And this is how they reward you? Well, here you go." She dragged the cart toward the guard. Soapy water splashed from a wheeled bucket fastened behind.

"What are you doing?"

"Handing over the cart. If you aren't going to let me do my job, I guess it falls to you. Now, if the linens are soiled, you'll want to sprinkle them with bicarbonate before rolling them up and tossing them in the bin. Try not to get any on you, or the smell will follow you the rest of the day. And if you find any patches of vomit, there's a sponge in the bucket. If it's dried on, be sure to scrub the area thoroughly—His Ordinence doesn't appreciate a sloppy cleanup."

"Vomit?"

"You really do have a lot to learn about tending the sick, don't you? Well, no time like the present. Who knows? If you manage to make the bed with military precision, maybe it could even earn you another one of those fancy commendations. You'll be the envy of the Inquisition."

A snicker escaped the guard's companion.

"What's so funny?"

His buddy snorted as he struggled to maintain composure.

"I'm glad you find this all so amusing. You'll need a good sense of humor while you're scrubbing down the place."

"Don't look at me. You're the one who told her she couldn't go in."

"Well, I'm not doing it."

"Oh, don't you worry," the old woman said. "I'm sure his Ordinence wouldn't think any less of his award-winning heroes just because they happened to be a little too squeamish to see to the Primal's comfort. After all, what's one more night in soiled linens?"

The old woman began pulling the cart away.

"Hey, where are you going?"

"Well, if I can't do it, and you two won't, there's no point in staying."

"Say we were to let you in. How long would it take?"

"Depends. If there's not too much vomit, maybe half an hour."

"We can't let her in anyway," the second guard said. "The door's locked."

She held up a stout ring of keys. "Not to worry, boys. I'm staff."

After a long pause, the first guard shrugged and stood aside. "All right—you have fifteen minutes."

The old woman turned the key in the lock "Typical. Too good to do the work, but not too good to tell someone else how to do it."

She was still muttering as the rectory door closed behind her.

· · · · ·

Thurman attended his uncle on his way back to his chambers. "Have they made any progress finding Laitrech? Everyone I talked to seemed to think he may have been found. They were all expecting some sort of announcement."

The Primal frowned. "No one has any patience anymore—or discretion, for that matter. As it happens, we think we have found him, but an announcement would be premature until Theratigan confirms the good news."

"You mean he won't just have him spit in a jar and send him on his way?"

Darron shot Thurman a sidelong look. "It's not as pointless as you seem to think. In any event, Theratigan is eager to know the details surrounding Laitrech's abduction to get some idea what we are up against. I am a little concerned, though. I'll be honest—even I believed the rumors that I'd be making that announcement this morning. I wonder what's keeping him?"

As they approached the rectory door, the guards parted and stood to either side at rigid attention.

The Primal fussed with the lock. "This will take some getting used to. Makes me feel a little like a prisoner in my own home."

"Guards are probably a good idea, at least until Theratigan sorts things out."

"As much as I hate to admit it, I suppose they are. Now come inside and tell me a little more about this family problem of yours. Does it have anything to do with your father?"

Thurman pushed the door gently closed behind him.

"Are you sure you're up to this?"

"Why don't we have a seat out in the garden? Nothing like a little fresh air to inspire a second wind."

"You must have slept out there, then. I haven't seen you this energetic in a long time."

"I am feeling better today. Laitrech's disappearance has given me something to focus on—something concrete I can achieve in the time left to me."

"You're sure that's all it is?"

"What else could it be? For what ails me, there is no cure."

Thurman shrugged. "Oh, I don't know—a miracle maybe?"

"Sarcasm isn't your strong suit."

"All right, how about a misdiagnosis then?"

The Primal shook his head. "There's no mistake. I've had Laitrech check it several times now. The result is always the same."

"And what if he's wrong?"

"He's very good at what he does. I have no reason to doubt him."

"It's cold out here," Thurman said. "Would you like a blanket?"

"That would be most kind of you. There should be one in the armoire near the desk."

"I'll be right back."

A moment later, he stood before the armoire. Its door swung effortlessly open to reveal a collection of blankets, walking sticks and cloaks. On its floor sat a wheeled bucket of water, still sporting a robust layer of foam. Thurman rolled up his sleeve and plunged his hand into the water. From its soapy depths, he retrieved a small box. Within lay a signet ring inscribed with the letters RS, which he slipped into his pocket. He dipped his hand into the bucket again, and it emerged clutching an odd-looking wand with a handle at each end. Inscribed along its side were the words Vis-à-vis.

Darron's voice drifted in. "Did you find them? They should be on the top shelf."

Thurman secreted the wand beneath his vestments. "Here they are. I'll be right there."

. . . . .

"And what was I supposed to say?" the second guard said. "'Beggin' your pardon, Your Primacy, but I just thought you should know the cleaning lady was by to collect your soiled linens?' I'm sure that's just the sort of thing he'd want his visitor to hear."

The first guard snorted. "You wouldn't have had to mention the soiled linens. You could just have said 'the cleaning lady was here while you were out.'"

"If you thought it was so important, why didn't you say something?"

"Because I wasn't the one having all the misgivings."

The rectory door opened, causing both guards to spring to attention.

The Primal stepped out, closed the door, and pulled out a ring of keys. He was dressed in his traveling cloak and carried a small satchel. Once the door was locked, he addressed the guards. "There's been a change of plans. Can I get a hand?"

"Of course, Your Primacy," the first guard said. "How can we help?"

"I need an escort to my carriage. I've decided it would be safest to go into hiding until the current situation is resolved."

Theratigan's distinctive voice reverberated down the corridor. "Your Primacy, the Palace has been infiltrated. Your safety is in doubt."

The Primal's keys clanged to the floor. He scooped them back up and turned to face the demon hunter and the two guards who accompanied him. "Infiltrated? What do you mean?"

"This morning I came across a suspect in the palace bearing the taint of Phrendonic Heresy. Of course, I had him taken into custody immediately."

"Was it our demon?"

Theratigan stopped abruptly and fussed with his monocle, switching it from one eye to the other, and then back. "Your Primacy," he said. "Listen to me carefully. You must order your guards to leave you at once."

"Theratigan, what's gotten into you? First you tell me the palace has been infiltrated, and then you want me to give up what little protection I have?"

"I know it sounds strange, but you must trust me. Order the guards away."

"I'll do nothing of the sort. Under the circumstances, I am better off not trusting anyone, particularly someone who admits recent contact with Phrendonic Heresy. If this demon could get to Laitrech in the Chapel, surely he could have gotten to you."

Theratigan's eyes widened, and he backed slowly away. "I see I was mistaken. I had suspected one of your guards might be an imposter, but were that true, he would surely have acted by now. If you'll excuse me, I'll redouble my efforts to track down this demon."

"I'm sorry, Theratigan, but I can't afford to trust anyone who is behaving strangely. Guards, take him."

The guards accompanying Theratigan each seized an arm.

"He is to be held in the interrogation chamber until further notice. And make sure you strip him of all his trinkets. There's no telling what horrors a demon could wreak with those."

Theratigan's eyes smoldered. "When I am cleared, rest assured I shall find this demon, and when I do, I shall see to it he is in no condition to ever trouble the Church again."

"And when you are cleared, we shall welcome your efforts—but not until."

The Primal watched as Theratigan's guards dragged him away. Then, his own guards escorted him from the Palace to the carriage house, where the Primal carriage awaited, ready, as ever, to leave at a moment's notice. He waved away the usual attendants and whispered into the ear of the driver, who nodded and climbed on board.

Once seated within, the Primal smiled and waved from the window until the carriage rounded a corner. At that point the Primal pulled the shades over the windows and opened his satchel, which was filled with street clothes. When he'd finished changing, he slid open a tiny window near the front.

"We are almost to the arena, Your Primacy," the driver said.

"Excellent. You understand that I am going into hiding?"

"If you say so, Your Primacy."

"When we get to the arena, slow the carriage to a crawl. The instant my feet touch the cobbles, resume your trip as though I never left. Do you understand?"

"Yes, Your Primacy. And my destination?"

"Caprian. Don't talk to a soul until you get there."

But when the carriage slowed, and its door slipped open, it was Thurman's feet that hit the cobbles.

. . . . .

Back at the rectory, an elderly cleaning lady whistled quietly as she let herself in, dragging her linen cart behind her. A few minutes later she emerged, her cart now plainly overloaded. But this curious fact seemed not to trouble her, and no one else was there to notice.

# CHAPTER 18

# A LITTLE FRIENDLY ADVICE

Michlos threw his coat over his arm as he strode through his mother's parlor. His jaw was set, and in his eyes, a storm simmered.

Arerio intercepted him. "I can take that, Master Michlos. Thank you for coming—I know you must be busy."

"Indeed I am, but don't let her use that against you. Whatever she says, you did the right thing by letting me know. Where is she?"

"In the solarium. I'll announce you."

"That won't be necessary."

Arerio bowed. "As you wish."

Michlos found her seated at a small table, a jeweler's loupe in one eye, examining intently something that glittered in the palm of her hand. She glanced briefly in his direction and then went back to her examination. "I don't know what's gotten into Arerio lately, but I apologize if his indiscretion pulled you away from something important. I'll have a word with him."

"Don't you dare take this out on him—not when your incredible lapse in judgment left him little choice."

Marguerite fixed him with an appraising look. "Conviction is rarely an excuse for a lack of civility. Perhaps when you calm down, we can discuss exactly what you mean by my 'incredible lapse of judgment.'"

Michlos took a deep breath and slowly exhaled. "You don't have that kind of time."

"Very well then, why don't you just go ahead and tell me what misimpression you are laboring under that could be responsible for such a juvenile display."

"Were you, or were you not, targeted for elimination by a Santine?"

"I was, but I've already dealt with that situation."

"By releasing him?"

"Of course. What did you expect me to do? Bury him in the basement?"

"I expected you to consult with me."

"Need I remind you that I am perfectly capable of making my own decisions. I've been doing it since before you were born."

"Before I was born, your daughter wasn't married to the Crown Prince."

"Oh, not this again. I am well aware of my relationship to my son-in-law."

"Are you? Do you have any idea what effect an accusation of heresy against you would do to him?"

"Is that what this is all about? Well, you needn't worry. Once Vane's associates report his own heresies to Father Cartier, he'll be in no position to accuse me of anything."

"He won't have to."

She eyed him more closely. "All right, out with it. What fresh torment beckons?"

"This morning three men were killed at St. Sophia's. One of them was the caretaker."

"I'm very sorry to hear that, but what does that have to do with Vane?"

"Another of them was dressed in a militia uniform. A donkey cart was found abandoned nearby."

Marguerite's eyes narrowed. "How did they die?"

"A witness reported multiple flashes of light followed by a fire that consumed most of the vicarage. All three men burned to death, but not beyond recognition. If, as Arerio reports, Father Cartier sent them to intercept you, he will undoubtedly be able to identify them. What conclusion do you suppose he's going to jump to?"

Marguerite paled. "We'll have to misdirect him. There must be some way."

"I am open to suggestions."

"Don't look at me like that. I couldn't have known he was a murderer."

"You pushed him to the edge. Desperate men do desperate things."

"There was a third man with them. Was there any sign of him?"

Michlos shook his head.

"Then there's a chance he could still be alive. If he is, we have to get to him before Vane does."

"To what end? You no longer have three witnesses to the Santine's heresy. At best, it's now his word against Vane's."

"To save his life—if he hasn't already gotten to Cartier, he's a marked man."

"A laudable goal, but your time would be better spent attending to your own circumstances. The lives of quite a few innocent people are riding on it."

Marguerite's eyes flashed. "I was. If Vane gets to him before we do, how do you suppose he'll stage the murder scene?"

"I hadn't even considered that. We have no choice. Vane must be stopped."

"Ideas?"

"It won't be easy. I don't even know what he looks like."

"I can give you a detailed description."

"Even if I do manage to find him," Michlos said, "what then? He's a Santine. If he activates his Amulet, there'll be precious little I can do against him."

Marguerite held out her hand, which still held the glittering object she'd been examining. "This Amulet you speak of. By any chance, might it take the form of a ring?"

Michlos gave a low whistle. "You took his Amulet?"

Marguerite shrugged. "Until he learns to play well with others, it seemed like a good idea to take away his toys. I'm not sure this is really it, though. I can't seem to get it to work."

Michlos nodded. "They're designed that way. They work solely for the intended user. They can't risk having them fall into the wrong hands."

Marguerite eyed the ring with renewed interest. "How do they do that?"

"You'd have to ask Magister Treust for the full explanation, but as I understand it, it makes use of a split attunement. The portion of the

Amulet that touches the flesh is Patterned with a decay Attunement, while another portion, usually the part that functions as a switch, is blocked. A third talis spans the two parts and is only detectable when the parts match and the switch is in the correct orientation. The rest of the spells are contingent on the presence of the third spell for function."

Marguerite raised an eyebrow. "So theoretically, it could be reset by temporarily suppressing the block and reattuning the entire Amulet to someone else?"

"I know what you're thinking, and I suggest you don't risk it. Each Amulet is hand-crafted specifically for the Santine to whom it is awarded. A general knowledge of the mechanism isn't a substitute for knowledge of the actual schematics. For all we know there could be some sort of defense mechanism built in to prevent just that sort of tampering."

"In any event, Vane won't have its defenses at his disposal. Assuming we can find him, he should be no match for you."

"That depends. I presume his defenses were fully engaged when he met you on the road. How did you manage to circumvent them, and could he do the same to me?"

Marguerite snorted. "All the hedges in the world won't stop a good old-fashioned Attunement-Extension."

"You mean he actually let you touch him?"

"Don't be so hard on the poor man. I doubt he's had much practice bullying people with my resources."

"Still, it highlights a serious flaw in the defenses. I'll have to give that some thought. All right, I'll see what I can do about neutralizing Vane. I'll need that description as soon as possible, as well as descriptions of the men who were with him."

"I'll prepare them immediately."

"And then, I think you should consider leaving town for a while."

"Leave town? Whatever for?"

"I can think of two compelling reasons. You hold the Amulet of one of them in your hand. The other is probably on his way back from Exidgeon to the blackened remains of his vicarage. Once he finds out what happened there, I expect the situation will escalate."

Marguerite crossed her arms. "I will not be driven from my home by the clumsy maneuverings of a renegade Santine and the mistaken assumptions of some bumpkin priest."

Michlos could tell from the set of her jaw that it was pointless to argue. "Very well. If you insist on being a sitting duck, at least promise you'll be more careful. I shudder to think what might have happened if Vane had been just a little less sloppy."

"He caught me with my guard down. That won't happen again. Remember, I'm not without defenses of my own."

"And, if anything out of the ordinary happens—and I mean any-thing—promise you'll send for me immediately."

"I don't see what—"

Michlos held a finger to her lips. "Promise."

"Oh, very well. I promise."

Michlos fell silent. He couldn't recall ever having successfully extracted a concession from his mother before, and it felt surreal. Had the circumstances been less dire, he might have paused to ponder the implications, perhaps even to toast the occasion, but this was no time for self-indulgent reflection.

.  .  .  .  .

Verone held out her hand to the ragged excuse of a man lying by the side of the road. He flinched and pulled back as though he feared she might strike him.

After a few moments, she withdrew her hand. "Poor dear. I expect the Inquisitors were none too gentle."

He just stared.

"Father Cartier sends his apologies for your harsh treatment. He said you'd understand that he couldn't take the risk that what you had to say would be appropriate for all ears."

The man dragged his arm across the blood seeping from his lip.

"Father Cartier has asked me to retrieve your message under more discreet circumstances. That's why he had the Inquisitors bring you here."

"Who are you?"

"My friends call me Verone. I'm a long-time confidante of Father Cartier's. And you are?"

"Aaron. How do I know you are who you say you are?"

Verone shrugged. "Surely you saw him consulting with me this morning. That's why he asked me to come—he knew you'd seen us together. Now, hold still." She drew out a kerchief and dabbed his lip. "There, not so bad—it should heal without a scar. Any broken bones?"

Aaron shook his head.

She gently patted his forearm. "You poor man—it must still have been a very trying experience. Do you feel up to giving a report?"

He nodded at last.

She mustered her warmest smile. "Excellent. What would you like me to tell the good Father?"

"Vane's a heretic. I saw it with my own eyes."

"Vane?"

"The Father will know."

"Yes, of course. I'm sure you're aware that heresy, particularly in our current situation, is a very serious charge. Can you tell me what makes you think he's a heretic?"

"I saw him create light without fire. He also made his shackles fall to pieces. Only a heretic could do that, right?"

"Shackles?" Verone asked. "What was he doing in shackles?"

"We were captured. The mission failed. I know we weren't supposed to have any further contact, but I had to warn Father Cartier. If the man who led the mission was a heretic, there might be others close to him as well. His life could be in danger."

"You did the right thing. Where was the last place you saw this heretic? We'll need to hunt him down as quickly as possible."

"In the big old estate up by the cliffs overlooking the river."

"You don't mean the Serrola Estate?"

"Yes, ma'am."

"You were captured and held there?"

He nodded.

"How did you escape?"

"She seemed interested only in Vane. She said he was duping us. At first, I thought she was lying—that she had staged it all to make it look like Vane was the heretic instead of her, but now I'm not so sure. If she was guilty, would she have released us all like that?"

"By 'she' do you mean Marguerite Serrola?"

"Yes, ma'am."

"Your mission was to capture Marguerite Serrola for the Inquisition?"

"So, Father Cartier did tell you?"

"We have been friends for a long time. So, the mission went wrong, and you were all captured. What happened to Vane?"

"I'm not sure. The Serrola woman seemed to think he would escape shortly."

"And the others?"

"We agreed that Vane's heresies were so important that Father Cartier needed to know right away. Since we didn't know if he was still at the college or back in town, we split up. The others went to St. Sophia's to see if he was there."

"You did the right thing."

"What am I to do now?"

"You're here from the Holy City?"

He nodded.

Verone considered for a moment. "Father Cartier is sending most of the Inquisitors back there today. I suggest you go with them. So long as no one else knows of your mission, you should be able to resume your previous duties as though nothing happened. I'll be sure Father Cartier gets your message, and I'll put in a good word for your bravery. Perhaps there will even be a reward in it for you."

For the first time since she'd seen him, he seemed genuinely relieved. "Bless you."

Verone flashed a cryptic smile. "Believe me—the pleasure was all mine."

．．．．．

Steaming puddles dotted the racetrack, remnants of the previous evening's storm, but plans to cancel the races due to the treacherous conditions were instantly scuttled upon Ordinal Lavicius's arrival. Instead, trumpets sounded, and the horses surged forward, their colors streaming blurs behind them. Up in his box, Ordinal Lavicius leaned forward, intent on the progress of his thoroughbred. His guest, a sallow, sharp-featured man, followed suit, his eyes shifting from horse to man and back again.

"I'll make a convert of you yet, Prentiss," the Ordinal said. "There's nothing quite like the thrill of the race."

"Oh, it's not the race I object to—it's my odds of turning a profit. Although you may view it as somewhat less than thrilling, I'm quite content to limit my risk to bets that qualify as a sure thing."

"Then it's not a bet," Lavicius countered. "It's a contract."

"A difference merely of degree."

A collective gasp rippled through the crowd as a yellow-swathed equine in the center of the pack lost his footing in the mud and tumbled to the ground, throwing his rider. Two others, who were too close to avoid a collision, went down as well. One of the riders did not get up. Although all three horses regained their feet, the one in yellow was favoring a foreleg.

"Ooh, tough break," Prentiss said.

"On the contrary—I'm almost certain to place now."

"How callous of me to have missed that."

Lavicius didn't take his eyes from the race. "You can't expect to appreciate all the subtleties overnight."

An Inquisitor stepped up from the rear of the box and whispered into the Ordinal's ear. Initially, Lavicius seemed inclined to wave the man away, but his hand froze mid-wave. With his horse only seconds away from the finish line, Lavicius turned to the messenger, focusing with even more intensity than he had on the race.

"He's fled the city?"

The Inquisitor nodded.

"And did he say where he was going?"

"He said only 'into hiding.'"

A cheer went up from the crowd, signaling the race was over.

Prentice applauded politely. "You took second place."

"Not now, Prentiss. This is important."

Lavicius turned back to the Inquisitor. "Did he leave anyone in charge?"

"No one seems to know."

"And where is Ordinal Laitrech?"

"Still confined to the interrogation chamber."

Lavicius eyed the man askance. "The Primal didn't see to his release before he left? Are you sure?"

The Inquisitor nodded. "In fact, he had Mr. Theratigan confined there as well."

"Curiouser and curiouser. I'm not sure what he has up his sleeve, but I can't pass up an opportunity like this. I'm calling an emergency Convocation for this evening."

"Ordinal Isrulian and Ordinal Shelby are out of town," the Inquisitor pointed out.

Lavicius shrugged. "We still have enough for a binding vote. Prentiss, if I call it for nine o'clock, would that give your Accipitrines time to ascertain the Primal's whereabouts?"

"I could certainly put some skilled people to the task."

The Ordinal rubbed his hands together in anticipation "Excellent. The Primal is missing, Armand is out of town, and Laitrech is in custody. Prentiss, I think I see your point."

"What point is that?"

"The thrill of a sure thing can be very seductive indeed."

. . . . .

At his makeshift desk in Canasty Hall, Cartier sorted through the stack of papers that had accumulated over the last few days, throwing some into the trash and placing others in a briefcase.

Verone appeared in the doorway. "So, I take it the Inquisition is almost completely out of Exidgeon, then?"

Cartier started. "Sometimes I wonder why I even bother to post guards."

"Don't be too hard on them—I can be very persuasive when I set my mind to it."

"I have no doubt. We finally got the last of the Inquisitors through the line a couple of hours ago. I'm just cleaning up a few last odds and ends, and then I'll be leaving as well."

"I presume the heretic responsible for this mess is in custody then?"

Something like fear flashed in his eyes. "I have that situation well in hand."

"You're a terrible liar, you know. How long before they let Isrulian out?"

Cartier sighed. "I don't know. Soon, probably."

"And when they do, how do you think he'll react to this little evacuation of yours if you haven't brought anyone to justice?"

He shook his head. "I don't know what happened. The plan was perfect."

"Care to tell me about it?"

He shrugged. "I suppose it wouldn't hurt anything now."

"Hurt anything? Why ever would you think that telling me something could hurt you?"

"I wasn't sure how you'd react. Many rank blood before justice."

"What are you talking about? Have I ever been anything other than supportive?"

"Of course not."

"Then why the reticence?"

"I suppose after all you've done, you are entitled to know. Perhaps you should have a seat."

Verone settled in and folded her hands in her lap. "Very well. Now what's this all about?"

"There's no delicate way to put this. Our prime suspect is none other than your Aunt Marguerite."

Verone's jaw dropped. "Aunt Marguerite?" And then she laughed. "You almost had me there for a second. Who is it really?"

"This is no joke."

"Oh, be serious. She's just an odd old lady."

"I am deadly serious. You yourself saw her standing outside the window before Dexter Hall went up in flames."

"There were countless people milling about outside that window. Why are you focusing on her so particularly?"

"Because of this." He reached into the briefcase and drew out a floral wrap still faintly redolent of roses. "Look familiar? We found it at the scene of the Hathaway fire."

"It's a floral wrap. It could belong to anyone."

"It could, unless you take the label into account."

"Label? Let me see that." Verone practically snatched the garment from his hands and studied the label.

"You see? All the evidence leads directly to your Aunt's doorstep."

"This means nothing. She could just as easily have gotten lost and dropped the wrap by accident."

"Your loyalty to her is commendable, but I'm afraid the evidence is easily sufficient to bring her in for questioning."

"Little old ladies just don't do this sort of thing. Are you sure you aren't trying to find a scapegoat to mollify Isrulian?"

Cartier shook his head. "I know this is difficult, but consider what we know about your Aunt. Remember how you told me she became estranged from your father?"

"Yes, of course, but that can happen in any family. It's no crime."

"Isn't it possible that somewhere along the line your father found out his sister was dabbling in heresy? How do you think he would react to that?"

"I don't suppose he would take it with grace."

"You must admit—the possibility bears investigating."

"And have you asked her to come in to clear up this mess?"

"That, I'm afraid, is a most delicate matter under the circumstances."

"So, you haven't then?"

"I was concerned if she were guilty she would simply decline. And with the Crown backing her, I'm not sure we'd ever get to the truth. Since our current position with the Crown is tenuous at best, I didn't want to risk agitating him further."

"So, you've done nothing?"

"Not exactly." He looked away. "I sent a small team of Inquisitors to arrest her for questioning."

"You ordered the abduction of the Crown Princess's mother?"

"Apprehending those suspected of heresy is well within the Church's jurisdiction. Besides, there seemed to be no better way to get at the truth."

"Where did they take her?"

"If all had worked as planned, she would be well on her way to the Holy City by now."

"But…?"

"But all didn't go as planned. The man who attacked me this morning was one of those I sent."

"But he was no Inquisitor."

"He just wasn't dressed as one. If they failed, I couldn't risk them being connected with the Church."

"But then they wouldn't have any authority. For all my Aunt would know, they could have been common brigands."

"Once she was in custody, they would have identified themselves."

"So now what?"

"I don't know. I don't know what went wrong. The plan should have worked."

"So Isrulian is going to show up any minute to discover you called off the Inquisition without actually making any progress?"

Cartier held up the wrap. "I still have strong evidence implicating your Aunt as the heretic."

"And no way of proving it, particularly if your clumsy attempt at abduction has tipped your hand." She shook her head sadly. "I do wish you'd talked to me beforehand. As things stand, I'm not sure I see any way out of this mess, unless…"

"Unless what?"

"Oh, I couldn't. I know my father and Aunt Marguerite haven't gotten along for some time, but I shudder to think what he'd say if he knew I was involved in some bizarre plot to arrest her and accuse her of heresy. Still, it certainly would be nice to clear this up as soon as possible."

"It would. Particularly since I can't guarantee what might happen if Isrulian removes me from the Inquisition. He'll be rabid to name a culprit, and once he has evidence to implicate a suspect, he may decide the actual truth of the matter is beside the point."

"Are you saying he'd convict Aunt Marguerite without a full investigation?"

"Stranger things have happened."

"But if that's true, he might go after the rest of her family as well— even those who have had nothing to do with her for over twenty years."

"I can't rule that out either."

"Even if I help you, you can't rule it out, right?"

"Actually, there might be something I could do. When Thurman left so suddenly, he put me in charge of this Inquisition, and Isrulian signed the paperwork to make it official shortly afterward."

"How does that help me? Isrulian could replace you at any time."

"In my official capacity, I can make agreements that bind the Church in return for cooperation in an investigation."

"So, if I help with the investigation, you can offer immunity for me and my family in return?"

"Immunity for past offenses only, but I would think that should suffice. It's called an Inquisitorial indulgence."

"Can you also make other kinds of agreements?"

"Such as?"

"Well, I don't for one minute think there's any substance to these charges, but Aunt Marguerite is a wealthy woman. Isrulian could be tempted to pursue these charges against her solely to acquire her estate."

"I don't think that's likely."

"You're the one who said he was rabid. Can you really predict what he'll do?"

"I suppose not. But what can I do about that?"

"Take the temptation away. If, in return for my help, you agree that the Church will disclaim any interest in Aunt Marguerite's estate, even if she is found to be a heretic, it would keep Isrulian honest. Then, the only reason he'd have for pursuing her would be if she really were a heretic."

"What sort of help are you offering?"

"I want to see this resolved as much as you do. If you agree to the indulgences for me and my family and have the Church disclaim her estate, I'd be willing to deliver Aunt Marguerite to you for questioning. The sooner we establish this heresy accusation is a bunch of nonsense, the sooner we can focus on finding the real heretics."

"And if it should turn out she really is a heretic?"

Verone shrugged. "Then I guess she'll just have to learn that bad decisions have consequences."

# CHAPTER 19

# TRUMPED

The six men shifted nervously as they waited for Ordinal Lavicius to call the meeting to order. The great round table in the Chapel Ordinalis had not been graced with so many Ordinals at one time since Darron Goodkin had been elevated to the Primacy. By now they were all aware their Primal, by all accounts a very sick man, had suddenly and unexpectedly gone missing. Following as it did on the heels of the unprecedented demon attack, many feared the worst.

Lavicius stood. "Thank you all for coming, gentlemen. Shall we get started?"

Ordinal Bittern cleared his throat. "Aren't we going to wait for Ordinal Laitrech?"

"I expect him momentarily," Lavicius said.

Ordinal Cronsett, whose rheumy eyes and deeply lined features marked him as the eldest of those assembled, raised an eyebrow. "Are we to assume Theratigan cleared him, then?"

Lavicius shrugged. "I imagine that depends on what you suspect him of. If you are asking whether Theratigan has determined that the individual claiming to be Ordinal Laitrech is not in fact the demon we've been hearing so much about, I expect the answer is no. It seems His Primacy decided to imprison Theratigan before the determination was made."

"You countermanded the Primal's order?" Ordinal Stohl asked. "Aren't you taking quite a risk? What if he turns out to be the demon after all?"

"Not at all, my friend. The Primal merely asked that Ordinal Laitrech be held until it could be determined that the demon had not taken his place. Of course, that order became a bit awkward when Theratigan was himself taken into custody. But the problem was solved easily enough. When Ordinal Laitrech's predicament came to my attention, I simply sent for someone else capable of making that determination. It's the least I could do for my fellow Ordinal under the circumstances, don't you agree?"

As several of the men nodded, Ordinal Bittern rose from the table.

"If you'll excuse me a moment, I'll go see what's keeping Laitrech."

"Oh, of course. How careless of me," Lavicius said. "Without his Relic, he'll need help getting past the Bastion, won't he? He's probably already waiting outside."

"What do you mean without his Relic?" Ordinal Kuypers asked. "You don't mean to say he's gone and lost it, do you?"

"He says it was stolen."

There was a moment of stunned silence, and then everyone spoke at once. Lavicius let them go on for several minutes before calling them to order.

"Please, gentlemen. One at a time."

Ordinal Marius's *basso profundo* was most clearly audible over the others. "Are you saying Laitrech permitted his Relic to fall into the clutches of a demon?"

"It wasn't his fault," Bittern said. "He was attacked."

"In all fairness," Lavicius said, "if what he says is true, the attack took place in this very room. Given the protection of the Bastion, could you really blame him if he let his guard down a little?"

Stohl ogled Lavicius in disbelief. "The demon struck here? How did it get in?"

"The Relic is used to bring down the Bastion around you," Bittern said. "That's how I was able to bring Laitrech out of the Chapel even though his Relic had been stolen."

Marius blinked. "Are you suggesting he brought the demon into the Chapel with him?"

"No. Laitrech said he had been sitting at the desk for some time when the Curator of Profanities came through the door, and that he remembers little else."

"The Curator doesn't have a Relic, does he? Has anyone talked to him?"

"The Curator is conveniently missing," Lavicius said. "It's possible the Curator could have been another one of the demon's victims. But as for Relics, as far as we know, only Ordinals carry them. Even the Primal doesn't have one. And as you know, it's not merely a matter of possessing a Relic—you need to know how to use it."

Cronsett's eyes narrowed. "You aren't accusing one of us, are you?"

"I'm simply answering your questions to the best of my knowledge, but if one of us didn't have something to do with it, what's the alternative?"

"That Laitrech is either lying or has been misled?" Marius said. "Both of which I find difficult to believe."

"Let's examine the rest of his story then. He says the demon in the form of the Curator used some sort of spell to make him sleep, and that the next thing he remembered was waking in Ordinal Bittern's chambers."

Bittern raised his hand. "That part is true. I found him down here shortly after he was discovered missing, and I was unable to wake him until late last night."

"So, he slept for nearly a full day and night?"

"Yes."

"But if that's true, doesn't it mean the demon's spell lasted far longer than it should have?"

Cronsett nodded slowly. "I'm certainly not as conversant with these things as I once was, but as I understand it, such a spell should have lasted no more than an hour or so. How does he explain such a spell lasting so long?"

"Isn't there a way to nullify the resistance from the Soul?" Marius asked. "I seem to recall such a trick was sometimes used to incapacitate the most dangerous Caprian Heretics during transport to the Holy City."

"Indeed," Lavicius said, "but as far as we know, that type of nullification was a secret the Phrendonic Heretics never mastered. That knowledge would have been available only to Ordinals exceptionally well-versed in the knowledge stored here. Let's have a quick show of hands. How many think we could actually pull it off?"

Cronsett was the only one to raise his hand. "Now that you mention it, I recall seeing it done on several occasions back in Caprian. Given several weeks to reacquaint myself with the technique, I might be able to get it to work."

"Can you think of anyone else who could do it?"

"Other than Laitrech, you mean?"

"You think Ordinal Laitrech could have done it?"

"Oh, unquestionably. He's got quite a knack for this sort of thing."

Bittern gaped at Lavicius. "Are you insinuating Laitrech put himself to sleep?"

"If he's telling the truth, he's the only person we know who could have. As for why he might want to? Well, let's see…during the attack on the Primal, that means he would have been both comatose and trapped in the Chapel without his Relic. As an alibi goes, it's not just airtight, it's overkill."

"How dare you," Bittern cried. "Ordinal Laitrech was a victim here. He would never collude with a demon. Never."

Lavicius shrugged. "My apologies, but in my defense, you did ask—"

"And the rest of you," Bittern said. "The least you could do if you're going to put him on trial is let him face his accuser."

"By all means," Lavicius said. "In fact, I thought you were going to get him some time ago."

The door slammed shut behind Bittern.

"Is an Ordinal even permitted in one of these meetings without his Relic?" Marius asked.

"I think that rule only applies during an Election," Cronsett said.

.  .  .  .  .

All conversation hushed as Bittern ushered Laitrech into the chamber. As Laitrech's eyes met those of his colleagues, he sensed the change immediately. Where there once had been a sense of collegiality coupled with a certain guarded admiration, all that remained was studied indifference.

He steeled himself to smile. He was going to have his work cut out for him.

. . . . .

Jonas's pipe billowed smoke as he considered his next play. Amberton had fled the tent when Jonas lit up, and Tilly had already folded, leaving only Reston to contend with. Each man had six cards laid out on the tablecloth, four face up and two face down. Between them lay the Hierophant that Reston had just played as a global trump. Jonas checked his cards again—Eight and Ten of Cups, Page of Swords, and Knight of Wands showing, for a possible straight, should one of his face-down cards happen to be a nine. Not bad compared to what Reston had—Page of Wands high.

"Personal trump," Jonas announced. He placed The World on top of the one of his face-down cards, converting it to a wild card and completing his straight. Reston would need a full house to beat him.

Reston drew a card and replaced one of his face-up cards with the Page of Pentacles from his hand to give him a pair. "I'll bid fifty," he said.

Jonas gave his pipe a vigorous puff. "I'll match and raise you a hundred.

Reston rubbed his chin, considering. "I also match." He moved a stack toward the mound of chips at the table's center.

"You can afford to lose all that on a Professor's salary?"

"You're assuming I'll lose."

Jonas drew a card—The Two of Pentacles. He tossed it directly on the discard pile. "Why mess with perfection? I bid another fifty."

Reston rubbed his temple and stared at his cards for a long moment. "All right," he said at last. "I'll match."

Reston drew another card. He spent a moment contemplating it, and then grinned wolfishly. He discarded his Page of Wands from its spot on the table and replaced it with a Seven of Cups from his hand.

Seeing Reston destroy his pair, Tilly chuckled and nudged her brother. "I don't imagine you thought far enough ahead to keep a trump in reserve. I haven't seen anyone actually fall for the Hanged-Man's gambit in a very long time."

"Global trump," Reston announced. "The Hanged Man." He discarded the Hierophant and replaced it with the card Tilly had foreseen.

"Just as I suspected," Tilly said. "If someone calls while it's in play, the lowest hand wins."

"I know how it works," Jonas growled.

In fact, he had not thought to retain a trump. Praying for another, he drew his card and turned up the corner to see The Fool peeking back at him. He smirked as he replaced his Ten of Cups with a Knight of Swords.

"Global Trump, The Fool," he said. He moved the dreaded Hanged Man to the discard pile.

With the Fool in play as a global trump, his personally trumped card counted as an Ace instead of a wild card. While that would cost him his straight, he still had two pair—Knights and Aces—far better than the nothing Reston was left with.

Again, Tilly chuckled. "And what trump could possibly have been more fitting than that?"

Reston drew another card and replaced one of his face-down cards with a card from his hand. "It seems my luck has changed. I bid another two hundred."

"Two hundred?"

"What? Too rich for your blood?"

"You're bluffing. I match and call."

"Suit yourself," Reston said.

Jonas flipped over his face-down ace. "Hah. I bet you didn't think I actually had the ace, did you? Combined with the wild card, which, by dint of the Fool, counts as an ace, I've got two pair. You have to be mighty careful if you are going to use the Hanged Man gambit and win. One well-placed trump, and the whole strategy falls apart like, well, a house of cards." Jonas reached for the mound of chips.

"Hold it right there, mister."

"What? You have a Four, a Deuce, a Seven, and a Page."

Reston turned over a facedown card. "And another Four."

"A pair of Fours isn't going to cut it."

"I'm not done yet."

Jonas blinked as Reston revealed a third Four.

"Where I come from," Reston said, "three of a kind beats two pair."

Jonas sat blinking. "But that means you had a full house. Why destroy it if you could have just won outright?"

Tilly snickered. "He probably noticed that when you think you're losing, the perfect card somehow has a strange tendency to mysteriously appear. He played you like a violin."

"Not to worry," Jonas said. "The night is young. My deal."

Amberton briefly popped his head into the tent, a handkerchief clamped over his face. "Michlos is coming."

"Looks like I'll have to take a rain check," Reston said.

Jonas shuffled the cards. "Nonsense. I'll deal him in, too."

Michlos opened the tent flap. "How is everyone doing tonight?"

"Michlos, my man," Jonas said. "Come in. Have a seat. The game is Trumps of Doom, two down, four up. Tilly, get the man some chips."

Michlos shook his head. "Sorry, I can't tonight. I do have good news, though. We've located Miss Merinne."

Reston leapt to his feet. "Did they try to smuggle her out in the last few carriages? Where do we need to intercept them?"

"No, it's nothing like that. It turns out that as of this afternoon, she's safe and sound in her dormitory. Apparently, she and Mr. Reysa did have a run-in with the Inquisition, but they managed to escape with the help of Monsignor Goodkin."

"The Monsignor?" Reston asked. "Why would he help them escape?"

"It's complicated. I'm not sure I completely understand it all myself yet, but it seems there was some sort of plot to discredit the Monsignor, and he was also taken into custody—the three of them escaped together."

"How do you know all this?"

"Simple, the Monsignor explained it when he rode into camp. I just came from his meeting with the Crown Prince."

"Did they say how they are going to resolve this Inquisition?"

"Given the involvement of an Ordinal and the failing health of the Primal, there are too many unknowns to say, but the Monsignor is promising his full cooperation, which is, I think, a good sign."

"And the University?"

"The Inquisition has pulled out almost completely. With any luck, things could be back to normal within a few days. In fact, Father

Cartier has agreed to relinquish control to the Crown as of tomorrow morning."

"So, it's settled, then," Jonas said. "You can't go back before tomorrow anyway, which means we have the entire evening. Michlos, you sure you don't want in?"

"Thank you, but no. I'll send word if anything else develops."

"Thank you," Reston said. "And good luck."

Jonas started dealing cards before the tent flap had fallen closed.

Reston held up his hand. "No more cards for me."

"It's poor etiquette to win a big pot and just quit."

"He doesn't want to play anymore," Tilly said. "I think it's time to settle up."

"Oh, all right. Did you want that in cash or merchandise?"

"Merchandise?" Reston asked. "I thought you lost your cart in the fire. Besides, I'm not much of a drinker."

"It's true, you aren't one of my run-of-the-mill customers."

"He's not your customer at all," Tilly said. "He's your creditor."

"Anyway," Jonas said, "that's what makes me think that you, of all people, might be interested in a very special item I just happen to own."

Reston perked up. "You mean the color wand?"

"Oh, I couldn't possibly part with that, given it's a family heirloom and all, but there is a certain medallion that I might be willing to sell for the right price. Assuming you're interested, we could just call tonight's winnings a small down payment."

"You aren't really suggesting that I buy the fruits of your graverobbing, are you?"

"If you don't have any interest in it for your own studies, you could always sell it to the Church. Given what Father Anton was offering, you could pay me off and still turn a tidy profit."

"Assuming they don't just send their Inquisitors after you to claim it," Tilly said. "If you think I am going to just stand here and let you sell Professor Reston something you've already sold, you've got another think coming."

Jonas glared at his sister. "Do I interfere in your business?"

"It's all right," Reston said. "I'm really not in the market for corpse parts. But there *is* something I'm interested in, and I suspect your specific skill set could prove quite useful for obtaining it. If you help me acquire this thing, I'd be willing to call it even. It should only take a few hours. What do you say?"

"I'm listening," Jonas said.

. . . . .

For the fourth time since she'd arrived, the peasants of the great grandfather clock in the library's Theology wing capered and cavorted, but Verone didn't even look up. In addition to the tome she was studying, several other musty volumes lay open on her table. She smiled, apparently pleased with what was written on the pages before her. Intent though she was, the telltale squeak of hinges caught her attention. A quick scan through the archway revealed nothing out of the ordinary. Taking no chances, she reached over and doused her lamp, plunging the Theology wing into darkness.

After only a few moments, the light of another lantern became visible.

"You got off easy," Reston said. "I had expected the door to be locked."

"A deal's a deal," Jonas said. "This little escapade still makes us even."

"As long as I get my book back, as far as I'm concerned we're even."

"Well, let's get it and get out of here. It's past my bedtime."

"Not so fast. We have to find it first."

"What do you mean? She didn't tell you where it was?"

"Only that it was in the Theology wing. But I know what it looks like. It shouldn't take long."

Jonas eyed the stacks dubiously. "I hope you're right."

"Well, here's the Theology wing. You may as well look too. It should say *Practical Phrendonics* on the spine."

"What about these books on the table here?"

"I certainly hope not. Too many people know about it already."

"Hmm, somebody has a guilty conscience."

Reston started scanning shelves. "Don't be ridiculous. The whole point of heresy is to enable the Church to censor the thoughts of its unwitting followers—they're terrified of what might happen if people actually contemplated the dogma they peddle. People willing to risk studying and debunking their myths and propaganda should feel heroic, not guilty."

"Umm, I meant whoever was reading these books here on the table. They're all open to pages that deal with Indulgences."

"Oh?" Reston said. "Probably just some student's class project. Students rarely reshelve books, and no doubt Mathers has been busy with too many other things to keep up."

"Your student must have left in a hurry," Jonas said. "He forgot to take his lantern with him."

"Happens all the time. They pull an all-nighter, fall asleep at the table, and when the morning sun wakes them, they rush off to class, totally forgetting they brought one."

Jonas reached for the lantern. "It would be a lot easier for me to help you look if we could light this one too."

Reston pulled out a large book swathed in red fabric. "That may not be necessary. I'm not sure if this cover was stupid or brilliant, but I guess it does hide the title, and even though it's red, you'd probably only really notice it if you were looking for something that didn't fit in."

"I don't think your student pulled an all-nighter…"

Reston placed the tome on an open shelf and paged through it. "Yes, this is it."

"…this lantern is still warm."

"Uh, what did you say?"

Jonas pulled his knife. "This lantern is still warm. We're not alone."

"Put that thing away. It's probably just some student who didn't want to be caught out studying after curfew."

Jonas eyed the rest of the darkened wing suspiciously. "Or some Inquisitor who didn't get the message that the Inquisition was leaving."

"Honestly, are you always this paranoid?"

Jonas pointed to the stacks beyond Reston. "There—something moved."

"Put the knife away. I'll handle this."

Reston took a deep breath as if to make some sort of announcement, but it never came. Instead, he wavered for a moment and collapsed. His fall extinguished the lamp, plunging the wing into darkness.

Jonas ducked and rolled toward the archway. He misjudged and bumped the clock as he regained his feet, causing the chimes to ring out his position. He dashed out through the archway and put his back against the wall, listening intently for pursuit.

He didn't have long to wait. Golden light blazed through the archway. A glowing inkwell flew into the main library. It rolled for several moments before coming to rest against a chair leg.

Now fully illuminated, Jonas fought to control his panic. Not daring to breathe, he pressed his back against the wall and waited.

Nothing. The longer he waited, the harder he found it to keep from bolting, even though he knew doing so would put him in plain sight. Then, at long last, he heard a footfall, soft, but unmistakable. Then another. Then a third, each one closer than the last. So close now he swore he could hear breathing. Finally, out of the corner of his eye, a glimmer of movement. In a flash, he slipped behind his adversary, wrapping his left hand around the waist and bringing his knife up to the throat. But then he wavered. Something didn't feel right—his opponent was a woman. Sharp pain pierced the back of his hand. Woman or no, he resolved to drive his knife into her throat, but his arm refused to work. The next thing he knew, he was sprawled helpless on the floor, unable to move, unable even to open his eyes.

He could still feel everything—the cold stone of the floor against his face, the throbbing pain in his hand, and most disturbingly, the moist warmth of an unwelcome voice in his ear.

"I'm flattered by the attention, really I am. And though I'd love to stay and get better acquainted, I'm afraid you've broken rule number one. I'm sure you meant well, or at least as well as a man is able, but you simply cannot expect a relationship to go anywhere if you can't abide by the rules. While I might possibly find it in my heart to forgive you, seeing as how you almost certainly couldn't help yourself, I feel it only fair to warn you—I never give second chances on rule number one. So, in case you find yourself inclined to renew our acquaintance, here's a little reminder: Don't touch me again…ever."

Unable to respond, Jonas heard her footsteps move back into the Theology wing. A few minutes later, the footsteps returned, and he had the distinct impression of being stepped over. Shortly thereafter, he sensed the inkwell's golden light winking out, leaving behind only the subtle flicker of what must surely have been lantern light. Finally, as the footsteps receded, that, too, dimmed, leaving him helpless in the darkness, with only Reston's silence and the relentless ticking of the clock for company.

# CHAPTER 20

# INδECENT pROpOSALS

For the first time she could remember, Verone actually enjoyed her stroll up the drive to her father's villa. The elms were showing signs of turning, painting the canopy with golden highlights that shimmered in the breeze. The subtle warmth of the crisp autumn sun was a perfect complement to the early morning chill. To be fair, though, she would have savored this moment even had it been cold and blustery. Morale, it seemed, was the natural hostage of immediate expectation.

As she approached the veranda, the comforting smell of Mum's signature breakfast biscuits enveloped her. She closed her eyes and inhaled deeply, envisioning delectable nuggets of crusty goodness. But the spell was broken when she realized that Mum rarely bothered with biscuits anymore without good reason—and for Mum, good reason usually meant company.

Verone's mind raced. Guests would be an unwelcome complication to plans that were already complex enough. She considered leaving and coming back another time, but only briefly. Too many other aspects of the plan had fortuitously aligned—she simply couldn't afford to wait any longer. If she was lucky, the guest might be someone innocuous, like Aunt Olivia.

Nathalie emerged from the villa. "Veronique, is that you? What a delightful surprise."

"Hi, Mum."

Nathalie took Verone's arm and ushered her inside. "You're just in time for breakfast. We were ready to sit down with Mrs. Merinne and her brother when Eloise told us that someone was lurking out on the veranda. Happily, there's plenty left, and it's still warm."

"Mrs. Merinne?"

"Why yes. She looked so despondent after we got back from misplacing her daughter again, I couldn't help myself. I invited them up to stay with us—at least until we can find out if the girl is all right. At first, I was a little worried about how they'd get on with Alistair, but if anything, your father seems more amused than annoyed by Mrs. Merinne's brother's…peculiarities."

"So, Dad is home then?"

Nathalie paused as the question registered. When she spoke again, her delight at seeing her daughter was tainted by a note of trepidation.

"Why do you ask?"

"I have something important to discuss with him."

"As I said, we have guests. You weren't planning to antagonize him, were you?"

"I'll take him aside, then."

The glass panels to the courtyard had been thrown wide to the crisp morning air. Beyond, Verone caught a glimpse of her father and his guests seated at a table. One of the guests stood as Verone and her mother approached.

"Miss Nevinander," Dona's mother said. "What a pleasant surprise."

"How nice to see you again."

Dona's uncle stood as well. "Once again fate smiles upon me. This day all my wishes are fulfilled."

"Always a pleasure, Mr. ah…Magnificent?"

"Please, call me Rayen."

Nathalie pulled back a chair for Verone. "Here, take my seat, dear."

"That's all right, Mum, I can get another."

"Sit. I'll only be a moment."

Verone settled between Amanda and Rayen.

Alistair finally spoke. "What a pleasant surprise, indeed. To what do we owe this rare pleasure?"

"Why to fate of course," Rayen said. "The air is thick with it. Can't you feel—"

Amanda glared. "Rayen, not now."

"Oh, it's quite all right," Alistair said. "I generally find Rayen's pronouncements to be fascinating."

Nathalie emerged from the villa. "Eloise is bringing a chair. Did I miss anything?"

"Rayen was just filling us in on Verone's fate," Alistair said. "Tell us, will she fare any better than her brothers have?"

"Now, that's unfair," Nathalie said. "You don't know that's why she's here."

"You mean she doesn't visit for years, and then, the minute she thinks the estate is up for grabs, she mysteriously reappears just to enjoy a rasher of bacon and our stimulating conversation? What an amazing coincidence."

Rayen shoveled a forkful of omelette into his mouth. "Unless, of course, she's here because of me."

"I knew it," Nathalie said. "I could sense there was something special between you two right from the start."

Verone reddened. "Mum, please."

A little smile played at the corner of Alistair's mouth. "How inconsiderate of me to jump to conclusions like that. Rayen, perhaps I should ask your intentions concerning my daughter. I'd hate to fall prey to any more misunderstandings."

"Of course," Rayen said. "Although she may not be quite ready to accept it, we are fated to be together. When the time comes, I intend to say 'I do.'"

"Enough," Amanda snapped.

Rayen started, and then looked down, focusing on a piece of cantaloupe.

"I apologize for my brother's inappropriate behavior. He's really not well, you know."

Alistair's eyebrow raised. "What's wrong with him?"

"He has seizures. Sometimes they make him delusional."

Rayen's eyes flashed. "They're not delusions." But, under the pressure of Amanda's gaze, his indignation gave way, and his attention returned to the cantaloupe.

A sturdy middle-aged woman wrestled a chair out from the villa and placed it next to Alistair.

"Thank you, Eloise," Nathalie said. "Could I also trouble you to bring another plate for Verone?"

"Really, Mum," Verone said, "don't bother. I just have a few questions for Dad, and then I'm off."

"These questions," Alistair said. "They wouldn't happen to involve the disposition of the estate, would they?"

"As a matter of fact, they do. Shall we retire to the study?"

Alistair dropped his napkin on his plate. "By all means. I can't wait to hear your take on why you're entitled to inherit over your brothers. I certainly hope you manage something less stultifying than Damien's spiel about the virtues of life-long loyalty, as though that somehow qualifies him to run a thriving business."

"Whenever possible, I do my best to avoid operating on a par with Damien. I don't promise you'll like everything I have to say, but I guarantee it won't be boring."

As Verone and Alistair disappeared into the villa, Amanda placed a hand over Nathalie's. "Are you feeling well? You're looking rather pale."

Nathalie dragged her gaze away from the villa and back to her guests. "Yes, of course. Can I get anyone some tea?"

. . . . .

Alistair's study was a testament to his interest in nautical gadgets. The walls that lacked bookcases bore navigational maps, while open spaces on shelves and tables displayed various sextants, astrolabes, and armillary spheres. Near the balcony, a telescope was perched atop a tripod almost as tall as Verone. As a girl, she had thought it resembled a huge spider, but that hadn't stopped her from sneaking into the study and using it to spy on her brothers.

Alistair offered Verone a seat and then sat at his desk, leaned back, and knit his fingers together behind his head. "I knew if I waited long enough, you'd come back to me."

"Don't flatter yourself. This is not a personal visit."

Alistair leaned forward. "All visits are personal. That's why they're done in person. In a way, I'm disappointed, though. While I fully expected a chance to inherit the estate would be tempting, a part of me hoped you'd have too much integrity to beg."

"When you're finished inflating your ego, let me know, and we'll get down to business."

Alistair waved his hand dismissively. "Oh, by all means, let the begging begin."

"Sorry to disappoint you, but when you sign over your holdings to me, it will be because you have no other reasonable alternative and because I am gracious enough to agree. Begging will not be necessary, but if you feel inclined, have at it. I'll try my best not to think less of you than I already do."

Alistair burst out laughing. "Well I must say that is a considerably different approach than your brothers took. So, tell me, since now I'm dying to know—what makes you think you have any chance whatsoever of inducing my agreement to terms like that?"

"Well for one, once the estate is safely in my possession, the Church won't be able to confiscate it anymore."

"You're implying, I take it, that this is a possibility I should be concerned about?"

"Well, it's up to you, of course. For all I know, you might donate it to the Church anyway and save them the trouble. But if that isn't your plan, you might be interested to know they have already attempted to arrest Aunt Marguerite on suspicion of heresy. Just how long do you think it will take for them to realize she has a long-lost twin brother?"

Alistair's smile faded. "What do you mean attempted?"

"Exactly what I said. They sent Inquisitors to take her into custody. They failed."

"The Crown intervened?"

"Not as far as I heard."

"Then how did she avoid arrest?"

"How do you suppose?"

Alistair stiffened. "She's not that reckless."

Verone shrugged. "She was probably desperate. As you may recall, she told you the Inquisition was getting out of hand. Maybe if you'd offered to help her instead of kicking her off your property, things would have gone differently. But you didn't, and here we are."

"When did all this happen?"

Verone removed a sheaf of papers from her leather case and placed them on his desk. "Sometime Saturday, I think, which means the Inquisition has had more than a day to plan their next move. Since time is clearly of the essence, I took the liberty of having the paperwork prepared. If you could just sign and date each page at the bottom…"

"You've known about this long enough to generate paperwork, and you're only telling me now?"

Verone smiled brightly. "Never go to a meeting unprepared—you taught me that."

"I know you have your issues with me, but did it not occur to you how this could affect your mother?"

Verone handed him the quill from his desk. "Of course it did. Once I control the estate, I'll be in a much better position to look after her."

Alistair snatched the quill out of her hand and placed it back on its stand. "Even if what you say is true, why should I sign over the estate to you? Why would you be in any better position to protect it from the Church than, say, Damien or the twins? You don't even have any children to use for a sympathy bid."

She produced another paper from her case and placed it before him. "Because I have something they don't. It's called an Inquisitorial Indulgence. It gives me immunity from prosecution by the Church for any heresies I may have committed. All you have to do is sign the papers and your precious legacy is safe."

"In return for what? What did you promise them to get this?"

"My cooperation in their investigation of Aunt Marguerite. And since I barely know the woman, how much help can they really expect?"

"So, what's to stop me from offering them my cooperation in return for one of these? Since I know her better, surely they would view my help as more valuable than yours."

"By all means, feel free to try. It might even work. Of course, you run the risk they'll view you as just another hapless heretic with a fat estate ripe for confiscation. And even if it does work, the estate will only be protected until you pass it on to someone who isn't. It seems to me you'd be better off just signing now and saving yourself the hassle."

"You overestimate how much I value this so-called legacy. If I'm just giving it away anyway, why should I care whether the Church ends up with it?"

Verone nodded slowly. "I see your point. Knowing your estate is in good hands is small consolation if you're entertaining that thought at the wrong end of an Inquisitor's branding iron. Very well, since I have an in with the Inquisitor, I'm prepared to throw in another Indulgence with your name on it."

"What about your mother?"

"Her's too."

Alistair regarded Verone thoughtfully. "It seems my little girl is all grown up. You make an impressive case, at least compared to your brothers. Of course, I'll need to check your facts before I can sign anything."

Verone gathered up the papers and slid them into her case. "What a pity."

"What are you doing?"

"Oh, I'm sorry. Didn't I make it clear? This is a one-time offer. By the time you check the facts, it will be too late to save either you or the estate. Don't worry, though. I've been saving up my allowance. I'll be able to live modestly but comfortably for a good long while, even without your estate."

"You honestly expect me to believe you don't care whether you inherit?"

"I am long past caring what you do or don't believe."

"You know, you were always my favorite—even after you left. Look at your allowance. None of the boys ever got an allowance like that."

"That's because you didn't need to pay them off to keep them from telling Mum just what kind of monster you really are."

"I did it because I cared."

Verone snorted. "You don't give a damn about anyone but yourself."

"You want proof? I'll give you proof. Give me the papers."

"You aren't begging, are you?"

Alistair threw up his hands. "What do you want from me?"

"What do you think?"

"An apology? Is that it? All right then, I'm sorry."

"It's *way* too late for that."

"Then what? Why did you come here at all?"

"To see you beg."

Alistair's mouth dropped open for several full seconds. Then he took a deep breath and set his jaw. When he finally spoke, his voice was measured.

"Give me the papers."

"To sign?"

"Yes, I'll sign them—under one condition."

"And what's that?"

"If I'm doing this to protect my so-called legacy, there's just one crucial thing missing."

"And that is?"

"Your heir. It's not much of a legacy if it ends with you, is it?"

"Well, I hardly think I have time to produce one under the circumstances."

"True enough. Therefore, I'd be willing to settle for a substantial step in that direction."

"What do you mean?"

Alistair snatched the quill from its stand. "I'm willing to sign—but only if the transfer is contingent on your being married first. All you have to do is say 'I do,' and you can take possession. Do we have a deal?"

"That's ridiculous. That could take months, or even years. It helps neither of us if the Church confiscates the estate before I take possession."

"Excellent point. Not only that, but you aren't getting any younger. If you're going to be producing heirs, the sooner you get started, the better. We'd best build in some incentive. Let's give it say, one week. If you aren't married by then, the whole deal is off."

"A week? How could I possibly get married in a week?"

"I'm sure your mother would be delighted to help with the planning." He held the quill poised above the first document. "We could just add one little clause right here and start signing."

"I think I could manage that. But I do have one condition of my own. I'd like Aunt Marguerite to attend the ceremony."

"Noble of you."

"And I'd like you to invite her—personally."

"She'd never agree to come if I invited her. You know that."

"Nevertheless, those are my terms. If you don't personally invite her or she doesn't attend, I can call off the wedding and still take possession of the estate. Deal?"

"I don't see how—"

"Take it or leave it."

"Would that include the Indulgences for your mother and me?"

"Of course."

"All right then, it's a deal. Maybe once you have children of your own, you'll be a little more forgiving of parental flaws."

"Don't hold your breath. You were warned at the time. I don't give second chances on rule number one."

.  .  .  .  .

While Cartier was relieved to have managed both the Hathaway fire and the Inquisition's evacuation in under two days, he was assailed by feelings of doubt as he and the last few Inquisitors passed beneath the arch that once had held Exidgeon's great gates. Until that moment, he hadn't appreciated the sense of security the fortress provided. But if Count Laslo had any intentions of reneging on his agreements, he gave no sign. He approached Cartier well in advance of his honor guard with a broad smile, his blond hair blinding in the sunshine.

"My thanks to you once more, Father, and that of the Crown as well. Your cool head and good judgment have no doubt averted disaster this day."

"And my thanks to you," Cartier said. "Your patience was critical to my efforts to defuse the situation. But let us not forget there are serious issues still to be resolved."

"Of course, Father," Laslo said. "Constable Connelly's investigation into these attacks is already underway. Access to the crime scenes will no doubt expedite matters, assuming the storm didn't wash away crucial evidence. The Crown is committed to seeing that justice is done, particularly in light of...recent developments."

"If I can be of any further assistance, please let me know."

As he made his way to his carriage, Cartier considered what Laslo could have meant by "recent developments," but then he dismissed the matter from his mind. His main priority was to apprehend the heretic before Isrulian could reappear and sabotage his plans, or worse yet, claim credit. The rest was just distraction.

When the carriage arrived at St. Sophia's, the meaning of Laslo's vague reference became clear. Smoke still rose in isolated spots from the ashes of Cartier's vicarage. The entire region had been roped off, and the militia was present to ensure the makeshift border was respected. In front of the church, several tables replete with baked goods heralded the presence of the Venerable Assembly of Church Mothers, complete with a colorful banner imploring the good citizens of Trifienne to "Help Rebuild Our Vicarage."

Cartier leapt from the carriage. "What happened here? Where is Garvin?"

The militiamen closed ranks.

"What's the meaning of this? This is my vicarage."

"Let him pass."

Cartier instantly recognized the Constable's voice. Brushing past the militiamen, he strode into the burnt-out shell of his vicarage and came face to face with not only the Constable, but with Monsignor Goodkin as well.

"Monsignor?"

"My deepest sympathies, Father," the Monsignor said. "I assure you the Constable and I will do whatever it takes to get to the bottom of these horrific attacks."

"Where is Garvin?"

The Constable looked away.

"I'm so sorry." the Monsignor said."

Cartier blanched.

"We're not sure of their identities yet," the Constable said, "but there were also two other victims. One was in a militia uniform, so we think we should be able to track down his identity eventually. The other we believe owned a donkey cart we found abandoned nearby. I know it's not a good time, but is there any chance you might be able to have a look? Knowing who the victims were could give us valuable leads. We've just moved them over into the church."

Cartier stooped to retrieve a charred candlestick from the ashes and stood for a few moments, turning it over in his hands. "What sort of monster torches a vicarage?"

The Monsignor shot the Constable a sidelong glance. "A heretical one, unless I miss my guess. I'm told you played a significant role in resolving the crisis up at Exidgeon, for which I am, once again, in your debt. But by doing so, you may have unwittingly made yourself a target."

"But I was up at the University. Why would they strike here?"

The Monsignor shrugged. "A warning, perhaps? Look here. See

how the grass is charred in a wide arc roughly centered on the vicarage entrance? I can think of only one thing that leaves that kind of mark, and that's Phrendonic Heresy.

"Are we talking a Sacrificer?"

"Not necessarily. Although the burn area is consistent, the sheer number of recent events suggests our arsonist may be surviving the deed. We may have a better idea once we identify the other victims."

"Could there be a connection to the Sacrificer at the brothel?" the Constable asked. "Maybe this is some sort of vendetta?"

"But I wasn't even in charge of the Inquisition then," Cartier said. "Why would they target me?"

The Monsignor steered them gently toward the Church. "We won't know for certain until we apprehend our arsonist. Shall we see if we can identify the victims?"

Cartier nodded and numbly followed the Constable's lead.

A lady called out from behind a table. "Constable Connelly, can I interest you or your men in a fresh-baked apple pie? It's for a good cause."

"Good morning, Mrs. Temrich," the Constable said. "I'll take five for my men, but I can't take them right now. We're going in to examine the victims. In the meantime, could I prevail upon you ladies to move a bit farther away from the church entrance?"

"Why, Constable Connelly," Mrs. Temrich simpered, "you're making me blush. But you were ever the charmer. And you aren't looking so bad yourself, I must say."

The Monsignor and the Constable exchanged puzzled glances.

"He said he'd take five," Mrs. Curtsik shouted into her ear. "And he wants us to move the tables away from the doors."

Mrs. Temrich primped her thinning hair. "Well after flattery like that, how could I refuse? If there's anything you need—anything at all, we'll be right over there."

"Father Cartier," Mrs. Curtsik said, "what a relief it is to have you back. We're doing the best we can, but we're in over our heads. Whatever are we going to do without a vicarage?"

Cartier smiled weakly. "Yes, well I'm sure we'll make do somehow. In the meantime, please try to keep out of the Constable's way."

"We will, Father. Poor Garvin. What a dreadful way to go."

The three men plodded down to the church basement, where the deceased had been laid out on tables and covered with sheets.

"Here is our militiaman," the Constable said. Grimacing at the smell, he lifted back the sheet from over the face. "Ring any bells?"

Cartier went parchment-white at the sight of the man's burn-ravaged features. The Monsignor squeezed Cartier's arm. "Are you all right, Father?"

He turned away. "I...I guess I just wasn't prepared."

"There isn't any way to prepare for something like this. Do you need a moment?"

He shook his head. "Let's just get it over with."

The Constable lifted back the second shroud. "Here's victim number two—probably the owner of the cart. Anyone you knew?"

Cartier's eyes widened, but shook his head. "I've never seen either of them before."

The Constable draped the shrouds back over the faces of the deceased. "Thank you, Father. I know that's not easy, even when you don't know them."

Cartier touched the Constable's arm. "What about the third?"

"We've already identified Garvin. There's no need to put you through that."

"Please? I can't just turn my back on him. I have to look—I owe him that."

"You're sure?"

Grimly, Cartier nodded.

"All right, then." He lifted the third shroud.

Cartier's hand went involuntarily to his mouth.

"I'm sorry," the Monsignor said.

The Constable released the shroud. "Perhaps we should head back upstairs—or did you need a few more minutes?"

Brushing back tears, Cartier shook his head, "No...I'm done here. Let's go."

"We'll get whoever did this. I promise."

Cartier's eyes flashed. "I'll thank you not to make promises you can't keep."

The Constable stepped back in surprise.

Cartier backed down immediately. "I'm sorry. It's just that I'm a little overwhelmed."

The Constable nodded. "I understand."

The Monsignor put a hand on Cartier's back. "In the meantime, my friend, we'll need to find you somewhere to stay. If you like, I'll see if they can put you up in the vicarage at Saint Bethany's over on the west side."

Cartier shook his head. "No, my family is here. I'll be all right, at least until after the funeral."

"As you wish. When you are feeling up to it, I'd like to have you bring me up to speed on the status of the Inquisition."

"Of course."

When they emerged into the sunlight, Mrs. Temrich was waiting. "Oh, Constable, I have your order ready. And I included a little something extra."

The Constable sighed. "I suppose I'd better get this over with. We'll be in touch, Father."

The Monsignor nodded. "And I should get back to my investigation." He turned to Cartier. "Father, if you need anything, let me know."

"I will."

"Oh, one last thing before you go? Do you have any idea what befell Ordinal Isrulian? The Constable says he hasn't been involved with the Inquisition for days now."

"Last I heard, the Sisters of Solace were holding him in quarantine up at the University. Apparently, they believed he was some sort of plague risk."

"Plague risk? You don't say."

Cartier shrugged and signaled his carriage. "For a while there, it seemed like there might actually even be a plague, but it seems it was a false alarm."

"I see."

The carriage pulled up to the church steps, and Cartier opened the door. "We'll talk soon."

The Monsignor nodded.

The Inquisitor driving the carriage shook the reins, and the carriage pulled away. "Where to, Father?"

Cartier had pulled out quill and parchment and was already writing. "To Tabalaria first."

"Tabalaria?"

"It's a restaurant. It's just around the corner. And then I have a mission for you."

"You can count on me, Father."

"I want you to saddle up one of these horses and ride toward the Holy City as fast as it will carry you." Cartier handed him the parchment. "Here are the new orders. You must overtake the battalion as soon as possible."

"To what end, Father?"

Cartier's eyes smoldered. "To bring that heretic murderess to justice."

. . . . .

Alexi stopped struggling to master his crutches long enough to protest. "I told you, I'm fine. Alphonse wrapped it again this morning, and it doesn't hurt nearly as much."

Dona set her jaw. "Don't argue with me. We're going to the infirmary, and that's final. Alphonse has no formal training in such things. What if there's a break that needs setting?"

The two of them were trudging across campus, which looked, in some places at least, nearly back to normal. With the final departure of the Inquisition, those who had been trapped at Exidgeon were making tentative forays into the sunlight, but classes had yet to resume. Unless someone stepped in to fill the void left by the disappearance of Chancellor Wiggins, regular University functions could still be days away.

Professor Reston waved from his office window. "Alexi. Miss Merinne. Over here."

Alexi waved back. "Hi Professor."

"Don't think for one minute he's going to get you out of this," Dona said.

Alexi's eyes twinkled. "Well we can't just turn our backs on him, can we?"

"Don't tempt me. I haven't quite forgiven him for abandoning me in the market."

"Give the man a break. After all, he did go out of his way to save your roommate."

"Oh, all right, but it's the infirmary for you the instant we're done with him."

A moment later, they entered the office to see Jonas seated in one of Reston's office chairs, drawing thoughtfully on his pipe. Reston offered Alexi and Dona the remaining chairs.

Dona eyed Jonas suspiciously. "Don't tell me you've let something happen to Tilly?"

Reston sat on the corner of his desk. "She's fine. She's back in town assessing the damage to her place of business. But there has been another complication I thought you should be aware of—the book is missing."

"I already told you," Dona said. "Miranda put it in the library."

"It's missing from the library."

"Do you want me to go and find it for you?"

"Perhaps I should have chosen my words with more care. It's been taken from the library."

Jonas leaned forward. "What the man means to say is that when we went to retrieve the book from the library last night, we were ambushed and the book was stolen."

Dona blinked. "Ambushed? But who else even knew it was there?"

"Other than your roommates?" Reston said. "You tell me."

"You can't think Miranda had anything to do with this."

"I don't know what to think. It was like they were there waiting for us."

"It wasn't 'they,'" Jonas said. "There was only one."

"A single person took the book away from the two of you?" Dona asked. "Good thing you've got that heresy thing going for you."

"They used it first," Reston said.

"So, if he used heresy, it must have been Everson, right?" Alexi asked.

Jonas shook his head. "Not unless Everson is currently disguising himself as a buxom woman. I didn't get a good look at our adversary, but she was undeniably female. Let's just say I have a feel for such things."

"I know all too well," Dona said.

"You think it was Miss Nevinander?" Alexi asked.

Reston shrugged. "I was out cold before I saw anyone at all, and Jonas never saw her face, so all we really know is that it was a heavy-set woman."

"With some knowledge of heresy at her command," Jonas added. The good Professor here was put to sleep, and I was paralyzed. We were lucky whoever it was didn't decide she'd be better off if we didn't make it."

Reston nodded his agreement. "As of right now, Miss Nevinander is our best suspect."

"Actually," Jonas said, "she's our only suspect."

"But that doesn't make any sense," Dona said. "Why would she go to all that trouble to help find me, then?"

"Why indeed?" Reston asked.

"You think she just wanted the book?" Alexi asked.

"Her involvement with both Everson and that effort does seem rather convenient, don't you think?"

"But why would she even need it?" Dona asked. "You said yourself she must already know this stuff, or she couldn't have been teaching Everson things he didn't otherwise have access to."

"I'd love to know the answer to that," Reston said, "but no one I've asked has seen Everson for several days now."

"We saw him." Dona said. "He was dressed as an Inquisitor at the gate when we were trying to leave the University with the church group."

"Yes, I remember you said that. Another coincidence?"

"He could be anywhere by now," Jonas said.

"Perhaps he'll reappear now that the Inquisition has withdrawn. By the way, what happened to your foot?"

"Just a sprain," Alexi said. "I hurt it when I fell from the cart after you rescued Miranda. I'll be fine."

"We were on our way to the infirmary to make sure it's not something more serious," Dona said.

"One other thing," Reston said. "When we discovered you hadn't made it out with the others, we were worried the Inquisition may have captured you."

"They did," Dona said.

"I was afraid of that. What did you tell them?"

"Nothing. Alexi's friend Alphonse rescued us while they were distracted by the rioting. They never even had a chance to question us."

"They had taken Monsignor Goodkin prisoner as well," Alexi said.

"So Michlos told us," Reston said.

"Michlos?" Dona said. "How would he know?"

"Turns out your Enforcer friend also happens to be the Crown's brother-in-law," Jonas said. "He was present when the Monsignor made his report."

"The Crown's brother-in-law?"

Jonas winked. "Yes, well, small wonder he could get an audience with the Princess, eh?"

"And you tried to kill him."

"A minor misunderstanding. Let's never speak of it again."

"But if Michlos is the Crown's brother-in-law," Alexi said, "does that mean the Crown Prince is also a heretic?"

"If he is," Reston said, "it seems the Monsignor is blissfully unaware—but even the rumor, if it got out, would be disastrous for the Crown. Unless we want to start another Caprian, we'll have to be extraordinarily careful not to let that slip. Anyway, regardless of whether the Inquisition has truly left the University, I can't imagine the Church is going to just let this matter drop. I'd like the two of you to keep a very low profile for the next few days. Is that clear?"

"Yes Professor," Alexi said.

"Miss Merinne?"

"Oh, all right, but after he gets his sprain checked out."

"Fine. In the meantime, I'll devise some plan for getting my book back before whoever took it uses it to get us into even more trouble."

. . . . .

"Good morning, Jamie," Cartier said.

"Good to see you again, Father," Jamie said. "The rest of your party is already seated. Right this way."

Cartier paused. "My…party?"

"Yes, they arrived about an hour ago, just as the church bells tolled nine. A lady and a gentleman. They did not give their names."

"No one you've seen before?"

"I'm afraid not. And here we are. Enjoy."

An elderly wisp of a man and a solid matron occupied one side of the table. The lady's cape partially concealed a vintage floral gown. As she stood, Cartier caught a whiff of roses.

The lady extended her hand. "Father Cartier, what a pleasure to finally make your acquaintance. I've heard so much about you."

"I'm afraid you have me at a disadvantage," Cartier said.

"My apologies, Father. I've grown so accustomed to being recognized by people I've never met that I'm losing my manners. I am Marguerite Serrola. Please, have a seat."

Realizing he'd just sent away what little defense he had, Cartier swallowed and sank into his chair. "Pleased to meet you, too."

"I understand you had some questions you wanted to ask me?"

"Where did you get that idea?"

"Why, from the men you sent to abduct me, of course."

"Arrest you, you mean? That's what we usually do with heretics."

"And here I was under the impression you dressed them as Inquisitors and sent them to do your dirty work. Or are you going to tell me you had no idea Josephus Vane was a Phrendonic Heretic?"

"I don't know what you're talking about."

"Then before you pursue the matter further, I suggest you get up to speed. Once Vane's heresy is generally known, do you suppose anyone is going to believe you sent him after me without knowing what he was? How do you think your precious flock will react to the news that their revered Father 'keeps the peace' with a secret force of Phrendonic Heretics?"

"You're just trying to divert attention from your own guilt. It won't work."

"I've been meaning to ask you about that. Who misled you into making these specious accusations in the first place?"

"If anything has 'misled' me, it's the evidence."

Marguerite cocked an eyebrow. "What evidence?"

"Well, for one, I, myself, saw you loitering outside Dexter hall just before it was attacked."

Marguerite's lips pursed. "And yet today, when I was standing right in front of you, you required an introduction to recognize me? Is the rest of your so-called evidence equally compelling?"

"I didn't need to recognize you," Cartier said. "You were wearing this." He produced the floral wrap. "Do you deny it belongs to you?"

Marguerite blinked at it. "Where did you find that?"

"It was entangled in the hedges next to the building in the Hathaway compound you set on fire to hide your involvement in a conspiracy to sell military secrets to the enemy."

"That wrap has been missing for weeks," Marguerite said. "And I haven't been up to the University in years."

"The evidence suggests otherwise."

"The evidence was planted."

"If you'll excuse my saying so—a likely story."

"Let me lay this out for you. Everything I've told you is true. If you insist on pursuing this matter, not only will you be wasting time chasing the wrong person, but you risk damaging the Crown with the fallout. That is something I cannot permit."

"What will you do? Burn me to death like you did my caretaker?"

Marguerite's eyes narrowed. "Don't try to pawn Vane's work off onto me. The truth of that matter lies with the remaining survivor, and I suggest you find him before Vane does. The sooner you do, the sooner you can appreciate your own complicity with the heretic who killed your caretaker. Now if you'll excuse me, I'll let you get to work. Time is of the essence."

"How generous of you."

Marguerite pulled on her gloves. "Come along, Arerio. We're done here."

. . . . .

"It's probably a sprain," Dona said, "but we'd like someone with actual expertise to check it out.

The woman in the amber habit nodded. "I'll add you to the list, but I can't make any promises. We are over capacity with injuries from the rioting and are still operating in triage mode. It could be many hours before someone is available to check a sprain. Or do you think it's serious enough that he should be admitted?"

Alexi shook his head vigorously.

"We'll wait."

"Very well. Have a seat over with the others."

"Would it be all right if we waited in the courtyard?" Alexi asked. "I don't feel I've been getting enough sun lately."

"I don't see why not. I'll put a note on the list to look for you there."

Dona led the way to the door. "It's going to be cold out there."

Alexi flashed his crooked smile. "Not if I can help it."

They stepped into the sunshine together. "Now, you behave yourself, Mr. Reysa, this is a public place."

The courtyard was home primarily to the Sisters' vegetable garden, which was populated by sere cornstalks and tangled tomato vines, now patchy and spent after a bountiful harvest. Not all areas, however, were devoted to necessities—one corner held a bed of dahlias still thick with blooms, and another, a splash of proud chrysanthemums. An ancient arbor leaned casually against the northern wall, entangled with an impenetrable mass of grape vines, its wares dangling in tantalizing aubergine clusters above a sturdy porch swing.

"Now what could be more private than that?" Alexi asked.

"Someplace not in the courtyard of the Sisters' enclave, perhaps? Still, this is a cozy little spot."

"Alphonse says privacy is a state of mind."

"No doubt he arrived at that conclusion during his visit to my dorm room."

"What?"

"So, he didn't tell you about that?"

Alexi took a seat next to Dona on the swing. "Seems he forgot to mention it."

"It's true. At some point Helena must have smuggled him up there. Did you know he's taken to calling her 'Binky?'"

"Binky? Are you serious?"

"You don't think it's adorable?"

"Tragic more like. Alphonse always seemed so in control of himself. It's disturbing to think he could have fallen so quickly and so completely."

Dona raised an eyebrow.

"Unless of course *you* think it's adorable, in which case I could also see how it might have its charming side."

Dona laughed out loud. "Now that was tragic."

"That's different."

"How so?"

Alexi nodded toward his crutches. "Unlike Alphonse, I can't run away if I say something other than what's expected of me."

Dona shook her head and sighed. "I'll never understand why men seem to think they are only attractive when they say what's expected of them. Don't you admire more a woman who holds to her principles over one who wavers with latest breeze?"

"You aren't saying you don't admire the man with the discretion to pick his battles, are you?"

"That's just it," Dona said. "What makes you think it would have been a battle?"

"I suppose you're going to say it wouldn't have been?"

"Don't be silly. How do you expect me to get to know you better if you're afraid to state your opinions?"

Alexi put his arm around her and gave the ground a slight push with his toe. "Look at it from my perspective. Why would I let a little offhand comment spoil a perfect morning with a lovely lady?"

Dona snuggled up against him. "Well, you do get points for flattery, and any woman who tells you otherwise is lying. But there comes a time when a girl would like to know a little more about her flatterer than just his brilliant smile and his rapier wit."

"And we're at that point?"

"Didn't you understand anything I just said?"

Alexi grinned. "I just like to hear you say it."

"All right then, I think we are at that point, but don't get me wrong—I wouldn't want you to think the brilliant smile is no longer a requirement."

"And the rapier wit?"

Dona eyed him sidelong. "Depends on the day. So, you can see why I might want to know if there's more to you than just that?"

Alexi shrugged. "There isn't that much to tell, really. I'm the second of two boys, and I have two younger sisters. My dad owns some land north of town he inherited from my grandfather, but he's a barrister by trade. Mostly he spends his time waging petty paper battles on behalf of overinflated egotists with way more money than is good for them. I think what keeps him going is the belief that one day, he'll have a case that's so important it will make the drudgery of the rest of his existence worthwhile—you know, a battle worthy of the name Reysa."

"You mean being a barrister isn't worthy enough?"

"Oh, not in his mind. My great-great-grandfather was a general in the war with Shune. He commanded at the Battle of Oskunga Wash—ever heard of it?"

Dona shook her head.

"It was a big deal. After the war, they made him a Count and gave him a huge estate. Dad's land up north is a tiny little slice of it."

"You're in line to be a Count?"

Alexi laughed. "Hardly. Dad was the fifth son of the fourth son of the sixth son of the Count, or something like that. There are probably hundreds of eager relatives in line ahead of me. I don't think Dad has even met the current Count, but that doesn't stop him being proud of where he's from."

"And you're not?"

"Oh, I'm proud to be a Reysa, but I don't intend to live my life in the shadow of someone who's been dead for generations."

"Then what do you intend to do with your life?"

"Well, Dad wants me to be a barrister like him."

"And is that what you want?"

"I'd rather gnaw my own arms off, but Dad's pretty set on it. When the time is right, I'm hoping I can somehow convince him that being an academic is equally honorable. He values education—he might even go for it."

"He doesn't know how you feel?"

"I haven't found the right time to discuss it. You know how dads can be."

All the mischief drained suddenly from Dona's face. She attempted a smile, but it was weak and unconvincing.

"Oh, I'm sorry. I didn't mean—"

"No, it's all right. It's ancient history. I need to let it go."

Alexi handed her a crutch.

"What's this for?"

"For beating me silly if I ever say anything so stupid again."

The glimmer of a smile returned. "No thanks, you're quite silly enough without my help."

"You're sure? You aren't just saying that to spare the invalid?"

"Actually, I was worried I might break the crutch."

"As merciful as she is beautiful. Such *noblesse oblige* shall not go unrewarded."

"A reward? For me?"

Alexi leaned closer. "I can think of no one more deserving."

"Whatever did you have in mind?"

"Close your eyes, and I'll show you."

Her eyes were barely shut when Ordinal Isrulian's sanctimonious voice rang out. The sound of it chilled her to the marrow.

"At last, Sister," he said. "I have you right where I want you."

# CHAPTER 21

---

# FACE-OFF

The narrow trail twisting its way up to the old Monastery was more overgrown than Michlos remembered. In his youth, it had seemed secluded—mysterious even—but now, the untended vegetation, interspersed with bleached trunks and moldering boughs, exuded an air of melancholy and neglect. He wondered briefly whether the Magisters were deliberately cultivating this effect or whether their endowment was running thin. He rounded the final bend, dismounted, and approached the heavy gate to the Monastery compound. That, at least, looked impregnable as ever. He tugged the bell pull and, from deep within, heard the old familiar chimes. After several minutes, a window slid open in the gate.

"State your business."

"Michlos Serrola to see Magister Treust. Is he available?"

"One moment."

A mechanism rumbled and the gates creaked open. Michlos hesitated, half expecting the young man to recognize him, but if he did, he gave no sign.

"Magister Treust is probably in his workshop, do you know the way?"

"I can find it. Out of curiosity, where's Stuart?"

The young man regarded him blankly. "Who?"

Stuart had been a fixture at the Monastery during Michlos's tenure there. He'd fixed whatever was broken, tended the gardens, and had usually been the first to respond whenever the bells signaled a visitor. His absence was another poignant reminder of how long it had been since he'd lived and studied within these walls.

"Never mind."

The Magister's workshop wasn't where he'd expected it to be. The converted pottery shed that had once served that purpose had been replaced by a new brick building, which housed long tables already set in anticipation of the noonday meal. Although no one was in sight as he peered through the doorway, the rattle of utensils reassured him that someone still lived here, other than the fading ghosts of his lost youth. He left without seeking directions—the grounds were small enough that he could find the workshop on his own, and he was loath to subject himself to any more reminders of just how out of place he had become.

The workshop turned out to be on the far side of the church. Magister Treust had apparently garnered enough clout to take over an old guesthouse. It was not only less drafty than the pottery shed, but also boasted an impressive view of the river below.

Michlos peered through the doorway. "You've come up in the world, old man."

Magister Treust looked up from his schematic and grinned. "It's nice, isn't it. Probably the last concession I'll be able to squeeze from them before they put me out to pasture."

"It certainly beats the pottery shed."

Treust set the schematic aside. "No doubt. Don't just stand there, come in. Here, let me get you some mead. I brewed it myself."

Michlos eyed Treust dubiously. "Mead?"

Treust shrugged and poured him a glass anyway. "The wine hasn't been drinkable since Stuart left us. Fortunately, unlike the grapes, the bees seem oblivious to his passing."

"How long has he been gone?"

"Almost six years. But I'm guessing you didn't come all this way to reminisce about the good old days. What's on your mind?"

"I need some information about a Santine."

Treust scowled. "You aren't planning to ask me something you know I can't answer, are you?"

"I'm hoping to convince you to make an exception. You know I wouldn't ask if it wasn't important. He's already murdered three people, and more lives may be at stake."

"Which Santine?"

"The White Spider. If it helps, he's been going by the name of Josephus Vane."

"What's he done?"

"He's become an Inquisitor."

"An eminently suitable position for a Santine, if you think about it. Whom did he kill?"

"Two other Inquisitors and the caretaker of St. Sophia's."

"Did they have information there was no other way to suppress?"

Michlos took a deep breath. "At least two of them did. They had discovered he was a heretic."

"There's more, I take it?"

"There is. He ambushed Mother with the intent of delivering her to the Inquisition."

Treust whistled. "Intent, you say? I take it he didn't succeed?"

"No. Instead, she took him captive. To keep him from returning to the Inquisition, she tricked him into revealing he was a heretic to his underlings and then set them all free, separately, of course. Two of the underlings became his victims shortly thereafter. I believe he murdered those men not just to suppress what they knew, but to frame Mother for the crime."

"What makes you think that?"

"He didn't merely kill them—he incinerated them on the doorstep of the man running the Trifienne Inquisition, the man who sent him to abduct Mother in the first place. I don't know what this Inquisitor thinks he has on her, but I don't believe for one minute it couldn't have been effectively misdirected or suppressed."

"Let me get this straight. The White Spider used Phrendonic Heresy to kill those men—not to suppress what they knew but simply to frame your mother for it?"

"That's right. She asked Vane for his evidence, but he never gave her a good answer. And even if he thought it necessary to kill them, he could easily have done that without raising further suspicion. It was a clear violation of his Oath."

Treust set down his glass. "Michlos, I won't presume to tell you the life of a Santine isn't fraught with difficult decisions. Some of them inevitably go awry. But our role here is merely to train them, not to police them, and certainly not to second-guess them. If he was convinced the evidence against your mother was unsuppressible, who am I to say his methods were unreasonable?"

"You know if this were just about Mother I wouldn't ask."

"You're worried about the potential to affect the Crown?"

"I am. A showdown between the Crown and the Church would be a disaster. And now, even if I could convince Mother to just up and disappear, I'm no longer convinced a clash can be averted."

"What would you have me do?"

"There's one more underling out there who knows about Vane's heresy, but he's still unaccounted for. I need to get to Vane before he finds him. This situation is already difficult enough—I can't allow Vane to use him as another opportunity to incriminate Mother. Is there anything you can tell me that might help track him down?"

"My hands are tied. You know I can't divulge specific information about previous students, even to you. It would destroy our credibility and undermine everything we've tried to accomplish."

"I'm sorry. I had to try."

"No harm done." Treust took up his schematic. "Say, as long as you're here, can I get your opinion on this?"

"Of course. What are you trying to do?"

"It's not something I've done before. I'm trying to figure out the best way to copy a namesake."

"I thought they couldn't be copied? Isn't that the whole point? It's what makes every Amulet unique to its Santine."

"Well, sort of. Since the owner must concentrate for the encryption to manifest, the owner couldn't himself cast anything else while activating it. But, in theory, that wouldn't prevent someone else from copying it while manifested."

"So, they can be copied?"

"Not a point we advertise, for obvious reasons, but even without the Amulet, the bulk of the encryption that encodes the namesake should remain Patterned on the individual. It should manifest just fine, provided the owner maintains concentration. You just won't be able to see it without the Amulet's contingent illusion to make it visible."

"At which point," Michlos said, "you could presumably copy it using some sort of displacement-cast detection to broadcast the namesake's pattern to a waiting Encryption spell."

Treust nodded. "Or you could just cast an Extension to spread it to anything that might be attuned to and touching him—like a new Amulet, for example. Pattern it while Extended like that, and I'm betting you could replace your Amulet without having to change the namesake."

"Wouldn't that create two overlapping copies of the namesake?"

"I think it would, but the Amulet's Illusion spell will only be able to read the one that's been Extended. It's a little sloppy, but I think it should work."

"I agree," Michlos said. "But why would you bother?"

"Why indeed?"

Michlos eyes widened as the implications of Treust's rhetorical question struck him. "Wait—you were working on this problem when I arrived, weren't you?"

"I was, but it's been a most delightful interruption. If only I could convince you to do it more often. You know you are always welcome."

"If you don't mind, then, perhaps I'll stay a bit longer. Drop in on some of the other Magisters, take a stroll around the place and see how things have changed—you know, that sort of thing."

"By all means. Perhaps we'll see you at lunch?"

Michlos rose to leave. "I'd like that."

Treust grabbed his arm. "Michlos?"

"Yes?"

"Be careful."

.  .  .  .  .

Nathalie Nevinander blinked, shook her head, and blinked again as her husband and daughter emerged from the villa—they appeared to be chatting amicably, and that was utterly outside the realm of her comprehension. She gaped as Alistair slid back the chair next to Rayen and offered it to Verone, who politely accepted. Amanda's eyes darted nervously among the three Nevinanders, while Rayen, seemingly oblivious, smiled, raised his teacup in salute, and turned his attention back to the remnants of a blueberry-slathered pancake.

"I'm glad you two were able to iron things out so quickly," Nathalie said. "Tea?"

"Forget the tea, dear." Alistair boomed. "An occasion like this calls for champagne. Have Eloise raid the cellars for that '19 we've been saving."

"I thought you were saving that 'to toast the passing of the estate. Does that mean you've decided?"

"Indeed, I have. What better dowry could a proud father provide?"

Nathalie eyed him skeptically. "Don't you mean inheritance?"

"No, I mean dowry—you know, the property the bride brings to the marriage?"

"What are you talking about? What marriage?"

"The one Verone needs to have within the week if she expects to get the dowry." Alistair glanced over to Verone. "Those are the terms, right?"

Verone shot her father a disgusted look. "Ass," she muttered.

"Oh, my apologies. I've gone and spoiled the surprise."

Rayen swallowed the last of the pancake. "It's all right. It wasn't really a surprise anyway."

Amanda sprayed her tea through her nose. "Rayen, stay out of this."

Rayen's eyes flashed. He stood and drew himself up to his full height. "Not this time, Mandy. For too long, out of gratitude, I have allowed you drag me on your fool's errand. Fate is not some credulous ingénue to be used and deceived as you see fit. You've spent your youth dodging destiny, and to what end? Mark my words—try as you may to conceal it, the taint will out, and when it does, what will you have left?"

Amanda regarded him coolly, but her teacup trembled. "If you're quite finished—"

"I most certainly am not." He turned to Verone and dropped smartly to one knee. "Vision of loveliness, lady of my dreams, though even in a thousand years I could never hope to merit the honor, will you marry me?"

He opened his hand. Nestled in his palm was a delicate ring of gold filigree set with a fiery crimson gemstone.

Verone sat transfixed. Never in any of her wildest fantasies had she permitted herself to envision a handsome man showing any interest in her at all, much less executing a flawlessly romantic proposal of marriage on her behalf. It was only when she felt tears welling that her skeptical nature reasserted its iron grasp on her heart.

*He just wants the estate.*

Amanda's jaw dropped nearly to the table at the sight of the ring. "That's not yours to give."

"I beg to differ," Rayen said. "It became mine once Mother abandoned it and I found it."

"Veronique, dear," Nathalie said. "It's impolite to keep the nice man waiting."

Verone's gaze strayed to her father. The corner of his mouth was pulled up in that maddening little smile of his—the smug bastard thought she'd never be able to go through with it.

She stood, cupped Rayen's outstretched hand in hers, and leaned down to plant a kiss on his forehead. "I will," she whispered.

. . . . .

Dona's eyes snapped open. She fully expected to be surrounded by a legion of Ordinal Isrulian's omnipresent sycophants, each armed to the teeth and grinning wickedly. To her surprise, other than the two of them, the garden was completely deserted.

"Did you just—"

Alexi clamped one hand over her mouth. With the other he put his finger to his lips, and then pointed upward. She let her gaze follow. Through the tangled grapevines, she could just barely make out a window, its sash slightly ajar.

Isrulian spoke again, his voice clear enough to suggest he must be at or very near the window. Despite the lush layer of vines that separated them, Dona felt helpless and exposed.

"I trust my release from this makeshift prison of yours was precipitated by an emphatic response to my letter to the Holy City. I hope this little escapade was worth the Primal's ire. I shouldn't be the least bit surprised if he orders this whole operation shut down."

A woman's voice responded. It was low, smooth, and accustomed to wielding authority—if the Ordinal's threat had made an impression on her, Dona surely couldn't tell.

"Ordinal Isrulian, you are being released from quarantine because we have determined that you no longer pose a plague risk. As for your letter to the Holy City, I expect you will find it among your belongings. I'm sure you'll appreciate that such things cannot be distributed while any risk of contagion exists."

Isrulian sputtered. "You never sent it? I was assured it was on its way. This is an outrage!"

"The sisters have been instructed to avoid agitating our guests. I'm afraid that sometimes involves humoring them."

"Just as well," Isrulian snarled. "I've come up with a few more things I'd like to add. And speaking of my belongings, where are they? Haven't you wasted enough of my time?"

"I expected them to be here by now. Wait here, and I'll see to it myself. Believe me, I have no desire to waste any more of your precious time than is absolutely necessary." The emphatic sound of door striking jamb belied the woman's apparent calm in the face of Isrulian's tirade.

Isrulian picked up on it instantly. "Well, it seems I'm finally making an impression."

"And long overdue it is, Your Ordinence."

"Orley," Isrulian said, "In case I haven't mentioned it, I want to thank you for being here when I was released. Such loyalty shall not go unrewarded."

"It was both my duty and my pleasure, Ordinence."

"The rest of my retinue apparently didn't share that point of view."

"In their defense, some waited for several days, but when Father Cartier ordered the evacuation, most were understandably reluctant to disobey."

"Ah yes, and speaking of the good Father, where was he while I was rotting in my cell?"

"I saw him speaking with the Sisters on several occasions. I can only imagine he did what he could."

Isrulian harrumphed. "Yeah, I bet. I'll deal with him in due course. In the meantime, I must get that letter to the Holy City. I'll wager even Goodkin won't allow such blatant disrespect of one of his Ordinals to go unpunished."

"But the Sisters aren't beholden to the Primal. What could he do?"

"Orley, this isn't about authority, it's about power—something our current Primal is apparently unfamiliar with. It's about time we had a strong Primal again—one who stands on principle and isn't afraid to defend the sanctity of his anointed officials."

"You think if Ordinal Laitrech had been Primal, he would have found a way to free you?"

"Not at all. I think if Laitrech were Primal, the Sisters would never have dared imprison me in the first place."

"So, when he becomes Primal, you think he will put them in their place?"

"Once Laitrech is Primal, it's only a matter of time before they no longer even have a place."

"Who will tend the sick if he excommunicates them?"

"Once he begins distributing Relics to all priests who show an aptitude, the Sisters will become obsolete. What patient in his right mind would choose to be merely 'tended' when he could be healed outright?"

"He plans to give Relics to priests? Won't the other Ordinals object?"

"When Goodkin is finally out of the way and Laitrech is Primal, they can object all they want, but I doubt they'll object for long. Once the Church establishes a monopoly on healing like the one it already has on spiritual well-being, no state will have the temerity to oppose it. Temporal powers like Trifienne wouldn't dare risk an affront to the Church like the one that just occurred at Exidgeon. Imagine the power of an interdict or excommunication that suspends not just spiritual functions, but all healing as well. The power of the Church will be absolute. Laitrech will usher in a golden age the likes of which the world has never seen, and we shall be a part of it."

The scraping of the door's latch announced the Sister's return, and Isrulian fell silent.

"Here, I've located your belongings," she announced. "Once you've checked through them, you're free to go."

"Yes," Isrulian said. "Well, everything seems to be here, including my letter, which will no doubt require significant amendment. I hope you've enjoyed your little victory over the Church. I intend to see to it that you have precious few such opportunities in the future." The door slammed behind him, interrupting the Sister's response.

. . . . .

"No really," the sister said sarcastically to the empty room. "The pleasure was all mine."

Out of the corner of her eye, she caught a flash of movement in the courtyard below. Her curiosity piqued, she lifted the window for a closer look, but the only thing moving was the swing under the grape arbor, which swayed silently in the still air as if motivated by a hushed conspiracy with an errant breeze.

. . . . .

The grounds of the old monastery were clearly in decline since Michlos's days as a student. It's not that they had become shabby or unkempt—quite the contrary. But the opulent groundskeeping, with its formal beds and exotic flora, had given way to a humbler rustic aesthetic of quiet trails and native plants that required little care. In the rare instance where a new building had been necessary, the materials and design were suited solely to fulfilling function, apparently at the lowest possible cost. Michlos found the new approach to be very much at odds with his grandfather's vision of an elite academy for training a force of gifted agents to address the unique needs of a network of powerful families who held in common a single nefarious secret. The original endowment had been engineered primarily by Marguerite's father, who had negotiated promises of ongoing contributions from several of the most influential families. It was, after all, a time when the deft intervention of a skilled Santine could make the difference between an isolated unresolved disappearance and wholesale Inquisitorial destruction of the entire familial network.

Initially, the endowment paid a generous stipend to each active Santine, but that practice had already fallen by the wayside before Michlos had enrolled. With it went any pretense of Academy oversight, resulting in what had essentially degenerated into a loose part-time confederacy of volunteers lacking clear standards or centralized control. Of course, against an Inquisition adept at turning friend against friend, the lack of organization was also a strength, but it did nothing to assure the continued integrity of the Santines themselves. It was presumed the high standards instilled during their rigorous training would suffice, and indeed, despite the lack of oversight, the track record for virtuous conduct had been impressive—until now.

And grateful as Michlos was for Magister Treust's subtle hint that Vane might be waiting nearby for a replacement Amulet, knowing he was there didn't solve the problem. The best he could do would be to keep Vane from further implicating his mother in additional crimes, but even if he found a way to neutralize Vane, it wouldn't change the fact that Marguerite was now under suspicion for both heresy and murder.

He'd already decided to decline Magister Treust's lunch invitation. He couldn't take the chance Vane would recognize him or that one of the other Magisters might unwittingly give him away. He'd also decided to move his horse from the hitching post at the gate to the stables proper, where it wouldn't announce quite so publicly that the Academy was hosting another guest. He was also eager to learn if Vane, too, had arrived on horseback, perhaps accompanied by saddlebags bulging with important information.

As he approached the stables, his heart skipped a beat. The gate stood ajar, and he could hear activity within. Instinctively his left thumb sought out the signet on his ring, but he stopped short of activating the switch.

"Who's there?" he asked.

"Master Michlos? Is that you?"

A congenial face topped by a black velvet hat sporting a cacophony of plumage poked out of the stable gate.

"Newcomb? What are you doing here?"

"I'm tending to her Highness's mare. No offense to the Magisters or anything, but Petunia's not exactly used to slumming like this, and it's making her nervous."

"Princess Celeste is here?"

Newcomb stepped fully into the daylight. His black-and-white-striped doublet stood out in stark relief against the stable's gray brick and aged wood. "We just arrived."

"May I inquire as to why?"

"Well, I probably oughtn't say—but, then again, her Highness does seem favorably disposed where you're concerned."

"I promise to be circumspect."

"It won't be secret for much longer anyway. She's decided to close the Academy. She's here because she thought it was only right that the Magisters be told in person."

The news hit Michlos like a punch in the gut. "Close the Academy? Why?"

"I think she views it as a danger to her reconciliation with the Church. She's afraid they may ask her to return the monastery as a show of good faith."

"And give them a foothold on the island? Why would she do that?"

Newcomb shrugged. "She doesn't always tell me her reasons. But she's never been fond of them, so I doubt she thinks she has any choice."

"I must speak to her before she makes the announcement. When is she planning to tell the Magisters?"

"I don't know—probably as soon as she can. She'd think it was rude to accept their hospitality for long without letting them know."

"Where is she now?"

"I heard them say something about lunch at the new commissary, and it's about that time."

"Can you do me a favor?"

"I'd be honored, sir."

"Can you see to my horse for me?"

"It would be my pleasure."

Michlos handed off the reins. "Thank you, Newcomb. I owe you."

Newcomb paused at the stable door. "Well, then, now that you mention it, if you wouldn't mind confiding in her Highness how much you admired the old uniforms, I'd be much obliged."

He turned to gauge Michlos's reaction, but the man was already gone.

. . . . .

Arriving at the commissary, Michlos took a moment to catch his breath. He could hear the clatter of dishes inside and the low rumble of distant conversation, but he couldn't make out the Princess's voice. Reluctantly he approached the front stoop, eager to locate her, but leery of revealing himself to Vane. He spent several long moments at the door hoping to overhear something that would make the choice easier, but nothing came. Finally, cursing his indecision, he reached for the latch.

"Michlos, is that you?"

Michlos's hand froze mid-pull. After an almost imperceptible sigh of relief, he smiled and turned to face the voice.

"Your Highness, what an unexpected surprise."

Celeste stood before him, tall and stately, a forest-green ermine-lined cloak across her shoulders and the platinum-and-emerald diadem of her office glinting on her brow. Beside her, Magister Wellsbrough, Provost of the Academy, paled to awkward insignificance, and when Michlos finally acknowledged him with a nod, it was almost as an afterthought. She clearly intended this visit to be official.

"Well that's reassuring," she said. "I confess I was beginning to feel like you could anticipate my decisions before I even make them—not that you'd let on, of course. Let me guess. You're going to tell me you have no idea why I'm here and that your visit at precisely the same time is pure coincidence?"

"It seems I am an open book, Your Highness."

"Don't worry, I'm not disappointed. I resigned myself long ago to never to expect a straight answer when dealing with you. I am curious though, do you come by it naturally, or does the Academy offer specific courses in tergiversation?"

The Provost raised an eyebrow. "I don't think there's anything like that among our current course offerings, but if you spell it for me, I can have someone look it up."

"No need, Provost," the Princess said. "If you offer it, I'm sure Michlos teaches it, and its title could be almost anything—other than what it actually is, of course."

"Alas, today I am not so much teacher as errand boy," Michlos said. "Could I interest Your Highness in an urgent message from the Crown, or do your misgivings extend to those as well?"

The Provost glanced from the Princess, to Michlos, and back. "I'll just head in to get some lunch, then. When you are finished, you are both welcome to join us."

The Princess inclined her head. "Thank you, Provost. I expect to be along presently."

Michlos stepped aside as the Provost disappeared into the dining hall. "Shall we head somewhere more secure?"

"Lead on."

Eager to get out of sight, Michlos led her away from the commissary.

"Where are we going?"

The steeple rising above the treetops ahead caught his eye. "I thought we'd try the church."

"The church? I was told that was off limits—something about it no longer being safe."

Michlos laughed. "That's one way to put it."

"Oh? Are you suggesting there may be a better way?"

"No, come to think of it, that probably was the best way, under the circumstances."

"I don't suppose Miss Merinne happens to be traveling with you?"

"I'm afraid not. Why do you ask?"

"Because I find I am a much more enthusiastic ally when I know what's going on than I am when I have the impression I'm being kept in the dark."

Michlos paused. "I mean no disrespect, Your Highness. It's just that some matters are best discussed with at least a modicum of privacy. They were correct when they told you the church is generally off limits, and it happens to be set off from the rest of the grounds by a fence. While it's not perfect, it's far more private than the dining-hall door at lunchtime."

"Very well, but once we get to the church, I expect your little sermons to start serving up some meaningful revelation. And, please, you can dispense with the formalities."

"As you wish, Highness."

The Princess sighed and let it drop.

A short walk brought them to the gate in the wrought-iron fence that surrounded the old churchyard. The individual bars were taller than Michlos could reach, each topped with a fleur-de-lis that came to a wicked point. The gate, also of wrought iron, was set between two massive stone pillars replete with decorative finials and intricate floral designs. A large padlock dangled from a heavy chain through the latch. As Michlos took it in his hand, it fell open.

"You made that look effortless," the Princess said.

"It was."

"Remind me not to let you anywhere near the royal vault."

"No, I mean I didn't do anything to it except lift it. The lock was already open."

"Careless caretaker, perhaps?"

"Maybe. They must be getting lax. This would never have happened on Stuart's watch."

"It's just as well. We'd have had to find a way to open it to get through anyway, unless you were planning to give your sermon here at the gate."

"I was thinking perhaps the old cemetery next to the church would be good. We should be quite a distance from prying ears there."

"The church itself wouldn't be better still? Is it really that dilapidated?"

Michlos opened the gate and stepped through, followed closely by the Princess. He left the lock hanging as it had been when they arrived—open, but seeming closed.

"At the risk of sermonizing," Michlos said with a smile, "the church isn't all that dilapidated."

"But the Provost said—"

"That the church wasn't safe. That's true enough, but you assumed the danger arose from age and lack of maintenance."

"Are you suggesting it was made unsafe deliberately?"

"In a manner of speaking. The building has been repurposed. Before students can graduate from the Academy, they must go through a rigorous set of tests to determine whether they are ready to face challenges a Santine is likely to encounter. Some of those tests are most conveniently carried out in a large indoor space."

"They've converted the church into a heretic testing station?"

"That's one way to put it."

The Princess frowned. "Has the heresy become integral to the structure, or can it still be removed?"

Michlos shrugged. "I only know how I was tested. When I was here, we were led to believe that the Magisters tailor each examination to the individual student, but I expect all the exams have at least some elements in common. In principle, anything they've done should be reversible, but you'd have to talk to them to be sure. Why do you ask?"

"A good landlord tends to worry even about the little things. What do they do in there that's so dangerous?"

Michlos thought for a moment. "Say, for example, your mission is to neutralize a renegade Phrendonic who is expecting trouble and has had time to prepare defenses. That sort of thing would be fair game."

"They litter the place with traps?"

"They're generally not as dangerous as the real thing. And they're not all traps, either. In fact, one of the toughest tests they gave me was the Eye of Moravidos, which isn't really a trap at all."

"What was it then?"

"I've told you about Amulets, right?"

"The talismans the Santines use to quench the magic of their adversaries?"

Michlos nodded. "Well, they were modeled on the Eye, but they're weak imitations at best."

"So, this Eye quenches magic too?"

"Indeed it does, and very effectively, as I found out."

"I don't understand. Either the Amulet quenches or it doesn't, right? Why would the Eye be any stronger than an Amulet that does the same thing?"

"It's not quite that simple. What most people don't realize about Amulets is that they each have a certain inherent strength. If you're strong enough and if you put enough effort into overcoming an Amulet's quenching effect, sometimes you can overpower it. However, no one has ever managed to overpower the Eye."

"What makes it so strong?"

"No one knows. You'd need to use magic to study it, but no one has been able to get magic to work on it. If you're the superstitious type, you might subscribe to the legend that it was created by an ancient god."

"So how did they test you?"

"I was to ring the church bell twelve times."

"That's a test?"

Michlos leaned back against a tree. "Well I admit it didn't seem like much of one at first. But I'd had to pass other parts of the examination to get to that point, and I was already tired. Once I got there, I found the bell rope had been removed, which meant I had climb up into the steeple. Imagine my surprise when I found Stuart already up there waiting for me."

The Princess settled on a nearby stump.

"He was there to prevent me from ringing the bell. At first, I was puzzled, since I was well aware he didn't know the slightest thing about the Phrendonic arts. I asked him politely to step aside, but he just as politely refused. I then realized he must be part of the test. I shrugged and worked a spell to put him to sleep—which he promptly ignored."

"That's where the Eye came in?"

"Yes, but I hadn't realized it yet. I thought maybe the Magisters had given him an Amulet to test my ability to overpower it. You see, the decision to overpower an Amulet is always a difficult one, particularly if you might need your abilities once you succeed."

"Why is that?"

"Because if you don't know how strong the Amulet is, your best chance for success is to put everything you've got into the attempt. But if you do that, you'll be too exhausted to work any other spells for some time after that. On the other hand, if you do less than your best and keep some reserves, your attempt might not be strong enough to succeed."

"What did you decide?"

"I kept reserves and tried again. I couldn't afford to assume that getting past Old Stuart was the final part of the test. I was devastated when he brushed that off too—I thought I'd made precisely the wrong choice."

The Princess reached up, removed her diadem, and shook her head. Her auburn tresses tumbled down around her shoulders. "Ah, that's better. What did you do then?"

"I was getting desperate. I'd nearly used up my biggest advantage, and it looked like what little I had in reserve was going to be equally useless. It finally dawned on me why they'd chosen Stuart for this task. Unlike me, he was no stranger to manual labor; there was almost no chance I was going to overpower him physically. The Magisters had skillfully driven home their point—I tended to rely too heavily on a single skill set and was at a loss when it was taken from me."

"Did you fail?"

"I really don't like to fail. Once I understood the point of the exercise, I considered what other skills I could bring to bear. I was not confronting an adversary in the usual sense. His goal was not to thwart everything I tried, but to make sure I didn't do one specific thing. I couldn't Sleep him, and I couldn't fight him, but that didn't mean I couldn't talk to him."

"What did you say?"

"We chatted for a long time. Although he'd been at the Academy the whole time I'd been there, it was the first time we'd had much of a conversation. He'd had what most would consider a hard life, but he survived it with a wry wit and a refreshing perspective on what really matters. I'd never met anyone quite like him before. In retrospect, I probably learned as much from that talk as I did from the entire examination."

"So, in the end, did you convince him to let you ring the bell?"

Michlos laughed. "No amount of persuasion could have shaken that man's loyalty once he'd given his word. I didn't insult him by trying. Instead I used one other advantage I had over him."

"Which was?"

"Youth. I was used to studying into the wee hours, while Stuart was generally asleep at dusk and out of bed again by daybreak. Once it got dark, it didn't take long for him to start nodding off, but that didn't seem to worry him much. No doubt he was counting on the first ring of the bell to wake him up in plenty of time to prevent me from finishing the rest."

"Wasn't he concerned you might knock him unconscious while he slept?"

"And maybe accidentally kill or maim him? I don't think the Magisters would have graded that a success, and I wouldn't have risked it anyway—not even to pass the exam. I'd already found out from questioning him that the Magisters hadn't given him an Amulet, and that told me there had to be something else operating in the steeple. Once he fell asleep, I was free to use his lantern to search the area."

"And that's when you found the Eye?"

Michlos nodded. "Near the bell was a pedestal resembling a sundial with a broad brass face numbered from one to eleven and an odd little crank sticking out of one side. The Eye was mounted on the face of the dial where the number twelve should have been—appropriate for a midnight-black star sapphire with twelve fully defined rays. The gem was as wide as my thumb—and instantly recognizable from descriptions I'd heard."

"It must be worth a fortune."

"Perhaps, to a rare private collector. The problem is that Phrendonic artifacts are subject to confiscation by the Church, and possession would probably lead to accusations of heresy. A prudent man wouldn't take the risk."

"So, how did you pass the test? Pry the gem out of the sundial and throw it away?"

Michlos shook his head. "I had nothing to pry with, but I did find something I could use—some old beeswax candles."

"I thought you already had a lantern."

"I did, but the candles weren't to help me see—they were going to help me inactivate the Eye."

"Didn't you say the gem couldn't be overpowered?"

"With the beeswax I didn't need to."

"I don't follow."

"Displacement-cast magic such as that on the Eye penetrates gasses well, but solids and liquids poorly. Regardless of their strength, the Eye's spells should not have been able to circumvent that basic law. I simply softened the wax with the lantern and molded a cylinder to place over the Eye, making sure I carefully sealed the bottom where the cylinder contacted the sundial."

"Couldn't you just have molded the wax over the Eye?"

"The seal needed to be airtight. This way, when I used Stuart's water bottle to fill the cylinder, a leak wouldn't stop me—I'd have at least until the water drained to do what I needed to do."

"Did the plan work?"

Michlos grinned. "I graduated, didn't I?"

She arched an eyebrow. "That doesn't answer the question—perhaps they pass unduly smug students just to be rid of them."

"I admit things didn't go quite as I'd expected. Getting the water bottle was easy enough—Stuart was a sound sleeper. But the instant I filled the cylinder, I realized my mistake. I'd forgotten the cardinal rule for dispelling Dispels: First make sure you aren't thereby activating something you would rather keep inactivated."

"What happened?"

"With a loud click, the sundial dial rotated slightly. Instinctively I jumped back, but in doing so I accidentally put out the lantern. And then, the bell tolled. I could hear Stuart scrambling in the darkness, but my eyes hadn't yet adjusted, so I couldn't see him. I thought about trying to evade him but decided the risk of falling out of the tower was too great."

"He caught you?"

"Not before the bell tolled again, but he had me pinned so quickly after that it made my head spin."

"The bell rang by itself?"

"No, the sundial contraption was doing it. The Eye had prevented its magic from working."

"The sundial was doing your job for you?"

"Yes, but there was just one little problem—I had no way of knowing how many times it was going to ring. Still, after four or five times, it started to seem at least possible that I might actually succeed."

"You mean he just held you there and let the bell ring?"

"Here's where his lack of training was a disadvantage. He had promised to keep me from ringing the bell, but now, despite having me pinned, the bell continued to ring, and he had no idea why. The longer it went on, the more confused he got."

"And the rest, I suppose, is history?"

"Not exactly. Fortunately, it was dark enough that he couldn't see me sweat. All he would have had to do was knock over the wax cylinder, and I would have been done for. I had to keep him away from the mechanism at all costs."

"How?"

"I did the only thing I could—I talked. I thanked him for participating in my exam and told him how much I'd enjoyed our little chat. I even offered to take him to dinner to celebrate—anything to keep him from meddling with the sundial or counting how many times the bell tolled."

"How many times did it ring?"

"Eleven,"

"So, he stopped you after all?"

"When the twelfth ring didn't come, I let out a whoop—as though I'd just succeeded."

"And that worked?"

Michlos shrugged. "Apparently, he'd lost count, because at that point he helped me up and shook my hand to congratulate me."

"But you weren't done yet."

"No, but he didn't realize that. And he seemed very puzzled as to how I'd rung the bell while pinned. So, I did what any gracious competitor would have done."

"You waited until he turned his back and put him to sleep?"

Michlos put his hand to his heart. "Highness, you wound me."

"You mean you didn't?"

"Of course not. Instead, I offered to show him how I'd done it."

"Don't tell me he actually fell for that?"

Michlos rubbed his knuckles on his chest. "One short turn of the crank later, and I had officially passed."

"What did he say when he found out he'd been duped?"

"Funny, that specific topic never came up."

"Amazing what you can get away when you fail to mention the relevant details, isn't it? Speaking of which, just how long do you intend to fail to mention that urgent message from the Crown?"

"Ah yes, that. The Crown would like to know your plans regarding the Academy."

The Princess began tucking her hair back under the diadem. "The Crown would like to know? Or you would?"

"Does it matter?"

"It does to me."

"Don't close it," he said softly.

She turned away. "You think I want to?"

"Why, then? Why, after you've accomplished so much?"

"You think I'm blind? This island is little more than an insignificant barnacle adrift in a sea of chaos—we currently survive only by the grace of some great sea creature that tolerates our presence. What happens if that sea creature flounders? Worse still, what if it foolishly wakes the leviathan and is consumed? What choice do we have but to cleave to another and pray we are not noticed?"

"I don't believe what I'm hearing. Is this really the same woman who braved the wrath of that very same leviathan for the noble cause of artistic freedom?"

"Back then I had the luxury of a stable and reliable ally."

"That hasn't changed."

The Princess rounded on him. "Really? Then look me in the eye and tell me this Inquisition poses no serious threat to the Crown."

Michlos paused—then sighed. "There may be some danger if the situation is mismanaged. But that doesn't change the Crown's commitment to the Colony."

"And you didn't think I needed to know that?"

"I didn't want to alarm you unnecessarily."

The Princess folded her arms. "I take it that means the Crown is unaware of this danger as well?"

Michlos shifted uncomfortably. "No, the Crown knows."

"I thought as much. Let's get something straight right now—though my realm is smaller, I am no less a head of state because of it."

"I never meant to imply—"

"And if you think that just because I'm a woman I need to be protected from vital information instead of kept apprised of it, well then, you can just find yourself another ally." She turned on her heel and stalked back toward the gate.

Michlos scrambled to keep up. "Celeste, wait. I can explain."

Her pace didn't slow. "It's 'Your Highness' to you."

At that moment, the distinctive sound of the church bell reverberated across the churchyard. Michlos stopped and glanced up at the steeple in confusion. Then he remembered the tampered lock at the gate, and somewhere deep in his mind, two met two—*Vane*.

The Princess whirled. "If this is some sort of joke, I'm in no mood."

Again, the bell tolled.

Michlos triggered his Amulet. "Get away from me."

"How dare you!"

"No, I mean get out of sight. I'll try to draw any fire."

The Princess wavered only a moment before diving unceremoniously behind a headstone.

The bell rang a third time.

Michlos sprinted for the church. "Vane is stealing the Eye. Get out of here—tell the Magisters."

"If he has the Eye, you'll be powerless against him."

"But if he escapes, the leviathan consumes us all."

For the fourth time the bell's doleful clang echoed across the island.

Michlos arrived at the Church and ducked inside.

The Princess winced in anticipation, but a fifth peal never came. An eerie silence descended over the churchyard. Leaning back against the headstone, her cloak now stained, her diadem askew, she blew a wayward lock of hair from her face and sighed. "Good thing he never bothered to mention who this Vane person was, or I would probably be unnecessarily alarmed right now."

. . . . .

Ordinal Lavicius surveyed the fairgrounds and beamed. Brightly colored tents had been erected around an elaborate but temporary central pavilion in the alpine meadow that served as this year's site for his beloved Accipitrine Festival. Nearby, the tantalizing aroma of roasting boar emanated from a makeshift fire pit, while numerous well-dressed participants milled about waiting for the festivities to begin. To one side, a cadre of falconers and owners tended their hooded charges, eager to test their mettle in competition. Lavicius stood among them, a great white gyrfalcon perched on his arm. He looked up as Prentiss approached.

"Good news, Your Ordinence. We've tracked down the Primal's carriage."

Lavicius handed off the gyrfalcon to his falconer. "That's reassuring news, Prentiss. I was beginning to think your Accipitrines weren't up to the task. And how is our beloved Primal?"

"Notably absent. It seems the carriage was accosted by brigands somewhere along the road to Caprian, but when they pried it open to greet their hostage, it was empty. Fortunately for the driver, our men intervened when they did, or things might have gone badly for him."

"How did he explain the Primal's absence?"

"For some reason, he was loath to speak of it."

"Was he? You don't suppose his reticence could indicate complicity in a plot against the Primacy, do you?"

Prentiss shrugged. "Hard to say."

"Have him brought to me. Perhaps after his ordeal, he needs a softer touch."

"And if that doesn't work?"

"Ready the Interrogation Chamber. In the meantime, I don't suppose you could find me some old-school Inquisitors. You know, the ones our well-meaning but misguided Inquisitor General dismissed as too efficient?"

"I'll see what I can do."

"We also must consider the possibility that the driver doesn't know the Primal's current location. Who was the last person to talk to him before he boarded the carriage?"

"Theratigan," Prentiss said.

"The demon hunter?"

Prentiss nodded.

"How convenient. I think he's already being held in the Interrogation Chamber. And who, before him?"

"I believe he was scheduled to meet with his nephew."

Lavicius raised an eyebrow. "Thurman, you mean?"

"So I've been told."

"Splendid. Could you find him and let him know I'd like to speak with him? And Prentiss, I hope I don't need to impress upon you that time is of the essence. I've only been voted temporary executive powers—I'm not Primal yet. Allowing Laitrech to find the Primal before we do would be an unmitigated disaster."

"I understand," Prentiss said.

. . . . .

Sunlight blazed through the rose window above the church entrance, splashing brilliant hues of, gold, azure, and crimson across the floor before Michlos. Rows of pews filled the space, split by an aisle of mosaic tiles stretching all the way to the altar. To one side, red and green votive candles flickered. The air was thick with incense, as though the building had been miraculously restored to its original purpose.

Perhaps the change was part of a test. He rubbed his chin, considering the best route to reach the bell-tower entrance. The most obvious path was the center aisle, but the tiles were a problem—touching them could trigger some test-related obstacle. The side aisles were equally suspect. He was considering hopping from pew to pew when the side stairwell caught his eye. It led to the crypts beneath the church, off limits for examination purposes. The bell tower might hold another entrance, which made the stairwell a safer option—but what if, while he was downstairs, Vane were to escape across the main floor?

His decision was made for him. A tall well-muscled man appeared within the sacristy arch. Michlos sensed his initial surprise, which was followed by a look of calculating appraisal.

"My apologies for setting off the bell," Vane said. "I went up for a look at how the Academy has changed, and I was intrigued by the mechanism. I'm pretty sure I reset it properly."

"You're aware this church is off limits?"

"I thought that was only for students, not graduates. Are you new here? I don't think we've met."

"You'll have to come with me. The other Magisters will be worried someone was injured or that an exam may be compromised."

"I'll head back through the crypts and meet you by the door."

Michlos suffered a twinge of panic. He couldn't lose sight of Vane now. "The center aisle is clear."

Vane eyed him dubiously. "I'd hate to risk setting something off."

"The center aisle is always the last area prepared for an exam."

"But I thought there was an exam tomorrow. Are the preparations not yet complete?"

Michlos's pulse quickened. The chances of an exam the next day were ridiculously slim. Vane could be fabricating an examination to test him. He improvised. "Actually, everything has been postponed due to the Royal visit."

He realized his mistake as soon as he'd said it.

Vane gasped. "The Crown is here?" Then his eyes narrowed. "What did you say your name was?"

Praying his slip hadn't caused Vane to recognize him, Michlos pushed on. "No, not the Crown—Princess Celeste. She arrived this morning. If you'll just come with me—"

"In that case, I shouldn't risk taking the aisle. We can't afford any more untoward disturbances."

Vane was gone before Michlos could react. With a resigned sigh, he worked a protective spell to avoid being incinerated like the men at St. Sophia's. He also activated one of his many rings—perhaps he could recapitulate his mother's victory despite the Eye. And then he waited.

Vane shouldn't have taken more than a minute or two, but minutes came and went. Had he slipped out a back door? Michlos's thoughts turned to the Princess—he hoped she'd locked that gate. Several more minutes passed.

Michlos approached the stairwell. "Are you all right down there?"

Silence.

Michlos extended his hand, and from it, a deadly looking blade materialized. The resulting breeze stirred his hair and produced scuttling momentary whirlwinds. A few whispered words, and the rapier glowed. Taking care to reactivate his Amulet, he descended.

The air became abruptly dank. Before him stood an ancient door. Tattered cobwebs suggested infrequent use—and that at least one was recent. He pushed. The decrepit hinges cried out, but yielded. Ahead lay a broad expanse of darkness. Here and there, pairs of tiny reddish eyes flashed into existence as they caught blade's light, then vanished.

"Hello?"

Great stone pillars loomed before him. Darker regions of blackness shrouded mounds of detritus—long-empty casks, rodent-ravaged furniture, and rusted tools. Several stone sarcophagi presided over the crypt's heart—a final obeisance to some of Ranselard's noble but ill-fated occupants.

Michlos began to doubt his choice. If Vane had escaped through a back door, he would be long gone before Michlos even made it across the crypt. But he was also mindful of the presence of a multitude of nooks and crannies capable of concealing someone determined to remain hidden.

"Are you down here?"

Something skittered in the darkness.

"Ah, so you are here."

"Who are you?" Vane asked.

Michlos tried to locate the voice, but sound echoed strangely in the crypt. "I'm here on behalf of the Magisters."

"You're a Santine."

Michlos edged forward but still couldn't pinpoint Vane. "What makes you think that?"

"Magisters don't carry Amulets."

The voice seemed to come from off to the right.

"And why not? Can't a Santine become a Magister?"

"Have I been Noticed, or haven't I?"

Michlos ground his teeth. Now Vane's voice seemed to be coming from someplace else. He focused instead on getting Vane to show himself.

"Let's just say your escapades at St. Sophia's didn't go unnoticed."

"Then I demand proof, as is my right."

"You know as well as I that it won't work in the presence of the Eye."

"The Eye? What are you suggesting?"

"You're denying you stole it?"

"If I did, then trying to provide your proof will betray me, won't it?"

"Very well," Michlos said. "Show yourself and you shall have your proof."

"Oh no, not while you're armed."

Michlos laid the sword across the nearest sarcophagus and took several steps back. He held up his hands.

Vane stepped out from behind a cask. "My proof, if you please."

Michlos held out his left hand and closed his eyes to concentrate on recreating the figment that would manifest his namesake. He could almost feel it squirming in his hand just as it had that day so many years ago, when Magister Treust worked the spells to make its image an indelible part of his being. Designed to withstand even his active Amulet, the illusion flickered once or twice and then stabilized. The serpent's sinuous scaled body coiled around his wrist and up the length of his arm. His hand gripped the beast just behind the neck where it split into two serpentine heads. Confident in his ability to maintain the figment, he opened his eyes. In the rapier's glow, Michlos clearly saw his namesake. He also saw Vane completing a spell.

The two-headed serpent vanished as weariness overwhelmed Michlos. Though he strove against it, he succeeded only in mastering himself long enough to settle slowly to the floor, where consciousness deserted him.

. . . . .

Cautiously Vane approached. He stared down at Michlos for a long moment before digging the toe of his boot into his side. When Michlos did not stir, he pulled a small lump of soft clay out of his pocket, pushing at it with his thumb until it revealed a black gem with a twelve-pointed star hovering beneath its surface. He grunted in satisfaction and slipped the gemstone back into his pocket.

Next, he approached the sarcophagus. The rapier-light illuminated the brightly colored lid, which was carved in the likeness of its long-dead occupant. The inscription identified her as Her Grace, Cecily Chartruvan, Duchess of Arusia. Taking up the rapier, he inspected the lid's edges for catches. Finding none, he tried lifting it. A lesser man would have despaired of the task, but Vane was both sturdy and determined. It yielded at last, and he slid it askew. Inside, skeletal remains grinned up at him from beneath bejeweled ducal regalia. Here and there, rotting fabrics still glinted with golden threads and other adornments that proudly proclaimed royal status, for whatever that was worth to a Ranselard alumna.

But Vane was not interested in baubles. Now that the sarcophagus was partly open, he leaned over, grasped Michlos beneath the arms, and dragged him toward it.

Michlos's eyes suddenly sprang open. He lashed out, striking Vane across the face with his ring, but Michlos's triumphant grin faded when, in response, Vane merely dropped Michlos and rubbed his jaw. Then, Vane's eyes narrowed, his nostrils flared, and his fist crashed into Michlos' nose with a satisfying crunch.

A few moments later, Vane wrestled the sarcophagus lid back into place. Still panting, he strode back to the crypt exit. From the steps, he turned and saluted the sarcophagus. "Give my regards to your mother." And then he was gone.

# CHAPTER 22

# Ꮄᴜsᴛʏ ᴏʟᴆ sᴋᴇʟᴇᴛᴏɴs

The floor-to-ceiling bookshelves in the Nevinander library were finished in a varnish so rich it was almost black. Rayen drew an overstuffed wingback chair up to the fireplace, removed his boots, and warmed his feet on the hearth. He rubbed the chair's orange-and-black-striped upholstery admiringly, wondering out loud what sort of exotic creature could have provided the hide. Nearby, Dona's mother peered through the crack in the door to make certain no one could overhear, and silently nudged it closed.

"Are you out of your mind?"

"Not at the moment," Rayen said. "Really, I've been feeling pretty good lately. Thank you for asking."

"Don't get smart with me. What do you think you're doing, proposing marriage to that woman like that?"

"I thought you rather liked her."

"It's not a matter of that. You don't know anything about her."

Rayen shrugged. "I know if I marry her, she stands to inherit all this. Is that really such a bad thing?"

"It makes no sense. You saw what they said to each other. He was practically goading her into it. Is that really the kind of marriage you want?"

Rayen glanced around and then nodded decisively. "Yes."

"Don't be ridiculous. That woman couldn't care less about what happens to you."

"I beg to differ. Unless she wants to forgo her inheritance, she has every reason to care."

"And once her father is out of the picture? What then? What's to stop her from tossing you out on your ear?"

"Not every marriage ends in happily ever after. That's hardly a reason not to try. Are you going to tell me you wouldn't have married Henry if you had known?"

"But I loved Henry."

"What makes you think the order of such things matters? Verone is intelligent, sophisticated, reasonably attractive, and she's been ex-traordinarily kind to us—she spent considerable effort helping us track down Dona. Even if I don't love her yet, she's just the sort of woman I think I could. If I don't marry her now, I'll never get the chance to find out."

"That may be, but if she's everything you say she is, then why, of all people, should she pick you?"

Rayen stared at her incredulously. "Madam, may I remind you that I have a gift, not some loathsome disability. I should think any woman would be delighted to land me."

"I was referring to your social status. But, while we're on the topic, just how delighted do you think your lovely bride is going to feel when your precious 'gift' puts in an appearance at the opera—or during tea with the Countess?"

"She is already aware of it, and she said 'yes' despite it. It's not like I kept it secret."

"Take it from me, there's a big difference between being aware of it and enduring it year in and year out."

Rayen trembled with indignation. "Then it's all worked out for the best, hasn't it? I suppose you'll be very relieved to finally be rid of me."

"Look, this isn't the most pleasant conversation for me either. I'm just pointing this out for your own good—it's far better that you to go into this with a realistic understanding of what this marriage is going to mean, instead of finding out later it never really stood a chance of working in the first place."

Rayen's face was ashen, and the trembling became more pro-nounced. "You're just jealous. Can you really be so crabbed and bitter that you would sabotage my happiness just because your husband ran out on you?"

Amanda gaped at him openmouthed. And then she slapped him.

Rayen's eyes rolled up, and he fell backward, his limbs twitching, froth accumulating at the corners of his mouth.

"Oh, not now. I'm so sorry. Oh Rayen, what have I done?"

As she had countless times before, she turned him on his side and moved away any hard objects. Then cradling his head in her lap, she rocked, tears streaming down her face, until the seizure at last subsided.

She was still there when Nathalie swept in, Verone in tow. "Now then, if we're going to have any chance of getting this done in time, we're going to need to get him measured right away. And, of course, we can't even start the invitations without a surname. Have you given any thought at all to where you'd like to hold the ceremony? Good heavens, what happened?"

"He's had another seizure," Amanda said. "He'll probably come around shortly."

Nathalie clucked consolingly. "Looks like as between the two of you, he got the better deal. Is there anything we can do?"

"Kind of you to ask, but I'll be fine. All the commotion of the past week must finally be catching up with me."

"And, after all you've been through, who could blame you. You stay right there, and I'll get Eloise to bring some water. Veronique dear, if you could, please try to get at least some of the relevant details."

Verone drew up a chair. "Does he always have visions when this happens?"

Amanda looked pained. "Don't tell me he's got you believing his nonsense, too?"

"Well, you must admit, his wedding prediction was pretty impressive."

Amanda shook her head. "I've seen this sort of thing with him before. He gets something in his head and keeps spouting it over and over until people actually start to accept it. This wedding situation was like that, too—you don't seriously think it would have happened if he hadn't put the idea in your father's head, do you?"

"You may have a point there, but even then, it's uncanny."

"Well I certainly hope for your sake that you didn't agree to marry him for his awesome powers as a seer, because even I can predict how that would end."

Rayen became suddenly restless. Amanda resumed rocking, her brow furrowed in concern.

"Is he coming 'round?"

"I'm not sure," Amanda said. "Usually he just wakes up."

"Looks like a bad dream. Should you wake him?"

"I don't know."

"Here, let me try." Verone leaned over and gently shook Rayen's shoulder. "Rayen, it's time to wake up."

Rayen shuddered, and his hand shot out and took hold of Verone's wrist. Verone recoiled, her eyes wide with revulsion. Steeling herself, she tried delicately to withdraw her hand, but his grip was vise-like.

"You can't have her," Rayen cried. He shuddered once more. His breathing became labored. Suddenly, he sat bolt upright, his eyes open, but still unseeing. "And only the taint remains," he said sadly, almost wistfully.

Verone finally lost her nerve and wrenched her wrist away. The shock of it finally brought him to himself, and he looked with surprise into the dubious eyes of his bride-to-be. He sighed contentedly. "Once again, you're here for me."

Verone rubbed her wrist. "Isn't that what fiancés are for? What did you see this time?"

"I'm sure he's exhausted from his ordeal," Amanda said. "It would probably be best if he got some rest."

"Oh, I don't mind," Rayen said.

Amanda put her hand to his forehead. "You're not well. You might even be feverish." She turned to Verone. "I really think I should take him up to the guest room and tuck him in until he's feeling better."

"I'm just a little tired. It will pass."

"You have others to think about now. You can't afford to go and get yourself sick—it would ruin all the plans. Is that what you want?"

"No, of course not, but—"

"All right then, let's get you upstairs."

Verone finally weighed in. "Amanda's right. We wouldn't want to risk anything interfering with the wedding, would we? Tell you what—I'll help her get you up there, and once you're safely tucked in, then, if you're feeling up to it, you can tell me."

His disappointment was plain. "If you say so."

"Oh, you don't have to trouble yourself," Amanda said. "I can handle this—I've been doing it for years now."

"It's no trouble," Verone said. "Besides, it would probably be good for me to learn what I should do if something like this happens when you aren't around—don't you agree?"

"But you have all that planning to get done and so little time—and really, I don't mind."

"Not to worry, Mum has all the planning covered. She just loves that sort of thing. In fact, my opinions generally end up just slowing things down. Since I have the opportunity, I think I'm better off spending a little quality time with my man. Don't you agree Rayen?"

Rayen beamed. "That would be delightful."

"There. It's settled, then. I'll take his right arm, and you take his left, and together we'll get him upstairs and taken care of."

Amanda wavered for a moment, then nodded.

Even though Rayen was recovering quickly, Amanda insisted they take the grand staircase with exaggerated caution, fussing over his health at every opportunity. Despite her delays, it was only a matter of minutes before he was safely tucked into the guestroom daybed.

Once there, Verone turned to Amanda. "And now it's your turn."

"Someone has to stay here and keep an eye on him. What if he has another seizure?"

"Don't argue with me. You've had a trying week so far, and the rest of it is unlikely to be any easier. Rayen and I will need you in top form for the ceremony"

"But I'm not tired."

"That is the single least-convincing lie I've ever heard. Now off to bed with you. I'll see to it Rayen has everything he needs."

"But—"

"If you don't go this instant, I'll be forced to sic Mum on you."

Despite her protests, Amanda really was too exhausted to truly argue. And besides, Rayen was already half asleep. The temptation finally convinced her—against her better judgment.

"I suppose I could use a tiny little nap."

"Now you're talking. I'll find a book and sit right here with Rayen until you come back. If there is any change, I'll let you know right away."

"You really *are* too kind."

Verone squeezed her hand. "Sweet dreams."

The instant Amanda was out the door, Verone sat next to Rayen's bed and leaned in close. "Rayen?"

Rayen started. "Oh, I'm sorry, I must have drifted off."

"I didn't mean to wake you. I was just seeing if you were up to telling me about your latest vision."

"You won't think it's nonsense?"

"Of course not. After all, you foresaw our wedding, didn't you?"

"Well, some things are clearer than others. Sometimes everything doesn't make sense right away."

"I promise to keep an open mind. Was it disturbing? You seemed like you were having a bad dream."

"It was far more menacing than usual. It was dark, and the walls were all closing in. I couldn't breathe."

"What else did you see?"

"I think I have it mostly prepared."

"What do you mean?"

"No one expects a true seer to just spout random bits and pieces of visions. The idea is to distill them down into their essence—you know, let the poetic form lend structure and meaning to the experience. Without that, they're no better than someone's random nightmares. Don't you agree?"

"Fascinating. I had no idea."

"Fortunately, I have rather a knack for this sort of thing."

"I'm sure you do. Now that I better understand the artistic element, I'm more eager than ever."

Rayen sat up and cleared his throat:

> *As Chervil beckons kin-to-be, before the final gasp,*
> *The frantic throes awaken she who flits outside his grasp.*
> *Enshrouded by a fair facade, yet deep beneath the paint,*
> *She stirs once more, malevolent, and redolent of taint.*

*She weaves a web of bitter tears—she sings the siren's cry,*
*She conquers houses, topples kings—bleeds even allies dry.*
*The doppleganger's secret trove could obviate the threat,*
*But use of it involves a choice the user may regret.*
*For it shall bring no accolades to expurgate this ghost.*
*And as was true in ages past, those closest suffer most.*

As he recited his masterpiece, Verone's initial reaction was to frown and raise her eyebrow, but by the time he finished and looked to her for approval, she was all smiles.

"Bravo. You've really outdone yourself."

"You're not just saying that?"

"Well, I don't pretend to be a great judge of poetry, but it sounded very skillfully crafted to me. I still can't say what it means though. It isn't about me, is it?"

"It's hard sometimes to know for sure, but that wasn't my impression. What made you think that?"

"Given our wedding is under a week away, I would have thought that conclusion inescapable from the words 'kin-to-be.' I certainly hope you're right, though. My schedule is full up—I don't have time to add being beckoned by the death god."

Rayen scowled at the suggestion. "Like I said, I'm not always able to figure everything out right away. Promise me you'll be extra careful."

"A wise man once told me there was no escaping fate."

"I certainly hope for his sake he's not always right."

"He might prefer it if he was. After all, if I'm so tainted and malevolent, wouldn't he be better off if Chervil took me?"

"Only if he would be better off inconsolable. Besides, I'm almost certain those words have nothing to do with you."

"You might be surprised."

"Well, no more than they apply to any other woman, then. What I mean is that the word 'taint' in these things usually arises from a very specific impression, and I've never had that feeling about you before. It must be someone else."

"Oh really. Not even married yet, and already dreaming about other women?"

"It's not like that at all. Usually when I have that impression, it's connected in some way with my niece."

"You mean Dona? She didn't seem all that tainted and malevolent."

"I don't normally think of her as malevolent either."

"But you do think she's tainted?"

Rayen stole a glance toward the door. "I probably shouldn't be talking about this. Amanda will flay me alive if she finds out."

"Dona is going to be my niece, too. If there's some dark family secret lurking in the closet, don't you think I have a right to know?"

"I doubt Amanda would see it that way."

"I certainly hope you aren't suggesting that Amanda is going to have veto power over how we choose to conduct our relationship, because that would be a very good way to start off on the wrong foot."

"It's not that—"

"Then what would you call it?"

Rayen began to pale again.

Verone waited a few moments longer and then patted his shoulder. "I don't mean to pressure you into things you don't want to do. If you don't want to tell me, it's all right. I was probably just being naïve in thinking we were really starting to connect as a couple. If you feel like we're rushing into things too quickly, I'll simply tell my father we aren't ready and that we are calling the whole thing off."

"But won't you lose the estate, then?"

"Probably, but better that than rush into an ill-fated relationship."

"But it's not ill-fated. I knew we were going to be together before we even met."

"That doesn't mean the time is right. Lots of men struggle with the idea of commitment. Particularly under these circumstances, if you need more time, I completely understand."

"I don't need more time. Really, I don't."

"Your reticence to talk about your family seems to say otherwise. Commitment is based on trust, and I don't think you're there yet."

"But I do trust you. I just don't want to offend Amanda."

Verone shook her head. "Amanda again? I really don't think you're ready."

"It's not that big a deal. It's just a little family legend."

Verone held up her hand. "No, stop right there. I don't want you to tell me—not unless you are absolutely sure you're comfortable with it."

"Amanda wouldn't want a little thing like this to come between us. I'm sure of that."

"Well, so long as you're sure." She folded her hands in her lap. "All right—tell me."

"I was very young the first time I ever heard of it, just a lad—too young to really understand what was going on. All I knew was that my grandmother was coming. She was a small woman, but she had tremendous presence. I was more than a little afraid of her but found her fascinating—this tiny woman who could order even my parents around. We had a game where I would hide when I knew she was coming, and I would wait to see how long it would take her to ask after me, and then I would surprise her by jumping out and shouting out 'here I am Grandma.' But this time she arrived with several other women who also seemed old to me—I think they were her sisters. All of them were very sad."

"Was there a funeral?"

"I don't think so. They brought with them a great dome-top trunk, which they presented to my mother. I remember my grandmother telling her the duty had fallen to her to safeguard the legacy—that Grandfather had been taken and all that was left to the rest of them was the sacrifice."

Verone perked up. "The sacrifice? Are you sure?"

Rayen shrugged. "I was very young—it's possible I misunderstood. Anyway, my mother wept, and even though there were tears in my grandmother's eyes as well, she admonished her to stay strong like the others in our family who had inherited the taint."

"What did she mean by that?"

"I never had the opportunity to ask. After seeing my mother crying, I was too afraid to come out of hiding. It took my father an hour to find me. We left our house that very night, never to return. I brought it up several times, but my parents acted like I made whole thing up. Later,

I suspected others in our family might have been seers like I am, and maybe that's what she meant, but now I'm not so sure."

"Why is that?"

"There came a day a few years after Dona was born that I had a particularly intense vision. In it I heard my mother's voice calling out to me over and over: 'Dona has the taint. Dona has the taint.' I was concerned for her, of course, but I couldn't help being ecstatic that someone else I knew might actually understand what it's like to have the Sight."

"Is she prone to seizures as well?"

Rayen shook his head sadly. "If she really did inherit the Sight, she's never shown the slightest sign of it. But then, it didn't come to me until I was in my teens, so I guess it's possible it may come later to her."

"I take it Amanda would not be thrilled by that?"

"She doesn't understand. She thinks the Sight is a terrible disease. The whole idea that Dona might have inherited it scares her to death. She's forbidden me to even bring up the topic—she has a fit if I so much as mention Dona and taint in the same sentence. That's why I hesitate to talk about it."

"What happened to the trunk?"

"My mother kept it locked and hidden away, but when she died, my father had it sent to Amanda. I have no idea what she did with it—I haven't seen it in years."

A smart rap came at the door.

Nathalie poked her head in. "How's our patient doing? Eloise has brought water."

"Bless you," Rayen said.

Nathalie gave Rayen a polite nod but didn't let him distract her from her mission. "So, have you made any progress finding out the relevant details?"

Verone sighed. "I'm afraid we aren't going to get any rest until she gets a start on those invitations."

"I am sorry to be such a nag. I don't know what's gotten into me—it's not like we have a deadline or anything."

"Well, Mr. Magnificent," Verone said. "The time has come to fess up. Who are you really?"

Rayen chuckled. "I have no idea how we could possibly have gotten to this point without a proper introduction. I guess when we met, I felt like we already knew each other."

Nathalie crossed her arms and tapped her foot. "The name, if you please?"

"Oh, sorry. It's Theratigan—Rayen Theratigan."

. . . . .

Taking the well-worn path back toward the commissary, Princess Celeste was relieved to see an older man striding purposefully in her direction.

"Come quickly. Michlos says Vane is stealing the Eye. He's trying to stop him but may need help."

"Stealing the Eye?" the man said. "Are you sure?"

"I'm just repeating what he told me."

"Any idea why he thought that?"

"Didn't you hear the bell?"

"I did. In fact, that's why I'm here. The Provost asked that I come check it out—you know, make sure nothing is broken, or that the students aren't meddling where they shouldn't. I'm Magister Treust, by the way."

"I'm Princess Celeste."

He winked. "Had I not already known, I would have surmised as much from the crown. Where is Michlos now?"

"After we heard the bell, he told me to come get help and went into the church. He was concerned the situation might turn dangerous."

"I certainly hope he doesn't intend to force the issue."

"What do you mean?"

"Vane is built like a bull. If I were Michlos, and if I truly suspected Vane of stealing the Eye, the last thing I'd want to do is confront him about it alone."

"Who is this Vane, and why would he want the Eye?" The Magister scratched his beard. Then his eyes widened. "Ah, I think I see the reasoning now. Michlos expects Vane to use it as a replacement."

"Replacement for what? Why are you people always so obtuse?"

"There's no time to explain. If Michlos was right, I'll just have to hope my title still carries some weight. You said he's in the church?"

"Yes, and I came straight here."

"Find the Provost. Tell him Vane may have stolen the Eye. Ask him to send armed backup, just in case."

"You have armed backup here?"

"It's possible he may have to improvise."

. . . . .

From the commissary's front stoop, Newcomb saw the Princess approaching. He scooped up his plumed hat, slammed it on his head, and sprang to attention. "Is everything all right, Your Highness?"

"I'm afraid not. Is the Provost still inside?"

"I don't know. I've been waiting here—I never went in."

"I'd like you to find him. Tell him Magister Treust needs armed backup at the church—someone named Vane has stolen the Eye."

"Right away, Highness. And where would you like me to meet you?"

"Bring them to the church. Make sure they come quickly."

"Pardon my boldness, but if there is some sort of conflict there, shouldn't you wait for the Provost to resolve it?"

She shook her head. "Michlos may need me. Just bring the Provost's men as soon as you can."

Newcomb started to object, but the Princess was already running back toward the church.

"Well," he said, "I guess she always has been prone to make exceptions where he's concerned."

. . . . .

After an entire morning of scrubbing smoke-damaged walls, the pain from Tilly's cracked knuckles and the throbbing in her back finally convinced her to take a break. She wiped the lye soap from her hands with the rag she'd been using to cover her face against the smoke smell and strolled through the brothel to inspect the ongoing work. She was heartened that a fair number of the girls had shown up to help with the cleanup. If they hadn't, she wasn't sure she could have forced herself to keep going. It wasn't just the hard work—she was used to that—it was knowing that at some point she would have to face the room at the end of the hall. When she caught herself complimenting each of the girls on their progress for the second time, she finally realized she couldn't put it off any longer.

She marched resolutely toward the stairway, but, at the last minute, veered into the adjoining warehouse. Before her stood Jonas's cart, none the worse for wear from the fire. After a glance over her shoulder, she reached up under it to retrieve a key and unlocked a fold-down panel. She pulled out a large bottle, and after a good long swig, she slipped it back onto the cart.

*No sense going in unprepared.*

The heat in her throat couldn't distract from the anguish in her soul as she climbed the stairs to the hallway where her mother had made her last stand. Nana's had been a tragic end to a tragic life, and Tilly couldn't help feeling partly to blame. If she'd kept a tighter rein on Jonas, or maybe if she'd realized Nana's intent a few moments sooner, there might have been something she could have done. The scorched walls conjured up the ghastly wails of those who had died there. But those memories paled in comparison to her recollection of the haunting beauty of Nanna's defiant lullaby—her anguished proclamation that life had finally become too cruel to endure. Tilly tried humming an old drinking tune, but ended up floundering on the chorus, which she usually managed flawlessly even after a long night of rum and revelry. She pushed on to the end of the hall through sheer force of will, pausing once, briefly, to wipe away tears.

Nanna's room, like the others near the end of the hall, had borne the brunt of the damage from Nanna's Sacrifice. Blackened wallpaper, once striped, peeled away from the plaster. The feather mattress had also gone up in flames, as evidenced not just by the remains of bedclothes, but also by the charred ceiling above. The trunk at the foot of the bed fared somewhat better, but its lid had been pried open and the contents strewn about the floor, presumably by the same agents of the Constable who had absconded with the bodies. Tilly bent to retrieve a jewelry box, its lid hanging by a hinge. From the rubble, she saved, one by one, inexpensive rings, chains and earrings, now soot-covered, many of which she'd given Nanna over the years. She spent a moment remembering each gift and its occasion before placing it solemnly back in its box. The remains of Nanna's hand-embroidered linens, once stored in the chest of drawers, were now scattered randomly about, as were the charred remains of hats and dresses that had once graced her treasured walnut wardrobe. Her most-prized possession, her wedding ring, was nowhere to be found. Above the chest of drawers was the little painting Jonas had given her from the Artist's Colony. It had always called to mind the proud towers of Caprian before the Inquisition. Singed though it was, she imagined she could still make out the skyline if she squinted hard enough. Setting the jewelry box aside, she took down the picture, wondering if there was any way it could be restored. As she moved it, something fell behind the chest of drawers.

The heavy paper that had sealed the painting's back had burned away. Likely whatever had fallen had been concealed within the stretcher that held the canvas. Her questing hand came upon a package tightly wrapped in scorched leather. The bindings offered little opposition, and the protective layers fell away to reveal a leather-bound book. The front cover, in embossed gold letters, said simply "Diary."

At first, she was reticent to open it—what if the artist left it there by mistake? Should she try to return it? If so, to whom? At last, she peeked at the title page to see whether the owner had signed it. It read: Francesca Ravennan.

Tilly's jaw dropped. Never had it crossed her mind that Nanna might have kept a diary. All these years never knowing what had happened to her, and now she could actually be holding in her hands the full explanation. The first entry was dated 882, when Nanna would have been in her late teens:

> *I met my future husband today—Mr. Giles Boothby Harcourt. He was sort of handsome, I guess, but he seemed a little old. Mother says a man of good breeding is hard to come by and that I should be grateful. He was very polite, and he gave me this diary as a gift, so I let him kiss me on the cheek when he left. FR, May 17, 881.*

Already Tilly had learned something—she hadn't known her parents' marriage had been arranged. She rifled hungrily through entries until another caught her eye.

*Last week our little girl finally arrived. We named her Mathilda after Boothie's grandmother. I think she looks more like me, but Mother says she favors the Harcourts. FRH, March 5, 882.*

Curious to see whether there was an entry for Jonas, she skipped ahead. Sure enough, Nanna had recorded the event:

*It's a boy! Boothie said it wouldn't matter either way, but he was so excited, you could just tell he didn't mean it. Boothie's mother insisted on the name Mapleton after her side of the family, and I agreed on condition his first name be Jonas. Jonas Mapleton Harcourt—can a name get any more distinguished than that? FRH, January 22, 883.*

Tilly smiled as she envisioned a young and vibrant Nanna cooing over her "distinguished" baby brother, and settled down on the cloth she'd thrown across the charred floorboards to read more:

*The cotillion was splendid. I admit I got a little pouty when Boothie up and left me without a partner, but what did he expect? I don't care how important he thinks his little meetings are, we'd been planning this for weeks. It would have been a complete disaster if it hadn't been for Barclay. He was so gallant, offering to step in and rescue me like that. I'm sure he could have had his pick of any number of younger prettier girls, but long after any reasonable person would have deemed his rescue obligations met, I still had his arm. Did I mention he said I looked radiant? FRH, April 2, 887.*

*Barclay?* On one hand, Tilly didn't want to think anything ill of her mother. On the other, she couldn't wait to see if the name showed up again. She didn't have to page very far:

*Boothie left again today for another week. It seems the Church has declared Phrendonics to be heretics, and the Accipitrines are debating whether to appeal to the Primal directly. Those who aren't would prefer they all stayed out of it, but Boothie thinks he might be able to convince at least a few of them to change their minds. Anyway, before he left, he gave me a little money to spend. I think I'll visit the racetrack. Barclay says it's a great way to meet important people. FRH, April 17, 887.*

This entry was followed immediately by:

*He was there, and what a lucky thing, too. He offered to help me place a little wager, and I won! I think he might be growing fond of me—he told me he'd be attending Lady Ashbury's costume ball, and he was fishing to find out if I'd be going too. Of course, I didn't tell him I was—that would have been far too forward. FRH, April 19, 887.*

Even though it had all happened so long ago, Tilly had a bad feeling about this Barclay character. Over the next few entries, Nanna had arranged to meet him several more times, each time without her husband's knowledge. What had seemed initially like a harmless flirtation had apparently developed into something far more serious. Though Tilly wanted desperately to believe her father never learned of it, she felt compelled to flip farther ahead regardless of what she might find.

*Apparently, my badgering Boothie to get Barclay Accipitrine membership wasn't enough for him—now he's starting to ask me personal questions about the members. It's a secret society—new recruits can't expect to get immediate access to everything just for signing up, especially with the threat of Inquisition hanging over us. I'm trying to convince him to be patient, but he's making me nervous. He can seem so poised and self-confident when he puts his mind*

*to it, but in his heart, he's not a patient man. FRH,*
*August 12, 887.*

Tilly wasn't sure what to make of this passage. Either her father must have been very distracted or her mother must have been a consummate liar. She couldn't imagine how Nanna could possibly have kept her relationship secret while at the same time promoting Barclay for membership in her father's secret society. The situation could not have been comfortable. Indeed, as a subsequent passage made clear, it was about to get worse.

> *The Primal negotiations have fallen through—the*
> *Accipitrines have been ordered to disband for the*
> *crime of abetting heresy. Despite the promise of*
> *diplomatic immunity, the Accipitrine representative*
> *barely escaped the Holy City alive. Unfortunately,*
> *he was forced to use his Phrendonic training, and*
> *several Inquisitors were killed in the process. Boothie*
> *says that until this blows over, all Accipitrine activ-*
> *ity will be suspended except at the highest levels.*
> *I doubt Barclay will be happy to hear that. FRH,*
> *November 4, 887.*

Tilly paused. Now that she was getting close to entries that dealt with the Inquisition, she wasn't sure she could bear to keep reading. Nanna's passing was still an open wound, and the details of Nanna's ordeal would do little to speed its healing—but she couldn't bring herself to put the little diary down. Instead, she told herself it would be better to know now and heal later rather than reopen the wound once it closed. Whether or not she was lying to herself, the need to know won out.

> *I've decided to call it off with Barclay. Our situation*
> *becomes less tenable every day, and my family must*
> *come first. Caprian has been ordered to turn over*
> *the leaders of the Accipitrines or face interdict. The*
> *King dithers, fearing, on one hand, the ramifications*

*of interdict, and on the other, the Accipitrines' wrath.*
*FRH, January 31, 888.*

Tilly felt an odd sense of relief that Nanna had finally decided to
end the relationship. While she knew they would not fare well during
the Inquisition, at least they could now face it united as a family. The
next entry chilled her blood.

> *I am undone! Barclay refuses to let me end it. If I*
> *insist, he says he will see to it that Boothie obtains*
> *all my letters to him. I can't risk it. I might never see*
> *Jonas and Mathilda again. FRH, February 5, 888.*

Tilly's heart sank at the thought of Nanna's dilemma. Once again,
she found herself wondering who this Barclay person was and why
she'd never heard of him.

> *The King is allowing the Church to station Inquisi-*
> *tors within Caprian. He seeks to avoid a confronta-*
> *tion with either faction by letting them fight it out*
> *among themselves. Boothie's sources tell him the*
> *Church plans to send Inquisitors in multiple waves*
> *to mask their true numbers. It is doubtful the King*
> *even realizes the danger. I suggested we send the*
> *children someplace safe, at least for the time being,*
> *and thankfully Boothie agreed. If they were here,*
> *Barclay might find a way to use them against me.*
> *FRH, March 12, 888.*

Tilly's mouth fell open. Could it be that she and her brother had
been spared the Inquisition not because of their father's foresight, but
because of their mother's indiscretion?

> *Today Barclay finally told me he would be willing to*
> *set me free—on condition that I tell him the identity of*
> *the Grand Eagle of the Order. I worked up the nerve*
> *to ask him why he wanted to know. To my amazement,*
> *he condescended to tell me, as if it were no great*

*thing. He wanted to deliver him to the Inquisition and end the madness in Caprian. I told him I'd sooner cut out my own tongue. He laughed, took me by the chin, and forced me to look him in the eye. He then asked if my answer would be different if that meant he would have no choice but to offer up Boothie in his place. FRH, March 23, 888.*

Tilly knew what Nanna must have done—what *she* would have done in Nanna's place, even if it ultimately would have led the Inquisition back to her husband. She shuddered to think a man Nanna had once loved could have been so cruel.

*They struck in the dead of night. Boothie didn't even find out until morning, and by then, there was no way to know where the Inquisition had taken the Grand Eagle. I've never seen Boothie so angry, but then, he is unused to feeling helpless. Only when I wept did he soften, mistaking my guilt for fear. He reassured me that we would be safe—that the Grand Eagle had prepared against this eventuality, and that he would sooner invoke the Sacrifice than betray the Order. He was baffled when, in response to his comforting words, I wept all the more. FRH, April 1, 888.*

Although her father may have been baffled, Tilly was finally beginning to understand the horror the Inquisition represented for her mother, who must surely have felt in some measure responsible for whatever atrocities the Church committed against the man she had named. She hoped Nanna had taken at least some small solace in the fact that what she had done she had been forced to do to protect her family. With a heavy heart, Tilly read on:

*He lied to me! There was a small gathering today at the Ashbury's and he was there. He cornered me alone and accused me of knowing the Grand Eagle would kill the Inquisitor General and that it would cast suspicion on him. He demanded another name—*

*this time, that of a leader unlikely to burst into flames.*
*Failing that, he said Boothie would be next. FRH,*
*April 12, 888.*

A gentle voice interrupted her reading. "Pardon me, are you by any chance Mathilda Harcourt?"

Tilly was so startled she nearly dropped the diary. She'd been so absorbed in her reading she hadn't noticed the approaching footsteps over the background hubbub of restoration efforts. The man leaning against the doorway was on the stocky side, plainly dressed, and his head sported a thin layer of salt-and-pepper stubble.

"We're closed."

"I'm not here for that. I was wondering if I could ask a few questions concerning your mother?"

Tilly tossed the diary into the open trunk. "You're a little late."

"I know. I've just come from the Constable. I'm sorry for your loss."

"I find that hard to believe—unless you mean the Constable is regretting the fire may have consumed something of value he didn't have a chance to either scatter or pilfer."

"I wasn't speaking for the Constable."

"Oh, well in that case I'm touched. There's nothing like the deepest sympathies of a total stranger to warm the heart when you've just lost your mother. Now, if you'll excuse me, I have a lot of work to do here, and I'd like to get started."

"I knew her. And I really am sorry."

"That's funny—I don't recall ever having to pencil you in on her social calendar—and I've been in charge of it for quite a long time."

"I lost track of her, and the last time I saw her, you probably weren't old enough to use a pencil."

Tilly froze. "Who are you?"

"I'm the man who adopted your baby brother. Did your mother never mention me?"

"If you really had known her, you'd know she couldn't speak."

"Even after all this time? I'd assumed she'd recovered. Does that mean you didn't know?"

"Maybe you'd better fill me in."

"Very well. It was in Caprian, many years ago. The Inquisition was out of control. The death of the Inquisitor General at the hands of a heretic had incited the Inquisitors to new levels of brutality. That, in turn, unleashed a spate of additional Sacrifices that decimated the ranks of the Inquisitors stationed there. In that poisoned atmosphere, my attempts to promote restraint were futile. My own father ordered me to hold my tongue—whether from fear for my welfare, or disagreement with my message, I never found out. I had little choice but to stand by and watch as the situation deteriorated still further. Innocent people were tortured on the strength of baseless accusations, entire families, including children, were branded and turned out of their homes to starve. Officially, my hands were tied. Unofficially, however, I was determined to mitigate these crimes as best I could."

"What did you do?"

"I cultivated trust among a small group of locals—no small task under the circumstances. Together we created a few secret shelters. We would take in refugees, branded or no. We provided food, shelter, and aid to those we could. I then used what little influence I still had with my father to keep them safe from the rest of the Inquisition. I think he agreed to it because he believed I was less of a problem if I was kept busy. He would warn me in advance of a raid, and I would make sure the place was abandoned in time.

"What does all this have to do with my mother?"

"I met her in one of the shelters. I recognized her immediately. She had a reputation among the leaders of the Inquisition as Lavicius's spy—the insider among the heretics who, out of profound loyalty to her faith, provided him with the identities of the Phrendonic leadership. Without her, the Caprian Inquisition would have been considerably longer and bloodier."

"And for her trouble, you had her branded?"

"That was a mistake. Lavicius was supposed to shepherd her to safety when the Inquisition ambushed your father, but she ran from him instead. I'm not sure why—perhaps she got turned around in the confusion. Since the Inquisition was under strict orders that she not be harmed, she escaped. Only much later did I find out she'd been captured in the presence of other accused heretics. No one recognized her until the damage was already done. My father ordered her release immediately when he found out what had happened."

"This Lavicius person—does he have a first name?"

The man raised his eyebrows. "You haven't heard of Ordinal Lavicius?"

"He's an *Ordinal?*"

"I suspect he has your mother to thank for that. He was so instrumental in the 'success' of the Inquisition at Caprian it catapulted him to prominence at a relatively young age."

"Yes, but what was his first name?"

"Back then, they called him Barclay."

Tilly nodded slowly. "And what's all this nonsense about a baby brother?"

"When I came across your mother in one of the shelters, she'd been badly beaten, despite being very expectant."

"The Inquisition again?"

"I doubt it. The wounds had none of the hallmarks of the Inquisitors' favored implements. I tried to find out what had happened, but she wouldn't speak, so we tended to her wounds as best we could and let her get some sleep. That night, she went into labor. I went to fetch the midwife myself. After my failure to get her to talk, I assumed she needed to see a familiar face. I told the midwife to let her know Lavicius would be there for her in the morning—that I would spend all night finding him if I had to."

"And did you find him?"

"Yes, but he declined to come back with me—said he was too busy. He did ask me to convey his best wishes though."

"And how did she react when you told her that?"

"I never got the chance. It was morning by the time I got back. The child had been born with little trouble despite your mother's injuries. The midwife had left her to rest. When I went to check on them, your mother was gone."

"And the baby?"

"Left behind."

"I don't believe any of this. My mother would never have abandoned her child."

"I'm not sure she had a choice."

"What do you mean?"

"Later that morning the shelter was raided without warning. Fortunately, the midwife had taken the child to find a wet nurse."

"So, your father went back on his word?"

"No, my father had nothing to do with it. But I think I know who did."

"Barclay."

He nodded. "He was the only one out of the ordinary who knew. I have since acquired a healthy distrust of Ordinal Lavicius."

"And what about the baby?"

"I told Lavicius it was stillborn. Then I took the child secretly away and placed him in my mother's care. When, after a year or so, I finally despaired of ever finding your mother again, I formally adopted him. You can imagine my shock when I recognized your mother's remains."

"You could still recognize her? Even after all these years, and the fire?"

"It was actually her ring I recognized. And then, when I found out you owned the building, it all made sense."

"Why do you even care? Nanna's dead. Your son no doubt has his own life to live, and we have ours. What possible good could it do to bring this all up now?"

"Because of the way she died."

"The Sacrifice? Is it really so strange to think that someone like her would choose that way to go? You said yourself that Caprian had a bunch of them."

"Trifienne has recently had quite a few as well. Unfortunately, there have been several examples where the Sacrificer seems to have escaped unharmed. That suggests to me someone has learned to incinerate from a nice safe distance."

"Are you saying you think someone else may have done this to Nanna?"

"I don't know—that's why I wanted to talk to you. Do you know what happened here?"

"Isn't it obvious from the Constable's corpse collection and all the devastation? The Inquisition cornered her at the end of the hallway behind you, and rather than risk another round of torture at their hands, she decided to end it all."

He nodded. "That's consistent with the evidence, but it leaves out one very important component."

"What's that?"

"Motive. Why were they interested in your mother in the first place?"

"You're the one with all the fancy Church connections. Why don't you just ask?"

"Oh, I intend to, but it's easier to get a truthful answer when you already know the truth before you ask the question."

"Out of curiosity, whom are you planning to ask?"

"My son."

"What? You mean the same one who's supposed to be my brother?"

"He's the only one I've got."

"Why would he know?"

"Because, according to the Constable, he ordered the attack."

"Wait a minute. What did you say you named him again?"

"Who?"

"Your son."

"I didn't say, but his name is Thurman."

"But that means that you must be—"

"Monsignor Armand Goodkin. A pleasure to finally meet you."

"I thought you walked with a cane?"

The Monsignor reached past the frame of the door and retrieved a sturdy walking stick. "I do, but given the fates of the previous Inquisitors, I wanted to talk with you before you knew who I was. I find the cane sometimes gives me away."

Tilly felt something snap. "Well, you're quite the piece of work, Mister. Your precious Church murdered my father, destroyed my mother, and left my brother and me to cobble together a meager living out of the ashes. Fully aware of all of this, you waltz in here with some ridiculous story about raising a long-lost brother I've never even heard of, and now you want me to tell you what could possibly have possessed him to send Inquisitors to chase down his own mother. Well that's just fine by me—one good turn deserves another, they always say. So, next time you two are having one of those little father-son chats, why don't you just go ahead and ask him how that little grave-robbing project of his is going. While you're at it, you can point out that, thanks to him, he can now add his own mother's bones to the list of potential lootables."

The Monsignor took a step back. "Perhaps it was insensitive of me to show up like this."

"You're damned right it was. Get out."

The Monsignor shook his head. "Please understand I only came with the best of intentions."

"Now."

Though he held his head high, it was with a profound air of sadness that he disappeared back down the blackened corridor.

Once she was certain the Monsignor had really left, she rubbed her palms against each other as though brushing off unpleasant grime and went back to considering how best to restore the room. She found concentrating difficult, however, since her mind kept returning to the chest where her mother's diary lay waiting for her. If there really had been a long-lost brother, wouldn't there be some mention there? Impatient with her own curiosity, she retrieved the book and paged through it, more to disprove the ridiculous story than anything else. Skipping ahead to the last entry, she read:

> *We are leaving Caprian. Boothie knows nearly ev-*
> *erything now—I couldn't bear to keep lying to him. I*
> *expected anger or rage or even despair, but not this.*
> *Now that I've given them Lord Amarose, Boothie is*
> *convinced they'll be coming for us all, and just when*
> *we need him most, I've made him lose the will to*
> *fight. He's considering the Sacrifice, and not just in*
> *self-defense. He denies it, but I can tell—and after*
> *what I've done, I've lost all hope of reaching him.*
> *Why was I so wicked? If I must be punished, then why*
> *not punish me alone? Instead, every time I open my*
> *mouth, someone else dies. And now, even the Sacri-*
> *fice is denied me—I can't punish an innocent life for*
> *my sins. And, after everything else, how am I ever*
> *going to tell Boothie that? FRH, April 25, 888.*

. . . . .

When Magister Treust arrived at the churchyard gate, it was stand-ing ajar, the lock still dangling open from its chain. He bent to retrieve it, wondering whether he should simply buy time by locking it. A quick examination revealed the lock had suffered no damage. Whoever opened it had either picked it or had stolen the key—but that didn't really tell him much, since neither option was likely to be beyond Vane, or Michlos either for that matter.

"Looking for this?" Vane held up a key as he approached through the graveyard.

"I was, now that you mention it. I wasn't aware we'd found a replacement for Stuart. When did you start?"

"I borrowed it from Magister Celeric. I was hoping to get a bird's-eye view of all the changes you've made here since I left. He suggested the steeple as the best place for that."

"Did he also suggest you ring out the joyous tidings of your arrival, or was that your idea?"

Vane pocketed the key. "I apologize for that. Once I got up there, I noticed the mechanism and couldn't resist trying to figure it out. I'm pretty sure I've reset it properly now."

"Is that so? How did you set it off in the first place?"

"Are you testing me?"

"Sorry. Force of habit—but I am curious."

"Who could forget the tale of how the wily Michlos Serrola bypassed the Eye of Moravidos to ring the bell?"

"Since when did privileged exam material become a part of the general curriculum?"

"It's not," Vane replied. "But students talk."

"I'll have to take that into account when I'm designing new tests. Shall we go make sure you didn't miss anything?"

"It was pretty straightforward—I hardly think that will be necessary."

"I don't mind at all. It's not every day I get the opportunity to show off my handiwork to someone with genuine interest."

"I've already been enough trouble. Besides, I should get this key back to Magister Celeric. Under the circumstances, he'll probably want to make sure it's back where it belongs as soon as possible."

"A few more minutes either way shouldn't matter. If you're in a hurry, you can just give the key to me, and I'll make sure it finds its way back."

"That's very kind of you, but I'd just as soon return it myself. I'd rather not risk him thinking I'm any more irresponsible than I must already seem for ringing the bell."

"Keep the key then. But I'd like you to come with me to check the mechanism in any event—if there's something amiss I might need your help to fix it. Not only that, but I think I've come up with a way to replace your Amulet, and we may as well take this opportunity to discuss it."

"Why don't we go return the key first. We can talk on the way."

"That would be a waste of time. You know very well I can't run off and leave the gate open—we'd have to turn around and bring the key right back to get through again. Come on, Josephus—I'm trying my best here. I'm not accusing anyone of anything, but if you should happen to need to put something back while we're inspecting the mechanism—as far as I'm concerned you could, no questions asked."

Vane rubbed his chin thoughtfully. Before he responded, however, Princess Celeste appeared. She had swept her hair back up under the diadem and managed to look regal despite the stains and the dust.

"The Magister may not have any questions, but I do."

Magister Treust nodded deferentially. "Your Highness, may I present Josephus Vane. He's one of our graduates, back for a visit."

"Princess…Celeste?" Vane asked.

"The same." She turned to Treust. "Magister, I've been renting this land for a pittance to your so-called 'elite' academy for eons now, but this is perhaps the first graduate I've ever seen. Doesn't that strike you as strange?"

Treust blinked. "Well, we do try to instill a sense of modesty in our students."

"Really? By ensuring they remain inconsequential? If that's your strategy, it seems to be working." She turned back to Vane. "Mr. Vane, who are you, and why haven't I heard of you before?"

A sly smile crept across Vane's face. "In my case, you may not have heard of me because after I graduated, I moved out of the area. I assure you I am well thought of within my circle."

"And what circle is that, pray tell?"

"I apologize in advance if my answer offends. Your stance on the matter is well known, but I am only here unofficially."

"Get to the point, Mr. Vane."

"I am employed by the Church as an Inquisitor. I'm only here visiting my *alma mater*, and even though I would certainly understand if you chose to evict me from the premises, I meant no disrespect."

"So, it appears the elite academy is actually more of an elite seminary. Excellent—that will make for a much gentler adjustment when I reconcile with the Church."

Magister Treust's jaw dropped. "Reconcile with the Church?"

"You aren't questioning my decision, are you?"

"Of course not, Your Highness."

"Wise. Now, Mr. Vane, if you are as respected as you let on, perhaps you'll have some suggestions as to how best to broach the subject with the Church."

Vane cleared his throat. "Typically, one would send an envoy to the Holy City to negotiate the terms of the reconciliation, preferably someone with expertise in Canon law."

"Someone like an Inquisitor?"

"Possibly, but where a Monarchy is involved, it would more likely be someone of higher rank."

"With commensurately greater incentive to favor the Church, I presume."

"I imagine that would depend on whom you chose."

"What about *you*, Mr. Vane? What if I were to choose you?"

"Then I would wonder about your motives."

"My motives are simple. Years of excommunication and interdiction have taken their toll. I can think of no one who remains on my little island with the type of expertise required for these negotiations. But if I recruit an expert from outside, he will probably be beholden to the Church instead of the Island. You may not feel you have sufficient expertise, but at least you have some, and the rest can be learned. What's more important is your connection to the Island. You've lived here. You understand who we are—what it means to be a member of this Colony. That's not something I'm likely to find anywhere else."

"I don't understand—are you asking me to be your envoy?"

"Not yet. We would need to speak at length—I'd need to get a much better idea of the extent of your qualifications and abilities. I merely suggest that you possess some unique qualities that might make you an attractive candidate. Are you interested?"

Vane nodded slowly. "I am."

"Good. I'll finish my business here shortly. Once I have, I'd like you to be my guest at Ranselard Keep."

"I would be honored."

"I'll be there as soon as I can manage it. Don't make me wait."

Vane bowed deeply. "I will head there directly, Your Highness."

The Princess acknowledged him with a nod.

With an inscrutable smile at Magister Treust, Vane slid out through the gate and headed down the path.

. . . . .

Once Vane was out of earshot, the Princess turned back to Treust. "You might want to call off the posse before he gets wind something is amiss, preferably before he makes it back to the dining hall."

"Right away, Your Highness."

As he made to pass her, she put a hand on his arm. "Did he take it?"

Treust nodded. "I'm pretty sure he did."

"There was blood on his sleeve. Did you see it?"

"I didn't notice."

"Have you seen Michlos?"

"No."

"Bring help."

Treust nodded again, and she sprinted for the Church. Thistles and grasses tore at her cloak and caught the heels of her dress boots, which were crafted more for marble floors and state occasions. Only when she finally felt the cool curve of the door latch did she hesitate. Based on Michlos's description, she envisioned the space beyond as a seething gantlet of dangerous heresies. She threw the door open but did not step inside.

"Michlos? Are you here?"

Candles flickered in the breeze, and the acrid scent of incense enveloped her.

She called again. "Are you hurt?"

Sunlight flooded through the rose window to create a spectacular display on the floor in front of her, but under the circumstances, it held for her all the charm of a great round target.

"Michlos, are you in here?" She began to second-guess herself. Was there any way he could have missed Vane? Could he still be searching out back of the Church? But her mind's eye kept returning to the crimson smear across Vane's sleeve. Squeezing her eyes shut, she took a deliberate step across the threshold into the light. Nothing untoward happened. She opened her eyes and looked both ways to make sure she hadn't missed anything. Only then did she resume breathing.

"Well, perhaps he exaggerated a bit. He is prone to that, after all."

She took another tentative step. "Michlos?"

Emboldened by her success, she started to relax.

"If this ends up being some sort of prank—"

She froze mid-step, her foot suspended above the first row of mosaic tiles that lined the aisle between the seats. She'd heard a noise—metal against stone, faint and oddly muffled. It wasn't coming from ahead of her—it was off to the side.

She took a step back. "Who's there? Michlos, is that you?"

Cautiously, she advanced toward the stairwell. "Are you there?" Peering down the steps, she could make out a glow reflecting off the open door from somewhere farther in. Unlike lamplight, the glow was strong and steady. It reminded her of the crystals suspended above her paintings—or the buckle of Michlos's hat.

"Michlos? I'm coming down."

She took the stairs as quickly as her boots allowed and threw the door open all the way. She'd hoped to see Michlos standing there with his crazy hat and an insouciant grin. Instead, she saw only a glowing rapier. It was lying against one wall, its light casting ominous shadows in the ceiling vaults. She approached cautiously, trying to determine whether it might be something Michlos would have willingly left behind. She'd just leaned over for a closer look when she again heard a faint sound of metal against stone. It was louder here.

She whirled, but nothing seemed amiss. In the rapier-light, she could make out hulking rectangular shapes in the room's center. They were too tall to be trunks and too massive for tables, and it took several seconds of squinting before it occurred to her she was standing in the presence of coffins.

Although she'd never been particularly superstitious, the idea of being alone this close to the dead with a mysterious rapier as the only source of light was more than a little unsettling. Then she heard the sound again. As best she could tell, it was coming from within one of the coffins.

She tried telling herself it must be a test, but her heart raced nonetheless. She asked herself what Michlos would do to pass such a test, but it wasn't clear what the test even was. Not to panic, maybe?

Gathering the tatters of her resolve, she pushed forward for a better look at the restless sarcophagus. The inscription read: Cecily Chartruvan, Duchess of Arusia. Why did that sound familiar? But the attempt to recall was promptly driven from her mind by faint scrabbling from deep within the sarcophagus.

"It's only a test, it's only a test, it's only a test." Despite the mantra, her pulse pounded in her ears. She took deep breaths to calm herself but only succeeded in making herself dizzy. Then, as she was regaining some measure of composure, the heavy stone lid shot up off the coffin base. It flipped head over foot, pivoting like a trapdoor along its bottom edge, and landed with a thunderous crash on the floor. She shrieked in terror. Had she been standing at the foot of the coffin, she would have been killed instantly, but that realization was not what kept her backing away aghast. A low agonized moan emanated from the coffin's dark depths. Then, to her horror, a bloody hand emerged—and groped its way toward her. As she watched, it trembled and collapsed back into the darkness. In response, Princess Celeste resorted to a response she had never before used in her life—she fainted.

. . . . .

In the rapier's glow, a violent wind arose that whistled through the cellar of the Academy's church, stirring up all manner of dust, grit, and litter. It formed, for an instant, a whirling vortex above the open sarcophagus of Cecily Chartruvan, Duchess of Arusia. How it resolved would have been of keen interest to both the room's occupants, had they had been conscious to see it.

. . . . .

Reston entered his office lost in thought. He'd checked for Everson three times now, and there was still no sign he'd been back. He would have to come up with a new strategy for tracking down the elusive Miss Nevinander if he was ever going see his precious book again. A pity, since Everson no doubt could have given him a reasonable assessment of what he might be up against. Then again, if it was just a matter of tracking her down, perhaps Miss Merinne's mother could be of assistance. After all, she had responded promptly the last time he'd sent word to her.

"Hello, Reston."

The tiny woman seated in his office chair rose to greet him. She was clad in a modest gown entirely of black silk. Her face was covered by a veil of black lace that completely obscured her features. As she approached, she lifted it to reveal her perfect heart-shaped face, with its pale complexion and rosebud lips—her only flaw, an angry purple bruise spattered across her right cheek. She regarded him coolly over the top of a fan of bone and black lace—her wide-set eyes twin pools of unfathomable melancholy.

Reston took a step back "Widow Bainbridge? What brings you here?" He made a mental note always to lock his office door.

"Let's see. You've only been here a few months, and already you've attracted the full attention of the Inquisition. What do you think?"

"That wasn't us."

"Really? Who was it then?"

Reston paused.

"Memory problems?"

"There are too many suspects to know for certain. Why didn't you warn me there were so many Phrendonics in Trifienne?"

She shook her head. "All those Phrendonics, and yet Trifienne was completely ignored by the Church until after you arrived."

"I'm telling you, it wasn't us."

She snapped the fan shut. "It doesn't matter. The experiment is over."

"But I'm making good progress."

"Don't waste your breath. I couldn't change the decision even if I were inclined to. I'm just the messenger. Hand over the book, and I'll be on my way."

Reston paled. "I don't have it here."

The Widow arched a perfect eyebrow. "No?"

"I had to hide it, you know—because of the Inquisition. I didn't dare risk them finding it here."

"I see."

"I'll get it for you as soon as I can."

"I don't have all day. Where is it?"

"Trifienne."

The widow sighed. "Very well. I'll be back for it in a week. I hope I don't have to warn you what will happen if you disappoint me."

"I'll have it for you then."

"See that you do."

She flipped down the veil and brushed past Reston.

Reston sank wearily into his chair as Jonas poked his head in.

"Who was that?"

"Just some poor widow looking for spare change. I gave her a few coins and sent her on her way. Say, are you free this week?"

"I was planning to help Tilly with the repairs. Why?"

"I have a little proposition for you."

"If this is about getting your book back, I'm not interested. Your last little deal almost got us killed."

"Just hear me out"

Jonas took a seat. "All right, but you're not going to change my mind. I'm only staying because hearing you out is slightly less annoying than stripping scorched wallpaper."

"You won't be sorry."

"If that's true, I expect it's only because I really hate stripping wallpaper."

# CHAPTER 23

# Apprehensions

There was light—blinding light, but she could ignore that. But then came the burning. She could feel it invading her mouth, her nose—her lungs. She gasped for breath, but that made it worse. She screamed, struggled, and finally opened her eyes. And then she remembered.

"She's coming around," said a familiar voice. "I think that's enough with the salts."

*Treust*, she thought. *That's Magister Treust.* And sure enough, now she could see his concerned face looming over her in the light.

"Well that's a relief," someone else said.

She struggled to put a name to this new voice. "Provost?"

"We're here, Highness."

"The coffin?"

"Michlos will be all right," Treust said. "He's in some pain and he's lost a bit of blood, but the injury doesn't look life threatening. It's probably just a broken nose. Are you feeling better?"

She nodded.

"Ready to try sitting up?"

She nodded again.

"Gently now," the Provost said.

She felt herself slowly being lifted to a sitting position. She was dizzy but recovering quickly. She was still in the church cellar near the coffins, but unlike before, the entire room was awash with light.

Candles had been placed at various points around the cellar, though they were not lit—instead, the candles themselves glowed. She spied Michlos sitting off to one side, his head tilted forward, applying a blood-spattered ball of cloth to his face to stanch the flow.

"There was something in the coffin," she said. "It reached for me."

"You mean something other than Michlos?" Treust asked.

"That was Michlos?"

"We got him out right away. I shudder to think of him passed out in those remains like that."

"What was he doing there?"

"He says Vane did it. Or, I think that's what he's saying. He's not so easy to understand at the moment. It seems sort of senseless to toss him into an open coffin though. Do you suppose it was intended as some sort of warning?"

"It wasn't open."

"What do you mean?"

"When I got here, the coffin was closed. I heard something moving inside, and when I got close to investigate, the lid flew off. I had no idea Michlos was in there. I guess I overreacted a little. Where is Vane now?"

"I presume he's on his way to meet you at Ranselard—he bypassed the dining hall and went directly to the gate. Either he's eager to meet with you, or he got what he came for."

"Or he was worried we might find Michlos sooner rather than later. Help me up. I have to get back there."

"I doubt he was worried about us finding Michlos," the Provost said. "There's not much air in these things when they're closed. It's a wonder he managed to get out before he suffocated. My guess is Vane thinks Michlos is safely dead with no one the wiser."

"Where is Newcomb?"

"I asked him to stand guard outside the Church. He was hot to get in here, but that really wouldn't be safe, either physically or from a security standpoint."

She nodded and took a few tentative steps. When that went well, she headed over to Michlos. Bending, she put a sympathetic hand on his arm. "Now don't try to talk. The Magisters think you have a broken nose but that you're going to be all right."

He nodded without taking the cloth from his face.

"I'll have you taken to Ranselard to have that looked at, but you'll need to stay here just a little longer, all right?"

He nodded again.

"Just until I deal with Vane."

He shook his head emphatically and winced. "He'ou kiou you."

"I'll be back as soon as I can. You stay here and rest."

"I can't yet you do yis."

"You can, and will. If you even so much as think about anything other than getting better, Provost Wellsbrough is under strict instructions to put you right to sleep. Have I made myself clear?"

Grudgingly, Michlos nodded.

"All right then, Magister Treust, if you would be so kind as to escort me out of here?"

"Right this way, Your Highness."

As the two of them emerged from the church, Newcomb's face lit up.

"They said you were hurt."

"Promise you won't tell anyone?"

"I swear."

"I only fainted. I'm perfectly fine. Can I trouble you to bring the horses?"

"I'll get them straight away. Will we be traveling incognito?"

"What do you mean?"

"Well, when we came here, you were wearing the diadem."

The Princess felt the top of her head. "It's gone."

"It must have fallen off when you fainted," Treust said. "I'll go back and check for it."

"I'll come with you. We can't leave until Newcomb is back with the horses anyway."

"As you wish."

"I don't think we're going to find it though."

"Why do you say that?"

"Because I just noticed the cloak I was wearing is missing too—unless you think that also rolled under something when I fainted. Are you sure Vane left the Academy?"

Treust nodded. "I watched him head out through the front gate. And you were wearing the diadem when I left you. I don't think there was time for him to get back in, steal your things, and get back out again."

"But if not Vane, who else?"

"Let's just go look. "No sense speculating when the evidence may be in plain sight."

No one below had seen either the cloak or the diadem, and a careful search yielded no clues.

"I can't spend any more time on this," the Princess said. "I must go deal with Vane. Will you keep looking?"

"Of course, Your Highness. One more thing before you go?"

"Yes?"

They started up the stairway. "I know you're determined to set things right, but now that it's certain he's gone rogue, Vane is especially dangerous. Are you sure you want to confront him?"

"He almost got away with murder. I intend to see him brought to justice. Besides, so long as he carries the Eye, he isn't any more dangerous than anyone else, right?"

"I see Michlos has already briefed you. Keep in mind, though, that for all its power, the Eye can easily be circumvented."

She nodded. "I've heard the story."

"The safest approach is to stay a long way away, preferably out of his sight. Barring that, you can hope the Eye will keep him in check. If that doesn't work, I'd like you to take this."

He removed the only ring he wore and handed it to her.

"What's this?"

"Has Michlos told you about Amulets? Normally I make these only for Santines, but this was my first functional prototype. It works when you depress the gem. If it's on, the gem turns red, like this, and that means it's protecting you."

He pushed down the gem and it clicked. The blue gem became a vibrant red. He pushed it down once more and it faded immediately back to pale blue.

"It's easily overpowered if someone is determined, but you still might find it useful."

"I don't know what to say."

"Say you'll be careful."

"I will."

Arriving outside, she hopped nimbly into the saddle before Newcomb could assist her. "Take good care of Michlos, won't you?"

"I'll keep my eye on him."

Once they were beyond the front gate, the Princess sent Newcomb ahead to quietly warn those at the keep. Meanwhile, she took a meandering route back to Ranselard, collecting one-by-one a small contingent of armed guards in the midst of their rounds. They slowly made their way up the twisting path toward the keep, allowing Vane plenty of time to arrive ahead of them. Just out of sight of the gate she called her troops to a halt. Newcomb was waiting for her.

He bowed deeply with a sweep of his plumed hat. "The rat has taken the bait, Highness."

"Where is he?"

"Waiting for you in the vestibule."

"Tell him I will see him now. Lead him around to the courtyard's back entrance but give him the artist's tour. We'll need time to get into position."

"As you wish, Highness."

"And Newcomb."

"Yes?"

"No heroics. I can't afford to lose you."

"You have my word." With a final nod, he was off.

The Princess gave him a few minutes of lead time and motioned for her men to follow. At the courtyard gate, she left behind several members of her force.

"No one is to pass through this gate until I give the order. Is that clear?"

They fanned out.

She led the rest of the men into the vestibule with bravado. If Newcomb hadn't managed to lead him away, she wanted to meet Vane radiating the impression of strength. It turned out not to be necessary—Vane wasn't there.

"From here, we'll be heading directly into the courtyard. You'll have only minutes to get into position. It's critical you remain out of sight and that you stay well separated. Prefer bows to blades where possible. Do you understand?"

The men nodded.

"Very well. Follow me."

Ranselard Keep's courtyard had a long and bloody history. As the site of the gallows for the old prison, it was commonly said that more of Trifienne's noble blood had been spilt there than on the battlefield.

And in those rare cases that called for it, the very center had been reserved for the stake and pyre. Even all these years later, the vegetation still grew sparse and sickly over that spot. Since those days, Trifienne had ceded sovereignty, prison had become palace, and repeated attempts had been made to adapt the area for recreational and ceremonial use. Skilled landscapers had been retained to create a welcoming space for the families of the palace staff. Famous sculptors had been awarded space there to showcase their labors—but to no avail. Whether because of its reputation, or for other reasons the Princess didn't fully comprehend, people occupied the courtyard only so long as they were obliged and not a moment more. The intricately carved throne her mother had commissioned for public events had seen less and less use over the years, since Celeste had little interest in forced participation. After all, she had the entire run of the island for hosting events.

For her meeting with Vane, however, the courtyard and its weathered throne seemed like just the place. She had no sooner taken her seat than a door opened across from her. Vane stepped into view, with Newcomb right behind.

The Princess stood as Vane strode toward her.

"Thank you for agreeing to see me, Highness. I have some new ideas to help with your reconciliation that I think you might like."

When he'd covered about half the distance that separated them, she finally spoke. "That's close enough, Mr. Vane."

Vane stalled. His eyes registered sudden suspicion. "I apologize if I've done something that's offended you."

She clapped her hands, and the armed men emerged from behind the trees and statues that lined the courtyard. As one, they leveled loaded crossbows at Vane's heart.

"I'm afraid, Mr. Vane, there are times when a simple apology just won't do."

Vane stiffened. "I don't understand."

"Listen carefully—your life depends on it. With your right hand, I want you turn out all your pockets onto the ground in front of you. Keep the left in the air."

Vane slowly raised his hands. "Your Highness, are sure you want to go down this path? As I told you before, I am an Inquisitor. Can you really afford to risk escalating hostilities with the Church just now?"

"Mr. Vane, you only have until the count of five. I suggest you get started."

"Perhaps there's been some misunderstanding?"

"One."

He swallowed hard and pulled things from his pockets. First to drop was a sack of coins, followed moments later by a handkerchief.

"Too slow. Just pull off your shirt and toss it on the pile."

"Are you serious?"

"Two."

He ripped off his shirt and discarded it.

"And now your drawers."

"What?"

"Three."

"Why are you doing this?"

"Now, take ten steps backward and put your hands behind you."

Vane glowered but complied.

"We may not be as large or powerful as the Church, or even Trifienne, but we take an equally dim view of murder on our soil."

On her cue, Newcomb snapped a set of iron manacles around Vane's wrists. "Should I take him below?"

"Not yet." She stepped down from the throne and approached the pile of garments. She poked the assorted clothing and items with the toe of her boot until she detected something in one of the trouser pockets. Reaching down, she retrieved a lump of soft clay. With her thumb, she dug into its soft surface to reveal the smooth black star sapphire beneath."

"Very clever, Mr. Vane. It seems I was at greater risk than I thought."

"You have no idea."

"All right. *Now* we take him below."

Minutes later Vane was escorted into a small stone cell. The door was forged of thick brass, a fact that caused his eyes to narrow as he passed through it.

"Yes, Mr. Vane. You're not the first Phrendonic to spend a little quality time here at Ranselard."

She slammed the door behind him.

He glared at her through the brass bars in the little opening at the top of the door.

"In fact," she said, "you might find it comforting to know you're in very good company. According to local legend, Dreamweaver once graced this very cell—just before they burned her at the stake."

. . . . .

Helena waved her hand at the coat in exasperation. "How do you expect me to fix this? If it were on a seam, maybe I could do something, but this goes right through the fabric. I can patch the hole, but the repair is going to show. And even if I could find a way to hide it, those soot stains aren't going anywhere. What did you do? Roll in the ashes?"

"Could you just make another coat?" Dona asked.

"With what fabric? It's not like I had that big a collection to begin with."

"All right, what about the hat, then?"

Helena frowned, giving it a once-over with her critical eye. "I suppose we could replace the feathers—assuming we can find a pheasant. The soot is still a problem, though."

"Well there must be something we can do. I can't afford to replace all this stuff."

"You were caught in a fire. Probably they'll understand."

"They might understand, but they're still going to expect their stuff to get replaced. Wouldn't you?"

Helena shrugged. "Maybe you could arrange to pay them over time. They're your housemates, not monsters—except maybe for Arietta."

"You borrowed something from Arietta?"

"Just the hat. It made the whole outfit."

"I'll never hear the end of it."

"It looked great though."

Miranda suddenly stepped into the doorway. "Speaking of looking great...Ta-*da*." She posed to show off her new ensemble—a smart cranberry dress with black accents, complete with matching hat.

"Welcome back," Dona said.

Helena rushed over for a closer inspection. "Look at you. Turn around. Where did you get this?"

"Well," Miranda said, "while I was stuck at home, I mentioned the cranberry fabric Dona had bought for me and that I wanted to talk to you about patterns for it. My mother was so afraid I might try to sneak back here that she took me out shopping to distract me."

"At least someone got a dress out of it," Helena muttered.

"And after all that, she just sent you back up here?" Dona asked.

"Oh, she has no idea I'm here," Miranda said. "Once I got the dress, I had to sneak up here to show it off."

"Weren't you afraid they might try to take you hostage again? It was quite a production to spring you last time, you know."

"I'm not stupid. I made sure to check Daddy's records before I came up. The Inquisition left this morning."

"Wait a minute, does he know you go through his records?"

"He ought to. He keeps the key in a place so obvious it might as well be in plain sight. It's like he's asking me to snoop."

Dona sighed resignedly. "Yeah, that's practically begging."

"That reminds me—there was something else in those records you should know. Do you remember that brothel you stayed at? It had a fire and a bunch of people were killed—including some Inquisitors."

"I never did get a chance to tell you about that, did I?" Dona said. "We got out of there just in time."

"You were there? What is it with you? First the Sultan's Respite, and now the brothel. I suppose you were also at St. Sophia's when that caught fire?"

"What? St. Sophia's burned, too?"

"Well, just the vicarage. It happened yesterday morning early. According to the records, they suspect foul play there as well. Both places apparently had 'some evidence of Phrendonic Heresy,' whatever that means. Say, maybe we could figure it out from that book of yours?"

"We should leave the book well enough alone until things have died down around here. We've already drawn more than enough attention."

"That's nothing compared to our story," Helena said. "While you were gone, we rescued the Monsignor and the Bursar from certain death. Tell her, Dona."

"Um, that was supposed to be a secret."

"Oh, let me shut the door then," Miranda said. Then she tossed her hat over Mr. Lop Ears and flopped on her bed. "Now what's this all about?"

Dona sat next to her. "If we tell, you can't tell a soul."

"Cross my heart."

"I don't know what you've heard, but rescuing you from Isrulian didn't go as smoothly as it might have."

"Daddy told me you were missing—that you'd fallen off the cart on the way out. He said so long as the Inquisition is in control here, there was no way to search for you—I have never been so relieved as when I heard you arguing with Helena just now."

Dona's eyebrow raised. "I take it you didn't sneak all the way up here just to show off the dress, then?"

"I did so. I just expected I might need to spend a little time rounding up my admirers first."

Dona hugged Miranda. "You're a dear friend, but I hope you don't get into too much trouble for it."

"There's no way it could be more trouble than you got me out of. Besides, other than the shopping, life at home gets dreadfully dull."

"Well it wasn't dull here," Helena said, "was it, Dona?"

"I heard there were riots."

"There were," Dona said. "In fact, we never would have escaped the Inquisition if it hadn't been for the riots. They had also taken the Monsignor into custody, and that's where we ran into him."

Miranda looked confused. "But doesn't he run the Inquisition?"

Dona nodded. "But there's some sort of power struggle going on at the highest levels of the Church. Ordinal Isrulian is on the other side, and he had the Monsignor arrested."

"He can do that?"

"I guess so, at least until the Primal countermands the order, and obviously, the Primal isn't here. The Monsignor escaped, but he then had to go under cover. The Inquisition caught him poking around the Hathaway compound and took him prisoner unaware of who he was, and he couldn't reveal himself with Isrulian lurking about."

Miranda shuddered. "I don't blame him—what a creep. How did you get away?"

Dona paused. Since the whole dormitory knew of their emergence from the caves, the promise to Brent seemed sort of pointless. Feeling only a modicum of guilt, Dona filled Miranda in on the details of their escape and their ordeal in the ossarium, through their escape out the garderobe.

Miranda's jaw dropped. "Our garderobe?"

"The very one. That part of the dormitory must have been retained from an older building. I suppose it makes sense—a good garderobe is hard to come by. Anyway, all I had to do was come up here and convince Helena to help."

"You convinced Helena to jump down the garderobe? That alone ought to get you a high pass from Hepplewhite."

"I made her go first," Helena said.

"To be fair," Dona said, "she did seem a little hesitant until I mentioned Alphonse was down there."

"That's cheating," Miranda said. "Even I might have jumped down there for Alphonse."

Dona grinned wickedly. "I know, but I was desperate. Once we got her down, though, she crafted a harness we used to get everyone across the gorge to safety."

"You're right," Miranda said. "That beats my story. I'm just glad yours had a happy ending."

Dona held up a moldering book. "Not only that, but while I was down there, I snagged a copy of next semester's extra-credit project. I'm going to learn Tep'Chuan. That ought to be worth a recommendation or two."

"I might have guessed. If anyone could turn a harrowing escape into an extra-credit project, it would be you."

"Whatever you do, don't tell anyone—I'm not sure the Inquisition would approve. Oh, that reminds me—we went to the infirmary this morning to get Alexi's ankle checked out, and Isrulian was there."

"What did he have to say?"

"Nothing, actually. At least, not to us. I don't think he even saw us. To create a distraction to free you, we told the Inquisitors that there was an outbreak of plague at the college. I guess the Sisters took it seriously, since he was still bristling about having been held in quarantine. You'll want to be especially careful you don't run across him while he's still loitering about campus."

"Oh, my. That wasn't mentioned in any of Daddy's notes. I hope he doesn't plan to stay long."

"Maybe you should let your father know."

"Good idea. He would definitely want to keep tabs on someone like that."

"By the way, how did you get to campus?"

"I borrowed one of Daddy's horses."

"And he didn't guess what you were going to do with it?"

Her eyes twinkled. "He probably will, once he finds the note."

"So, you'll need to head back to town to return it soon anyway?"

Miranda nodded. "I've already caused more than my share of trouble by coming up here."

"Would you mind terribly if I tag along?"

"I'd be glad of the company, but how will you get back?"

"Maybe I can impose on Gregory to borrow the carriage again. Then we could both get back in style."

"I'd love that."

Helena's brow darkened. "Hey, what about me?"

Miranda frowned. "I'm afraid there's only room for two on horse-back."

Dona grabbed her coat. "We'll bring you something from town. What would you like?"

"It's all right," Helena said. "I'll see if Alphonse is free. Maybe I can get him to take me dancing again."

"I doubt any dances will be happening tonight," Miranda said. "Everything is still locked down."

"I guess it will just have to be the two of us then. Such a pity."

Miranda harrumphed. "I never stood a chance, did I?"

Helena just smiled. "Well, you two have fun."

Miranda turned to Dona. "Ready?"

Dona nodded. "We'll try to be back later tonight if we can find Gregory. If not, I'll stay at Miranda's parents' house, so don't worry if we don't show. You can tell Alexi if he comes looking."

"Do try to stay out of trouble," Helena said. "And when you come back, please—use the front door."

. . . . .

The taller buildings were cloaking their neighbors in heavy shadow as Miranda untied her horse from the post. "What did you need to do in town? Or are you planning to unwind a bit after all your adventures?"

"I was hoping we could swing past St. Sophia's."

"So, you want to see that 'evidence of Phrendonic Heresy' for yourself, eh? What happened to your plan of not drawing attention?"

"We can just go have a quick look—we don't need to be obvious about it."

"This is for that extra credit project of yours with Reston, isn't it? Must you always go above and beyond on everything?"

"Oh, the extra credit project—well, I did miss several classes."

"With everything going on here, I doubt anyone would even remember—and I certainly don't think Reston could hold it against you. Why don't we head over to Darcy's Pub and toast your safe return instead? I bet Gregory would be amenable."

"Maybe after. You know my philosophy on grades—better safe than sorry."

Miranda sighed. "You can't blame me for trying."

The ride to Trifienne was almost unnaturally uneventful—the University had suddenly become a singularly unpopular travel destination. By the time they arrived at the church, the hubbub surrounding St. Sophia's was almost a welcome contrast.

A great bonfire had been thrown together in the square before the church. In the roaring flames, St. Sophia's somber façade flickered in sharp relief against the twilight. Nearby, a fiddler, a banjo player, and a flutist had set up shop, furiously improvising a catchy dance tune. The fiddler, standing on a crate, called out moves as a small impromptu cast of dancers twirled, dipped, and pranced to the music. Others browsed makeshift tables near the church steps that offered a mouth-watering display of homemade desserts. To one side, a covered basket hung suspended from a pole. A hand-painted sign beneath the basket urged the good folk of Trifienne to "Buy a ticket—win a prize—build a Vicarage." Around the outside of the square, several booths had sprung up, each offering a unique opportunity for patrons to show off their manly skills and impress the ladies. In the church's shadow, the vicarage ruins stood forlorn and empty.

"Looks like we might be able to slip in and get a quick look without anyone noticing," Dona said.

"I'll drop you off here and find someplace to hitch the horse."

Dona made her way around the crowd's periphery until the vicarage's gutted shell loomed before her. Even in the dim half-light, the scorched semi-circle of turf was unmistakable—no normal fire would have left such a regular pattern. She edged as close to the ruins as she could, and when no one was looking, ducked quickly under the crime-scene rope and into the vicarage proper.

Once inside, she realized it was too dark to investigate anything. She had hoped to find some telltale clue that would reveal the identity of the arsonist, but other than the turf circle, it looked simply like a burnt-out building. Here and there she recognized charred bits of personal effects—a watch fob, a shaving mug, a brass cufflink—but there was nothing about them that seemed the slightest bit out of the ordinary. Dona wondered whether she should have found a way to bring Alexi. Maybe with his greater familiarity with all things Phrendonic, he would have spotted something her untrained eye was missing. Mindful to avoid the soot, she grudgingly picked her way back outside. Unless his eye was better than hers, if Alexi was going to fulfill his promise to the Monsignor, he would have to seek his evidence elsewhere.

After a quick peek to make sure no one was watching, she slipped back under the rope. She found Miranda at the crowd's edge, clapping her hands and bobbing in time to the music.

"Find anything?"

"Nothing."

"I didn't think you would. Daddy and the Monsignor already searched it. They didn't find anything useful either."

"The Monsignor was here? When?"

"This morning," Miranda said. "I told you they suspected heresy—who did you think made that call?"

"Well it's good to know things are beginning to work themselves out. It was looking pretty scary there for a while."

"The Crown Prince is a shrewd negotiator, or so Daddy says. Not only that, but it's bad politics to be at odds with the Church. I'm not surprised they've managed to resolve things. You should have more faith."

"No thanks. I tend to get on better with truth."

Miranda smiled. "Sometimes they're not so different, you know."

"When that's true, you don't need faith."

"You never need it, but sometimes when there's no way you can know the truth, it's nice to have."

"All that does is keep you from planning for the worst—and then, when the worst happens, you're in real trouble."

"But who would want to live life expecting only the worst?"

Dona opened her mouth to deliver a snappy comeback, only to realize she didn't have one. She'd never really looked at it from that perspective before, and she found it disconcerting. Instead, she changed the subject. "Maybe we should hit Darcy's after all. A little unwinding would do me good."

"You and me both," Miranda said. "Let me see. Where did I put that horse?"

Dona pointed. "I think you went that way."

Miranda squinted. "Hey, isn't that Miss Nevinander, from up at the College?"

Once Miranda had pointed her out, Verone was easy to spot. "I think you're right. Quick, you get the horse, and I'll keep my eye on her."

"Keep an eye on her? Whatever for?"

"Hurry, we need to follow her."

"Wouldn't it be easier just to flag her down?"

"I don't want her to see me."

"I thought she was your friend? What's this all about?"

"There's no time for truth right now. Could I trouble you for a little faith instead?"

Miranda crossed her arms. "I might have known you'd find a way to get the last word. Oh, all right. But when this is over, I expect a full explanation."

As Miranda scurried off, Dona scanned once more for Verone. Though she had been plainly visible just moments before, now she was nowhere to be seen.

"Figures."

She jostled her way through the crowd, hoping to pick up the trail while there was a chance the woman was still nearby. Since she was focused on looking for Verone, she was almost on top of it before she realized she'd found Verone's horse tethered at a restaurant.

Good enough. If she wanted to find Reston's book, keeping track of either the horse or the rider would probably suffice.

Across the square, she saw Miranda was mounted. Dona started off in her direction, formulating a plan as she went. She would tell Miranda to bring the horse close enough to the restaurant that they could keep an eye on Verone's horse, but far enough away to not be obvious. Then, when Verone came back, they'd follow her home at a safe distance. That way, at least she'd be able to tell Reston where to start looking. It was the least she could do. After all, she couldn't help feeling she was at least a little responsible for losing Reston's book, even though really it was more Alexi's fault than hers. And if she happened at the same time to find out something Alexi could use for his penance, so much the better.

Halfway to Miranda, her plan fell apart. As Dona gaped in surprise, Miranda turned her horse about and galloped off. When she didn't reappear after several long minutes, Dona got a sinking feeling that she was on her own. Well then, if she couldn't follow Verone, maybe she could eavesdrop and overhear something that would prove useful.

She took up a position in the alley just around the corner from the restaurant entrance, leaning as casually as she could against the wall. With all the activity in the area, she was hoping to be, if not inconspicuous, then at least less obvious than some of the others around her. Given that the bonfire was now taller than she was, and even more dancers had joined in, she was confident she wouldn't be noticed. What she hadn't counted on was how long she wouldn't be noticed. As a brisk breeze clawed its way through her coat, she eyed the dancers with envy. She'd almost decided it might be worth a quick trip to the fire to warm her hands when she finally heard Verone's voice.

"Thank you again, Father. I really do appreciate your willingness to perform the ceremony in the face of such horrific circumstances and on such short notice."

"A wedding will do me good," Cartier said. "I could use an excuse to take my mind off the funeral."

Fortunately, neither of them heard Dona's gasp. The possibility of being recognized by Verone was one thing, but she hadn't bargained for the risk of being caught by Cartier. She shuddered to think of how he might react upon coming face to face with the young Sister who had disrupted his Inquisition with tales of a false plague. Instantly, she revised her plans for the evening—to find Gregory and get herself back to Exidgeon as soon as possible. Careful to face away from the restaurant, she tried to slink nonchalantly back into the crowd. She didn't exhale until she was halfway to the bonfire.

Before she could take another breath, the music and dancing wound down abruptly. A small cadre of armed men had entered the square and was clearing a path through the crowd directly toward Dona. Praying she was not their target, she fell back with those around her and breathed another sigh of relief as the soldiers passed, but her relief was short-lived. Ordinal Isrulian trailed along behind them. He passed so close she could have touched him.

Isrulian barked an order and the cadre halted in unison. As Isrulian strode forward, the soldiers stepped smartly aside to let him pass.

"Father Cartier," he said, "you're a difficult man to find of late."

"I've been busy."

"Yes, I see that—busy dismantling an active Inquisition while the heretics are burning your house down."

"I didn't—"

"Don't try to deny it. I just saw the vicarage ashes. And since you've gone ahead and dismissed all those Inquisitors, it can only mean that you've brought our arsonist to justice. Am I right?"

"If I may, Your Ordinence," Verone said.

"You again? The last time I let you butt in, you were trying to smuggle that young heretic out of the University."

Dona took this statement as her cue to leave. She edged her way back toward the church.

"I was merely going to point out that Father Cartier lost a dear friend in the vicarage fire," Verone said. "He has every incentive to bring this arsonist to justice."

"Is that right?" Isrulian said. "As long as you are so well-versed in Father Cartier's motivations, perhaps you can explain his rationale for allowing the band of heretics who attacked me right under his nose to escape?"

Verone folded her arms. "I don't know what you're talking about."

"I do hope you'll forgive my skepticism, given one of them was one of your charges. Perhaps a little Inquisitional therapy would help jog your memory."

Dona stopped short as an elderly lady thrust a warm apple pie under her nose. "Buy a pie for a good cause?"

"Um, not today thanks," Dona whispered. She gently pushed the pie out of her face and made to move on, but the pie lady stopped her once more.

"Say, aren't you that young lady we spent all that time looking for up at the University?"

To her horror, Dona realized the pie lady was Mrs. Temrich. She shook her head vigorously. "You must have me confused with someone else."

"Speak up, dear," Mrs. Temrich shouted. "Can't you see there's a crowd? They're drowning out everything you say."

"Isrulian," Cartier said. "If you have a problem with me, I'll thank you to take it up with me instead of taking it out on my congregation."

"Oh, I wouldn't dream of leaving you out," Isrulian said. "But it's a little selfish for you to expect you will be the only guest with an invitation to the party, don't you think?"

"I can't tell you how worried we were when we discovered you were missing again," Mrs. Temrich said. "The ladies will be so relieved to hear you made it back safe and sound. We must tell them. Look, there's Mrs. Curtsik."

Dona shook her head even more vigorously. Oblivious, Mrs. Temrich waved to her friend. "Myra, over here. I just found Miss Merinne again."

Isrulian froze.

"What?" Mrs. Curtsik called back.

"I said I've found Miss Merinne. She's right here. She made it down from the University after all."

Isrulian slowly pivoted toward Mrs. Temrich's voice. It took him only a moment to spot Dona. "Ah, there you are, Miss Merinne. I guess I shouldn't be surprised—you do have a habit of showing up anytime things get interesting. I imagine you overheard I'm planning a little party. Consider yourself invited."

Hearing this, Mrs. Curtsik skidded to a halt.

Mrs. Temrich, however, only heard part of the conversation. "A party? What a wonderful idea. We can charge admission on behalf of the vicarage, and I, of course, shall bring the pies."

Isrulian motioned to his mercenaries. "Take all three of them. Bind their hands and make sure their heads are covered. If they resist, shoot them."

Several of the mercenaries raised their crossbows. The weapons incited panic, causing everyone to flee at once. Dona was knocked to the ground instantly. A mercenary misinterpreted her fall as an attempt to escape and let fly his bolt, which made things even worse. Verone ducked back into the restaurant. She managed to get the door closed just before, in rapid succession, three crossbow bolts buried themselves deep into the wood. One of them missed Cartier by a handbreadth.

Isrulian stamped about, berating the mercenaries as fools and ordering them to stand down. His efforts did little to abate the stampede.

A shrill horn pierced the chaos. Several squads of the Crown's militia approached in rigid formation. Marching across the square, the formation tattered as individual soldiers dropped ranks to attend the injured. By the time the front line made it to the restaurant, the stampede had run its course. Most who were able had scattered, but a few still lurked nearby, taking cover behind booths or trees in the hopes of finding those they'd lost in the fracas.

A few moments after the militia appeared, several figures on horseback made their way across the square to where a defiant Isrulian stood surrounded by his mercenaries. "If it isn't the esteemed Count Laslo and his lackey, Constable Connelly. Gentlemen, you are a little late."

Dona thanked her lucky stars when she heard the names. Still, while Isrulian had armed men under his command, she had no intention of drawing his attention. She remained motionless on the ground, her eyes closed.

"What happened here?" Laslo asked.

Cartier instantly intervened. "Ordinal Isrulian started a panic when he had his men aim their crossbows at the crowd."

Laslo raised a blond eyebrow. "Is this true?"

Isrulian glared at Cartier a long moment before answering. "I was surrounded by suspected heretics. The crossbows were a necessary precaution for taking them into custody."

"You mean to tell me these men are Inquisitors?"

"My Inquisitors were dismissed without my knowledge or consent. I was forced to improvise."

"You realize, of course, that mustering a military force within the city violates any number of treaties with the Holy City."

"This isn't a military force. They're just my bodyguards."

"Bodyguards protect one from physical threats. They do not take potential heretics into custody."

A third horseman galloped in to join the Count and the Constable. "Sorry I'm late."

"Welcome, Monsignor Goodkin," Laslo said. "We were just having a little conversation with Ordinal Isrulian here about his violation of certain treaties. You are the Inquisitor General, are you not?"

"I am."

"It seems the Ordinal incited a stampede during an attempt to take supposed heretics into custody. Did you give him authority to do so?"

"I did not."

"This is ridiculous," Isrulian said. "In case you haven't noticed, I'm an Ordinal. If anything, he would get his authority from me, not the other way around."

"And who appointed you Inquisitor General?" Laslo asked.

"The Primal, of course," the Monsignor said.

"And isn't it true within the Church Hierarchy that the Primal out-ranks an Ordinal?"

"Indeed, it is."

"So, would it be fair to say that if the Ordinal here were in fact trying to take purported heretics into custody using hired mercenaries, he would not have been acting in an official capacity?"

"That is correct."

"Thank you, Monsignor. I've heard enough."

"You're wasting time with this nonsense," Isrulian said. "Even if I had violated some treaty or other, I'd simply claim diplomatic immunity."

Laslo waved to indicate the mercenaries. "That may be an option for you, Your Ordinence, but it isn't for them. Gentlemen, drop your weapons."

"Don't listen to them. I have every right to travel with bodyguards, and they know it."

"Do as I ask, and your sentences will be light," Laslo said. "Disobey me, and the penalty will be severe."

After a tense pause, one of the mercenaries set his crossbow on the ground. A flurry of weapons dropped as the rest followed suit.

Laslo signaled to his men, who moved in to restrain the mercenaries. "Take them to lockup until we decide what to do with them."

Near where Dona lay, a militiaman called out to the Count. "Your Excellency, I think you should see this."

Dona opened her eyes, praying she wasn't about to become the center of attention. To her relief, the soldier was looking at someone else. She got up and started brushing herself off—and caught a glimpse of the soldier's charge.

"Oh no, Mrs. Temrich." She rushed to the woman's side. A crossbow bolt had found its mark in her ribcage beneath her right arm. Her breath was labored.

Mrs. Curtsik hovered over her. "Laverne, you just hold tight. These nice men are going to help you get better."

Mrs. Temrich shook her head weakly. "I still can't hear you. Oh, now don't cry, Myra. Someone's got to put in a good word for the rest of you. May as well be me. Dear, quiet Myra. I'll save all my best words for you. Is Miss Merinne still here?"

Dona squeezed her hand and fought back tears of her own. "I'm here."

"There's a slip of parchment in my apron pocket. Can you get it?"

Dona found the tattered parchment. "It's a recipe."

Mrs. Temrich coughed. "I never had a daughter. Promise my pies won't die with me."

Tears flowing in earnest, Dona nodded. "I promise."

Laslo knelt next to her. With help from the Constable, the Monsignor dismounted and joined them. Cartier was the last to arrive.

"Isn't there anything you can do?" Dona asked.

The Monsignor shook his head. "I doubt even Ordinal Laitrech could save her now."

Father Cartier knelt and prayed, while Mrs. Curtsik sobbed loudly into her kerchief. One by one, the other members of the Venerable Assembly of Church Mothers gathered round with bowed heads. With a final rattling breath, Mrs. Temrich passed.

Laslo's face was grim. "So, this was the dangerous heretic you needed a dozen mercenaries to protect you from?"

Isrulian was unrepentant. "Rooting out heresy is dangerous business. Sometimes innocent people get hurt." He pointed at Dona. "If you must know, she was the real suspect. The old woman must have gotten in the way."

Dona felt heat creep into her face and braced herself to be taken prisoner along with Isrulian's Mercenaries, but if possible, Laslo's eyes narrowed even further. "You mean to tell me you flouted our treaties and endangered our citizens for the vaunted purpose of hunting down unarmed schoolgirls and helpless grandmothers?"

"This outcome was unintended and regrettable, but heresy is an insidious beast. Often the most fair-seeming are the first to succumb."

"Heresy isn't the only beast here. If you didn't have immunity, I'd see you hang for this."

"I think you forget whom you address."

Laslo turned to the Constable. "Is there no way we can circumvent the immunity?"

The Constable shook his head. "I think it would be ill-advised. Even if the Primal were inclined to waive it in this case, the other Ordinals would be outraged."

"What do you suggest, then? Exile?"

The Constable nodded. "Once so warned, if he comes back we could argue his immunity is forfeit."

"How long should we give him to leave?"

"I would think a few hours should suffice."

"You can't exile me," Isrulian protested. "You don't have the authority."

"Watch me. You're lucky I don't have a carriage handy, or I'd stuff you in it and send you off this instant."

He'd no sooner said the words than a carriage pulled into the square and came to a stop right in front of him. A grey-haired man popped his head out of the window.

"I'm looking for a Father Cartier. I was told I could find him here."

The Monsignor's face lit up. "Albert? What are you doing here?"

"Armand? What luck! I expected you to be much harder to find than this. I was told you could use my help. Any pesky Profanities you need curated?"

"If not, I'll certainly see if I can dig some up. How fares the Primal?"

The Curator stepped stiffly down from the carriage and checked his pockets. "Let me see. I have a letter for you here from Thurman. It's supposed to explain everything. Ah, here it is."

"Excuse me," Laslo said. "Is your carriage by any chance bound for the Holy City?"

"I have no idea. Thurman rented it on my behalf."

"I had intended to return there," the driver said. "But if you have another destination in mind, I'm open."

"Not at all—the Holy City will do just fine." He looked pointedly at the Ordinal and nodded in the direction of the carriage. "You heard him, Isrulian. Get in."

"I shall do no such thing. Ordinals wouldn't be subject to such orders even if they came from the Crown Prince himself, let alone some minor functionary."

Laslo advanced on the Ordinal. "You seem to be under the mistaken impression your consent somehow matters."

Isrulian backed away. "You won't get away with this. The *new* Primal won't be such a puppet to temporal authority. I shall see to it."

"If you're determined to appeal to a higher authority," Laslo said. "I can arrange that."

The Monsignor looked up from Thurman's note. "Good news, Your Ordinence. The Primal is doing much better. It seems he's expected to make a full recovery."

Isrulian's jaw dropped. "That's not possible."

"Not possible? You mean to say you don't think the sick can get well? Or do you know something about his illness you aren't telling us?"

"I…it's just that he seemed too far gone to recover."

"It appears he was being slowly poisoned. You wouldn't happen to know anything about that, would you?"

The Ordinal's eyes narrowed. "What are you implying?"

The Monsignor leaned forward. "Nothing the ensuing investigation won't uncover, I'm sure. No doubt they'll find your assistance invaluable."

"This is your last chance," Laslo said. "In the carriage—now."

Isrulian sniffed and strode toward the carriage. "Very well, but for the record, I'm only doing this because the Monsignor seems to think I can be of service to the Primal."

"If I might make a suggestion?" the Monsignor asked.

Laslo nodded. "Of course, Monsignor."

"It seems such a shame that after His Ordinence went to all that trouble getting those bodyguards that he should end up losing them over a misunderstanding just before his trip back to the Holy City. An Ordinal should never travel such long distances without proper protection."

"Hmm, I see your point," Laslo said. "You there."

Several militiamen snapped to attention.

"See to it His Ordinence makes it to the Primal safely—and no-where else."

The men nodded and boarded the carriage.

"Since they're all going to be seeing the Primal," the Monsignor said, "I think a note of introduction is in order. This will only take a moment." He scribbled on a piece of parchment, while Laslo finalized arrangements with the carriage driver. Once the Monsignor passed the document to the driver, Laslo said the word, and the carriage rolled out of sight.

Verone peeped out of the restaurant. "Is it safe to come out yet? Oh my heavens, is that Mrs. Temrich?"

Cartier shook his head sadly. "It looks like there will be another funeral this week. I'm afraid we may have to postpone the wedding."

Verone stopped short. "You mean a day or so?"

Cartier shook his head. "After all this, and with two funerals, I probably won't be able to get to it until next week."

"But...I can't wait until then."

"Verone, you know if there were any way I could possibly fit it in for you, I would, but there's really no way I can put off a funeral."

"But the invitations—all the hours of planning—"

"Pardon me," the Monsignor said. "I couldn't help but overhear. It seems Father Cartier has his hands full. Could I perhaps be of assistance?"

Verone gave him an appraising look. "I'm sorry, I don't believe we've met."

"Miss Verone Nevinander," Cartier said, "let me present Monsignor Goodkin. He's the Primal's brother."

She extended a flawlessly manicured hand. "A pleasure. I wasn't aware the Primal's brother did weddings."

"It's the least I can do under the circumstances. I was planning to return to the Holy City as soon as the situation here stabilized, but now that my brother seems to be recovering, my reasons for going back are no longer pressing. So long as I still have work to do here, I'm happy to help."

Verone turned to Cartier. "You wouldn't be insulted, would you?"

He smiled. "Not provided I get an invitation. If it goes late enough, I might even be able to catch the reception."

"Very well then, Monsignor. I accept your gracious offer. Here's an invitation. It should have all the information you need. And while I'm at it, here's yours too, Father. Oh, and Miss Merinne, here's yours as well. So glad you happened by—you know how difficult you can be to track down. Now, let's see about tending to the injured, shall we? I propose we move them out of the cold and into the church. The ladies and I will make sure they have a place to sleep and are well fed. Constable, if you would be so kind as to send for the Sisters, we can get those with only minor injuries treated and released. By morning we can come up with a way of transporting anyone who might have more serious injuries wherever the Sisters think is best."

Count Laslo hopped on his horse. "Since matters seem to be in good hands, I have a report to make. Send word if you need me."

"Thank you, Your Excellency," the Constable said.

Laslo saluted. "My thanks to you and your daughter for the heads up." With a nod, he was off.

Dona marveled at her luck as she broke the seal on her invitation. Finally, she had some sort of address for the elusive Miss Nevinander. Even better, she didn't need to resort to subterfuge to get it.

She marveled even more once she opened it. "What an amazing coincidence. Your fiancé has the same name as my uncle."

Verone spared a glance in her direction. "Dona dear, do try not to be so dense. He is your uncle."

. . . . .

"Oh great," Miranda said. "As if the cart wasn't bad enough."

Dona was about to ask what she was talking about when a large wet droplet pelted her forehead.

Gregory gave the reins a shake. "Don't blame me. It's not my fault Morissant was already off somewhere with his carriage. Besides, it's not like you gave me any warning. I know this oxcart isn't much, but it's better than walking, isn't it?"

"Yes, it is," Dona said. "And I'm sure Miranda feels the same way. She's just worried about her new dress getting wet."

"I've never even had a chance to wash it," Miranda said. "What am I going to do if the colors run? Can't we do this tomorrow?"

Dona stifled a chuckle at the mental image, which sent Miranda into even a deeper funk.

"We should be almost there," Gregory said. "At this point it would be farther to turn around."

"But it might be pouring later," Miranda said. "If we turn around now, we might make it back before the worst of it starts."

Dona shook her head. "I promised Miss Nevinander I'd stop there tonight and let her mother know where she is. Not only that, but my mother is probably worried sick. The last time she saw me was up at the University when Isrulian was taking you hostage. She shouldn't have to wait another day to find out I'm all right."

Miranda lapsed into a sullen pout.

"Wait, I never heard about this," Gregory said. "Someone took her hostage?" Was it that same guy who ran off with our carriage after the opera?"

"No," Dona said. "This was an Ordinal."

"A real Ordinal," Gregory asked. "Or just someone dressed like one?"

"This one was real."

"What's this about someone running off with your carriage?" Miranda asked.

Dona sighed. "It was probably the same person who broke into my hope chest. You two must promise me you won't mention any of this stuff to anyone else. I still don't know what I'm up against."

"If someone was willing to go to such lengths," Miranda said, "shouldn't Daddy know?"

"Maybe. I'll give that some thought, but in the meantime, tell no one. Promise?"

"If you're sure that's what you want."

Gregory drew back on the reins. "Here we are."

"They have a gate guard?" Miranda asked. "Are you sure this is the right place?"

As Gregory shrugged, Dona was already off the cart and presenting her credentials to the sleepy guard.

"Well?" Miranda asked.

"He will let them know we are here."

"They aren't going to make us wait here in the rain, are they?"

"It's only sprinkling. You'll live."

Miranda hooked a finger in her sleeve and eyed her wrist for any sign of leaching cranberry. "But it's got to be half a mile up to that house."

"I said you'd live—I didn't say you wouldn't dye."

Miranda tried to make a show of harrumphing, but an involuntary smile broke through. "I'll never know why I keep bothering to save your skin when you clearly have so little regard for mine."

It was only a short time before the gate swung open to admit them, but by the time the rickety cart pulled up in front of the Nevindander villa, Dona had to admit she was getting uncomfortably damp. She found herself stealing furtive glances in Miranda's direction for signs of unnatural redness, but the sputtering lantern light was too dim to reveal anything conclusive. The light was sufficient, however, for her to make out the profiles of her mother, her uncle, and Verone's mother Nathalie waiting on the veranda to greet them.

Amanda embraced her daughter. "Thank heavens you're safe. I've been so worried. What happened up there? Why weren't you with us when we left the University?"

"There were some complications. Ma, you remember my room-mate, Miranda, don't you?"

"Of course," Amanda said. "What a lovely dress."

Miranda beamed and curtseyed.

"And this is my good friend, Gregory Delauren."

"A pleasure," Amanda said. "Aren't you the singer?"

Gregory nodded. "I can carry a tune in a pinch."

"Carry a tune?" Dona said. "He's just being modest. Actually, he's the most transcendent voice in a generation."

"They don't really say that, do they? Honestly, I never bother to read those rags."

Dona winked. "Right—of course you don't. And Uncle Rayen, you're looking dapper."

"Your mother takes good care of me."

She gave him an expansive hug. "Looks like it's paid off. What's this I hear about a wedding?"

"Why does everyone always seem so surprised? It's not like I've kept it a secret."

"No offense, but sometimes there's a wide gulf between a gentle-man's intentions and a lady's acceptance."

"I'll say," Nathalie said. "Why don't we move this out of the evening damp and inside next to a nice warm fire? I'll have Eloise make us something warm to drink."

Dona's jaw dropped as they entered the villa. Never had she seen such opulence. Massive black pillars topped by ornate gold-leaf capitals held aloft the foyer ceiling, itself a showcase of vibrant cherubic frescoes. The space housed a vast round table sporting a tableau of bronzes engaged in the hunt. Fresh florals were arranged about them to convey the impression of a forest. The table was embraced by a grand stairway, its two great arms gently curving around behind them on their way up to the second floor. Ahead was a bank of stained-glass panels that could be thrown wide for access to the courtyard beyond. As they moved on to the great room, Dona beheld new wonders wherever she looked. Even Gregory, who'd had more exposure to wealth on a grand scale, seemed a little awestruck.

Alistair Nevinander presided over the great room from a wingback chair near the gaping maw of an enormous fireplace, his slippered feet resting on an antique ottoman. He set aside his book as they entered, adjusted his smoking jacket, and peered at his guests over the tops of his reading glasses. Across the fireplace from him, Nathalie's sister Olivia was seated at a broad table amidst towering stacks of stationery. She frowned as they entered.

"Verone isn't back yet? The girl left hours ago. Weddings don't plan themselves—if she doesn't trouble herself to lend a hand, we're never going to get all this done in time."

"She sent us," Dona said. "She's been held up by a mishap at Saint Sophia's. She said to tell you she'd be back as soon as she could."

"The fire you mean? Why would that keep her?"

"No, there's been another incident." She described the confrontation between Ordinal Isrulian and Count Laslo.

"My word," Nathalie said. "Is my daughter all right?"

Verone chose that moment to stride in. "She is just fine. The Sisters arrived quite promptly, and I left the matter in their capable hands."

"Poor Mrs. Temrich," Nathalie said.

Verone shook her head. "Unfortunately, the circumstances necessitate a slight change of plan. Since Father Cartier will be occupied with two funerals this week, he had to decline to officiate at the wedding. Now, before you panic, Monsignor Goodkin has agreed to do the honors."

Alistair finally pulled himself up out of the chair. "Well, that's going to necessitate another change of plans, isn't it?"

"I don't think so," Verone said. "Why should it?"

"What do you mean, dear?" Nathalie said.

"While I am in charge, Inquisitors General are not welcome in this house. If he's officiating, the wedding isn't happening here."

"But where else could we possibly have it on such short notice?"

"Now you're just being obstructionist," Verone snapped.

"A common complaint of the reckless and the irresponsible," Alistair said. "If that's any example of your executive decision-making skills, then I'd be foolish to be any other way. My decision stands— your Monsignor is not welcome here. Now if you'll excuse me, it's getting late."

Nathalie pecked him on the cheek. "Good night, dear."

Once Alistair left, the room fell silent for several minutes.

Finally, Olivia spoke up. "Well, if neither Cartier nor this Monsignor can do it, then who?"

"I have no intention of replacing the Monsignor," Verone said.

Nathalie shrugged. "I think your father's mind is made up."

"So is mine. If that means we can't have the wedding here, then so be it."

Olivia shook her head. "What other venue could possibly accommodate all these guests on such short notice? I don't think you have a choice."

"What about Ranselard Keep?"

Olivia grimaced. "The prison? I know we all appreciate a little symbolism at a wedding, but normally we sacrifice honesty in favor of at least the illusion of romance. You might as well forget the rings and just exchange shackles."

"I was just there recently. It's been completely made-over since the prison days. It's really very nice, now. I think it would be perfect."

"There's just one small problem," Nathalie said. "The whole island is under interdict—the Church won't perform a wedding there, and even if they did, it wouldn't be valid."

Verone waved dismissively. "A minor concern at most, particularly if the Primal's brother is on your side. The more I think about it, the more I like it. I have some arranging to do, but the new plan is to hold the ceremony at Ranselard. Time is short—I'd best get started right away if I'm going to pull this off. I'll try to be back tomorrow sometime."

She was gone as quickly as she'd appeared.

Olivia grumbled as she slid stack after stack of completed invitations off the table and into the trash. "Nevinanders."

With Alistair's and Verone's departures, the evening settled into something more comfortable—indeed, almost festive. Eloise appeared with steaming mugs of cider, Dona's mother offered to assist with the invitations, and a lively discussion ensued about ceremony particulars. Nathalie's enthusiasm for her only daughter's wedding was contagious, and soon the three women were laughing and chatting like old friends. Rayen took a seat in Alistair's chair, while Dona, Miranda, and Gregory gathered round on the ottoman near the fire's warmth. To everyone's delight, Dona eventually cajoled Gregory into singing for them. He started off with a wedding song, but somewhere along the way it took a ribald turn and ended up a drinking song. Dona was initially mortified, but Nathalie sprayed cider across the invitation she was working on, and Olivia laughed so hard she had tears in her eyes.

His next piece was a well-known sing-a-long, and Gregory played the room like the expert he was, serenading the ladies until they joined in the melody, and then delighting them by switching to harmony. He was on the fourth chorus when Dona felt a tap on her shoulder.

"Do you think you could convince him to sing at the wedding?" Rayen asked.

"I can ask. Are you sure you shouldn't run it past Verone first?"

Rayen shook his head. "I would really like to contribute something. So far I haven't had a say in anything but the proposal."

"That's a pretty major contribution."

"I know, but I'd like the ceremony to include something from our family, too. He's your friend, and he'd be fantastic. If he'll do it, I'll feel like we really brought something of value to the table."

Dona squeezed his hand. "They're already getting something pretty valuable, but I'll ask. Just don't spring it on Verone at the last minute. Brides and wedding surprises are a volatile combination."

Gregory continued to take them on a tour of his repertoire for another hour or so before Olivia crumpled an invitation and tossed it in the trash.

"Looks like I've had one too many ciders for detailed work. I'm better off calling it a night and getting an early start. Young man, you've got quite a talent. Thank you so much for sharing it with us old ladies."

Gregory bowed theatrically. "It was an honor and a pleasure."

"We really should think about getting back up to the college, too," Dona said.

"In the rain?" Nathalie protested. "On an open cart? I won't hear of it. You'd all catch your deaths. Eloise, would you be so kind as to make up some additional guest rooms."

"I've already seen to it, ma'am."

"There, it's been decided."

Dona looked to her compatriots. Gregory shrugged and Miranda nodded subtly, with perhaps a hint of desperation. "That's very kind of you. We'd be delighted."

"Splendid. Eloise will show you up to your rooms. We'll breakfast at nine."

Dona hugged her mother goodnight. "Sorry for all the trouble I've caused lately."

"It's a mother's job to worry. Just do me a favor and try not to get lost on your way to bed."

Dona eyed her surroundings. "In this place? No guarantees."

With Eloise to lead them, they arrived at their appointed rooms without difficulty. Dona's bed was magnificent—four-poster, covered with a stark white comforter, and stacked with emerald and burgundy feather pillows. A white cotton nightgown with red and green ribbon accents lay neatly folded next to the pillows. The walnut vanity was backed with the most ornate mirror Dona had ever seen. The vanity held a complicated array of the latest implements deemed essential for assisting the modern woman to look her best. Dona didn't even recognize most of them. She had a seat and sorted through them, trying to imagine their uses. Finally, she seized a brush and pulled it through her hair, resolving with all the earnest naïveté of youth that if beauty ever truly became as complicated as all that, she would simply settle for ugly and be done with it.

She caught her reflection's eye. "Well, this is a fine situation you've gotten me into, isn't it?"

The Dona in the mirror stared accusingly but said nothing.

"So, Miss Smarty Pants, now that I'm here, do I search for the book to fulfill an obligation to my professor, or do I refrain out of deference to my future aunt?"

Reflected Dona looked suddenly puzzled and a little disturbed.

"And why is she, of all people, going to be my aunt? You don't suppose she's just using Uncle Rayen to get to me? But if she already has Reston's book, why would she need to get to me at all? What if she set this up before she got the book and now has no intention of going through with it?"

A very suspicious-looking Dona frowned back at her.

"I think it's time I had a little heart-to-heart with Uncle Rayen."

The other Dona nodded her approval.

Dona cracked the door and checked the hallway. It was dark, and all was quiet. She knew Rayen was in the other wing, because Eloise had dropped him off before the rest of them. She thought she should be able to find it—it was just a matter of crossing the balcony above the stairs and finding the right room. She grabbed her lamp from the vanity and ventured out into the hallway. Padding softly on bare feet, she made her way past Miranda's room. At regular intervals. she passed alcoves on either side of the hall, each occupied by yet another demonstration of Nevinander excess, whether a marble bust or a gleaming suit of armor. She paused briefly to look down at the foyer below. Enormous shadows played across the walls and ceiling, and the glass panels of the far wall splashed them with sparkling motes of reflected lamplight. Satisfied nothing was amiss, she was about to go back to finding Rayen when the colored glass panels blazed momentarily electric. In that instant, Dona could have sworn she caught the silhouette of a crouched figure. She froze and listened intently, but even after the thunder rumbled through, all she heard was the gentle patter of rain on the roof and the staccato thumping of her heart. She had to wait several minutes for the next flash, but by then, there was no sign anything was amiss. Roundly chastising herself for an overactive imagination, she scurried across the balcony at twice her previous pace.

To her relief, Rayen was awake.

"What took you…?"

"It's me," she said. "You don't need to play the little games, remember?"

"Sorry, force of habit. What's on your mind?"

"This wedding, mostly. I don't understand it."

"What's not to understand? I proposed, and she said yes."

"I understand the procedure—it's the motivation I'm not so clear on."

Rayen shrugged. "Why does anyone get married? Sometimes the reasons are obvious, I suppose, but I doubt that's generally the case. I don't see how this is so unusual."

"Forgive me for being blunt, but what does she see in you?"

"You know, a relationship is one of those rare things so delicate it can be analyzed to death. So far, I've resisted the urge, despite your mother's position that, at worst, it would be a mercy killing."

"Would you view it any differently if you knew that when she met you, Verone thought I had something she wanted?"

"So? I wouldn't mind having some things she has either."

"But would you still marry her if she didn't have them?"

"Of course."

"Can you say the same for her?"

Rayen shrugged again. "Whatever she wanted from you, I doubt it compares to the estate she inherits from her father for marrying me."

"You mean she only inherits if she marries you? Doesn't that bother you?"

"Why should it? I only inherit if I marry her too."

"You really think she's going to be willing to share?"

"I'm pretty easy to share with. It's certainly worth a shot."

"You wouldn't be crushed if she tossed you out a week after the wedding?"

"I'd be unhappy about it, but let's face it, it's not like I'd be any worse off than I am now."

"There seems to be an awful lot at stake here. Aren't you worried for your safety?"

"You're treating this as though I have a choice. On my honor and all games aside—I've seen this coming for a long time now. There's no point in wasting time second-guessing the inevitable."

Dona nodded. "If you say so." Once Rayen had decided he'd truly seen something, there was no convincing him otherwise, and although she found the inheritance aspect of the arrangement unsettling, she couldn't fault his logic.

"How's Ma taking the news?"

"Not so well. I would have thought she'd be happy—I know I haven't been an easy charge. Without me, she'll finally have the opportunity to live a normal life."

"Did you ever stop to think maybe you were more than just a burden to her? Without you to worry about, she'll finally have time to focus on herself."

"Exactly. You'd think she'd be ecstatic."

Dona shook her head. "For a seer, you sometimes have a surprising knack for overlooking the obvious. Once you're gone, she'll have no one."

"She's a fine woman. She'll find someone."

"I imagine it's much easier to see that from the outside looking in. From the inside, I bet the view is terrifying. Not everyone has the luxury to foresee the success of his or her next relationship. While she had you, she was never forced to come to grips with the possibility that she might end up living out the rest of her days alone."

"Oh, now I think I see your point. And here I thought she was just upset about the ring."

"The ring? What ring?"

"Well, she did seem a bit taken aback when I presented Verone with your grandmother's ring."

"Her wedding ring?"

"No—that, she took with her. This was an heirloom piece."

"I don't recall Grandma having jewelry of any value. When did she give it to you?"

"She didn't. She threw it away, and I pulled it out of the trash."

"I didn't know she was so well off that she could afford to throw away jewelry."

"Yeah, I always felt a little guilty about that."

"Guilty? Why?"

"It was sort of my fault. You may not remember, but your grandmother was deathly afraid of spiders."

"I've heard stories."

"In my defense, I was just a kid. We had an argument. I don't even remember what it was about, but I got the bright idea to tell her I'd dreamt there was a spider in her jewelry box."

"And you'd dreamt no such thing?"

"No. I made it up just to be spiteful. It was right after the Sight first manifested, before I understood the responsibility that accompanies such a gift."

"And she believed you?"

Rayen nodded. "Ironic, isn't it? She was the one person in my life to recognize my gift for what it truly was, and I used it against her. When I found the ring, I felt terrible. I had no idea she'd take me that seriously."

"What did she say when you confessed?"

"I never did. I wanted to, but I couldn't bring myself to do it. I always came up with reasons to put it off."

"You never told her?"

"She was the only person who ever believed in me. How could I tell her I'd lied? I kept the ring, always intending to find the right time, but it never came, and then it was too late."

"So, when I was a little girl and you took me out digging for buried treasure—that was just more of grandma's jewelry she'd thrown away?"

Rayen chuckled. "You still remember that?"

"Hard to forget. I still have the loot."

"No, that was your mother's doing. It was only a short time after your father disappeared that I saw her out burying something. I was dying to know what it was, but I figured if she caught *me* digging it up, there'd be a scene. On the other hand, she could hardly fault us if we came across it innocently, could she? I had no idea she was burying part of your inheritance."

"That's why you wanted me to keep it secret?"

He winked. "You aren't losing faith in the pirate's curse, are you?"

"I had nightmares about that, you know."

"And I had nightmares of your mother finding out. I expect mine were worse."

"So why bury this stuff in the first place? If she really wanted to get rid of it, why not just pawn it? It's not like we couldn't have used the money."

He gave her a sly grin. "I wondered the same thing, but I wasn't about to invoke the curse to find out. I didn't need to know that badly."

"So, if I want to know anything else, I'm going to have to ask Ma?"

"I'm afraid so, but do me a favor—could you wait until after the wedding? I'd rather not get her too worked up until after the knot is formally tied."

"I've waited this long, I suppose a few more days couldn't hurt."

He made the secret sign. "Pirate's honor?"

"Pirate's honor. Well, I suppose I should let you get some sleep. Even old buccaneers need to rest up before a big day of nefarious adventures."

He raised his hand. "Guilty, as charged."

She gave him a goodnight hug. "Thanks for being the best uncle ever. I do so hope everything works out for you."

"It will. After all, I've seen it, and they don't call me Rayen the Magnificent for nothing."

"You realize, you're the only one who calls you that, right?"

Rayen shrugged. "Can you think of anyone in a better position to know?"

Dona chuckled. "Sleep well."

"You too."

Rayen hadn't resolved all her doubts, but she was relieved he seemed to be fully aware of the risks he was taking. He always had been more resilient than anyone gave him credit for. Given Rayen's reticence, she wasn't sure she cared to brave her mother's wrath, even to find out about more about her pirate hoard. When she first noticed the jewelry's resemblance to those in Princess Celeste's Dreamweaver portrait, it was easy to get excited about the possibility of a connection, but finding out her mother had done the burying came as a bit of a shock. Now she hoped it was all just a strange coincidence. The situation was made even more bizarre by the discovery of the matching ring and a Mr. Lop Ears look-alike in the caverns beneath the college—caverns that, according to Brent's journal, had once been occupied by the mysterious Mistress, whom Brent himself had identified as Dreamweaver.

As she crossed the balcony, Dona was startled out of her reverie by the sound of a soft footfall in the foyer below.

She held her lantern over the railing and squinted down into the shadows. "Who's there?"

Silence.

She backed away from the balcony. "I know you're down there. Show yourself this instant."

As she turned to run, a dark shape sprang from the alcove. Before she could react, her arm was twisted behind her, and she felt something sharp press against her throat. Stubble tickled her cheek as her captor, reeking of sweat and tobacco, breathed a warning into her ear.

"One peep, my pretty little two-timer, and you're a goner."

# ACKNOWLEDGEMENTS

**Jean Jenkins**, whose breathtaking editorial expertise has once again helped me produce a product of which I am immensely proud.

**Mike Curdie**, whose enviable artistic gifts made Trifienne leap from the page and helped make my vision for the cover a reality.

**Adeela Syed**, whose incisive feedback helped not just with the story, but with my whole perspective.

**Brett Barbaro**, whose interest in the manuscript ranged beyond mere text. I hope one day to oblige him with a game of Trumps of Doom.

**Cindy Pury**, whose thoughtful and meticulous suggestions on motivation and plot were absolutely indispensable.

**Mary Vensel White**, wordsmith extraordinaire and Author of *The Qualities of Wood* and *Bellflower*. Her keen eye ferreted out the dull spots and helped make them gleam.

**Elspeth (Beth) Riley**, editor par excellence, whose seemingly effortless facility with language informs not just my fiction, but my life.

**Daniel Mendyke**, whose keen ability to think several steps ahead helped lay a solid magical foundation and may even have won him a game or two of chess.

**James Czarnik**, who read despite all the other demands on his time—he taught me, once again, that "love is a verb."

**Yergalem Meharenna**, whose inexhaustible enthusiasm keeps me going even through the hard parts.

**Marianne Smith**, who believed enough in my writing and editing that she hired me to do it, and thereby changed everything.

**Tam Czarnik**: As did the Elves for the Ents, Tam gave me my voice.

**Lisa McLendon**, whose boundless editorial expertise guided the resolution of various pesky last-minute issues.

**Genelle Belmas**, my inspiration and my love. I strive to make her proud in ways she does not expect, as she continues to do for me.

**The Southern California Writers' Conference**, who opened my eyes to the existence of publishing conventions and practices and made me appreciate their value. Their tireless efforts help me "suck less."

**Nero**, who warmed my feet throughout those long first-draft years. I shall miss him always.

**Reshi**, who after Nero left, decided I needed him and moved in. He was right.

The Pocket Watch used for the spine cover image was designed and crafted by **Lady Pirotessa** (at Blue Rose Creations). I *still* marvel at it.

# GLOSSARY OF TERMS

**Attunement:** This property determines what constitutes a single object for purposes of vesting a spell—two or more objects attuned and in contact means a spell cast on one will spread to all of them. In general, items that remain in close contact for extended periods of time (about a year or so) become naturally attuned to each other. Thus, if a dagger blade is attached to a handle, and the two remain together for long enough, they become a single object for purposes of vesting spells (as long as they remain in contact as the spell vests) (see Vest). Certain Phrendonic spells from the Category of Enchantment can accelerate this process. In general, objects that are 95 percent attuned to each other behave as though they are 100 percent Attuned, while objects less than 95 percent Attuned behave as though they are not Attuned. Thus, once separated, Attuned items can lose their Attunement comparatively rapidly.

**Category:** Phrendonic spells can generally be grouped into one of seven categories based on how they function. Category dictates not only a spell's function, but also places limits on spells that affect it. For example, a Dispel spell cannot generally affect more than one category. Thus, if two spells on the same object hail from different Categories, to dispel both, two different Dispels are required—one tailored to each of the Categories represented by the affected spells. The seven Phrendonic Categories are: Alteration Divination, Enchantment, Encryption, Evocation, Kinesis, and Summoning.

**Charge:** Some spells, referred to as Numeni (plural of Numenus), require an energy supply to maintain their effects. Charge spells collect and provide that energy—termed a 'charge.' A Numenus can only accept a new charge when it is empty of charge or very nearly so. A Reservoir spell can hold a charge until a Numenus vested on the same item is ready to receive one. Numeni, Charge spells, and Reservoirs all possess a trait called Tolerance. A charge can flow from a Charge spell or Reservoir with a higher Tolerance to a Reservoir or Numenus with a lower Tolerance. If multiple receptive Numeni are available, the charge flows to the one with the lowest Tolerance. Once a Numenus receives a charge, it retains it until the charge is exhausted. Thus, if an Incinerate spell and a Light spell are both vested on the same item, casting a Charge spell on the item will have different results depending on the Tolerances of the three spells. If the Light spell has the lowest Tolerance of the three, the Light spell will receive the charge and the object will light up. If the Incinerate has the lowest Tolerance, the object will instead blow up. If the Charge spell has the lowest tolerance, the charge will have nowhere to go and will dissipate without effect. Only the Tolerances of empty or (nearly-empty Numeni capable of accepting a Charge) are considered for purposes of distributing charges.

**Demon/Daemon:** A soul displaced from its native body. The Church uses the term "Demon." Phrendonic practitioners prefer "Daemon."

**Diffract:** A type of Suppression spell that works on radiant effects (effects that extend beyond the target object in a radius, such as Darkness). Typically, a Diffraction spell is limited to affecting spells within a single category, e.g., Summoning. Since it only suppresses the effect without disturbing the spell's pattern, a Diffraction will not prevent a spell of the Diffracted Category from vesting within its radius. For that, one would use a Hedge, which is the corresponding radiant Dispel. See Dispel.

**Dispel:** A spell of the category of Alteration that disrupts the pattern of another spell vested on the same object causing it to dissipate. It is distinguished from a Suppression, which disrupts the effect of another spell, but leaves the pattern intact. If a Dispel is subsequently removed, the affected spell is still gone (provided it wasn't

Patterned). By contrast, if a Suppression is removed, previously suppressed spells can often reassert themselves. A given Dispel is generally limited to Dispelling only spells within a single category. To be successful, the Dispel must be inherently stronger than the spell to be dispelled. Ordinals use the term Disrupt for essentially the same effect.

**Evoke:** To use a spell from the Phrendonic Category of Evocation. Evocation encompasses a Category of magic in which surrounding gasses are recruited into the pattern of a spell as it vests. Thus, solid objects may be created from air, although the spell itself must generally be cast upon an object to seed the effect. If the Evocation is dispelled or expires, the gas returns to its previous gaseous state. See also Category.

**Kinesis:** The Phrendonic category of magic associated with spells that attract or repel.

**Numenus:** See Charge.

**Ordinal:** The nine Ordinals are appointed by the Primal, customarily for life terms. They rank just beneath the Primal, and upon a Primal's death, the Ordinals vote to determine his successor. Beneath the Ordinals are Archbishops, Bishops, and Priests, in that order. The Inquisitor General is not technically part of that hierarchy—his role is to administer the Inquisition, and he serves at the pleasure of the Primal. Thus, in his official capacity, the Inquisitor General reports only to the Primal, and his authority is as extensive or as limited as the Primal allows.

**Passive Charge:** Passive Charges are a special form of Charge Spell that collect energy over time and, when full (usually after about an hour), dump the accumulated Charge into an available Reservoir or Numenus vested on the same item. Once emptied, they resume gathering energy, and the process repeats as long as the spell remains in effect. See also Charge.

**Patterning:** A Patterned spell is one that has undergone the process of Patterning to make the spell's pattern integral to that of the object on which it is vested. In essence, a Patterned spell becomes permanent, as long as the object it's vested on remains intact. Thus, a Color spell Patterned on a Promise Stick to turn it red would no longer have a duration—instead, the stick would remain red indefinitely. However, if the stick is broken in half, the spell dissipates like normal, except that if the stick is reassembled (provided the two halves remain attuned), the Patterned spell manifests once again and the red color returns. Patterned Numeni still require Charges to take effect. Like Attunement spells, Patterning spells reside in the Category of Enchantment.

**Phrendonic Heresy:** Practicing Phrendonic magic, as outlined in the work Practical Phrendonics, was officially declared heresy by the Edict of Caprian in the year 887. Some related practices, such as demonology, had been deemed heretical long before that. Prior to 887, a number of canon scholars viewed Phrendonic practices as already subject to those previous edicts. To them, the Edict of Caprian was little more than a clarification of existing canon.

**Profanity:** This term is used by the Church to denote an object upon which a Phrendonic spell is vested. Since Phrendonic spells generally don't last long unless they've been Patterned, it is usually presumed that a Profanity bears spells that have been Patterned.

**Promise Stick:** In its simplest form, a Promise Stick is a stick notched so that it may be easily snapped in two, usually to quickly break a spell without the bother of having to dispel it. In general, once a spell is vested on an object, at least 80 percent of the object must remain intact, or the spell is broken. Thus, if a Color spell is cast upon such a stick to turn it red, when the stick is broken, the spell is broken as well, and both pieces return to their normal color. However, if the stick is broken unevenly such that one piece retains at least 80 percent of its mass, the spell remains in effect on the larger piece, and dissipates from the smaller.

**Reservoir:** See Charge.

**Sacrifice (Incinerate):** Incinerate is a Summoning spell that instantaneously converts a Charge into light and heat in a radius around the targeted object. During the Caprian Inquisition, a number of Phrendonic Heretic prisoners used this spell to immolate themselves rather than endure torture that might induce them to betray their compatriots. Inquisitors who got too close were often injured or killed as well. The Church's term for the practice, "Infernal Sacrifice," gained traction at that time. Such a Sacrifice was an avenue of last resort for a heretic, usually attempted after having been bound and masked or blinded. By casting the Sacrifice on themselves, they obviated the general requirement for the caster to see a spell's target to vest it. Since it's a Numenus, the Incinerate additionally requires a Charge to take effect.

**Slept:** Term of art used by Phrendonic practitioners to indicate that someone under the influence of a Sleep spell.

**Sorcel:** Phrendonic term for spell, specifically, one that has not been Patterned and is therefore ephemeral.

**Spell Radius:** Radiant spells generally affect a 30-foot radius surrounding the targeted object. Skilled Phrendonic practitioners can modify radiant spells to have a smaller radius, but not a larger one. Spell Radius is to be distinguished from Casting Distance, which is generally line-of-sight up to a maximum of 150 feet.

**Spells vested on persons vs. Spells vested on objects:** Spells vested on people or animals behave differently in some particulars than they do when vested on inanimate objects. For example, the maximum duration of a spell on a person is approximately an hour, whereas on an object, a spell can last up to a day. The difference is thought to result from an interaction between the spell and the person's soul.

**Tag:** A Phrendonic spell that creates a standard (though invisible) magical pattern, generally useful for interacting with other spells, such as Attractions or Repulsions. The term is also used to refer to spells that create non-standard patterns that are able thereby to avoid interaction with the standard spells.

**Talis:** Phrendonic term for a Patterned spell effect.

**Vest/vesting:** The nearly instantaneous process whereby the pattern of a spell spreads across the target object. Once initiated by casting, a spell spreads to encompass all solid material that is both attuned to and touching the point at which the vesting initiated. Thus, if one were to cast a Color spell on the blade of a knife to turn it red, the spell would initiate at a point targeted by the caster and spread until it encompassed everything that was attuned to the blade. If the handle had been in association with the blade long enough, they would be Attuned, the spell would vest on the handle, and the handle would turn red as well. If the blade and handle were only recently assembled and therefore not Attuned, the Color spell would vest on the blade only, and the handle would not be affected.

# ABOUT THE AUTHOR

Doug Bornemann was a jealous child. When his cousin Margaret got a two-octave toy organ that played real notes, he wanted one too. It took wheedling, but he was eventually successful. Proud of his achievement, he took his bright-red battery-powered Jaymar organ to his second-grade class for show and tell. Blue-haired Mrs. Mueller was so impressed by his enthusiasm for hammering out the melody to *You're a Grand Old Flag,* she made it her mission to arrange piano lessons. Shamelessly exploiting his parents' secret hopes that their child might actually be talented at something, she convinced them to devote a fraction of the meager monthly household income to renting a piano—a fine blond spinet with waterfall keys. For a music teacher, Mrs. Mueller recommended Marilyn, one of her former Brownies who had recently returned from college with shiny new degrees in math and music. Marilyn demonstrated prodigious talent with numerous instruments, including piano, though her specialty was the accordion. For 10 years, Marilyn stoically endured Doug's keyboard antics and even managed to instill some musical wisdom—as well as an appreciation for classical music that still baffles his long-suffering wife. Marilyn's brilliance in math and business whisked her away to strategic corporate jobs in Michigan and, eventually, Southern California. Many years later, when Doug's academic pursuits took him to UC Irvine—only a few miles away from Marilyn's California home—they renewed their acquaintance. During that time, Doug took up writing as a hobby. By serendipitous accident, he emailed Marilyn an early copy of his first work-in-progress, and she has been an unflagging advocate for his writing ever since. In 2020, they will celebrate the 50th anniversary of their friendship. In a way, she's still stoically enduring his keyboard antics, and Doug couldn't be more grateful. Caring teachers really do change lives.